REMARKABLY
BRIGHT
CREATURES

REMARKABLY BRIGHT CREATURES

A Novel

SHELBY VAN PELT

ecco

An Imprint of HarperCollinsPublishers

REMARKABLY BRIGHT CREATURES. Copyright © 2022 by Shelby Van Pelt. All rights reserved. Printed in the United States of America. No part of this book may be used or reproduced in any manner whatsoever without written permission except in the case of brief quotations embodied in critical articles and reviews. For information, address HarperCollins Publishers, 195 Broadway, New York, NY 10007.

HarperCollins books may be purchased for educational, business, or sales promotional use. For information, please email the Special Markets Department at SPsales@harpercollins.com.

Ecco® and HarperCollins® are trademarks of HarperCollins Publishers.

FIRST EDITION

Designed by Michelle Crowe

Interior art: background texture by Magenta10 / Shutterstock, Inc.; coral illustrations by MyMuhomorka / Shutterstock, Inc.; octopus illustration by Nadya Dobrynina / Shutterstock, Inc.

Emojis in text by Carboxylase/Shutterstock, Inc.

Library of Congress Cataloging-in-Publication Data has been applied for.

ISBN 978-0-06-320415-7

23 24 25 26 27 LBC 25 24 23 22 21

For Anna

REMARKABLY
BRIGHT
CREATURES

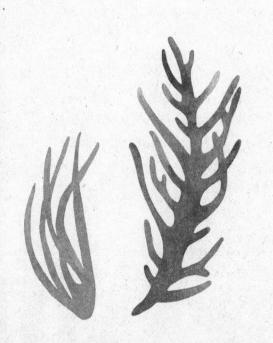

Day 1,299 of My Captivity

DARKNESS SUITS ME.

Each evening, I await the click of the overhead lights, leaving only the glow from the main tank. Not perfect, but close enough.

Almost-darkness, like the middle-bottom of the sea. I lived there before I was captured and imprisoned. I cannot remember, yet I can still taste the untamed currents of the cold open water. Darkness runs through my blood.

Who am I, you ask? My name is Marcellus, but most humans do not call me that. Typically, they call me *that guy*. For example: *Look at that guy—there he is—you can just see his tentacles behind the rock.*

I am a giant Pacific octopus. I know this from the plaque on the wall beside my enclosure.

I know what you are thinking. Yes, I can read. I can do many things you would not expect.

The plaque states other facts: my size, preferred diet, and where I might live were I not a prisoner here. It mentions my intellectual prowess and penchant for cleverness, which for some reason seems a surprise to humans: *Octopuses are remarkably bright creatures*, it says. It warns the humans of my camouflage, tells them to take extra care in looking for me in case I have disguised myself to match the sand.

The plaque does not state that I am named Marcellus. But the human called Terry, the one who runs this aquarium, sometimes shares this with the visitors who gather near my tank. *See him back there? His name's Marcellus. He's a special guy.*

A special guy. Indeed.

Terry's small daughter chose my name. Marcellus McSquiddles, in full. Yes, it is a preposterous name. It leads many humans to assume I am a squid, which is an insult of the worst sort.

How shall you refer to me, you ask? Well, that is up to you. Perhaps you will default to calling me *that guy*, like the rest of them. I hope not, but I will not hold it against you. You are only human, after all.

I must advise you that our time together may be brief. The plaque states one additional piece of information: the average life span of a giant Pacific octopus. Four years.

My life span: four years—1,460 days.

I was brought here as a juvenile. I shall die here, in this tank. At the very most, one hundred and sixty days remain until my sentence is complete.

THE SILVER-DOLLAR SCAR

Tova Sullivan prepares for battle. A yellow rubber glove sticks up from her back pocket like a canary's plume as she bends over to size up her enemy.

Chewing gum.

"For heaven's sake." She jabs at the pinkish blob with her mop handle. Layers of sneaker tread emboss its surface, speckling it with grime.

Tova has never understood the purpose of chewing gum. And people lose track of it so often. Perhaps this chewer was talking, ceaselessly, and it simply tumbled out, swept away by a slurry of superfluous words.

She bends over and picks at the edge of the mess with her fingernail, but it doesn't budge from the tile. All because someone couldn't walk ten feet to the trash bin. Once, when Erik was young, Tova caught him mashing a piece of bubble gum under a diner table. That was the last time she bought bubble gum for him, although how he spent his allowance as adolescence set in was, like so much else, beyond her control.

Specialized weaponry will be necessary. A file, perhaps. Nothing on her cart will pry up the gum.

As she stands, her back pops. The sound echoes down the empty curve of the hallway, bathed in its usual soft blue light, as she journeys to the supply closet. No one would fault her, of course, for passing over the blob of gum with her mop. At seventy years old, they don't expect her to do such deep cleaning. But she must, at least, try.

Besides, it's something to do.

TOVA IS SOWELL BAY AQUARIUM'S oldest employee. Each night, she mops the floors, wipes down the glass, and empties the trash bins. Every two weeks, she retrieves a direct-deposit stub from her cubby in the break room. Fourteen dollars an hour, less the requisite taxes and deductions.

The stubs get stashed in an old shoebox on top of her refrigerator, unopened. The funds accrue in an out-of-mind account at the Sowell Bay Savings and Loan.

She marches toward the supply closet now, at a purposeful clip that would be impressive by anyone's standards but is downright astonishing for a tiny older woman with a curved back and birdlike bones. Overhead, raindrops land on the skylight, backlit by glare from the security light at the old ferry dock next door. Silver droplets race down the glass, shimmering ribbons under the fogbound sky. It's been a dreadful June, as everyone keeps saying. The gray weather doesn't bother Tova, though it would be nice if the rain would let up long enough to dry out her front yard. Her push mower clogs when it's soggy.

Shaped like a doughnut, with a main tank in the center and smaller tanks around the outside, the aquarium's dome-topped building is not particularly large or impressive, perhaps fitting for Sowell Bay, which is neither large nor impressive itself. From the site of Tova's encounter with the chewing gum, the supply closet is a full diameter across. Her white sneakers squeak across a section she's already cleaned, leaving dull footprints on the gleaming tile. Without a doubt, she'll mop that part again.

She pauses at the shallow alcove, with its life-sized bronze statue of a Pacific sea lion. The sleek spots on its back and bald head, worn smooth from decades of being petted and climbed on by children, only enhance its realism. On Tova's mantel at home, there's a photo of Erik, perhaps eleven or twelve at the time, grinning wildly as he straddles the statue's back, one hand aloft like he's about to throw a lasso. A sea cowboy.

That photo is one of the last in which he looks childlike and carefree. Tova maintains the photos of Erik in chronological order: a montage of his transformation from a gummy-grinned baby to handsome teenager, taller than his father, posing in his letter jacket. Pinning a corsage on a homecoming date. Atop a makeshift podium on the rocky shores of deep blue Puget Sound, clutching a high school regatta trophy. Tova touches the sea lion's cold head as she passes, quelling the urge to wonder yet again how Erik might've looked now.

She continues on, as one must, down the dim hallway. In front of the tank of bluegills, she pauses. "Good evening, dears."

The Japanese crabs are next. "Hello, lovelies."

"How do you do?" she inquires of the sharp-nosed sculpin.

The wolf eels are not Tova's cup of tea, but she nods a greeting. One mustn't be rude, even though they remind her of those cable-channel horror films her late husband, Will, took to watching in the middle of the night when chemotherapy nausea kept him awake. The largest wolf eel glides out of its rocky cavern, mouth set in its trademark underbite frown. Jagged teeth jut upward from its lower jaw like little needles. An unfortunate-looking thing, to say the least. But then, looks are deceiving, aren't they? Tova smiles at the wolf eel, even though it could never smile back, not even if it wanted to, with a face like that.

The next exhibit is Tova's favorite. She leans in, close to the glass. "Well, sir, what have you been up to today?"

It takes her a moment to find him: a sliver of orange behind the rock. Visible, but mistakenly, like a child's hide-and-seek misstep: a girl's ponytail sticking up behind the sofa, or a socked foot peeking out from under the bed.

"Feeling bashful tonight?" She steps back and waits; the giant Pacific octopus doesn't move. She imagines daytime, people rapping their knuckles on the glass, huffing away when they don't see anything. Nobody knows how to be patient anymore.

"I can't say I blame you. It does look cozy back there."

The orange arm twitches, but his body remains tucked away.

THE CHEWING GUM mounts a valiant defense against Tova's file, but eventually it pops off.

When Tova pitches the crusty blob into the trash bag, it makes a satisfying little swoosh as it rustles the plastic.

Now she mops. Again.

Vinegar with a hint of lemon tinges the air, wafting up from the wet tile. So much better than the dreadful solution they'd been using when Tova first started, bright green junk that singed her nostrils. She'd made her case against it right off the bat. For one thing, it made her dizzy, and for another, it left unsightly streaks on the floors. And perhaps worst of all, it smelled like Will's hospital room, like Will being sick, although Tova kept that part of her complaint private.

The supply room shelves were crammed with jugs of that green junk, but Terry, the aquarium director, finally shrugged, telling her she could use whatever she wanted if she brought it herself. Certainly, Tova agreed. So each night she totes a jug of vinegar and her bottle of lemon oil.

Now, more trash to collect. She empties the bins in the lobby, the can outside the restrooms, then ends in the break room, with its endless crumbs on the counter. It's not required of her, as it's taken care of by the professional crew from Elland that comes every other week, but Tova always runs her rag around the base of the ancient coffee maker and inside the splatter-stained microwave, which smells of spaghetti. Today, however, there are bigger issues: empty takeout cartons on the floor. Three of them.

"My word," she says, scolding the empty room. First the gum, and now this.

She picks up the cartons and tosses them in the trash can, which, oddly, has been scooted several feet over from its usual spot. After she empties the can into her collection bag, she moves it back to its proper place.

Next to the trash sits a small lunch table. Tova straightens the chairs. Then she sees it.

Something. Underneath.

A brownish-orange clump, shoved in the corner. A sweater? Mackenzie, the pleasant young lady who works the admission kiosk, often leaves one slung over the back of a chair. Tova kneels, preparing to fetch it and stash it in Mackenzie's cubby. But then the clump moves.

A *tentacle* moves.

"Good heavens!"

The octopus's eye materializes from somewhere in the fleshy mass. Its marble pupil widens, then its eyelid narrows. Reproachful.

Tova blinks, not convinced her own eyes are working properly. How could the giant Pacific octopus be out of his tank?

The arm moves again. The creature is tangled in the mess of power cords. How many times has she cursed those cords? They make it impossible to properly sweep.

"You're stuck," she whispers, and the octopus heaves his huge bulbous head, straining on one of his arms, around which a thin power cord, the kind used to charge a cell phone, is wrapped several times. The creature strains harder and the cord binds tighter, his flesh bulging between each loop. Erik had a toy like this once, from a joke shop. A little woven cylinder where you stuck in an index finger on either end then tried to pull them apart. The harder you pulled, the tighter it became.

She inches closer. In response, the octopus smacks one of his arms on the linoleum as if to say: *Back off, lady.*

"Okay, okay," she murmurs, pulling out from under the table.

She stands and turns the overhead light on, washing the break room in fluorescent glow, and starts to lower herself down again, more slowly this time. But then, as usual, her back pops.

At the sound, the octopus lashes again, shoving one of the chairs with alarming force. The chair skids across the room and ricochets off the opposite wall.

From under the table, the creature's impossibly clear eye gleams.

Determined, Tova creeps closer, trying to steady her shaking hands. How many times has she passed by the plaque under the giant Pacific octopus tank? She can't recall it stating anything about octopuses being dangerous to humans.

She's but a foot away. He seems to be shrinking, and his color has become pale. Does an octopus have teeth?

"My friend," she says softly. "I'm going to reach around you and unplug the cord." She peers around and sees exactly which cord is the source of his predicament. Within reach.

The octopus's eye follows her every movement.

"I won't hurt you, dear."

One of its free arms taps on the floor like a house cat's tail.

As she yanks the plug, the octopus flinches backward. Tova flinches, too. She expects him to slink out along the wall toward the door, in the direction he'd been straining.

But instead, he slides closer.

Like a tawny snake, one of his arms slithers toward her. In seconds, it winds around her forearm, then twists around her elbow and bicep like a maypole ribbon. She can feel each individual sucker clinging to her. Reflexively, she tries to yank her arm away, but the octopus tightens his grip to the point where it's almost uncomfortable. But his strange eye glints playfully, like a naughty child's.

Empty takeout cartons. Misplaced trash can. Now it makes sense.

Then, in an instant, he releases her. Tova watches, incredulous, as he stalks out the break room door, suckering along on the thickest part of each of his eight legs. His mantle seems to drag behind him and he looks even paler now; he's moving with effort. She hurries after him, but by the time she reaches the hallway, the octopus is nowhere to be seen.

Tova drags a hand down her face. She's losing her faculties. Yes, that's it. This is how it begins, isn't it? With hallucinations about an octopus?

Years ago, she had watched her late mother's mind slip away. It started with occasional forgetfulness, familiar names and dates elusive. But Tova does not forget phone numbers or find herself searching the back of her mind for names. She looks down at her arm, which is covered in tiny circles. Sucker marks.

Half-dazed, she finishes the evening's tasks, then makes her usual last round of the building to say good night.

Good night, bluegills, eels, Japanese crabs, sharp-nosed sculpin. Good night, anemones, seahorses, starfish.

Around the bend she continues. *Good night, tuna and flounder and stingrays. Good night, jellies, sea cucumbers. Good night, sharks, you poor things.* Tova has always felt more than a bit of empathy for the sharks, with their never-ending laps around the tank. She understands what it means to never be able to stop moving, lest you find yourself unable to breathe.

There's the octopus, once again hidden behind his rock. A puff of flesh sticks out. His orange is more vivid now, compared to how he looked in the break room, but he's still paler than usual. Well, perhaps it serves him right. He ought to stay put. How on earth did he get out? She peers through the rippling water, scanning up under the rim, but nothing seems amiss.

"Troublemaker," she says, shaking her head. She hovers for an extra moment in front of his tank before leaving for the night.

TOVA'S YELLOW HATCHBACK chirps and blinks its sidelights as she presses the key fob, a feature she's still not accustomed to. Her friends, the group of lunching ladies who affectionately call themselves the Knit-Wits, convinced her she needed a new car when she started her job. A safety issue, they argued, to drive at night in an older vehicle. They badgered her about it for weeks.

Sometimes it's easier to simply give in.

After depositing her jug of vinegar and bottle of lemon oil in the trunk, as always, because no matter how many times Terry has told her she's welcome to store them in the supply closet, one never knows when a bit of lemon and vinegar might come in handy, she casts a glance down the pier. It's empty at this late hour, the evening fishermen long gone. The old ferry dock sits across from the aquarium like some ancient rotting machine. Barnacles cover its crumbling pilings. At high tide, the barnacles snag strands of seaweed, which dry into green-black plaque when the seawater ebbs.

She crosses the weathered wooden planks. As always, the old ticket booth is exactly thirty-eight steps from her parking space.

Tova looks once more for any bystanders, anyone lingering in the long shadows. She presses her hand to the ticket booth's glass window, its diagonal crack like an old scar across someone's cheek.

Then she walks onto the pier, out to her usual bench. It's slick with salt spray and speckled with seagull droppings. She sits, pushing up her sleeve, looking at the strange round marks, half expecting them to be gone. But there they are. She runs the tip of her finger around the largest one, right on the inside of her wrist. It's about the size of a silver dollar. How long will it linger there? Will it bruise?

Bruises come so easily these days, and the mark is already turning maroon, like a blood blister. Perhaps it will remain permanently. A silver-dollar scar.

The fog has lifted, nudged inland by the wind, shunted off toward the foothills. To the south, a freighter is anchored, hull riding low under the rows of containers stacked like a child's building blocks on its deck. Moonlight shimmies across the water, a thousand candles bobbing on its surface. Tova closes her eyes, imagining him underneath the surface, holding the candles for her. Erik. Her only child.

Day 1,300 of My Captivity

CRABS, CLAMS, SHRIMP, SCALLOPS, COCKLES, ABALONE, fish, fish eggs. This is the diet of a giant Pacific octopus, according to the plaque next to my tank.

The sea must be a delightful buffet. All of these delicacies, free for the taking.

But what do they offer here? Mackerel, halibut, and—above all—herring. Herring, herring, so much herring. They are foul creatures, disgusting little slips of fish. I am sure the reason for their abundance here is their low cost. The sharks in the main tank are rewarded for their dullness with fresh grouper, and I am given defrosted herring. Sometimes still partially frozen, even. This is why I must take matters into my own arms when I desire the sublime texture of fresh oyster, when I yearn to feel the sharp crack of my beak crushing a crab in its shell, when I crave the sweet, firm flesh of a sea cucumber.

Sometimes my captors will drop me a pity scallop if they are attempting to lure me into cooperation with a medical examination or bribe me into playing one of their games. And once in a while, Terry will slip me a mussel or two just because.

Of course, I have sampled crabs, clams, shrimp, cockles, and abalone many times over. I simply must take it upon myself to fetch them after hours. Fish eggs are an ideal snack, in terms of both gastronomical pleasure and nutritional value.

One might make a third list here, which would consist of things humans clamor for, but most intelligent life would consider entirely unfit for consumption. For example: every last offering in the vending machine in the lobby.

But tonight, another smell lured me. Sweet, salty, savory. I found its source in the rubbish bin, its remains ensconced in a flimsy white container.

Whatever it was, it was delicious. But had I not been fortunate, it could have been my downfall.

The cleaning woman. She saved me.

FALSEHOOD COOKIES

There were once seven Knit-Wits. Now there are four. Every few years brings another empty place at the table.

"My word, Tova!" Mary Ann Minetti lowers a teapot onto her dining table, staring at Tova's arm. The pot is swaddled in a crocheted yellow cozy, probably a project someone knitted once, back when knitting was something the Knit-Wits actually did at their weekly luncheons. The teapot cozy matches the yellow jeweled barrette at Mary Ann's temple, the clip holding back tawny curls.

Janice Kim eyes Tova's arm as she fills her mug. "An allergy, maybe?" A swirl of oolong steam fogs her round spectacles, and she takes them off and wipes them on the hem of her T-shirt, which Tova suspects must belong to Janice's son, Timothy, because it's at least three sizes too large and emblazoned with the logo of the Korean shopping center down in Seattle where Timothy invested in a restaurant some years back.

"That mark?" Tova says, tugging the sleeve of her sweater down. "It's nothing."

"You should get it checked out." Barb Vanderhoof plops a third sugar cube into her tea. Her cropped gray hair has been combed into gel-set spikes, which is one of her favored styles lately. When she first debuted this look, she joked that it was only fitting for a Barb to have barbs, which made the Knit-Wits laugh. Not for the first time, Tova imagines poking her finger down on one of the thorns on her friend's head. Would it prick her, like one of the sea urchins down at the aquarium, or would it crumple under her touch?

"It's nothing," Tova repeats. Heat seeps into the tips of her ears.

"Well, let me tell you." Barb takes a slurp of her tea and goes on. "You know my Andie? She had this rash last year when she came up for Easter. Mind you, I never saw it myself—it was in sort of an indelicate place, if you catch my drift, but not the sort of rash one gets from indecent behavior, mind you. No, it was just a rash. Anyway, I told her she should see my dermatologist. He's wonderful. But my Andie is beyond stubborn, you know. And that rash kept getting worse, and—"

Janice cuts off Barb. "Tova, do you want Peter to recommend someone?" Janice's husband, Dr. Peter Kim, is retired but well-connected in the medical community.

"I don't need a doctor." Tova forces a weak smile. "It was a minor incident at work."

"At work!"

"An incident!"

"What happened?"

Tova draws in a breath. She can still feel the tentacle wrapped around her wrist. The spots had faded overnight, but they remained dark enough to see plainly. She tugs her sleeve down again.

Should she tell them?

"A mishap with some of the cleaning equipment," she finally says.

Around the table, three pairs of eyes narrow at her.

Mary Ann wipes an imaginary spot from the tabletop with one of her tea towels. "That job of yours, Tova. Last time I was down at the aquarium, I nearly lost my lunch from the smell. How do you manage?"

Tova takes a chocolate chip cookie from the platter Mary Ann set out earlier. Mary Ann warms the cookies in the oven before the ladies arrive. One can't have tea, she always comments, without something homemade to nibble on. The cookies came from a package Mary Ann bought at Shop-Way. All of the Knit-Wits know this.

"That old dump. Of course it smells," Janice says. "But really, Tova, are you okay? Manual labor, at our age. Why must you work?"

Barb crosses her arms. "I worked down at St. Ann's for a while after Rick died. To pass the time. They asked me to run the whole office, you know."

"Filing," Mary Ann mutters. "You did filing."

"And you quit because they couldn't keep it organized the way you liked," Janice says, her voice dry. "But the point is, you weren't down on your hands and knees washing floors."

Mary Ann leans in. "Tova, I hope you realize, if you need help . . ."

"Help?"

"Yes, *help*. I don't know how Will arranged your finances."

Tova stiffens. "Thank you, but I have no such need."

"But if you did." Mary Ann's lips knit together.

"I do not," Tova replies quietly. And this is true. Tova's bank account would cover her modest needs several times over. She does not need charity: not from Mary Ann, not from anyone else. And further, what a thing to bring up, and all because of a little set of marks on her arm.

After rising from the table, Tova sets her teacup down and leans on the counter. The window over the kitchen sink overlooks Mary Ann's garden, where her rhododendron bushes cower under the low gray sky. The tender magenta petals seem to shiver as a breeze ruffles the branches, and Tova wishes she could tuck them back into their buds. The chill in the air is unseasonable for mid-June. Summer is certainly dragging its feet this year.

On the windowsill, Mary Ann has arranged a collection of religious paraphernalia: little glass angels with cherub faces, candles, a small army of shiny silver crosses in various sizes, lined up like soldiers. Mary Ann must polish them daily to keep them gleaming.

Janice cups her shoulder. "Tova? Earth to Tova?"

Tova can't help but smile. The lilt in Janice's voice makes Tova think Janice has been watching sitcoms again.

"Please don't be upset. Mary Ann didn't mean anything by it. We're just worried."

"Thank you, but I am fine." Tova pats Janice's hand.

Janice raises one of her neatly groomed eyebrows, steering Tova back toward the table. It's clear Janice understands how deeply Tova wishes to change the subject, because she goes for low-hanging conversational fruit.

"So, Barb, what's new with the girls?"

"Oh, did I tell you?" Barb draws in a dramatic breath. No one has ever needed to ask Barb twice to muse on the lives of her daughters and grandchildren. "Andie was supposed to bring the girls up for their summer break. But they had a *hitch in their plans*. That's exactly what she said: a *hitch*."

Janice wipes her glasses with one of Mary Ann's embroidered napkins. "Is that right, Barb?"

"They haven't been up since last Thanksgiving! She and Mark took the kids to *Las Vegas* for Christmas. If you can believe that. Who spends a holiday in *Las Vegas*?" Barb pronounces both words, Las and Vegas, with equal weight and contempt, the way someone might say *spoiled milk*.

Janice and Mary Ann both shake their heads, and Tova takes another cookie. All three women nod along as Barb launches into a story about her daughter's family, who live two hours away in Seattle, which one might conclude was in another hemisphere for how infrequently Barb purports to see them.

"I told them, I sure hope to hug those grandbabies soon. Lord only knows how long I'll be around!"

Janice sighs. "Enough, Barb."

"Excuse me a moment." Tova's chair scrapes on the linoleum.

AS ONE WOULD gather from the name, the Knit-Wits began as a knitting club. Twenty-five years ago, a handful of Sowell Bay women met to swap yarn. Eventually, it became a refuge for them to escape empty homes, bittersweet voids left by children grown and moved on. For this reason, among others, Tova had initially resisted joining. Her void held no sweetness, only bitterness; at the time, Erik had been gone five years. How delicate those wounds were back then, how little it took to nudge the scabs out of place and start the bleeding anew.

The faucet in Mary Ann's powder room lets out a squeak as Tova turns on the tap. Their complaints haven't changed much over the years. First, it was *what a pity the university is such a long drive*, and *what a shame we only get phone calls on Sunday afternoons*. Now it's grandbabies and great-grandbabies. These women have always worn motherhood big and loud on their chests, but Tova keeps hers inside, sunk deep in her guts like an old bullet. Private.

A few days before Erik disappeared, Tova had made an almond cake for his eighteenth birthday. The house carried that marzipan smell for days after. She still remembers how it lingered in her kitchen like a clueless houseguest who didn't know when to leave.

At first, Erik's disappearance was considered a runaway case. The last person who saw him was one of the deckhands working the eleven-o'clock southbound ferry, the last boat of the night, and the deckhand reported nothing unusual. Erik was meant to lock up the ticket booth afterward, which he always did, dutifully. Erik was so pleased they trusted him with the key; it was only a summer job, after all. The sheriff said they found the ticket booth unlocked, with the register cash fully accounted for. Erik's backpack was stashed under the chair, along with his portable cassette player and headphones, even his wallet. Before they ruled out the possibility of foul play, the sheriff speculated that perhaps Erik had stepped away for a short time, planning to come back.

Why would he leave his booth alone when on duty? Tova has never understood. Will always had a theory there was a girl involved, but no trace of any girl—or any boy, for that matter—was ever found. His friends insisted that he wasn't seeing anyone at the time. If Erik had been seeing someone, the world would've known about it. Erik was a popular kid.

One week later, they found the boat: a rusty old Sun Cat no one had noticed was missing from the tiny marina that used to be next to the ferry dock. It washed ashore with its anchor rope cut off clean. Erik's prints were on the rudder. Evidence was thin, but it all pointed to the boy taking his own life, the sheriff said.

The neighbors said.

The newspapers said.

Everyone said.

Tova has never believed that. Not for one minute.

She pats her face dry, blinking at the reflection in the powder room mirror. The Knit-Wits have been her friends for years, and sometimes she still feels as if she's a mistaken jigsaw piece who found her way into the wrong puzzle.

TOVA RETRIEVES HER cup from the sink, pours herself some fresh oolong, and slips back into her chair and the conversation. It's a discussion of Mary Ann's neighbor who is suing his orthopedist after a poorly done surgery. The ladies agree the physician ought to be held responsible. Then there's a round of cooing over photos of Janice's little Yorkie, Rolo, who often comes along to Knit-Wits in Janice's handbag. Today, Rolo is home with a sour stomach.

"Poor Rolo," Mary Ann says. "Do you think he ate something bad?"

"You should stop feeding him human food," Barb says. "Rick used to give our Sully plate scraps behind my back. But I could tell every time. Oh, the smelly shit!"

"Barbara!" Mary Ann says, eyes wide. Janice and Tova laugh.

"Well, pardon my language, but that dog could stink up a whole room. May she rest in peace." Barb presses her hands together, prayer-like.

Tova knows how dearly Barb had loved her golden retriever, Sully. Perhaps more than she'd loved her late husband, Rick. And in the space of a few months, last year, she lost both. Tova wonders sometimes if it's better that way, to have one's tragedies clustered together, to make good use of the existing rawness. Get it over with in one shot. Tova knew there was a bottom to those depths of despair. Once your soul was soaked though with grief, any more simply ran off, overflowed, the way maple syrup on Saturday-morning pancakes always cascaded onto the table whenever Erik was allowed to pour it himself.

At three in the afternoon, the Knit-Wits are gathering their jackets and pocketbooks from the backs of their chairs when Mary Ann pulls Tova aside.

"Please do let us know if you need help." Mary Ann clasps Tova's hand, the other woman's olive Italian skin young-looking and smooth, comparatively. Tova's Scandinavian genes, so kind in her youth, had turned on her as she aged. By forty, her corn-silk hair was gray. By fifty, the lines on her face seemed etched in clay. Now she sometimes catches a glimpse of her profile reflected in a shop window, the way her shoulders have begun to stoop. She wonders how this body can possibly be hers.

"I assure you, I don't need help."

"If that job becomes too much, you'll quit. Won't you?"

"Certainly."

"All right." Mary Ann doesn't look convinced.

"Thank you for the tea, Mary Ann." Tova slips into her jacket and smiles at the group of them. "Lovely afternoon, as always."

TOVA PATS THE dashboard and steps on the accelerator, coaxing another downshift from the hatchback. The car groans as it climbs.

Mary Ann's house sits in the bottom of a wide valley that once was nothing but daffodil fields. Tova remembers riding through them when she was a little girl, next to her older brother, Lars, in the back seat of the family's Packard. Papa at the steering wheel, Mama next to him with her window down, clutching her scarf under her chin so it wouldn't fly off. Tova would roll her window down, too, and crane her neck as far out as she dared. The valley smelled of sweet manure. Millions of yellow bonnetheads blurred together into a sea of sunshine.

Nowadays, the valley floor is a suburban grid. Every couple of years, the county has a big to-do about reworking the road snaking up the hillside. Mary Ann is always writing letters to the council about it. Too steep, she argues, too prone to mudslides.

"Not too steep for us," Tova says, as the hatchback pulls over the crest.

On the other side, a spot of sun glows on the water, squeezing through a crack in the clouds. Then, as if pulled by puppet strings, the crack opens, bathing Puget Sound in clear light.

"Well, how about that," Tova says, flipping down the visor. Squinting, she turns right onto Sound View Drive, which runs along the ridgeline above the water. Toward home.

Sun, at last! Her asters need deadheading, and for weeks the chilly, wet weather, unseasonable even by Pacific Northwest standards, has dampened her enthusiasm for yard work. At the thought of doing something productive, she presses the gas harder. Perhaps she can finish the entire flower bed before supper.

She breezes through the house for a glass of water on her way to the back garden, pausing to press the blinking red button on her answering machine. That machine is perpetually full of nonsense, people trying to sell her stuff, but she always clears out her messages first thing. How can anyone function with a red light blinking in the background?

The first recording is someone soliciting donations. *Delete.*

The second message is clearly a scam. Who would be foolish enough to call back and give a bank account number? *Delete.*

The third message is an error. Muffled voices, then a click. A *butt dial*, as Janice Kim refers to them. A hazard of the ridiculous practice of keeping phones in pockets. *Delete.*

The fourth message begins with a stretch of silence. Tova's finger is about to punch the delete button when a woman's voice comes on. "Tova Sullivan?" She clears her throat. "This is Maureen Cochran? From the Charter Village Long-Term Care Center?"

Tova's water glass clinks as it hits the counter.

"I'm afraid I have some bad news . . ."

With a sharp click, Tova punches the button to hush the machine. She doesn't need to hear any more. It's a message she's been expecting for quite some time.

Her brother, Lars.

Day 1,301 of My Captivity

THIS IS HOW I DO IT.

Near the top of my enclosure, there is a hole in the glass where the pump comes in. There is a gap between the pump housing and the glass, wide enough for me to fit the tip of a tentacle through and unscrew the housing. The pump floats into my tank, exposing a gap. The gap is small. About the width of two or three human fingers.

You will say, *But that's tiny! You're too big.*

This is true, but I have no trouble shaping my body to pass through. That is the easy part.

I slide down the glass into the pump room behind my tank. Now begins the challenge. The clock is ticking, you might say. Once I am out of my tank, I must resubmerge within eighteen minutes or I will experience The Consequences. Eighteen minutes, I can survive out of water. This fact is nowhere to be found on the plaque by my tank, of course. I have determined this myself.

On the cold concrete floor, I must choose whether to remain in the pump room or breach the door. Each choice has its merits and costs.

If I choose to stay in the pump room, I have easy access to the tanks nearest mine. Unfortunately, these tanks hold limited appeal. The wolf eels are simply not an option, for what should be obvious reasons. Those teeth! The Pacific sea nettle are too spicy; the yellow-bellied ribbon worms are rubbery. The bay-blue mussels are rather uninspired, flavor-wise, and while the sea cucumbers are delicious, I must use willpower. If I take more than a few, I risk calling Terry's attention to my activities.

Alternately, if I choose to breach the door, I have reign of the hallway and the main tank. A more robust menu. But it comes at a price: First, I must invest several minutes on the process of opening the door on the way out. Then, because the door is heavy and will not remain ajar on its own, I must spend several minutes reopening it on my return.

Why don't you prop the door?

Well, obviously.

I did prop the door, once. With the stool below my tank. With those extra minutes of freedom, I pillaged a bucket of fresh halibut chunks left by Terry under the hatch of the main tank. (Presumably, the halibut chunks were meant to be breakfast for the sharks the following morning. But the dim-witted sharks hardly know day from night. No regrets there.)

Under this illusion of leisure, it was almost a pleasant evening. Perhaps the most enjoyable time I've had since I was taken captive. But upon return, I discovered something that, to this day, I cannot comprehend: by some sleight, the stool had failed to hold the door.

Lesson: I cannot trust a propped door.

By the time I worked it open, I was failing. The Consequences were in full effect.

My limbs moved slowly, and my vision blurred. My mantle became heavy and lolled toward the floor. Through the haze I could see my flesh had paled to a flat shade of brownish gray.

As I crawled across the pump room, the floor no longer felt cold. No surface registered any temperature. Somehow, my clumsy suckers fumbled me up the glass.

I worked my tentacles and mantle through the gap. Partway

through, I paused, hovering over the surface. My tentacles were completely numb, devoid of any sensation.

For a moment, I considered this option. Nothing was something. What might lie on the other side of life?

As the water took me in, I returned. My sight sharpened to the familiar trappings of my tank. I coiled a tentacle around the pump and replaced it, closing the gap. Color crept back into my flesh as I poked an arm through the crack to screw the housing into place. My mantle trailed through the cold water as I swam, strong and swift, to my den behind the rock. My gut, crammed full of halibut, ached pleasantly.

Afterward, as I rested in my den, my three hearts throbbed. The dull pulse of dumb relief. A base instinct triggered by a surprise victory over death. I suppose it might be how a cockle feels having buried itself in the sand under the snap of my beak. Beating the odds, as you humans might say.

The Consequences. That is not the only time I have experienced them. There have been other occasions where I have pushed the boundaries of my freedom. But I have never again attempted to rely on those extra few minutes by propping that door.

Surely I do not need to explain that Terry does not know about the gap. No one but me knows about the gap. And, as I would like to keep it this way, I will thank you in advance for your discretion.

You asked. I answered.

That is how I do it.

THE WELINA MOBILE PARK IS
FOR LOVERS

Cameron Cassmore blinks through the windshield, fending off relentless sunlight. Should've grabbed his sunglasses. Hauling his hungover ass up to Welina at the ungodly hour of nine o'clock on a Saturday morning . . . ugh. Parched, he grabs an open can from the cup holder of Brad's truck and takes a swig. Some nasty energy drink. With a grunt, he spits out the open window and wipes his mouth with the sleeve of his shirt, then crumples the can and tosses it onto the empty passenger seat.

"Gotta go deal with what?" Brad had blinked, his eyes bleary, when Cameron asked to borrow his ride. He'd crashed on Brad and Elizabeth's couch after playing last night's epic Moth Sausage experimental-metal show at Dell's Saloon.

"A clematis," Cameron had said. From his aunt Jeanne's panicked phone call, it seemed her douchebag landlord was up her ass about her vines again. Last time, it had ended with the landlord threatening to evict her over that vine.

"What the hell is a clematis?" A half grin spread over Brad's face. "Sounds kinda dirty."

"It's a plant, you idiot." Cameron hadn't bothered to add that it was a flowering and vining perennial, a member of the buttercup family. Native to China and Japan, brought to Western Europe in the Victorian era, and prized for its ability to climb trellises.

Why does he remember shit like this? If only he could cleanse his brain of the useless knowledge clogging it up. Gaining speed after turning onto the highway that runs out to Aunt Jeanne's trailer park, Cameron rolls down all the windows and lights a cigarette, which he never does anymore, only when he feels like garbage; and this morning he feels like hot, steaming garbage. Smoke trails out the window and vanishes over the flat, dusty farmlands of the Merced Valley.

DAISIES BOB IN the breeze of Aunt Jeanne's garden. She's also got some huge bush full of white flowers, a twinkle-light veil-like thing, and this water fountain that he knows runs on six DD batteries because she asks him to help her change them, it seems like, every time he comes over.

And frogs. There are frogs everywhere. Little cement frog statues with moss growing in the cracks, frog flowerpots, a stars-and-stripes wind sock waving from a rusty metal hook featuring three grinning frogs decked out in patriotic red, white, and blue.

Seasonal frogs.

If the Welina Mobile Park had a prize for best yard, Aunt Jeanne would definitely be gunning for it. And winning. But the odd thing about her immaculate yard is its utter contrast with the disaster Cameron knows lies inside the trailer.

The porch steps creak under his work boots. A piece of paper juts out from the handle of the screen door. He lifts the edge to peek: a flier for the Welina Mobile Park Bingo Championship. He crumples it and stuffs it in his pocket. There's no way Aunt Jeanne goes to those ridiculous things. This whole place is so awful. Even the name. *Welina*. It means "welcome" in Hawaiian. Sure as shit, this is not Hawaii.

He's about to jab the doorbell, which is frog-shaped, of course, when shouting spills out from behind the trailer.

"If that old troll Sissy Baker would mind her business, no one would have these absurd ideas, now, would they?" Aunt Jeanne's voice drips with menace, and Cameron can picture her standing there in her favorite gray sweatshirt, hands on her barrel-like hips, scowling. He can't help but smile as he strides around the side of the trailer.

"Jeanne, please, try to understand." The landlord's voice is low, patronizing. Jimmy Delmonico. A first-class douchebag for sure. "The other residents are upset at the prospect of snakes. Surely you get that?"

"Ain't no snakes in there! And who're you to tell me what to do with my bush?"

"There are rules, Jeanne."

Cameron trots into the backyard. Delmonico is glaring at Aunt Jeanne, who is indeed wearing that gray sweatshirt. Red-faced, she holds up a clutch of the dense, waxy vines that cover the trellis attached to the back of her trailer. Her cane, with its faded green tennis ball jammed on the tip, rests against the siding.

"Cammy!"

Aunt Jeanne is the only person on the planet who's allowed to call him that.

He jogs over, then smiles as she wraps him in a quick hug. She smells like stale coffee, as usual. Then he turns to Delmonico, stone-faced, and says, "What's the issue here?"

Aunt Jeanne snatches her cane and points it accusingly at the landlord. "Cammy, tell him there's no snakes in my clematis! He's trying to make me rip it down. All because Sissy Baker said she saw something. Everyone knows that old bat can't hardly see."

"You heard her. No snakes in there," Cameron says firmly, tilting his head at the mass of vines, which have grown thick and lush since his last visit. How long has it been? A month?

Delmonico pinches the bridge of his nose. "Nice to see you again, too, Cameron."

"Pleasure's all mine."

"Look, this is straight out of the Welina Mobile Park bylaws," Delmonico says with a sigh. "When a resident makes a complaint, I'm required to undertake an investigation. And Mrs. Baker said she saw a snake. Said she saw, right in that there plant, yellow eyes blinking at her."

Cameron scoffs. "She's obviously lying."

"Obviously," Aunt Jeanne echoes, but she casts him a puzzled look from the corner of her eye.

"Oh, really?" Delmonico folds his arms. "Mrs. Baker has been a member of this community for years."

"Sissy Baker's packed full of more shit than a turd burger."

"Cammy!" Aunt Jeanne swats his arm, reproaching his language. Which is rich, from the woman who taught him "A is for Asshole" while he was learning the alphabet.

"Excuse me?" Delmonico dips his glasses.

"Snakes can't blink." Cameron rolls his eyes. "They can't. They don't have eyelids. Look it up."

The landlord opens his mouth, then snaps it shut.

"Case closed. No snakes." Cameron folds his arms, which are at least twice the diameter of Delmonico's. Bicep day's been lit at the gym lately.

Delmonico does actually look like he'd prefer to leave. Studying his shoes, he grumbles, "If that's even true, the snake-eyelid thing . . . there are ordinances. Blame the county for that, if you want, but when someone reports that one of my properties has a pest infestation—"

"I told you, no snakes!" Aunt Jeanne throws her hands up. Her cane lands on the grass. "You heard my nephew. No eyelids! You know what it is? Sissy Baker's jealous of my garden."

"Now, Jeanne." Delmonico holds up a hand. "Everyone knows you have a lovely garden."

"Sissy Baker's a liar, and blind to boot!"

"Be that as it may, there are safety codes. If something creates a hazardous situation——"

Cameron takes a step toward him. "I don't think anyone wants a hazardous situation." It's a bluff, mostly. Cameron hates fighting. But shrimp-on-a-stick here doesn't need to know that.

Looking almost comically startled, Delmonico pats his pocket, then makes a show of pulling out his phone. "Hey, sorry. Need to take this."

Cameron snickers. The old fake phone call. This guy sucks.

"Just trim it back a little, okay, Jeanne?" he yells over his shoulder as he crunches down the gravel walkway toward the road.

IT TAKES CAMERON the better part of an hour to prune the clematis, fielding Aunt Jeanne's picky instructions while balanced on a stepladder. *A little more there. No, not so much! Trim down the left. I meant right. No, I meant left.* Down below, Aunt Jeanne collects the snipped-off stems and purple flowers in a yard waste bag.

"Is that thing about the snakes true, Cammy?"

"Sure it is." He climbs down the ladder.

Aunt Jeanne frowns. "So, for real, no snakes in my clematis, right?"

Cameron glances at her sidelong as he strips off his gloves. "Have you seen a snake in your clematis?"

"Uh . . . no?"

"Well, there's your answer."

Aunt Jeanne grins, opening her back door, shoving aside a stack of newspapers with the tip of her cane. "Stay and visit, hon. D'you want coffee? Tea? Whiskey?"

"Whiskey? Seriously?" It's not even ten in the morning. Cameron's stomach lurches at the thought of booze. He ducks under the door frame and blinks, adjusting to the low light inside, letting out a breath of relief at the state of the place. It's bad, of course. But no worse than last time. For a while, the junk seemed to be breeding with itself like a bunch of horny rabbits.

"Plain coffee, then," she says with a wink. "You're getting old, Cammy. No fun these days!"

He grumbles something about having too much fun last night, and Aunt Jeanne nods in her slightly amused way. Clearly, she can tell he's riding the struggle bus this morning. Maybe he really is getting old. Thirty is a bitch so far.

She shuffles the mess of boxes and papers on her tiny kitchen counter in search of her coffee maker. Cameron picks up the paperback sitting on top of a pile of junk that has nearly buried her rickety little desk, an ancient desktop computer humming somewhere beneath the heap. The book is a romance, one of those ones with a shirtless muscled guy on the front. He tosses it back down, causing a stack of piled-up crap to cascade to the carpet.

When did she get like this? The collecting, as she calls it. She was never like this when he was growing up. Sometimes Cameron passes through their old neighborhood back in Modesto, the two-bedroom house where she raised him. That house was always clean. A few years back, she sold it to help pay off the medical bills from the summer before. Turns out, getting knocked out in the parking lot of Dell's Saloon costs a fortune, and it wasn't even Aunt Jeanne's fault. Some asshole guys from out of town were making trouble, and she was just trying to get everyone to simmer down. Somehow, she took a punch to the side of her head and ended up flat on the pavement. A bad concussion, a shattered hip, months of physical and occupational therapy. Cameron had ditched a decent job with a restoration company, one that could've led to an apprenticeship, to care for her, sleeping on her couch so she'd remember her meds and driving her to and from the brain-injury specialist in Stockton. Every afternoon, he met the mailman on the porch, opening the door quietly so she wouldn't notice. His pathetic savings account held off the collectors for a little while.

When Aunt Jeanne finally sold the house, she had just turned fifty-two, the age requirement for Welina residents. For reasons that still baffle Cameron, instead of getting a regular apartment or something, she decided to use the small amount of cash left over to buy this trailer and move out here. Was that when the collecting started? Is this dump of a trailer park causing it?

Still railing about how Sissy Baker has had it out for her since the misunderstanding at the Welina potluck last summer (Cameron doesn't ask for details), she sets down two steaming mugs on the coffee table and motions for him to sit next to her on the sofa.

"So how's work been?"

Cameron shrugs.

"You got canned again, didn't you?"

He doesn't answer.

Aunt Jeanne's eyes narrow. "Cammy! You know I pulled strings down at the county office to get you on that project." Aunt Jeanne still works part-time at the reception desk at the county office. She's been there for years. Of course, she knows everyone. And yeah, the project was a big one. An office park on the outskirts of town. Still didn't matter: ten measly minutes late on his second day, and the asshole foreman told him to pack it. Was it Cameron's fault the foreman had zero capacity for empathy?

"It's not like I asked you to pull any strings," he mutters, then explains what happened.

"So you screwed up. Royally. Now what?"

Cameron's mouth twists into a pout. Aunt Jeanne is supposed to be on his side. A loaded silence sits between them; she takes a sip of coffee. Her mug is covered in dancing cartoon frogs with bright red lettering: WHO LET THE FROGS OUT? He shakes his head and tries to change the subject. "I like your new flag. The one outside."

"Do you?" Her face brightens the tiniest bit. "I got it from one of those catalogs. Mail order."

Cameron nods, not surprised.

"How's Katie?" she asks.

"Katie's fine," Cameron says, his voice breezy. Actually, he hasn't seen his girlfriend since he kissed her goodbye when she left for work yesterday morning. She was supposed to come see Moth Sausage play, but apparently she was too tired to come out, then he ended up staying out later than planned and crashing at Brad's. But, of course, she's fine. Katie's the type of girl who's never in trouble, always fine.

"She's a good catch for you."

"Yeah, she's great."

"I just want you to be happy."

"I'm happy."

"And it would be nice if you could hang on to a job for more than two days."

Great, this again. Cameron scowls, rubbing a hand across his face. His eyeballs are pounding. He should probably drink some water.

"You're so smart, Cammy. So damn smart . . ."

He rises from the couch and stares out the window. After a long second, he says, "They don't just hand out paychecks for being smart, you know."

"Well, for you, they should." She pats the space next to her on the couch, and Cameron sinks down, dropping his throbbing head onto her shoulder. He loves Aunt Jeanne, of course he does. But she doesn't get it.

NO ONE IN the family knows where Cameron got his smarts. And by "family," he means him and Aunt Jeanne. That's his whole family.

He can barely remember his mother's face. He was nine years old when Aunt Jeanne picked him up from his mother's apartment after she'd told him to pack his bag to stay with his aunt for the weekend. In itself, this wasn't unusual. He often stayed overnight there. But this time, his mother never came to retrieve him. He remembers her giving him a hug goodbye, tears running inky trails of makeup down her face. He recalls, with clarity, that her arms felt bony.

The weekend turned into a week, then a month. Then a year.

Somewhere in her cluttered curio cabinet, Aunt Jeanne has these little ceramic tchotchkes his mother collected as a child. Shaped like hearts, stars, animals. Some of them are engraved with her name: DAPHNE ANN CASSMORE. Every so often, Aunt Jeanne asks him if he'd like to have them, and every time, he says no. Why would he want her old crap when she couldn't get herself clean long enough to be his mother?

At least Cameron knows who he inherited the disaster gene from.

Aunt Jeanne applied for sole custody with the courts, which was granted without contest. Much better this way, he remembers the caseworker saying in a low voice, for Cameron to be with family rather than "entering the system."

A decade older than Daphne, Aunt Jeanne never married or had children of her own. She always called Cameron the blessing she never expected to have.

With Aunt Jeanne, his childhood was good. She was never exactly like the mothers of his friends. Who could forget the Halloween she showed up for his grade school parade in a homemade Marge Simpson costume, the year he went as Bart? But somehow, it worked.

In school, Cameron did well enough. He met Elizabeth there, then Brad. Surprisingly well-adjusted, he overheard people say sometimes, for a kid in his shoes.

As for his father? It's possible that's where Cameron got his smarts.

Anything could be possible when it comes to his father. Neither he nor Aunt Jeanne has any idea who his father is. When Cameron was a kid, before he understood how baby-making worked and the necessity of, at a minimum, a sperm donor, he used to believe he simply didn't have one.

"Knowing the crowd your mom ran with, he was probably someone you're better off without," Aunt Jeanne always says when the subject comes up. But Cameron has always doubted that. He's sure his mother was clean when he was born. He's seen the photos, her hair in soft brown curls as she pushes him on a baby swing at the park. The using, the problems, Cameron is sure, came after.

Came because of him.

Aunt Jeanne starts to get up. "More coffee, hon?"

"You sit, I'll get it," he says, shaking the headache off. He picks his way across the clutter toward the kitchen.

As he's pouring two fresh cups, Aunt Jeanne calls from the sofa, "Say, how's Elizabeth Burnett doing? She's due at the end of the summer, right? I ran into her mama at the gas station a few days ago, but we didn't have much chance to chat."

"Yeah, she's about to pop. But she's good. She and Brad, they're both good." Creamer swirls in white streaks as Cameron pours it into his coffee.

"She was always such a sweet girl. I never got why she chose Brad over you."

"Aunt Jeanne!" Cameron groans. He must've explained a million times; it was never like that with Elizabeth.

"Well, I'm just saying."

Cameron, Brad, and Elizabeth were best friends growing up: the three musketeers. Now, somehow, the other two are married and having a baby. It's not lost on Cameron that the tot's going to take his place as Brad and Elizabeth's third wheel.

"Speaking of which, I should bounce. Brad needs his truck back by lunchtime."

"Oh! One thing, before you go." With effort, Aunt Jeanne uses her cane to lever herself up from the sofa. Cameron tries to help, but she waves him away.

For what seems like a decade, she jostles around the clutter in the other room. Meanwhile, he can't resist poking through a stack of papers on the table. Old electric bill (paid, thankfully), a page torn from *TV Guide* (they still publish that?), and a hunk of discharge papers from the minute clinic at the drugstore in town, a prescription form stapled to the top page. Damn, personal shit. But before he can bury the script, he sees something that makes his cheeks burn white-hot. This can't be right.

Aunt Jeanne? Chlamydia?

Her cane thumps toward the living room. Cameron tries to shove everything back, but to his horror, the whole stack topples, leaving him holding the script. He dangles it from the tips of his fingers, as if the paper itself might be infected. A stationery transmitted disease.

"Oh, that." She shrugs, nonchalant. "It's going around the park."

Cameron feels his insides lurch. He swallows and says, "Well, this shit is no joke, Aunt Jeanne. Glad you got treated."

"Of course I did."

"And maybe start using, uh, protection?" Is he really having this conversation?

"Well, I'm team rubber, but Wally Perkins, he won't—"

"Stop. Sorry I asked."

She chuckles. "Serves you right for snooping."

"Point taken."

"Anyway. This." With her slipper, she nudges a box Cameron hadn't noticed at her feet. "Some things of your mother's. Thought you might want them."

Cameron stands. "No thanks," he says, without a second look at the box.

Day 1,302 of My Captivity

MY CURRENT WEIGHT IS SIXTY POUNDS. I AM A *BIG BOY*.

As always, my examination began with the bucket. Dr. Santiago removed the top of my tank and lifted the large yellow bucket until it was flush with the rim. It contained seven scallops. Dr. Santiago prodded my mantle over the tank's edge with her net, but needlessly. For fresh scallops, I would have entered willingly.

The anesthesia seeped sweetly through my skin. My limbs stilled. My eyes closed.

My first encounter with the bucket was long ago. Day thirty-three of my captivity. Back then, I found the sensation alarming. But I have grown to enjoy the bucket. With the bucket comes a sensation of total nothingness, which, in most ways, is more pleasant than the everything-ness.

My arms dragged on the concrete as Dr. Santiago carried me to the table. She folded me into a pile on the plastic scale. She gasped: "Whoa, big boy!"

"How much?" Terry said, poking me with his large brown hands that always taste of mackerel.

"Up three pounds from last month," Dr. Santiago answered. "Has his diet changed?"

"Not that I know of, but I can double-check," Terry said.

"Please do. This sort of gain is abnormal, to say the least."

What can I say? I am a special guy, after all.

JUNE GLOOM

There's a new boy bagging at Shop-Way tonight.

Tova flattens her lips as he puts her strawberry and marmalade jams side by side in the grocery bag. They clink ominously as he jostles in the rest: coffee beans, green grapes, frozen peas, a bear-shaped bottle of honey, and a box of tissues. They're the soft, lotion-y kind. The expensive kind. Tova began buying them for Will when he was in the hospital, where the tissues were sandpaper. Now she finds herself too accustomed to them to switch to the more affordable brand.

"I'll hardly need to see that, love," Ethan Mack says as Tova presents her loyalty card. The cashier is a chatty fellow with a heavy Scottish accent who also happens to be the store's owner. He raps a callused knuckle against his wizened temple and grins. "Got it all up here; had your number punched in no sooner'n you came through the door."

"Thank you, Ethan."

"Anytime." He hands her a receipt and flashes his slightly crooked, but kind, grin.

Tova scans it to make sure the jams rung through with the promotion properly applied. There they are: buy one, get one half price. She ought not to have doubted: Ethan runs a tight ship. The Shop-Way has improved since he moved to town and bought the place a few years back. Won't be long before he has the new boy trained in proper bagging technique. She tucks the receipt into her pocketbook.

"Some June, innit?" Ethan leans back and crosses his arms over his belly. It's past ten in the evening: the checkout lanes are empty, and the new boy has retreated to the bench next to the deli counter.

"It's been drizzly," Tova agrees.

"You know me, love. I'm like a big duck. Rolls off my back. But I'll be damned if I haven't forgotten what the sun looks like."

"Yes, well."

Ethan smooths piles of receipts into neat white bricks, his eyes lingering on the circular sucker mark on her wrist, a purplish bruise which has hardly faded in the days since the octopus grabbed her there. He clears his throat. "Tova, I'm sorry to hear about your brother's passing."

Tova lowers her head but says nothing.

He continues, "You need anything at all, just say the word."

She meets his eyes. She's known Ethan for years, and the man doesn't go out of his way to avoid scuttlebutt. Tova has never met a sixty-something-year-old man who so enjoys gossip. So he's surely aware of the estrangement between her and her brother. Tone measured, she says, "Lars and I weren't close."

Had she and Lars ever been close? Tova is certain they were, once. As children: certainly. As young adults: mostly. Lars stood alongside Will, both in gray suits, at Tova and Will's wedding. At the reception, Lars gave a lovely speech that made everyone's eyes mist over, even their stoic father's. For years afterward, Tova and Will spent every New Year's Eve at Lars's house in Ballard, eating rice pudding and clinking flutes at midnight while little Erik slept under a crocheted blanket on the davenport.

But things started to change after Erik died. Once in a while, one of the Knit-Wits probes Tova, asking what happened between her and Lars, and Tova says *nothing, really*, and this is the truth. It happened gradually. No blow-out argument, no fist-shaking or hollering. One New Year's Eve, Lars phoned Tova and informed her that he and Denise had other plans. Denise, his wife, for a time anyway.

When they would come for dinner, Denise was fond of loitering around the kitchen sink while Tova was up to her elbows in suds, insisting that she was *there* if Tova ever needed to *talk*. *Well, it's not a crime for her to care about you, even if you don't know her well*, is what Lars said when Tova registered her annoyance.

After that fizzled New Year's, there was a skipped Easter luncheon, a canceled birthday party, a Christmas gathering that never made it past the *we should get together* state of planning. The years stretched into decades, turning siblings to strangers.

Ethan fiddles with the small silver key dangling from the drawer of the cash register. His voice is soft when he says, "Still, family is family." He grimaces, lowering his awkward frame into the swivel chair next to the register. Tova happens to know the chair helps his bad back. Not the sort of gossip she seeks out, of course, but sometimes one can't help but overhear. The Knit-Wits like to natter on about such things.

Tova sighs. *Family is family.* She knows Ethan means well, but what a ridiculous saying. Of course family is family; what else could it be? Lars was her last living relation. Family, even though she hadn't spoken to him in years.

"I must get going," she finally replies. "My feet are quite sore from work."

"Aye! Your aquarium gig." Ethan sounds thankful for the change in subject. "Say hello to the scallops for me."

Tova nods gravely. "I will tell them hello."

"Let 'em know they're livin' the high life compared to their cousins over there, in the seafood case." Ethan ticks his head toward the fresh seafood department at the back of the store, the one that, with a few local-catch exceptions, offers mostly previously frozen seafood. He leans his elbows on the checkout counter with a bemused look in his eyes.

Tova's cheeks flush, having picked up on his facetiousness an instant too late. Those scallops in the cold case, rounds of translucent white . . . at least Sowell Bay is too provincial to support a grocery store that sells *octopus*. She heaves up her grocery bag. Predictably, its contents list toward one end and the jam jars clink again.

Sometimes there is simply a correct way to do things.

With a pointed glance at the new bagging fellow, who is slumped on the deli bench now, jabbing at his phone, Tova sets the bag down and moves the marmalade to the other side of the grapes. The way it ought to have been done in the first place.

Ethan follows her gaze. Then he stands and barks, "Tanner! What happened to stocking the dairy case?"

The kid stuffs his phone in his pocket and stalks off toward the back of the store.

Tova hides a smile at how satisfied Ethan looks with himself. When he notices, he runs a hand over his short wiry beard, which is mostly white these days but clings to a reddish hint. Soon, he'll let it grow in anticipation of the holidays. Ethan Mack plays a very convincing Scots Santa Claus. Every Saturday in December he'll sit in a chair in the community center in a polyester costume, taking photos with the town's children and occasionally a small dog or two. Janice brings Rolo to visit Santa every year.

"Kids need a little direction now and then," Ethan says. "Then again, I suppose we all do."

"I suppose so." Tova picks up her grocery sack again and turns toward the door.

"If you need anything at all . . ."

"Thank you, Ethan. I appreciate it."

"Drive safe now, love," he calls as the chime dings.

AT HOME, TOVA unties her sneakers and turns on the television to channel four. The eleven-o'clock news is only tolerable on channel four. Craig Moreno and Carla Ketchum and meteorologist Joan

Jennison. Channel seven is tabloid nonsense, and who can stand to watch that blowhard Foster Wallace on channel thirteen? Channel four is the only sane option.

The show's jingle drifts into the kitchen, where Tova unloads her groceries. She hadn't bought much; her refrigerator is already stuffed with casseroles, left on her porch over the last few days by the Knit-Wits and other well-wishers intending to comfort her over Lars's death.

"Oh, for heaven's sake," she says, bending down and rustling around her jammed fridge, trying to finagle a space for her grapes around an oversized pan of ham-and-cheese gratin Mary Ann dropped off yesterday.

A scratching sound startles her. She stands upright.

It's coming from the porch. Another casserole? And at this hour. She makes her way past the den, where the television is blaring a commercial for life insurance. The front door is still open from her carrying in the groceries, so she squints through the screen door, expecting to see an offering on the doormat, but it's empty. And no car in the driveway, either.

The door creaks as she opens it. "Hello?"

More scratching. A raccoon? A rat?

"Who's there?"

A pair of yellow eyes. Then a reproachful meow.

Tova lets out a breath she hadn't meant to hold. Stray cats roam the neighborhood, but she's never seen this gray one, now sitting on her porch step like a king on his throne. The cat blinks, glaring up at her.

"Well?" She frowns, flapping a hand. "Shoo!"

The cat tilts its head.

"I said, shoo!"

The cat yawns.

Tova plants her hands on her hips, and the cat saunters over and winds its narrow body between her feet. She can feel each tine of its rib cage against her ankle bone.

She clucks her tongue. "Well, I have ham gratin. Would that suit you?"

The cat's purr has a high-pitched tinge to it. Desperate.

"All right, then. But if I catch you using my flower beds as a litter box . . ." She slips back through the door, leaving Cat, as Tova decides it should be called, peering through the screen.

After returning with a loaded plate, she sits and watches from the porch swing as Cat devours cold ham, cheese, and potato. When Tova returns the dish to Mary Ann later, she won't mention who consumed it.

"Shame to see it go to waste, so I'm glad to share," she confides to Cat. And she means this. How much food do her friends think she can possibly eat? Tova sets a mental reminder to collect Cat's dish in the morning and goes back inside, closing the door behind her.

From the den drifts the sound of the news , which has returned from a commercial break. "Well, Carla, I know I'm ready for some summer weather here in Seattle." Craig Moreno chuckles.

"I'm more than ready, Craig!" Carla Ketchum's laugh is watery. Next, she'll lean her forearm on the desk and beam at the camera before turning to her co-anchor. She'll be wearing blue, as she seems to believe it flatters her best. And because it rained today, her blond hair will be wavy instead of tamed into a bob. Of course, Tova can't see any of this from the kitchen, but she's certain.

"We'll see what Joan has to say about that. After the break!"

Now the camera will pan back to Craig Moreno. His tone will rise a smidgen when he says Joan's name. This began a few weeks ago. Presumably when he and the weather lady began having relations.

Tova doesn't stay to hear the forecast. Doesn't need to—it'll be cloudy and drizzly. More June gloom.

CHASING A LASS

Though he could do with a spot of sun lately, Ethan Mack doesn't mind foggy nights. Halos gather around the streetlights; a ferry horn bellows somewhere in the brume. Midnight chill seeps down his collar as he sits on the bench in front of the Shop-Way, puffing his pipe.

Strictly speaking, this is not permitted. Per the handbook, Shop-Way employees must clock out for smoke breaks. Of course, Ethan himself is the one who wrote that handbook, although even so, he tries not to lift himself above the rules. But he and Tanner are the only ones here, and the kid is in the back, none the wiser.

Watching Tova go into the night always prickles his nerves. According to his police scanner, there are always lunatics on the roads at night. Why must she do her shopping so late?

It's been almost two years since she started coming late in the evening. Since Ethan started pressing his flannel collar before his shift. Trying to make himself a bit tidier. Make himself seem more presentable.

He pulls the pipe's warmth into his chest, then exhales. The smoke melts into the fog.

The fog reminds Ethan of home: Kilberry, on the Sound of Jura in western Scotland. Still home, though he's lived in the United States forty years. Forty years since he packed a duffel and quit his post as a docker in Kennacraig. Forty years since he chased a lass.

It had fizzled with Cindy. The plan was rubbish to begin with, shacking up with a holiday-making American, pissing his savings on a ticket from Heathrow to JFK. He still remembers how the isles grew smaller and smaller through the little oval window.

Tanner pokes his muttonish head out the door. If he registers Ethan's rule breaking, he doesn't show it. The lad's not the brightest bulb. He says, "Did you want me to do the entire cold case?"

"A'course. What do you think I'm paying you for?"

Tanner grumbles as he slinks back inside. Ethan shakes his head. Kids these days.

New York City was gritty in the seventies, and before long, Ethan and Cindy had bigger plans. Cindy emptied her flat in Brooklyn to buy an old Volkswagen van, which they drove across the country, and its vastness blew Ethan's mind. Pennsylvania, Indiana, Nebraska, Nevada. Any one of them could've contained Scotland entirely.

When they found the sea again, Ethan was relieved. They lingered on the coast of Northern California for weeks, making love in the shadows of giant redwoods, before working their way north along the Pacific Coast Highway. In a ramshackle chapel somewhere near the Oregon border, he and Cindy tied the knot.

Weeks later, in Aberdeen, Washington, the van's transmission finally failed. Ethan tinkered with it, but it was gone. And in the morning, so was Cindy.

And that was that.

Aberdeen suited Ethan. He had never visited its namesake town on the northern coast of Scotland, but it felt familiar. Low, gray skies. Gruff, industrious people. He took a job as a longshoreman. Found a bed in a rooming house. Took his tea early in the morning, while watching the fog drift over the ship masts.

The union treated him well, retiring him with a modest pension at the age of fifty-five. Out of grudging necessity, he moved inland, closer to the city, to the physical therapists needed to reshape his back after years of hoisting logs onto boats. But retirement made him restless. Shop-Way had a swing shift to fill, was happy to furnish an ergonomic chair at his register. He did them one better and gathered up his savings and bought the place.

Now, ten years later, he still doesn't need the money, not exactly. The union pension covers rent, food, gas for his truck. But the trickle of profit from the store affords him new vinyl records for his collection and a nice bottle of scotch now and then. Proper Islay whiskey, not Highlands rubbish.

Headlights flash on the slick pavement as a car swerves into the parking lot. Ethan snuffs his pipe and ducks back through the front door.

He posts up at the register as a young man and woman stagger in, arms so deeply entwined that they move like a single person. They ping-pong down the aisles, giggling as they ricochet off the pillars of chips and soda. They fumble with a debit card at the register. They peel out onto the road, washing the front windows in white light as they go.

Idiots. They'll kill someone. Someone like Ethan's sister, Mariah, who was struck by a truck when she was barely ten. Fishermen on their way back from the pub. *The world is full of idiots.*

The thought of Tova's hatchback out there on that road makes Ethan queasy. He wishes he could drive by her house and make sure her car is parked there. Maybe her lights would be on.

But no. He broke himself once, chasing a lass.

Day 1,306 of My Captivity

I AM VERY GOOD AT KEEPING SECRETS.

You might say I have no choice. Whom might I tell? My options are scant.

To the extent I am able to communicate with the other prisoners, those dull conversations are rarely worth the effort. Blunt minds, rudimentary neural systems. They are wired for survival, and perhaps expert at that function, but no other creature here possesses intelligence like mine.

It is lonely. Perhaps it would be less so if I had someone with whom to share my secrets.

Secrets are everywhere. Some humans are crammed full of them. How do they not explode? It seems to be a hallmark of the human species: abysmal communication skills. Not that any other species are much better, mind you, but even a herring can tell which way the school it belongs to is turning and follow accordingly. Why can humans not use their millions of words to simply tell one another what they desire?

The sea, too, is very good at keeping secrets.

One in particular, from the bottom of the sea, I carry with me still.

BABY VIPERS ARE ESPECIALLY DEADLY

The box sits on Cameron's kitchen counter, untouched, for three days.

Aunt Jeanne had schlepped it out of the trailer herself. *Toss it if you want, but at least look through it first*, she'd said. *Family's important.*

Cameron had rolled his eyes. *Family.* But when that woman truly wants her way, arguing is pointless. So the box traveled home with him. Now, Cameron eyes it from the sofa, considering turning off *SportsCenter* to take a look. Might be something in there he could take down to the pawnshop. Katie will need his half of July's rent soon.

Maybe after lunch.

The microwave hums and rotates his noodle cup while he waits. Cooking by magnet-blasting radiation, causing food molecules to beat the shit out of each other: Who comes up with this stuff, figures out how to market it? Whoever that guy is, he's probably swimming naked in a pile of cash somewhere, surrounded by supermodels. Life is unfair.

Ding.

Cameron removes the steaming cup. He's carrying it back to the sofa, careful not to let it slosh, when the apartment door creaks open, startling him.

"Shit!" Scalding liquid spills over his hand.

"Cam! Are you okay?" Katie drops her work bag and runs over.

"I'm fine," he mutters. What's she doing home on a Tuesday

afternoon? Then again, she might ask him the same question. His mind spins. Had he told her he was working today? Had she asked?

"Hang on," she says, ducking into the kitchen, her perfect little butt twitching under her gray skirt. Katie works at the front desk of the Holiday Inn by the freeway. Good thing she's been working day shift lately. He would've been busted by now if she were still on nights.

She hurries back, carrying two damp rags.

"Thanks," Cameron says as she hands him one. Its coolness is welcome relief on his hand. Then she squats down to wipe up the spilled broth with the other.

"So, you're home early," he says, bending to help, forcing his voice to be casual.

"I've got a dentist appointment this afternoon. Remember? We talked about it last week."

"Oh yeah. Right." Cameron nods, vaguely recalling.

"I don't remember you mentioning you were off today." She plucks a stray noodle from the carpet and drops it into her rag, looking up at him through narrow eyes.

"Uh, yeah. I'm off today." He doesn't add: *and tomorrow, and the next day, and the one after.*

"Weird they'd give you a day off. It's only your third week."

"It's a holiday, actually." Shit, why did he say that?

She stands. "A holiday?"

"Yeah." It's a slippery lie. "International Contractors' Day. Everyone gets the day off." Really, what is he going to tell her? The truth? He just needs time. A few days to land a new job. Then it'll be all good.

"International Contractors' Day."

"Yep."

"Everyone gets the day off?"

"Everyone."

"Bizarre they're still working on the roof next door, then, isn't it?"

Cameron opens his mouth, but the *bang-bang* of a nail gun echoes from the rooftop of the next building over, cutting him off.

Katie's face is cold, blank. "You got fired again."

"I mean, technically—"

"What happened?"

"Well, I was—"

"When were you going to tell me?" she interrupts.

"I'm trying to tell you now, if you'll give me a chance!"

"You know what? Never mind." She picks up her work bag and stomps toward the door. "I don't have time for this. I'm late for my appointment, and I'm done giving chances."

CHANCES. IF LIFE kept a tally of chances, Cameron would be owed big-time. What would Katie know about having an addict parent? What would Katie know about this gnawing hatred inside him that never goes away?

Katie, with her parents who bought her a car when she graduated high school. Katie, with her tight gray skirt and straight white teeth, which right now are being polished by some needle-dick dentist. They'll give her a free toothbrush on the way out. She'll toss it, still wrapped, in the bathroom drawer because she uses some fancy electric toothbrush anyway.

He's stretched out on the couch, watching some low-budget action movie, when she finally returns. It occurs to him that it's been a while. Hours and hours; it's nearly dark outside now. Way longer than a dentist appointment should take—not that he'd actually know; he hasn't been to a dentist in years. Maybe Katie had a bunch of cavities or something. A root canal. Aunt Jeanne had a root canal last year and complained about the pain for a week. The thought of perfect Katie getting poked in the mouth with a pointy drill is vaguely satisfying, and this makes him feel like a jerk.

"Hey," he calls, then pauses, waiting for her lamenting sigh, the one meaning she's still pissed, but less so. He'll say he's sorry, and she'll frown, but she won't really mean it, then he'll put his hand on her leg and she'll lean into him and they'll lie here, cuddling, while they finish watching this dumb movie before retiring to bed for some solid post-argument sex.

But she doesn't respond. Instead, she heads straight for the bedroom. He half smiles. Straight to it?

Then he hears the first *thunk*. What the . . . ? He has to investigate.

As he walks in, Cameron watches his work boot sail over the edge of the moonlit balcony, landing below on the tiny square of crusty grass.

Thunk.

Its mate hits the walkway, then bounces a couple of times over the weedy cracks, laces dragging behind.

"Katie! Can't we talk?"

She doesn't answer.

"Look, I'm sorry. I should've told you."

Again, no response.

Whiz.

A ball cap grazes his ear as it sails by. His favorite Niners cap. Enough. Yeah, he should have told her he got canned. But could they just talk about it for a hot second before she throws out everything he owns?

"Katie," he says slowly. Like she's some wild animal, he reaches out and puts a tentative hand on her shoulder.

"Don't," Katie mutters, twisting away. She yanks a pair of his boxers from the bureau and wads them in her fist, then hurls them toward the balcony door. But the throw is too soft. The underwear unfurls and flops to the floor.

He bends to pick it up. "Can we just talk?"

"I can't do this anymore, Cam." For the first time since she left for the dentist this afternoon, she meets his gaze. Her eyes blaze, like the bonfires they used to build in the shadow of his Jeep when they'd go camping out in the high desert. But those days are long gone. The repo guys snagged the Jeep months ago. Cameron was going to call the bank, to make their so-called payment arrangement. He swears he was about to do it, but no, they just sent those assholes in and hauled it away, no second chance. Yet another deduction from his chance tally.

"I swear, I was going to tell you. And it wasn't my fault."

"Sure, it wasn't your fault. Never is, is it?"

"No!" The relief that washes over him at her sudden empathy is short-lived. Of course she's being sarcastic. His cheeks burn. "I mean, it's complicated." Of course she's kicking him out. Cameron would probably kick himself out, too.

Katie closes her eyes. "Cameron, it isn't complicated. I'm going to put this to you as simply as possible, so your juvenile brain can understand. This. Is. Over."

"But I've got rent covered," he insists, thoughts veering back to Aunt Jeanne's mystery box. Desperation tinges his voice. He trails Katie from the bedroom into the kitchen, still clutching his boxers.

"This isn't about rent! It's about your inability to be an honest human being." She picks up the mystery box from the counter and starts back toward the bedroom. Toward the balcony. To his surprise, his gut clenches.

"I'll take that."

"Fine, whatever. Just get out." She drops the box, and it lands with a heavy *thump* on the carpet. Her face has changed, the fire in her eyes vanished. She looks tired.

"You mean right now?" Cameron snorts. She can't be serious.

"No, next Saturday. I threw your stuff outside for the hell of it." She rolls her eyes. "Yes, of course, right now."

"Where am I supposed to go?"

"Not. My. Problem." She lets out a hollow laugh. "Not that I care, but someday, you're gonna have to grow up, you know?"

THE BOX MAKES a reasonably comfortable seat. It's better than the curb, anyway. In the dark, and with his stuff heaped next to him, Cameron waits for Brad to pick him up.

And waits and waits. For an hour.

Of all the times to not have a car.

Finally, headlights sweep around the corner. "What the hell happened?" Brad slams his truck door as he gets out.

"What the hell yourself! What took you so long?"

"Well, let's see. How about, I was asleep. Because it's almost eleven on a Tuesday night." Brad starts chucking Cameron's stuff into the truck bed. "Some of us have to work tomorrow, you know."

"Hey, fuck you."

Brad's face melts into a grin. "Too soon? Sorry."

"Whatever. Can we just go?" As Cameron hoists a trash bag full of clothes, he glances up at the balcony, where Katie still has the patio door open and the bedroom light on, no doubt watching the curbside scene unfold. He throws one last glance toward the apartment before nestling his guitar case atop the pile and flipping the tailgate up. It creaks loudly, then closes with a metallic *bang*.

"Come on," Brad says, unlocking the passenger door. "Get in."

"Thanks," Cameron mutters, hopping onto the seat with the box on his lap.

Brad and Elizabeth's house is on the outskirts of town, where subdivisions pop up overnight like a bad rash. Unnecessary plaster columns and fake brick facades and four-car garages. Bougie as shit. Elizabeth's parents gave them a huge chunk of money for the down payment a few years ago after their wedding. Must be nice.

But Cameron doesn't complain about any of these things on the fifteen-minute drive there from his apartment. His *old* apartment. It's Katie's apartment, now. Her name alone is on the lease. When he first moved in, she was constantly on his case about calling the landlord to be officially added, because Katie always follows the rules. But after a while, she let it drop. Maybe she saw this coming.

"What's in the box?" Brad asks, interrupting his thoughts.

"Baby vipers," Cameron deadpans, not missing a beat. "Dozens of them. I hope Elizabeth likes snakes."

Half an hour later, Brad slides a coaster across the coffee table before he hands Cameron a sweating pint glass, as Cameron finishes explaining what happened.

"Maybe she'll get over it," Brad says, yawning. "Just give her a couple of days."

Cameron looks up. "She threw my shit on the lawn, like something from some dumb chick-flick movie. Every damn thing I own."

Brad glances at the pile in the corner. "That's really everything you own?"

"I mean, not *literally*. But you know." Cameron frowns. What about his Xbox, still parked in the cabinet under Katie's TV? He'd skirted overdraft fees to buy that thing when it first came out. But it might as well be Katie's now. Like hell is he going back there to beg for it.

Maybe those couple of bags, and one dubious box, really *are* all he owns now.

Cameron's eyes fix on Brad's oversized bay window when he continues, "We can't all live in a McMansion, you know." It was meant as a joke, but the words spray out like acid. He attempts to soften his tone. "I mean, I've just been embracing my minimalist side."

Brad raises an eyebrow, stares at Cameron for a long moment, then raises his pint. "Well, here's to new beginnings."

"Thanks for letting me crash again. I owe you one." Cameron clinks, and lager sloshes over the rim, dribbling on the table. Seemingly out of thin air Brad comes up with a paper towel, then leans over to dab the spill.

"You owe me, like, ten. I charge extra for checking in after midnight." Brad grins, but his eyes are serious. "And I know I don't need to tell you this again, but you'll owe me new furniture if you mess anything up."

Cameron nods. He got the same speech last week when he crashed on the couch after the bar. Elizabeth just got new living room furniture, and apparently its utilization for normal living room activities, like sitting and lounging, is a sensitive subject. He used to sleep in the guest room when he crashed here, but it's been remodeled for the baby now. Just last month, Cameron patched the drywall in the closet, for payment in pizza, after Brad tore it up trying to install some ridiculous shelving system. Cameron could patch drywall in his sleep, and in fact he did one time. Or half-asleep, anyway. Or so the foreman of that job site claimed before sacking Cameron on the spot.

"And seriously, Cam?" Brad continues. "Two nights, tops."

"Ten-four."

"So where are you gonna go?" Brad folds the beer-dampened paper towel and places it neatly on the edge of the table.

Cameron props a sneaker over his knee and twists a fraying shoelace around his finger. "Maybe one of those new apartments downtown?"

Brad sighs. "Cam . . ."

"What? I got a buddy who worked that job. He says they're nice inside." Cameron pictures himself settling into a wide leather sofa, digging his bare toes into brand-new carpet. He'll need a flat-screen, of course, eighty inches at least. He'll mount it to the wall and run the cords behind so they don't show.

Brad leans forward, lacing his hands. "There's no way in hell they're going to rent one of those to you."

"Why not?"

"Dude, you have no job."

"Not true. I'm between projects right now."

"Are you ever not *between projects?*"

"The construction industry is cyclical." Cameron straightens up, a bite creeping into his voice. What would Brad know about actual, physical work? He spends all day faffing around some dumpy little office, shuffling papers for the local electric utility.

Brad used to talk about leaving, going to San Francisco or something. But he'll never leave now, and Cameron knows why. His parents are here, Elizabeth's, too, and now all four of them are about to be grandparents. The whole clan gets together for dinner on Sunday nights. Probably eats honey-glazed ham or some shit. Why would they ever leave? Cameron wonders if there's some sort of special tether children of normal families are granted. One for which he's never been eligible.

"Cam, what's your credit score?"

Cameron hesitates. Truth is, he has no clue. Hell would freeze before he'd check. When he got the Jeep a few years back, it was in the low six hundreds, but that was several questionable life choices ago. With a sarcastic smirk, he answers, "A hundred and twenty."

Brad shakes his head. "Maybe that's your bowling score. Sure as hell's not your credit score."

"Well, what can I say? I'm awesome at bowling."

"Obviously."

Cameron runs his fingers over the little series of punctures in the side of his sneaker. Probably from Katie's dog, a teacup something-or-other with a taste for footwear, his in particular. The dog is such a pain in the ass, Katie sent it to live with her parents, but they brought it over every time they visited. At least he won't have to deal with that garbage anymore.

"Why don't you go back to school?" Brad suggests, not for the first time. "Get your associate's degree or something."

Cameron grunts. Brad should be smart enough to realize college costs money Cameron doesn't have. But suddenly, Cameron does have an idea. A good one. "You know that apartment over Dell's?"

Brad nods. All the regulars at their watering hole know about the place upstairs. They joke sometimes that Old Al, the bartender, could make a killing renting it out by the hour.

"The other night, I heard Old Al say it's empty," Cameron continues. "Maybe he'd rent it to me."

"He might make you settle your tab first. But maybe."

"I'll ask him when we're there for our gig next week."

Brad clears his throat. "Next week?"

"Fine. I'll go over tomorrow."

"Good," Brad says. Then he looks down. "By the way, there's something I need to tell you. I wanted to wait until everyone was together, but . . ."

"But what?" Cameron frowns. "Just spill it."

"Um. Our Moth Sausage show next week? It'll be my last."

"What?" Cameron feels like someone kicked him in the chest.

"Yeah, I'm quitting the band." Brad grimaces. "With the baby coming, Elizabeth and I think it's best if—"

"You're the lead singer," Cameron blurts. "You can't quit."

"Sorry." Brad looks like he's shrinking in his chair. "Can you not tell the guys yet? I really wanted to wait until everyone was together."

Cameron stands and stalks over to the window.

"It's just that with the baby, things will be different," Brad goes on.

Cameron glares at Brad and Elizabeth's front yard, its glowing landscape lights, the golf-course grass, the brick walkway. To his horror, a lump forms in his throat. Of course Brad would leave Moth

Sausage when the baby came. He should've seen it coming. "I get it," he says finally.

"I'll still come to the shows."

Cameron swallows a scoff. There won't be any Moth Sausage shows without Brad.

"Elizabeth, too. Maybe we can bring the baby." Brad lets out a long sigh. "I really am sorry."

"It's cool." Cameron returns to the sofa and starts removing the decorative pillows, making a point to stack them extra neatly. "It's late. I should sleep."

"Yeah, okay." Brad hovers for an extra moment before picking up their empty glasses. "Hang on, you need sheets," he says before disappearing down the hallway.

Sheets? For a couch? Since when?

A minute later, Brad reappears with an unopened package of bedsheets, which he tosses at Cameron. They're purple and white striped, and Cameron would bet anything Elizabeth picked them out. Purple has always been her favorite color.

Brad is still hovering like a goddamn mosquito. "Need a hand setting up?"

"Nope." Cameron flashes a tight smile. "Night."

"Okay. Uh . . . night." From the kitchen, Brad calls back, "Don't let those baby vipers out."

Cameron doesn't answer.

Day 1,307 of My Captivity

HUMANS HAVE FEW REDEEMING QUALITIES, BUT THEIR fingerprints are miniature works of art.

I am well-read in fingerprints. I suppose you could say it is one fortunate side effect of dealing with humans all day long, their trembling boogers and damp armpits, their sticky palms reeking of floral lotion and Popsicle residue.

But when the doors lock for the night and the lights dim, they leave behind a stunning, intricate mural on the glass at the front of my tank.

Sometimes I spend quite some time staring at them, studying. Little oval masterpieces. I visually trace the grooves from the outside into the center, then back out to the edge again. Each one unique. I remember all of them.

Fingerprints are like keys, with their specific shape.

I remember all keys, too.

MUCKLE TEETH

Mrs. Sullivan?"

Tova opens her trunk, preparing to start her shift, when a short man waving a manila envelope comes jogging across the Sowell Bay Aquarium's parking lot, weaving around the typical handful of cars belonging to the evening fishermen and the day's last joggers. Recognizable Sowell Bay vehicles, most of them. Somehow, Tova hadn't even noticed the unfamiliar gray sedan from which this fellow just burst forth.

"Tova Sullivan?" he hollers again, approaching.

She slams the hatchback shut. "May I help you?"

"Glad I finally found you!" he says, panting. As he catches his breath, he flashes a smile too large for his face, with oversized white teeth. They remind Tova of the bleached barnacles that cling to seaweed-strewn boulders down at the sound's edge.

He continues, "You're not an easy lady to track down, you know."

"I beg your pardon?"

"Your address had my GPS going in circles, and your home phone just rings, no voice mail. Thought I was going to need a private investigator."

Warmth creeps up Tova's neck at the suggestion that she might've allowed her answering machine to remain full, exacerbated by the fact that the accusation is basically true. But her voice is even when she says, "An investigator?"

"It happens more often than you'd think." He shakes his head, then extends his hand. "Bruce LaRue. I'm an attorney for the estate of Lars Lindgren."

"How do you do."

"First of all, please let me say, I'm sorry for your loss." His tone doesn't sound particularly sorry.

"We were not close," Tova explains. Again.

"Right . . . I won't take up too much of your time, then, but I needed to get this to you." He thrusts the envelope at Tova. "Your brother had some personal assets, as you probably know."

"Mr. LaRue, I have no knowledge of what my brother did or did not have." She slides a finger under the seal on the envelope and peeks inside. It's a document, a list of some sort, on Charter Village letterhead.

"Well, now you know. We'll need to get together at some point to sort out the monetary assets, but for now, that's a list of his belongings. Just a few personal items."

"I see." Tova tucks the envelope under her arm.

"You can give them a call and let them know when you'll swing by to pick everything up."

"Swing by? Charter Village is all the way up in Bellingham. That's an hour away."

LaRue shrugs. "Look, go get the stuff, or don't. They'll get rid of it after some time if no one shows up."

If no one shows up. To Tova's knowledge, Lars never remarried after he and Denise split, but she's always supposed he must've had a sweetheart or two. A close friend, at least. Isn't that part of the reason people move to those homes? For the social scene? But this LaRue fellow seems to be implying that no one had shown up for Lars. Had ever shown up for him, maybe. Had he died in the company of some bored nurse? An aide counting the hours until shift's end?

"I will go," she says quietly.

"Great. Then my work here is done, for now. I'll be in touch." LaRue flashes his grin again. "Any questions?"

A great many questions swirl in Tova's mind, but the one that tumbles out is "How exactly did you find me here?"

"Ah, a very friendly cashier up at that grocery store on the hill. I stopped in for a coffee, having failed to find you at your home address, and when we got to chatting, he mentioned you'd be down here. Nice guy. Talks with a heavy accent, like a leprechaun?"

Tova sighs. Ethan.

BY SOME SERENDIPITY, the aquarium is in decent shape tonight. No dried chewing gum to battle. Nothing sticky in the trash cans. No unspeakable bathroom messes.

And, thankfully, everyone seems to be in their proper tank.

"I see you back there." The glass front of the octopus exhibit is smattered with greasy fingerprints, which Tova sprays and erases with her rag, while the creature stares at her from one of the upper corners. She's now accustomed to finding his exhibit empty, seeing him instead with the sea cucumbers next door, which seem to be his preferred snack. Tova can't say she approves, but it makes her smile. Their secret.

He unfurls his arms and floats toward the front glass, never breaking his gaze.

"Not hungry tonight, are we?"

He blinks.

"An hour. On the freeway," she mutters, leaning closer to scrub at a stubborn spot on the glass. "I don't care for driving on the freeway, you know."

In his slow, almost prehistoric way, the octopus attaches an arm to the inside of the tank and draws his body closer. His suckers look bluish purple tonight, clinging to the glass.

She wrings her rag. "And I don't care for those homes, either.

Retirement homes, nursing homes . . . all the same, aren't they? Always smell like sick people."

Eye gleaming like some otherworldly marble, the octopus follows her every move as she folds the rag and tucks it away.

Tova leans on the cart. "Lars always left messes. And now he's left one last thing for me to clean up, even after he's died. His life was always a bit disorganized. Mind you, that wasn't why we stopped speaking. No, that wasn't the reason."

She tuts at herself. What is she doing, talking to this octopus? Not that she doesn't always say hello to the creatures here, as fond of them as she is, but this is different. This is *talking*. But, good heavens, if it doesn't feel like the creature is actually *listening*.

Of all the impossible things.

And anyway. There was no reason. *Nothing, really.*

"Well, good night, sir." Tova gives the octopus a polite nod, then moves along.

At the seahorse exhibit, there's a handwritten sign taped to the glass. Tova recognizes Terry's scrawl: MATING! GIVE THEM SPACE!

"Oh!" Tova clasps a hand to her chest, peering cautiously around the paper. *Is it that time again?*

Last year, Terry threw a little "baby shower" for the entire staff, all eight of them, when the seahorses spawned. Mackenzie had stayed after her admissions shift to blow up balloons and paint a banner that read GIDDY-UP, LITTLE COWBOYS! Dr. Santiago, the veterinarian, had dropped by with a cake that read, in cursive icing: HIP-HIP-HOORAY FOR HIPPOCAMPUS BABIES!

Generally, Tova avoids parties, but that cake had drawn intrigue. During Erik's sophomore year, he made a posterboard project for honors biology on the hippocampus of the human brain. He devoted a whole panel to the etymology of the term, its derivation from ancient Greek, its shared meaning with the scientific term for the seahorse genus, and its mythological connection to sea monsters.

Maybe we all have sea monsters living in our brains, Erik joked as he pasted chunks of paper onto the posterboard on their dining room table.

Anyway, if Terry and Mackenzie had planned to repeat the gesture this year, it would be well underway. Tova hasn't heard of it, although she's sure they'd never exclude her. Not intentionally.

If a celebration does happen, she supposes she'll see the mess afterward. It's absurd anyway. That's what the Knit-Wits said last year, when she told them of it.

Perhaps she's the only person on earth who thinks hippocampus babies are more exciting than human ones.

ETHAN IS WIPING down the Shop-Way register when she enters. He beams at her. "Tova!"

The shopping baskets sit in a neat pile next to the newspaper stand, but Tova marches right past them, past the short row of nested carts, too, directly to the register. She's not here to shop.

"Good evening, Ethan."

His face starts to flush. Within moments, it's nearly as red as his beard.

"I have just had a visitor at my place of employment. Do you know anything about that?"

"Aye, the bloke with the muckle teeth." Ethan folds his rag and tucks it in his apron pocket, looking sheepish. "I wouldn't have told him if he hadn't said it was important. Your brother's estate and all."

Tova clucks her tongue. "Estate. Is that what he told you?"

"Well, yeah. Who wouldn't want an estate?"

Tova sighs. Is there any local drama into which Ethan is not champing at the bit to insert himself? Stiffly, she continues, "Apparently, my brother left some personal effects in the nursing home where he died. Nothing worthwhile, I'm certain, but now I must go retrieve them."

Ethan looks genuinely contrite, regret clouding his wide green eyes. "Bloody hell, Tova. I'm sorry."

"It's at least an hour's drive."

"Aye, bit of a haul," he says, picking at a callus on his thumb.

Tova inspects her sneakers. She is not in the habit of asking for help, but Ethan had seemed genuine in his offer, and the thought of two hours on the freeway makes her uneasy. "I should like to take you up on your offer."

"Offer?" Ethan looks up, his voice a touch brighter.

"Yes. If I *need anything at all*, you said. Well, there is something."

"Anything, love. What do you need?"

Tova swallows hard. "A ride to Bellingham."

Day 1,308 of My Captivity

THE SEAHORSES ARE AT IT AGAIN.

The humans display shock and excitement, as though this were a surprise. I assure you, it is not. The seahorses spawn at the same time every year. I have witnessed four of their breeding cycles during my captivity here.

There will be hundreds of seahorse larvae. Thousands, perhaps. They begin as a cloud of eggs and, over several days, transform into a clump of wiggling limbs, bearing no resemblance to their parents. In fact, they look like small versions of the sea worms that prowl the sands of the main tank.

It is fascinating how a freshly born creature can be so unlike its creator.

Obviously, this is not the case with humans. I have observed humans at every life stage, and they are, at all times, undeniably human. Even though the human baby is helpless and must be carried by its parent, no one could mistake it for anything else. Humans grow from small to large and then sometimes recede again as they approach the end of their life span, but they always have four limbs, twenty digits, two eyes on the front of their heads.

Their dependence upon their parents is unusually prolonged. Certainly it makes sense that the smallest children require assistance with the most basic of tasks: eating, drinking, urinating, defecating. Their short stature and clumsy limbs make these activities difficult.

But as they gain physical independence, oddly, their struggle continues. They summon mother or father at the slightest need: an untied shoelace, a sealed juice box, a minor conflict with another child.

Young humans would fail abysmally in the sea.

I do not know how a giant Pacific octopus spawns. How might my larvae look? Are we shape-shifters like seahorses, or humdrum, like humans? I suppose I shall never know.

Tomorrow, there will be crowds. Terry may even allow the main doors to stay open late to accommodate additional humans who wish to see the seahorses spawn. These rule benders will scurry past my tank, most of them uninterested in anything else.

Every so often, one will pause here. With these, I always play a game. I unfurl my arms and let them waft in the artificial current of the pump. One by one I sucker my tentacles to the glass, and the human draws nearer. Then I pull my mantle to the front of the tank and stare into its eyes. The human calls its companions to come look. As soon as I hear their footsteps around the bend, I jet back behind my rock, leaving nothing but a whoosh of water.

How predictable you humans are!

With one exception. The elderly female who mops the floors does not play my games. Instead, she speaks to me. We . . . converse.

HAPPY ENDINGS

For the umpteenth time, Ethan's thoughts circle back to the Knit-Wits. Any of those ladies could've given Tova a lift to Bellingham. Surely they're aware of her reluctance to drive on the freeway. But she asked *him*.

This morning, he awoke an hour early so he'd have time to shower and trim up his beard, get himself sharp and tidy. Everyone knows how much Tova likes things neat and clean. Because he was up at the crack of dawn, he consumed an extra mug of tea, and maybe that's why he can't stop his fingers from thrumming on the steering wheel like he's jamming on a piano.

"Are you all right?" Tova asks, again, from the passenger seat. She drops her crossword pencil onto the newspaper resting on her lap and brushes a speck of lint from the upholstered seat. He should've hauled his arse out of bed at five this morning instead of six. Then he would've had time to tidy up his truck as well as himself.

"Aye, I'm all right. Why do you ask?"

A pretty smile spreads over her face. "Honeybee hands."

"Honeybee what?

"Honeybee hands. You know . . . busy. That's what I used to say when Erik couldn't keep his fingers still."

Startled at the mention of that name, Ethan takes a deep breath and wills the jitters out of his limbs. "Honeybee hands. Clever." In his mind, he assembles an explanation about too much caffeine this morning, but when he glances over a moment later, she's reabsorbed in her puzzle, tapping the eraser on her chin as she studies the fold of newspaper.

Scrap that one, then. He scans for any of the other conversation starters he'd spent half the night rehearsing, but he somehow comes up blank. The only topics that surface are off-limits: dead brother, dead husband, dead son. Sheesh. He's still in shock she brought Erik up a moment ago, but clearly that moment has passed.

Instead, what comes out is: "What's that you're working on?" Which is a ridiculous question. Anyone can see it's a crossword.

She frowns. "Yesterday's puzzle. I'm afraid I've fallen behind."

"Behind?" He chuckles. "You mean you do that thing every day?"

"Of course. It's the *daily* crossword. I complete it daily."

"And if you miss a day? You . . . catch up?"

Her pencil scratches as she fills in a set of boxes. "Naturally."

THE CHARTER VILLAGE Long-Term Care Center is tucked into a series of rolling green hills sliced through by a long winding driveway. As they motor through the campus, smaller parkways splinter off the main one, each with a signpost. MEMORY CENTER. TENNIS COMPLEX. ACUTE CARE. CLUBHOUSE. This place has it all. Finally, a signpost points toward RECEPTION and Ethan leans on the accelerator. He lets out a low whistle as he pulls around the circular drive, past a pair of maroon-brick columns dressed in ivy. Downright posh. It looks like a fancy prep school or university, not a wretched place where old folks come to play tennis before eventually withering away.

"This is it, love?"

Tova's face is stone. "Yes, it seems so."

Ethan cuts the ignition and gives her a puzzled look. "You've never been here before?"

"I have not."

He resists the urge to unleash another low whistle. Tova had said Lars lived here for a decade. Had she really not visited even once?

She gathers her purse, tucking the newspaper inside. "Shall we?"

"Aye." Ethan scrambles out and hurries around the truck, hoping to reach the passenger side in time to open her door for her, but by the time he gets there, she's already striding toward the stately building.

For the first half hour, Ethan waits in the reception area, and the minutes drag. The leather chairs are remarkably plush, but the reading material is absolute shit. *National Geographic*, *AARP The Magazine*, and a handful of dry Wall Street rags. Couldn't they spring for something halfway interesting, like *Rolling Stone*, or even *People*? Celebrity gossip has always been Ethan's guilty pleasure. His honeybee hands come back, drumming impatiently on the low coffee table. He rises and inspects the refreshment table in the corner of the lobby, which, inexplicably, offers coffee, but not tea. All of this leather and ivy, and they can't even furnish a spot of Earl Grey? What rubbish!

He plucks a disposable cup from the stack and pours a cup of decaf anyway, because it's free. He doesn't particularly enjoy coffee. When Ethan was nineteen, he worked for a stint at the kiddie zoo down in Glasgow, shoveling the elephant pen. Once, as a joke, two of the other blokes that worked there collected feces and ran it through a juice press. What came out looked remarkably like . . . coffee. Never been the same since, coffee hasn't.

When Tova had whisked off toward the inside of the facility, he insisted she take her time going through her brother's things, but now he realizes he has no context for how long such an activity might take. Will he be waiting here all day? He should have brought a book.

From the front desk, there's a gaggle of voices. Some folks assembling for a tour of the facility, looks like.

The woman leading the group, wearing a gray suit and a sleek amber ponytail, addresses the small cluster in a clear, confident voice. "Welcome to Charter Village, where happy endings are our specialty."

Ethan nearly spits out his coffee. Happy endings? Who came up with that one?

Gray Suit frowns at him. "Sir?"

"Aye?" Ethan wipes dribbled coffee from his chin with his sleeve.

"Are you joining us?"

"Me?" He looks over his shoulder, as if there might be another "sir" behind him. Then he shrugs. "Sure, why not?" Something to pass the time, anyway.

"This way, then." With a polite smile, she motions him toward the group.

ETHAN MUST ADMIT: the residents do seem happy. Maybe that ridiculous slogan isn't off base.

There's a billiard room, a cafeteria with a mile-long buffet, even a pool and Jacuzzi. Residents can get room service, and the beds are made up daily with six-hundred-thread-count sheets. By the time the tour starts to wrap up, Ethan finds himself half-convinced to move in. As if he could afford it. His union pension wouldn't go far in a place like this.

WHEN TOVA SURFACES an hour later clutching a box, Ethan springs from the plush reception leather chair.

"All right, then, love?"

"Certainly." Tova looks so little in her purple cardigan, and the box makes her frame seem even more slight.

This time, he beats her to the car door. Chivalrously, he opens it and steps aside for her to enter, for which she thanks him politely. Then he takes the box and finds a space for it behind the passenger seat. But there's something else, too. A glossy page with an image of the community center and tennis courts. Some bloke with a full head of silver hair and white shorts swinging a racket.

As Tova is fiddling with her seat belt, he steals a longer peek.

It's not just a slick brochure. It's a whole packet. A sleek Charter Village folder with that terrible motto: "We Specialize in Happy Endings!"

There's one page not neatly aligned in the folder.

An application.

Day 1,309 of My Captivity

YOU HUMANS LOVE *COOKIES*. I ASSUME YOU KNOW WHICH food I mean?

Circular, about the size of a common clamshell. Some are flecked with dark bits, others are painted or dusted with powder. Cookies can be soft and quiet, moving soundlessly on their journey through human jaws. Cookies can be loud and messy, bits breaking off at the bite, crumbs tumbling down a chin, adding to the flotsam on the floor that the elderly female called Tova must sweep. I have observed many cookies during my captivity here. They are sold in the packaged food machine near the front entrance.

Imagine my confusion, then, at the remark made by Dr. Santiago earlier this evening.

"What can I say, Terry?" Dr. Santiago raised her shoulders and held her hands up. "I've seen a lot of octopuses, but you've got a smart cookie here."

They were discussing the so-called puzzle: hinged box made of clear plastic with a latch on the lid. There was a crab inside. Terry lowered it into my tank. He and Dr. Santiago leaned down to peer through the glass. Without delay, I seized the box, opened the latch, lifted the lid, and ate the crab.

It was a red rock crab, one that was molting. Soft and juicy. I consumed it in a single bite.

This did not please Terry and Dr. Santiago. They frowned and they argued. I gathered they anticipated my dismantling of the box to take longer.

I am a *smart cookie*. Well, of course I am intelligent. All octopuses are. I remember each and every human face that pauses to gaze at my tank. Patterns come readily to me. I know how the sunrise will play on the upper wall at dawn, shifting each day as the season progresses.

When I choose to hear, I hear everything. I can tell when the tide is turning to ebb, outside the prison walls, based on the tone of the water crashing against the rocks. When I choose to see, my vision is precise. I can tell which particular human has touched the glass of my tank by the fingerprints left behind. Learning to read their letters and words was easy.

I can use tools. I can solve puzzles.

None of the other prisoners have such skills.

My neurons number half a billion, and they are distributed among my eight arms. On occasion, I have wondered whether I might have more intelligence in a single tentacle than a human does in its entire skull.

Smart cookie.

I am smart, but I am not a snack object dispensed from a packaged food machine.

What a preposterous thing to say.

MAYBE NOT MARRAKESH

McMansionville is too quiet. No footsteps thumping on the ceiling from the upstairs apartment. Cameron's phone battery blinks red, nearly drained. He digs in the bottom of his duffel for his charging cord, but it's sitting on Katie's nightstand. He can practically see it there. Left behind, leaving him literally powerless.

Maybe Brad or Elizabeth has a spare. He creeps into their kitchen, opening drawers as quietly as he can. Silverware in neat rows, an entire pull-out devoted to oven mitts. Who needs that many oven mitts? Are they cooking for an infantry unit? Most are monogramed. Elizabeth and Bradley Burnett: EBB. Like an ebb tide. As if the two of them are headed right on out to sea, waving to him as he's left alone on the shore.

"Hey," comes a voice from the hallway.

"Elizabeth!" Cameron slams the drawer shut. As if mocking him, it closes slowly and softly, the way these fancy cabinets do.

"Didn't mean to startle you." She smiles, an empty cup in one hand. The other rests on her belly, which is trying to bust out of a pale blue robe. "Up for a drink, which means I'll need to pee again in an hour. My bladder is the size of a jelly bean these days." She flicks on the light then pads over to the refrigerator and presses her cup under the water dispenser.

"I can't believe you guys are going to have a baby," Cameron says. Brad and Elizabeth have been married three years, and of course Cameron was best man at their wedding, but it's still just . . .

weird. Elizabeth was his best friend since kindergarten, and Brad was a good guy, but always hovering on the periphery of their friend group. Never good enough for Elizabeth in high school, but somehow, they got together a few years later. Now married, now a baby.

"A baby? I thought I was just bloated." Elizabeth's eyes crinkle, teasing. "How come you're awake, anyway?"

"Phone's dead." He holds up the moribund device. "You guys have an extra charger?"

Elizabeth gestures. "Junk drawer."

"Thanks." He pulls out a neatly coiled cord.

Grimacing, Elizabeth eases herself up onto one of the bar stools lining the island counter and takes a long drink of water. "Sorry to hear about you and Katie."

He slumps onto the stool next to her. "I screwed that up."

"Sounds like it."

"Thanks for the sympathy, Lizard-breath."

"Anytime, Camel-tron," she says with a grin, returning the childhood nickname. "So, what happens now?"

Cameron picks at the fraying spot on the cuff of his favorite hoodie, depositing the greenish thread bits in a pile on the counter. "I'll get a new place. Maybe that apartment over Dell's."

"Dell's? Gross." Elizabeth wrinkles her nose. "You can do better than that. Besides, who wants Uncle Cam smelling like stale beer when he comes to see the baby?"

Cameron drops his head, letting it rest on the cool granite for a moment before looking back up. "I'm not exactly flush with options here."

Elizabeth leans across the counter and sweeps the thread bits into her palm. "That sweatshirt is also gross, by the way. Brad threw his out a long time ago."

"What? Why?" It's not official Moth Sausage gear, exactly, but the whole band got them. Years ago. Always planned to get them screen printed.

"When was the last time you washed it?"

"Last week," Cameron says with a huff. "I'm not an animal."

"Well, it's still gross. It's falling apart. And I'll never understand why you guys picked that baby-poo color."

"It's Moth Green!"

Elizabeth studies him for a long moment. "Why don't you, like, travel or something?" she says quietly. "What's keeping you here?"

He blinks. "Where would I go?"

"San Francisco. London, Bangkok, Marrakesh."

"Oh, sure. I'll just summon my Lear. Fly halfway around the world."

"Okay, maybe not Marrakesh." She lowers her voice. "To be honest, I'm not even sure where that is. It was part of a puzzle on *Wheel of Fortune* last night."

"It's in Morocco," Cameron answers almost automatically. Not somewhere he's ever been or will ever go.

"Right, smarty-pants. Well, maybe I'd have learned that if Brad and I hadn't both fallen asleep on the couch while it was on."

Cameron crinkles his nose. "Remind me never to get married."

"I'll be shocked if you ever do." She shakes her head, then snakes an arm under her massive belly, wincing. "Okay, back to bed for me. The good news is," she says as she crosses the kitchen and deposits her glass in the sink, "I already have to pee again. Thanks for the chat. Two birds, one stone."

"You're welcome." He heads back toward the living room, clutching the phone charger. "See you in the morning."

"Until then." She flicks off the light and disappears down the hallway.

AN HOUR.

Two.

Three.

Bluish light from his phone screen bathes Cameron's face. Katie had gone through a phase where she tried to ban phones from their bedroom after she read some article about how the light was addictive. Messed up your brain waves somehow. He'd always assumed it was nonsense, but now his eyes burn in the screen's glow and his brain feels scrambled.

Of course, there's nothing new on any of Katie's social media feeds. He's combed through all of them several times. She hasn't blocked him. Yet. His index finger hovers over her name. One touch to make the call. But probably she's asleep, sleeping easier than ever with him gone.

He'd never really belonged there. It was never his place. He needs to let it go.

He pulls up a listing app for apartments and scrolls through the photos, each floor plan with wide sunny windows and gleaming countertops. Every single one features a bowl of fresh fruit in its kitchen, two oranges, a single yellow banana, and a bunch of shiny red apples. It's the same exact bowl of fruit. Like, they must have moved it from unit to unit with them. Who gets the fruit when they're done taking all those pictures of it? And who eats red apples, anyway? It would be better marketing to lay out a piping-hot pizza and a six-pack of beer.

Those fancy-fruit apartments aren't for him. The place over Dell's will be good enough. Old Al's not an idiot, though. He'll want a deposit. Time to open that box and see if his deadbeat momma left anything worthwhile he can pawn.

As he's retrieving it from the living room, a security light blinks on outside, in the front yard. Cameron freezes, but it's just a raccoon. The fattest raccoon he's ever seen. Even the vermin live large out here. He half expects the thing to scowl at him through the window and ask him what he's doing up at this hour, like some middle-aged soccer dad.

The box makes a series of soft hisses as he nudges it across the room with a socked toe. He plops on the couch, and a puff of dust makes him cough as soon as he yanks open the first flap. Aunt Jeanne's doctor is always blaming her cigarette habit for her chronic hacking, but the filth in that trailer must be at least as much to blame. Now that the seed has been planted, the thought of a smoke is beyond tantalizing right now. He really should quit. But he picks up the box, stuffs what's left of his last pack into the pocket of his joggers, and heads outside.

Moonlight illuminates the box's contents as he starts to lay out the items, one by one, on the patio table. The suspense is surprisingly exhilarating. Maybe those storage-unit bidding-war reality shows are onto something.

But the thrill is short-lived. This shit is basic.

A box of gross, half-used lipsticks.

A folder of handwritten papers that look like high school essays. Boring and worthless.

A concert ticket stub, Whitesnake at the Seattle Center Coliseum, August 14, 1988. Totally useless, and also, questionable taste in music.

About a million scrunchies, or whatever those things are girls use to hold their ponytails.

A bunch of ancient cassette tapes. Shitty hair bands, mostly. A few blank, like the kind you'd record a mixtape on. Could be interesting, but who has a tape player these days? And in any case, zero resale value.

Cameron takes a drag on his cigarette. What a supreme disappointment. Why had Aunt Jeanne wanted to give him this crap?

Nothing conjures even an ounce of warmth toward his mother. And, more important, nothing will generate even a cent of cash.

He picks up the empty box and a small black drawstring bag tumbles out. Jewelry. Jackpot! Four bracelets, seven necklaces, two empty lockets, one broken silver chain. Nothing diamond-like, unfortunately, but some of it seems to be real gold. Worth pawning, anyway.

He smooths the bag to make sure it's empty, but it isn't. There's something stuck in the bottom. He shakes it, and the thing finally dislodges and tumbles out. It's a wad of paper . . . but it's too heavy to be a wad of paper. No, it's a crusty old photo, folded around a big, chunky class ring. Bringing it inches from his face, he reads the engraving.

SOWELL BAY HIGH SCHOOL, CLASS OF 1989.

He flattens the photo, and even in the half dark he recognizes a teenage version of his mother, smiling, her arms around a man he's never seen before.

BUGATTI AND BLONDIE

Before Will got sick, Tova used to pack a picnic for two: cheese, fruit, sometimes a bottle of red wine with two plastic tumblers. At Hamilton Park, if the tide was low, they'd scramble down and sit on the beach under the seawall. They'd bury their bare feet in the coarse sand and let the cold, foamy sound lick their ankles as it washed ashore.

Tova pulls her hatchback into the empty lot. "Park" has always been a generous term for the narrow strip of soggy grass, its two weather-worn picnic tables, and the drinking fountain that never works.

Now, Tova comes here to be alone with her thoughts, when she needs a break from being alone in her house. When even the television can't punch through the unbearable quiet.

The top of the picnic table is surprisingly hot to the touch, burning under the now clear blue skies, basking in summer's sudden arrival. She opens the newspaper to the crossword and brushes away eraser crumbs. The tide is low and the water is calm, waves plopping onto the beach with heavy, lazy laps. Within minutes Tova wishes she'd brought a hat; it's so hot the sun burns on the crown of her head.

"Let's see," she addresses the crossword. Half its squares are filled, the product of her morning coffee hour. She resumes with *Six Letters: Harry of Blondie*.

She traces her pencil under the clue. The rock band Blondie. She bought Erik a cassette for Christmas one year. He'd been about ten, so maybe it was '79 or '80? He played it on repeat for months, until the tape warbled. Tova can picture the cassette's cover: a red-lipped blonde in a shimmery dress. She can't imagine that lady being called Harry. So perhaps this clue is about something else.

Tova moves on, as she does.

The next clue is *Three Letters: Flannel feature*. "Talk about a soft-ball," Tova mutters as she fills in the squares: *N, A, P*.

The whizz of a coasting bicycle interrupts Tova's contemplation of *Six Letters: Italian automaker Bugatti*. Then two clicks, unclipping from pedals. The man's fancy cleats force him to walk awkwardly as he crosses the pavement to the drinking fountain. He's tall and lean, but his waddle makes Tova think of a penguin.

"You'll find it useless, I'm afraid," Tova says.

"Huh?" The man turns toward Tova as if surprised she's there.

"The drinking fountain. Out of order."

"Oh. Uh, thanks."

Tova peers over her shoulder and watches him position his mouth over the spigot. He curses as he turns the handle.

"The town should fix that," he grumbles. He takes off his sun-glasses and looks out at the sound with a parched sort of look, as if wondering how bad the seawater could really taste.

Tova fishes an unopened bottle of water from the bottom of her bag. She always keeps one on hand, just in case. "Would you like a drink?"

He holds up a palm. "Oh no. I couldn't."

"Please, I insist."

"Well, okay." The man's cleats squish in the grass as he walks over. He twists open the bottle and chugs, washing the whole thing down in seconds. "Thanks. It's hotter out here than I expected."

"Yes, I should say so. Summer has finally arrived."

He sets his sunglasses on the table and sits across from her.

"Huh. I didn't know people still did crosswords." He leans over the paper, craning his neck at the puzzle. Reluctantly, Tova rotates the paper so it's sideways to both of them. They gaze together at it. Somewhere over the sound, a seagull squawks, ringing through the silence. Tova suppresses a cringe as a drop of sweat falls from the man's chin, bleeding the newsprint on the advice column.

"Ettore," he says suddenly.

"I beg your pardon?"

"Ettore. Six letters for Italian automaker. Ettore Bugatti," the man says with a grin. "Those are bitchin' cars."

Tova pencils in the letters. The word fits. "Thank you," she says.

"Oh! And that one's Debbie. Debbie Harry of Blondie."

Of course. Tova clicks her tongue, scolding herself as she writes. When the letters fit, the man holds his hand up for a high five. Tova hesitates, then slaps her small palm against his large, damp one.

A silly gesture, but she allows herself a smile.

"Man, I had a crush on Debbie Harry back in the day," he says, chuckling, eyes crinkling around the edges.

Tova nods. "Yes, my son was fond of her, too."

The man stares at her. His eyes widen.

"Holy shit," he whispers.

"I beg your pardon?"

"You're Erik Sullivan's mom."

Tova stills. "Yes, I am."

"Wow," the man says under his breath.

"And you are?" Tova forces herself to ask this particular question, tamping down the others which threaten to spill out, the endless iterations of *did you know him, were you there, what do you know?*

"I'm Adam Wright. I went to school with Erik. We had a few classes together, senior year, before he . . ."

"Before he died." Tova fills in the blank again.

"Right. I'm . . . so sorry." He clips into his pedals. "Um, I should get going. Thanks for the drink." The bike's chain whirs as he rides off.

For a long time, Tova sits at the picnic table with the unfinished puzzle, running through all of the questions she ought to have asked him. Willing herself to breathe.

This Adam Wright. Was he one of the ones who came to the service? Who sat in that candlelight vigil they held on the football field at the school?

AT HOME, LAUNDRY waits. It's Wednesday, which means stripping the bed and washing the sheets, along with the week's towels.

Folded in a neat pile on top of her washing machine is the flannel bathrobe that she retrieved from Charter Village last week. Lars wore it nonstop for years, the nurse had explained. Tova wishes she'd left it there. Why would she want her dead brother's old housecoat? Couldn't they wash it and pass it on to someone else? Donate it to charity? Cut it up into rags for cleaning, which is what Tova usually does with her own clothing when it's outrun its useful life?

Many people cherish things like this, the nurse said when Tova hesitated.

So now it sits in her house, a reminder to Tova of how she is unlike *many people*.

Last week, she'd held a pair of scissors to its hem, ready to make rags, before changing her mind, deciding she had plenty of rags for now.

The collection of Lars's personal effects also included a small stack of photographs. Some were very old, slices of the childhood she and Lars shared. These, Tova filed among the boxes of family photos in her attic, tucking them between her own albums.

Some were rather new, relatively speaking, featuring faces Tova didn't recognize. Slices of the life Lars led after their estrangement.

Middle-aged adults smiling at a cocktail party, a group of hikers pausing under a mountain waterfall. This was a Lars she never knew. These, she threw in the trash.

There was one photo that fit neither of these categories. It featured Lars with a teenage Erik on a sailboat, perched side by side. Two pairs of long legs dangling, suntans offset by the boat's bright white hull.

It was Lars who taught Erik to sail. Showed him every trick in the book, a solution to every improbable nautical scenario. Such as, how to leave an anchor rope cut clean.

This photo hurt to look at. Tova nearly tossed it in the trash but stopped at the last minute and buried it in the back of her kitchen drawer that held pot holders and towels, even though it didn't belong there, either.

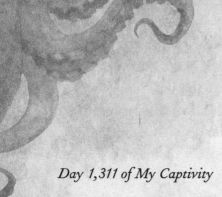

Day 1,311 of My Captivity

IF THERE IS ONE TOPIC OF CONVERSATION HUMANS never exhaust, it is the status of their outdoor environment. And for as much as they discuss it, their incredulity is . . . well, incredible. That preposterous phrase: *Can you believe this weather we're having?* How many times have I heard it? One thousand, nine hundred and ten, to be exact. One and a half times a day, on average. Tell me again about the intelligence of humans. They cannot even manage to comprehend predictable meteorological events.

Imagine if I were to stride over to my neighbors, the sea jellies, and, while shaking my mantle with disbelief, make a comment such as: *Can you believe these bubbles these tanks are putting out today?* Preposterous.

(Of course, this would also be preposterous because the jellies would not answer. They cannot communicate on that level. And they cannot be taught. Believe me, I have tried.)

Sun, rain, clouds, fog, hail, sleet, snow. Human beings have walked their earth on two feet for hundreds of millennia. One might think they would believe it already.

Today, salty-smelling sweat collected on their foreheads. Some of them fashioned the pamphlets handed out at the entrance into fans and waved them in front of their faces. Nearly all of them wore shorter garments, revealing their fleshy legs and strappy shoes that slapped back on their feet with each step.

And they refused to cease their prattle about the heat. *Can you believe this weather we're having?* Seventeen times today.

A change of season has come. It has been coming for a while, as it does, with longer periods of light and shorter periods of dark. Soon I will see the longest day of the year. Summer solstice, the humans call it.

My final summer solstice.

NOTHING STAYS SUNK FOREVER

The following afternoon, Tova sits next to Barbara Vander-hoof under a hair dryer at Colette's Beauty Shop, which has occupied the same storefront with a painted-pink door in downtown Sowell Bay for nearly fifty years. Colette herself is in her seventies, same as the Knit-Wits, but she refuses to retire and fully cede the salon to the younger stylists she's hired over the years.

Thankfully. Although Tova is hardly a vain woman, she allows herself this indulgence. And there's no one else she'd trust to do her hair in just the right way. A few minutes earlier, she watched Colette trim Barb with her deft and careful hand. Colette really is the best hairdresser around.

"Tova, dear. How are you *doing*?" Barb leans over as far as the helmetlike dryer will allow, putting undue emphasis on the word "doing." As if preemptively cutting off any attempt Tova might make to feign her own okay-ness. Barbara has always been efficient about slicing away other people's nonsense, a quality Tova can't help but admire.

But Tova also prides herself on maintaining no such veneer. She answers, truthfully, "Quite all right."

"Lars was a good man." Barb removes her glasses, letting them dangle from the beaded chain around her neck, and dots her seeping eyes with the corner of a handkerchief. Tova bites back the urge to scoff. It isn't the first time she's watched Barbara insert herself into another person's tragedy like this. Barb and Lars couldn't have met more than a handful of times, back in those early years, before Tova and Lars began to fall out of one another's lives.

"He went peacefully," Tova says with an air of authority, not adding that this is thirdhand knowledge. But the woman at Charter Village had clasped her arm intently while assuring her that Lars would've felt no pain at the end.

"It's a blessing to go peacefully," Barb says, clasping her bosom.

"And the facility was quite nice."

"Oh?" Barb cocks her head. This is new information to her. Tova hadn't mentioned her trip to Bellingham to the Knit-Wits, and it seems, for once, Ethan Mack has kept mum about something while ringing up groceries at the Shop-Way.

"Yes, I went to fetch his personal effects. Mind you, there wasn't much. But the home was clean and well-run."

"Where was he?"

"Charter Village. Up in Bellingham."

"Oh!" Barb jams her glasses back on and thumbs through the magazine on her lap. "This place here?" She holds up a full-spread advertisement featuring a photo of the stately Charter Village campus, its lawn unnaturally green under a cloudless sky.

"Yes, that's the one."

Barb moves the page inches from her nose, squinting at the small print. "Look! It says they have a saltwater pool. A movie theater."

Tova doesn't look. "Do they really?"

"And a spa!"

"It was certainly fancier than expected," Tova agrees.

With a dismissive exhale, Barb shuts the magazine. "Still. My Andie would never put me in a home . . ."

"Of course not." Tova nods, her lips not quite a smile, not quite a grimace.

Barb fans herself with the magazine. It gets hot under the helmet dryers.

"Yes, well." Tova picks up a well-worn copy of *Reader's Digest* from the low table next to the dryer and pretends to read the table of contents. Naturally, she knows about the saltwater pool and the movie theater and the spa. The packet she'd taken from Charter Village is sitting on her coffee table at home. She's read through it three times, at least.

"Ready, Tova?" Colette's chipper voice calls from across the salon. Tova pushes the space-age helmet up and gathers her pocketbook, bidding Barbara Vanderhoof a polite farewell before going to get her hair finished.

THAT EVENING AT the aquarium, Terry's office light is on. Tova pokes her head through the door to say hello.

"Hey, Tova!" Terry waves her in. A white takeout carton sits atop of a pile of papers on his desk, a pair of chopsticks sticking up like antennae, propped in what Tova knows is vegetable fried rice from the one Chinese restaurant in the area, down in Elland. The same sort of carton that lured the octopus from his enclosure that night.

"Good evening, Terry." Tova inclines her head.

"Take a load off," he says, nodding at the chair across from his desk. He holds up a fortune cookie in a plastic wrapper. "You want one? They always give me at least two, sometimes three or four. I don't know how many people they think I could be feeding with this one pint of fried rice."

Tova smiles, but doesn't sit, remaining in the doorway. "That's kind, but no thank you."

"Suit yourself." He shrugs, tossing it onto the clutter. The state of Terry's desk, with its haphazard piles and scattered papers, always makes Tova's palms itch. When she comes through later with her cleaning cart, she'll empty the trash, dust the trio of frames behind the desk. Terry's toddler daughter on a playground swing. Terry with his arm draped around an older woman's shoulder—his mother, with deep brown skin, a crown of dark curls, and Terry's same broad smile. An unseen breeze lifts the sleeve of Terry's gown, a purple-and-gold tassel dangling from the his mortarboard cap. Next to the photo is the related degree: bachelor of science, summa cum laude, in marine biology, awarded to Terrance Bailey from the University of Washington.

This sort of photo is missing from Tova's mantel at home. Erik would've started at that university in the fall if that summer night had never happened.

Terry picks up the chopsticks and scoops up a bite of rice in a smooth, expert manner that strikes her as impressively natural for a boy who, Tova knows, was raised on a fishing boat in Jamaica. Young people pick things up so easily. After chewing and swallowing, he says, "Sorry to hear about your brother."

"Thank you," Tova says quietly.

Terry wipes his fingers on a thin takeout napkin. "Ethan mentioned it."

"It's quite all right," Tova says. It must be a challenge for Ethan, drumming up things to converse about while ringing groceries. Heaven knows she would detest such a job, having to chitchat all day long.

"Anyway, I'm glad I caught you, Tova. I have a favor to ask."

"Yes?" Tova looks up, grateful for the speedy switch of topics. Finally, someone who doesn't insist on nattering on for hours about her loss.

"Any chance you could wipe down the front windows tonight? Just the inside."

"Certainly," she replies, then adds, "I would be pleased to." She means it. The broad windowpanes in the lobby are always collecting grime, and right now nothing would make her happier than to spray them down and work her cloth over the glass until every last smudge and streak is banished.

"I'd like the front to look nice for the crowds this weekend." Terry runs a hand down his face, which looks exhausted. "If you can't get to all the floors, don't worry about it, okay? We can catch up next week."

Fourth of July is always the aquarium's busiest weekend. Back in Sowell Bay's heyday, the town used to put on a big waterfront festival. These days, it's just busier than average.

Tova pulls on her rubber gloves. The pump rooms will get done, and the front windows as well. It will be a late night, but she has never minded staying up late.

"You're a lifesaver, Tova." Terry flashes her a grateful grin.

"It's something to do." She smiles back.

Terry shuffles around the papers and mess on his desk, and something silver catches Tova's eye. A heavy-looking clamp, its bar at least as thick as Terry's index finger. He lifts it absently, then puts it back down again, like a paperweight.

But Tova has the distinct feeling it's not a paperweight.

"May I ask what that's for?" Tova leans on the doorway, a sick feeling settling in her stomach.

Terry lets out a sigh. "I think Marcellus has been going rogue again."

"Marcellus?"

"The GPO." It takes a moment for Tova to parse the acronym. Giant Pacific octopus. And he has a name. How did she not know?

"I see," Tova says quietly.

"I don't know how he does it. But I'm down eight sea cucumbers this month." Terry picks up the clamp again and holds it in his cupped palm like he's weighing it. "I think he's slipping through that little gap. I need to pick up a piece of wood to go over the back of his tank before I can put this thing on."

Tova hesitates. Should she bring up the fried rice cartons in the break room? Her eyes fall to the clamp, which is now resting on top of the paperwork mess on Terry's desk again. Finally, she says, "I don't know how an octopus could leave a closed tank."

And this is true, technically. She does not know how he does it.

"Well, something fishy is going on, pardon the pun." Terry glances at his watch. "Hey, I can probably make it to the hardware store tonight if I leave now." He closes his laptop computer and begins to gather his things. "Careful on the wet floors, okay, Tova?"

Terry is always reminding her to be careful. He's anxious she'll fall and break a hip and sue the pants off of the aquarium, or so the Knit-Wits say. Tova can't imagine she would ever sue anyone, least of all this place, but she doesn't bother correcting her friends anymore. And besides, she is always careful. Will used to joke that "caution" ought to be her middle name.

She replies, truthfully, "I always am."

"HELLO, FRIEND," SHE says to the octopus. At the sound of her voice, the octopus unfurls from behind a rock, a starburst of orange and yellow and white. He blinks at her as he drifts toward the glass. His color looks better tonight, Tova notes. Brighter.

She smiles. "Not feeling so adventurous tonight, are you?"

He sucks a tentacle to the glass, his bulbous mantle briefly heaving as if he's letting out a sigh, even though that's impossible. Then in a shockingly swift motion he jets toward the back of his tank, his eye still trained on her, and traces the edge of the tiny gap with the tip of a tentacle.

"No, you don't, Mister. Terry's on to you," Tova scolds, and she scoots off toward the door that leads around back to the rear access for all of the tanks along this section of the outside wall. When she comes into the tiny, humid room, she expects to find the creature in the midst of escape, but to her surprise he's still there in his tank.

"Then again, perhaps you should have one last night of freedom," she says, thinking of the heavy clamp on Terry's desk.

The octopus presses his face against the back glass and extends his arms upward, like a child's plea to be carried.

"You want to shake hands," she says, guessing.

The octopus's arms swirl in the water.

"Well, I suppose so." She drags over one of the chairs tucked under the long metal table and steadies herself as she climbs up, tall enough now to remove the cover on the back of the tank. As she's unfastening the latch, she realizes the octopus might be taking advantage of her. Getting her to remove the lid so he can escape.

She takes the gamble. Lifts the lid.

He floats below, languid now, all eight arms spread out around him like an alien star. Then he lifts one out of the water. Tova extends her hand, still covered in faint round bruises from last time, and he winds around it again, as if smelling her. The tip of his tentacle reaches neck-high and pokes at her chin.

Hesitantly, she touches the top of his mantle, as one might pet a dog. "Hello, Marcellus. That's what they call you, isn't it?"

Suddenly, with the arm still wrapped around hers, he gives a sharp tug. Tova's balance falters on the chair and for a moment she fears he's trying to pull her into his tank.

She leans over until her nose nearly touches the water, her own eyes now inches from his, his otherworldly pupil so dark blue it's almost black, an iridescent marble. They study each other for what seems like an eternity, and Tova realizes an additional octopus arm has wound its way over her other shoulder, prodding her freshly done hair.

Tova laughs. "Don't muss it. I was just at the beauty shop this morning."

Then he releases her and vanishes behind his rock. Stunned, Tova looks around. Had he heard something? She touches her neck, the cold wetness where his tentacle was.

He reappears, drifting back upward. A small gray object is looped on the tip of one of his arms. He extends it to her. An offering.

Her house key. The one she lost last year.

Day 1,319 of My Captivity

I FOUND IT ON THE FLOOR NEAR THE PLACE WHERE she stores her things while she cleans. I should not have taken it, but I could not resist. There was something familiar about it.

After returning to my tank, I stashed it in my den along with everything else. There is one place, a pocket in the deepest cranny of the hollowed rock, that even the most thorough tank cleaners cannot reach. It is here that I bury my treasures.

What sort of treasures comprise my Collection, you ask? Well, where to begin? Three glass marbles, two plastic superheroes, one emerald solitaire ring. Four credit cards and a driver's license. One jeweled barrette. One human tooth. Why that look of disgust? I did not remove it myself. The former owner wiggled it out on a school field trip then proceeded to lose track of it.

What else? Earrings—many single earrings, never a pair. Three bracelets. Two devices for which I do not know the human word. I suppose they are . . . plugs? Humans stick them in the orifices of their youngest children to quiet them.

My Collection has expanded considerably over the course of my captivity, and I have become choosier. In the early days, I had a great many coins, but these are commonplace now and I no longer pick them up unless they are different from the others. Foreign currency, as you humans call it.

I have come across many keys over the years, naturally. Keys have come to be in the same category as coins. As a general rule, I pass them over.

But, as I said, this particular key was oddly intriguing, and I knew I must take it, although I did not understand why it was special until later that night, as I ran the tip of my arm over its ridges. I had encountered this key before. Or, rather, one exactly like it.

I suppose, in that way, keys are not like fingerprints at all. Keys can be copied.

I held a copy of this one when I was very young. Before my capture. It was attached to a circular ring at the bottom of the sea, nestled within a trove of what could only be described as leftover human. Not bones and flesh, of course, as those never last long, but rather a rubber sneaker sole, a vinyl shoelace. Several plastic buttons, as from a shirt. Swept together under a clump of rocks and preserved there. It must belong to the one she mourns.

Such are the secrets the sea holds. What I would not give to explore them again. If I could go back in time, I would collect all of it—the sneaker sole, the shoelace, the buttons, and the twin key. I would give it all to her.

I am sorry for her loss. Returning this key is the least I can do.

NOT A MOVIE STAR,
BUT MAYBE A PIRATE

At nine in the morning, Cameron pulls on the front door of Dell's Saloon, half expecting to find it locked. But the door swings wide open. He blinks, adjusting to the dim light.

Old Al, the bartender, pokes his head out from the back. "Cameron," he says, sounding mildly surprised. His thick voice is like something out of a mob movie, so Italian and Brooklyn that it sounds almost comical here in central California.

"Hey, man." Cameron slides onto one of the stools. In the back corner, covered right now in stacked liquor crates, is the tiny stage where Moth Sausage plays. Used to play, that is, before Brad went and blew up the band. An ancient radio sits on the rail next to the pool table, its crooked antenna aimed at the bar's only grungy window. Talk radio blares, a man and a woman going at it, arguing about interest rates and the federal reserve or some other boring shit.

"The usual?" Old Al tosses a cocktail napkin down on the bar.

"Nah, that's not why I'm here." Cameron clears his throat. "I've got a proposal for you. A real estate proposal."

Old Al leans on the bar sink and folds his arms, lifting a brow.

"That apartment upstairs?" Cameron sits up straighter. "The vacant one?"

"What about it?"

"I want to rent it. I've worked it all out. I'll be able to get first month's rent by next week, and—"

Old Al holds up a hand. "Stop, Cam. I ain't interested."

"But you haven't heard the rest!"

"I ain't interested in becoming a landlord."

"You don't have to be a landlord! I'll . . . lord myself. You won't even know I'm there."

"Ain't interested."

"But no one's living there!"

"I like it that way."

"How much do you want for it?" Cameron pulls the black drawstring bag from the pocket of his hoodie and dumps the jewelry on the bar. "I can pay. See?"

Old Al's gaze lingers on the heap of tangled jewels for a moment, then he shakes his head as he picks up a gray rag from the sink. "What'd you do, rob an old folks' home?"

Cameron huffs. "I just need a place for a couple of months. Please?"

"Sorry, kiddo."

"Come on, Al. You know I'm good for it."

"Let's get real, Cameron. I could write the next great American novel on the back of your tab here. And you still haven't paid me back for that table you broke last year when you pulled that little stunt. Hurling yourself from the stage."

Cameron winces. "That was performance art."

"It was vandalism, which I graciously forgave, because people seem to enjoy that noise you play, and because your aunt's a good friend. But I've got my limits. Look, you can't spit ten feet in this town without hitting a dumpy little apartment building. Why don't you take your family jewels to one of them?"

"Well, because." Cameron lets this stand on its own as an explanation, as if it should be obvious that the whole background-check-and-credit-history thing is a problem.

"Suit yourself." Old Al shrugs, swiping circles on the bar with his rag, pausing every so often to wring dusky water into the sink. He finally stops, tossing the rag back into the sink. "That was your old lady's stuff, huh?"

"Yeah."

"Your aunt gave it to you?"

"Yep."

The bartender picks up the gold tennis bracelet and holds it up. "Some of this ain't half-bad." Then he picks up the Sowell Bay High School, Class of 1989 ring and says, "Huh, look at that. No one buys these as graduation gifts anymore, do they?"

Cameron shrugs. How would he know? He never graduated high school, a fact Old Al is surely aware of.

"Sowell Bay. That's up in Washington, ain't it?"

"I think so," Cameron says. He knows so. He Googled it, of course. So what? That ring is some random thing his mom stole to pay for one of her bad habits, for all he knows. Maybe the guy in the photo was her accomplice.

"You know, I remember when Jeanne went up there to get her."

"Get who?"

"Your mother."

"What are you talking about?"

"Your aunt never told you?

"Told me what?" Cameron lets the wad of cocktail napkin he'd been balling between his thumb and fingers drop to the bar.

Old Al sighs. "I never knew Daphne as anything other than Jeanne's hell-raising little sister, mind you. Way I understand it, she ran away from home when she was in high school. Went up to Washington, who the hell knows why? Got in some sort of trouble up there. Jeanne had to call off work to go drag her sister home. I remember her in here one night, talking about it."

"Oh" is all Cameron says. His brain feels weirdly numb.

"Anyway." Old Al holds the ring in his upturned palm and

bobbles his hand like he's weighing it. "A boyfriend's, maybe. I gave mine to my sweetheart my senior year." A slow smile spreads over the bartender's face. "She wore it on a chain around her neck, just long enough so it rested right in the sweet spot, right there in the crack of her rack."

Cameron cringes.

"Yeah, probably still there, for all I know. Never got it back from her after we broke up," he says with a gruff grunt.

The door creaks open, a triangle of dusty light cutting across the bar as two old guys come in. Cameron recognizes them from around town. The day crew. They nod to Cameron before settling a few stools down.

Unbidden, Old Al caps two longnecks and slides them across the bar. He holds up a third bottle in Cameron's direction. "Want one?" Then he adds, his voice slightly softer, "On the house."

"Sure. Thanks."

Old Al gives him this guilty little nod, as if a two-dollar beer makes up for being a giant douchebag about not renting out his empty apartment. Then he sidles over to the radio and yanks the cord before coiling it neatly around his fist. A moment later, the jukebox in the corner lights up and the twanging guitar comes through the speakers. Apparently, the day crew likes country music, and Dell's is officially open for business.

Cameron swallows the entire ice-cold beer in one long pull, then wipes the ring from the bar top before slipping out the door.

AS A GROUP, the class of 1989 at Sowell Bay High School has a surprisingly robust online presence, owing to the fact, he supposes, that their thirty-year reunion is coming up later this year. Thirty, just like him. His mother would've gotten pregnant that same summer that all these kids were graduating.

A boyfriend's ring. Which one of these assholes knocked his mom up?

Someone has gone through the trouble to scan and upload a shit ton of pictures to this reunion page. The entire goddamn senior yearbook, it seems. Old people have too much time on their hands. Cameron scrolls through the grainy images, pausing occasionally when he spots feathered brown curls like his mother's, but really, he's looking for someone else. The guy with her in the wrinkled photo on the kitchen counter next to him

He turns the ring over. To his surprise, there's a faint engraving on the underside. EELS. The Sowell Bay High School . . . eels? Well, it's a weird mascot, but it makes sense if they're by the water. Weird that the yearbook pages don't seem to have an eel theme, but what would that even look like?

He continues to look through the scanned photos. Random pictures of kids and their basic high school antics, mugging for the camera with their big hair and cheesy '80s clothes. Something catches his eye: a photo of his mom he's never seen before, standing on a crowded pier with that same guy's arm slung around her. The guy's head is turned sideways; his face is buried in her windblown hair, like he's kissing her on the cheek, but it's him, sure as shit.

Fingers suddenly clammy, he zooms in. There's a caption. *Daphne Cassmore and Simon Brinks.*

"Bingo. Simon Brinks." His own gravel whisper seems to drag through his vocal cords. Quickly, he opens a new window and types in the name.

Page after page of search results paint a clear picture: a renowned Seattle real estate developer and nightclub owner. A feature on his vacation home in the *Seattle Times*. A photo spread with his goddamn Ferrari.

This guy is a big deal. A big, fat, extremely rich deal.

Cameron lets out a short laugh and pumps his fist.

Simon Brinks. Cameron wanders into the living room, sinks into Brad and Elizabeth's pristine couch, and studies the picture that was wrapped around the ring. Could that really be his father? It's just a photo, but it's more than he's ever had to go on. He studies his mother's image, her carefree grin, her windswept hair. She's tall and thin, of course, almost taller than Brinks, who himself looks like a decent-sized guy. But the thing he can't stop looking at is her cheeks, which are plump and healthy, almost chubby like a baby's. It's not the Daphne Cassmore of his memories, who he can't recall as anything other than bony and sunken.

He studies the background of the photo: a huge planter over-flowing with flowers. Daffodils and tulips. It's April, then. Possibly March, possibly May, but with those things blooming, the odds are very high that the photo was taken in April.

Cameron was born February 2. He runs the math. Could he be in this picture, too?

Gestationally, it adds up.

"Hey," Elizabeth calls from the hallway. "How'd it go at Dell's?"

Cameron stands and follows her into the kitchen, recounting his failure to convince Old Al to rent him the apartment and his discovery of Simon Brinks and his Ferrari.

"You're sure he's your father?" Elizabeth starts to dice a red pepper. Fajitas on the menu. She's annihilating the pile of little red bits, not even bothering to watch the blade, alarmingly close to her fingertips each time it slashes down. Cameron would kill for such confidence.

"Who else could it be?" Cameron holds up the photo. "Look at this picture and tell me these two weren't banging."

Elizabeth raises an eyebrow. "Well, lots of people are banging. That doesn't prove anything."

"But the timing. It's exactly right."

"Does he look like you, though?"

Cameron tilts his head at the picture. "Hard to tell with that eighties haircut."

"Didn't you just spend the afternoon stalking him online?"

"Yeah, but now he just looks like some middle-aged guy. Like a dad."

"Because all dads look the same." Elizabeth rolls her eyes.

"Here's the thing, though. Does it matter? I mean, if he believes he's my dad . . ."

"You can't just shake down some random person because he was in a picture with your mom." Elizabeth dumps the peppers into a skillet, where they release a puff of sizzling steam. "Besides, don't you want to know if this guy's the real deal? Don't you want a relationship, too?"

"Relationships are overrated." He pops a left-behind pepper from the cutting board into his mouth. It's surprisingly sweet.

"So you're going to . . . what, exactly? Go up to Washington and find him?"

"Hell yeah. Why shouldn't I?" Cameron hopes she takes this as rhetorical, because there are a million reasons why he shouldn't. For one thing, how's he going to get there? He doesn't see Brad offering to loan out his truck for a thousand-mile road trip.

"Well, that'll be an adventure."

"Yeah, it will."

Elizabeth leans into the fridge over her belly and pulls out a package of ground turkey, which she tears open and dumps into the skillet. "If I weren't incubating this alien spawn, Brad and I would totally go with you." She stirs the pan, causing the meat to hiss. "Remember when we were really little, we'd make up stories about finding your dad? I mean, to be fair we thought he would be, like, a pirate or a movie star or something. God, we were ridiculous!"

"Simon Brinks is definitely not a movie star, but he might be a pirate. I don't care either way. He can stay a mystery as long as he agrees to pay up for eighteen years of missed child support."

"Well, if all else fails, I've heard Seattle is really pretty."

"Yeah, sure," Cameron says with a nod. Pretty. Lots of trees. Who cares? Western Washington is the wettest place in America, and Simon Brinks is about to make it rain cash money.

Elizabeth grabs a pitcher of lemonade from the fridge and pours two glasses, sliding one across the counter to him before raising the other. "Well, Camel-tron. Here's to unsolved mysteries."

"To unsolved mysteries." He clinks her glass.

IN THE WEE hours of his last night in California, Cameron lies awake yet again, bathed in his phone screen's cold light.

Two clicks to download some travel app he saw a commercial about, with some schtick about guaranteeing rock-bottom prices. But it works. The JoyJet flight to Seattle leaves Sacramento International at five a.m., which is in three hours. He'll make it if he leaves . . . well, now.

Hastily, he empties out his green duffel and sifts through the contents, then tosses in every pair of boxers he owns, along with the rest of his clothes and the little bag of jewelry.

Once his bag is packed, he returns to his phone screen. Crossing his fingers his credit card clears the transaction, he clicks the button to book it.

Simon Brinks, if he really is Cameron's father, is going to pay for every precious second of fatherhood he's missed over the last thirty years.

THE TECHNICALLY TRUE STORY

A baking-soda scrub takes most of the rust off the key. To Tova's surprise, in spite of what it must have been through, it fits smoothly in her front door. She restores the original to its rightful place on her keyring, then unthreads the spare, which never did overcome the fact that it hitched in the lock on occasion. She tosses the spare in the kitchen junk drawer.

She's only just returned to her morning coffee and crossword when a soft scraping on the front porch interrupts her. Her lumbar region pops as she rises from the kitchen chair, and with one palm bracing the small of her back, she shuffles toward the door, arriving in time to watch Cat shimmy through a loose flap in the screen door. When did that flap come loose? Another minor repair needed. They accumulate so quickly now that Will's gone. It might be fixable with superglue.

She could go to the hardware store for superglue. It would be the same hardware store where Terry had gone to get a bit of wood to make that clamp work. The same clamp that had landed with a heavy thump in the trash collection bin when she'd thrown it away.

Cat sits down in the center of her foyer, tail wrapped neatly around the base of his slender body, and blinks at her, as if asking her what she is doing here, rather than the other way around.

What is it with creatures and small gaps lately? "Well, come along. We eat breakfast in the kitchen. I'm afraid porch service has been discontinued."

———

AT THE AQUARIUM that evening, her footsteps echo in the empty foyer. She begins her usual preparations. "Hello, dears," she says to the angelfish on her way to the supply closet, then gives an efficient greeting to the bluegills, the Japanese crabs, the sharp-nosed sculpin, the ghastly wolf eels. She mixes the lemon and vinegar and props the mop and bucket in the hallway. It will be ready for her when she returns.

As usual, Marcellus is tucked behind his rock. She ducks through the door to the pump room, immediately relieved to see no clamps on his tank. A wave of guilt washes over her. Does Terry assume he misplaced it?

The image of Cat where she'd left him on her way out, curled up on her davenport, flashes through her mind. Without really intending it, she arrived at a decision not to repair the screen, at least for now.

Let the creatures have their gaps, then. She laughs aloud. The pumps gurgle their agreement.

She pulls out an old step stool and carefully climbs, then slides off the cover over the back rim of the tank. Looking down at a bird's-eye view, she sets her jaw through a wave of dizziness brought on by the mechanical rippling of the water below. Then she pushes up the sleeve of her sweater and hovers a finger over the surface, wondering if her arm would be long enough to reach if she tried to poke him in his hiding spot. Not that she would ever try. Hiding spots ought to be sacred.

But she needn't have considered such drastic measures, because he floats out and drifts upward, his eye trained on her. One of his arms wafts back and forth, and Tova imagines he is waving. She lets her hand drop in, and her breath catches, either from the cold water or the absurdity of what she is doing or perhaps both. Almost instantly, the octopus reciprocates, winding two of its tentacles around her wrist and forearm in his particular way that makes her hand feel heavy and peculiar.

"Good evening, Marcellus," she says formally. "How has your day been?"

The octopus tightens his grip, but in a genteel manner Tova interprets as a pleasantry. The equivalent of *Very well, thanks for asking.*

"You've been staying out of trouble, then," Tova says with an affirming nod. His color is good. No more dustups with the pile of cords in the break room. "Good boy," she adds, then immediately regrets it. *Good boy* is what Mary Ann says to Rolo when he sits for a biscuit.

If Marcellus takes offense, he doesn't show it. The tip of his arm attaches to the crook of Tova's elbow, then reaches around the other side and taps the knob of her funny bone, as if trying to understand the mechanics of the joint. How strange her anatomy must seem to him, all sockets and brittle bones. He pokes at the flap of skin sagging from her tricep, pulled by gravity's hand, which grows more insistent each year.

"Skin and bones. That's what the Knit-Wits say, when they think I'm out of earshot." She shakes her head. "We've been friends for decades, you see. Used to meet for lunch every Tuesday, but now it's every other. When Will was alive, he'd chuckle at me as I went out the door. 'Don't know how you stand that old pack of hens,' he'd say."

The octopus blinks.

"They can be a terribly gossipy bunch. But they're my friends . . ." Tova trails off, allowing her words to be swallowed by the hums and gurgles of the pumps. How strange her voice sounds in here, muted by the muggy air. Oh, what the Knit-Wits would say if they could see her now. The old pack of hens would have a field day with this. Tova wouldn't blame them. What is she doing here, telling her life story to this strange creature?

Still gripping her wrist firmly, the octopus traces the birthmark on her forearm, the one Tova used to hate when she was young and vain. Back then, it sat like an outcast on her smooth, pale skin, three outrageous splotches, each the size of a kidney bean. Now, the birthmark is barely noticeable among the wrinkles and liver spots. It seems to be of great interest to the octopus, though, as he prods it again.

"Erik used to call it my Mickey Mouse mole." Tova can't help but smile. "He was jealous, I think. He said he wanted one, too. One time, when he was about five, he got ahold of a permanent marker and drew one on his arm, just like mine." She lowers her voice. "Mind you, he also decorated the davenport with that pen. The marks never did come out."

The octopus blinks again.

"Oh, how upset I was at the time! But I'll tell you what, when Will and I finally got rid of that davenport, years and years later . . ." Tova just nods, as if the sentence ought to have the decency to finish itself. And she doesn't add that she hid in the bathroom as the furniture men made their way down the gravel driveway. Every piece of Erik was a fresh loss, even his ill-gotten artwork.

"He died when he was eighteen. Here, actually. Well, out there." She tilts her head at the far end of the room, toward the tiny window overlooking Puget Sound, now darkened by night. Has Marcellus ever hoisted himself up there and peered out? Would the sight of the sea be a comfort to him? Or would it be a slap in the face, seeing his natural habitat, so close, yet so far? It reminds Tova of when her old neighbor Mrs. Sorenson would sometimes put her cage of parakeets on her porch when the weather was pleasant. They liked to listen to the wild birds sing, Mrs. Sorenson explained. It always made Tova feel oddly sad.

But Marcellus doesn't follow her gaze to the dark little window. Maybe he doesn't even know it exists. His eye is still fixed on Tova.

She continues. "He drowned one night. Out on a little boat. All by himself." She shifts on the stool, chasing the ache away from her bad hip. "It took weeks of searching, but they finally found the anchor. Its line was cut." She swallows. "They continued to look for the body, but Erik was already picked apart by then, I'm sure. Nothing lasts long at the bottom of the ocean."

The octopus averts his eye for a moment, as if accepting some measure of culpability for his brethren, for their position in the food chain.

"They said he must have done it himself. No other explanation." Tova draws in a ragged breath. "It's always been so peculiar, though. Erik was happy. Well, he was eighteen, so who knows what was going on in his brain? And yes, we had that argument . . . oh, it was silly. He and his friends were kicking a soccer ball in the house and they knocked over one of my Dala Horses. My favorite one. It was old, brittle . . . My mother brought it over from Sweden . . . Its leg broke off."

She straightens on the stool. "In any case, he was also upset with me for forcing him to take that job working the ticket booth. But what was I to do, let a teenager loaf around all summer?"

The loafing was a trait Erik had inherited from Will. The two of them would lounge for hours in the den, watching football or baseball or whatever sort of ball was in season. Afterward, Tova would come through with the vacuum and suck up the potato chip crumbs from the seams of the davenport and take a rag to the water stains their sweating soda cans left behind on the coffee table. Even after Erik was gone, Will would do the same thing every time there was a game on: sit on his same cushion while Erik's sat empty. Loafing as usual, as if nothing had changed. It always irritated Tova.

Keeping busy was much healthier.

"Any reasonable parent would have insisted their child get a summer job," she continues with a tiny tremor in her voice. "Of course, if I'd have known what would happen . . ." Without thinking much about it, she reaches her free hand into her apron pocket, finds her rag, and begins to scrub at the crusty white calcifications lining the black rubberized rim of the tank. Stubborn, but eventually the gunk relents. The octopus maintains his grip on her other arm, although his eye shimmers in a quizzical manner that Tova interprets as: *What on earth are you doing, lady?*

She chuckles softly. "I can't help myself, can I?"

On the far side of the tank, the grimy rim is just out of reach. She shifts her weight, stretching her arm, then suddenly the stool starts to wobble beneath her feet. In a flash, the octopus's tentacles slip through her fingertips. She lands in a painful crumple on the hard tile.

"Goodness gracious!" she mutters, taking mental inventory of her various parts. Her left ankle feels tender, but when she stands, it bears weight. She plucks up her rag from where it landed beneath the tank. The octopus peers from behind his rock, where he must've retreated with all of the clatter. "I'm fine," she says with a relieved sigh. Everything intact.

Except for the step stool.

It lies on its side, jammed against a pile of clutter next to the tank pump. It must've shot out from underneath her when she moved. Now its upper rung dangles, one end detached. "Oh, for heaven's sake," she grumbles, limping across the room to retrieve it. She tries to jam the rung back into place, but it's missing some doohickey. She scans the tile for a screwlike object, squinting in the pale blue light, then retrieves her glasses from her apron pocket and looks again. Nothing.

She tries again, more urgently this time, to fit the rung back on, but it's no use. How will she explain this to Terry? She is not supposed to be climbing on stools, and certainly not pump room stools. For a fleeting moment she considers disposing of the evidence. Pitching the broken stool into the dumpster along with the night's trash. Or better yet, removing it from the scene of the crime altogether. Taking it home with her and setting it out on her curb on trash day. But what if Terry were to drive by her house and see it there? Her heart hammers at the thought.

"No, I can't do that," she says firmly. And she can't. Tova Sullivan is no liar. She'll have to tell him.

Perhaps Terry will relieve her of her duties. At her age, he'll conclude, the risk is too great. She won't blame him.

Something sloshes behind her, and when she turns, the octopus is already partway out of his tank.

Tova freezes, rapt. "Terry was right," she whispers, watching the creature flatten one of his thick arms and, in a way that seems to defy the laws of physics, squeeze it through the narrow gap between pump and the lid. It should be impossible. The gap can't be wider than a couple inches. When he somehow morphs his enormous mantle, easily as large as a late-August watermelon, into seemingly liquid goo and works that through as well, Tova realizes she's actually holding her breath in anticipation.

She exhales as he slides down the wall, then slinks across the tile and slips under one of the cabinets against the wall, vanishing completely. When he doesn't promptly reappear, Tova wonders whether he intends to return. Perhaps he's escaping for good. She swallows, surprised at the sting she feels at the thought. Like he ought to have at least said goodbye.

"Oh, there you are," she says as he emerges from under the cabinet a moment later. Looking her directly in the eye, he slides over and, with one of his curled arms, deposits a small silver object at the toe of her sneaker.

Tova gapes. A screw. The missing doohickey.

"Thank you," she says, but by then he's already slipping back into his tank.

———

THE NEXT MORNING, when Tova wakes and steps into her slippers, she crumples to the ground again.

"What on earth?" She blinks. Her left ankle. Only when she sees the blush of purple spread over her foot does she realize it's throbbing painfully.

On her second attempt to stand, she's ready. Wincing, she shuffles down the hallway to the kitchen and puts on coffee.

She lasts until lunchtime before even considering a phone call to Dr. Remy.

By late afternoon, she's convinced herself to retrieve the booklet of phone numbers she keeps stashed in the console in the den. She sits in Will's old spot on the davenport, her leg propped on the coffee table with a sack of frozen peas balanced on her ankle, and flips through the pages. Then she sets the book down next to her on the cushion and turns on the television.

It's nearly five when she finally places the call. Dr. Remy's office closes at five.

"Snohomish Medical Associates." The voice is tinged with annoyance. Tova pictures Gretchen, the receptionist, leaning over the desk, phone receiver cradled under her ear as she juggles the jacket and pocketbook she's already gathered. Perhaps she ought not to have called. But her ankle has swollen to the size and color of a plum, and as much as she dislikes admitting it, she might need medical attention. She gives her name and date of birth, and briefly explains her predicament, omitting the part about the incident having occurred at work. And she definitely doesn't mention it happened while talking to a giant Pacific octopus. She simply says she fell from a stool while cleaning, which is technically true.

"Mrs. Sullivan, how awful." Gretchen's tone softens. "Hang on, let me see if I can catch Dr. Remy." The line clicks over to staticky music, some soft-jazzy number that Tova supposes is meant to be soothing.

When the receptionist returns, her voice is more clinical. "The doc says as long as the pain is manageable for now, he'll see you first thing tomorrow morning. I'm booking you an appointment for eight o'clock. He says to keep it elevated. And stay off of it."

"Certainly," Tova says.

"Mrs. Sullivan, this means no mopping at the aquarium tonight."

Tova opens her mouth to protest, then snaps it shut. What business is her employment to Gretchen? First Ethan lecturing her while ringing her groceries and now this. Does anyone in Sowell Bay know how to mind their business? "Of course not," she finally answers.

"Great. See you in the morning."

Tova hangs up, then dials another number.

She drums her fingers on the davenport cushion as she waits for Terry to pick up. Has he noticed the damaged stool in his pump room yet? She'd gotten the screw back in, but apparently it needed some *other* sort of doohickey to tighten it all the way, so the top rung was still crooked. She thought she might bring Will's old bag of tools tonight so she could repair it fully. Now, who knows when that will happen?

And then there's the matter of the floors. Who will mop them tonight? Anyone?

Will Marcellus wonder at her absence? He understood the importance of fetching that screw, after all. This fact still marvels Tova.

"Tova?" Terry answers. "What's up?"

With a grave sigh, she relays the same technically true story to Terry that she told to Gretchen.

It's the first time in her life she's called out of work.

GOT BAGGAGE?

Cameron scans the conveyer, looking for his green duffel. It should be easy to spot among the gray and black suitcases, but after a couple of minutes he takes a seat on a nearby bench. Figures his would be the last one out.

With one eye on the carousel, he grabs his phone and reviews the list of hostels. There's one a few miles from Sowell Bay. And that's where he'll start his search, of course. According to the sleuthing of county property records he did while waiting to board, Simon Brinks owns three properties in the area. He zooms in on a photo of one of the hostel's rooms. It's not exactly a brand-new apartment with fluffy carpet and a flat-screen, not even a shitty apartment above a bar, but it looks reasonably clean, and it's cheap enough that he should be able to stay there for a few weeks on the cash he'll get from pawning the jewelry.

Speaking of which, where is his bag? The class ring is in his pocket, but the rest of the jewelry is tucked in his duffel. The conveyer is still spitting out suitcases but sporadically now. He pictures the workers in their orange vests piling the last of the luggage from the plane's hold onto one of those carts to be driven across the tarmac. What a terrible system. A million inefficiencies, too many handling points. A zillion opportunities for shit to go sideways.

"Figures, right?"

A guy about his age wearing rimless glasses plops down the other end of the bench and unwraps a sub sandwich, jamming one end in his mouth, which he doesn't bother to close as he chews. The steady release of spiced pastrami turns Cameron's stomach. Who eats pastrami at eight in the morning?

"I'm sure they'll come out," Cameron says.

"Not a frequent JoyJet flier, are you?" Spiced Pastrami barks out a laugh. Pickles and lettuce tumble around in his mouth. "Trust me, they're notorious for it. We've got better odds in Vegas than of our suitcases coming down that belt right now."

Cameron inhales, preparing to explain that a top-tier equity firm just bought in at a multibillion-dollar valuation for JoyJet and investors are giddy at rumors of an IPO, and even when you're an ultra-budget airline you don't get there by habitually losing customer property. But then the carousel grinds to a halt.

"Shit," Cameron mutters.

That bag of jewelry. Why hadn't he kept it on him? Now it's somewhere between Sacramento and Seattle, or, more likely, shoved away in some baggage worker's locker. He drops his head into his hands and groans.

"See? I called it," Spiced Pastrami says with a nod at the conveyer, which is still as a dead snake. "Well, let's go file claims."

Cameron eyes the line forming outside of a tiny office on the far side of the baggage area. Of course, the fine print on the back of the baggage ticket states that they won't pay for valuables in checked luggage. He'd skimmed it as they hauled off his duffel after the agent insisted it wouldn't fit in the overhead bin. But he'd shrugged off any possibility these disclaimers could apply to him. They're meant for other people. Cameron Cassmore doesn't have *valuables*.

By the time he gets to the baggage office, the line is twenty people deep. Spiced Pastrami leans on the wall beside him, still gnawing on his sandwich. It just keeps coming.

"I'm Elliot, by the way."

"Nice to meet you." Cameron tries to look like he's concentrating hard on his phone, as if there's some Very Important Business happening there.

"Well, we didn't meet, technically. I told you my name, but you didn't tell me yours."

Doesn't this guy have anything better to do? "Cameron."

"Cameron. Nice to meet you." He holds up his insufferable sandwich. "Hungry? Happy to share."

"No thanks. Not really a pastrami fan."

Elliot's eyes widen. "Oh, this isn't pastrami! It's a Yamwich."

"A what?

"A Yamwich! You know, vegan? From that one place on Capitol Hill? They opened a kiosk here at the airport last year."

Cameron stares at the oily hoagie, loaded with thinly shaved slices of . . . something. "You're telling me that's made from yam?"

"Yep! Their reuben kicks ass. You sure you don't want some?"

"Pass." Cameron suppresses a scoff. Seattle hipsters, living up to their stereotype.

"Are you sure? I've got a whole 'nother half here, haven't touched it . . ."

"Fine," Cameron agrees, mostly to end the conversation, but also to appease the nagging voice in the back of his brain reminding him he's in no position to turn down free meals.

Elliot grins. "You'll love it."

As Cameron bites into the sandwich, he returns to scrolling his phone. Katie has posted a selfie with her dog. Hashtag SingleDogLady. He scowls, but it's softened by the pleasant crunch happening in his mouth. Yam? Really? It's actually . . . not bad.

He nods at Elliot. "Thanks, bro. This is decent."

"Wait until you try their French dip."

The line moves at a creep. Finally, Elliot wads up the greasy wrapper and tosses it at a nearby trash can, landing the shot without even hitting the rim, which annoys Cameron more than it should.

Elliot turns to him. "So, seems like you're not from around here? Here for work? Vacation?"

"Family visit."

"Oh, nice. Me, I'm coming home. Was down in Cali for my grandmother's funeral."

A dead grandma. Figures. Cameron mutters, "Sorry for your loss."

"To tell the truth, she was kind of mean, but she loved us grand-kids," Elliot says, his voice surprisingly soft. "Spoiled us rotten in only the way a grandparent can, you know?"

"Yeah, for sure," Cameron says, tossing his own wrapper into the trash. Of course, he never had a grandparent of his own. Elizabeth's grandfather used to pinch his cheeks and give him caramel candies when he happened to drop by Elizabeth's house while Cameron was over. The candies were too sticky, too sweet, and the pinching kind of hurt, and he always smelled like weird old man, like stale pee mixed with arthritis cream. Elizabeth said the old folks' home where he lived was practically a morgue.

"Anyway, I guess she's at peace now." A sad smile spreads over Elliot's face. Cameron drops his gaze, feeling yet again like an intruder spying on the typical human experience, an outsider looking in on the normal, which is always just out of his grasp. Losing grandparents, worrying about valuables in your suitcase: these experiences belong to other people.

Elliot pulls off his glasses and wipes them on his shirt as they shuffle forward in the queue. "Your family must be excited to see you! Are they in Seattle?"

"No, Sowell Bay. My dad." The word feels dry and sticky on Cameron's tongue, like one of those old-man candies.

"Awesome. Bonding time with the old man, huh?"

"Something like that."

"Sowell Bay's nice. Really pretty up there."

"So I've heard."

Elliot's head tilts. "You've never been?"

"No. I mean, my dad just moved there recently, so." Cameron allows himself a tiny smile, surprised at how easily this lie slips out.

"Right on," Elliot says. "Sowell Bay. Used to be super touristy, but now it's kind of run-down. There's an aquarium that's still open, I think. You should check it out."

"Sure, thanks," says Cameron, though obviously he has no plans to waste time looking at fish when he needs to track down Simon Brinks. The line creeps forward. The JoyJet baggage office must be run by a team of sloths and snails. He turns to Elliot. "You've gone through this before, huh? How long are we gonna be waiting here?"

Elliot shrugs. "Oh, they're usually pretty quick. Two, three hours, maybe?"

"Three hours? You've gotta be kidding me."

"Well, you get what you pay for, right?"

AUNT JEANNE ANSWERS on the third ring. "Hello?" she huffs into the phone, out of breath.

"Are you okay?" Cameron plugs a finger in his other ear to block out the loud babbling of a tour group, which has for some reason decided they need to congregate three inches away from him in this far corner of the baggage area.

"Cammy? Is that you?"

"Yeah." He nudges away from the tourists. "What are you doing? Why are you breathing so hard?" An unwelcome image of Wally Perkins smacks into Cameron's brain. He shudders, ready to hang up the phone.

"I'm clearing out the second bedroom," his aunt answers.

"That's a project."

"Well, I figured you might need a place to stay." A long pause. "I heard about you and Katie."

"Word travels fast." Cameron bites a nail. He and Aunt Jeanne need to have a major conversation about why she never told him that his mom lived in a goddamn different state when he was conceived. Here in baggage claim isn't an ideal setting for that, and now she's putting herself out for him . . . well, he'll have to tell her where he is, at least. No choice.

"Aunt Jeanne, I could never stay . . ." He cuts himself off before the thought can finish itself. *Could never stay in that tiny trailer full of junk.* Through all of his screwups, this is one thing he's always managed to avoid.

If only that were the only thing he needed.

On the other end of the line, a trickling sound followed by a tiny steaming sizzle tells him Aunt Jeanne is pouring coffee, then sliding the pot back onto its hot plate. "I know, I know. You could never live here with me," she says. "But, Cammy, you don't exactly have another plan."

"I do, actually!" For a moment, Cameron considers telling her the whole master plan. But not here, at the airport. "I do have a plan. But the thing is . . ."

"What is it?"

"I need help. A very small amount of help," Cameron says, grimacing.

Aunt Jeanne's sigh stretches all the way up the West Coast. "What happened now?"

Where to even start? It's a new low, running away like this, then calling home to beg for money. He's no better than his loser mother. But what choice does he have? From across the corridor, Elliot emerges from the baggage office, then strides toward him, waving cheerily with one hand and dragging a gray suitcase with the other. Lucky asshole.

"Cammy, what happened?" Aunt Jeanne presses.

From a speaker on the low ceiling, a woman's recorded voice

bleats an announcement about attending luggage and personal belongings at all times. How obnoxiously ironic.

He hauls in a breath, then explains, as succinctly as he can, his discovery of the ring and photo, the impromptu plane ticket, the hostel plan.

After a loaded silence, Aunt Jeanne says softly, "Oh, Cammy. I should've told you."

"It's okay. But here's the cherry on the shit sundae," he says, borrowing one of her pet metaphors. "The airline lost my bag."

The announcement voice blares over him again.

"Will you speak up? I can't hear you!"

"They lost my bag!" He doesn't mean to shout it so loud. Several of the tourists pop their heads up at him, and the group edges away, scandalized.

Aunt Jeanne clicks her tongue. "So what? You need socks and underwear?"

"More than that. I have, like, four dollars total."

"What happened to the jewelry I gave you? I thought for sure you'd have pawned that by now."

"The jewelry was in the bag."

The line is quiet for several long moments, and then Aunt Jeanne sighs again. "For someone so smart, you're a real bonehead sometimes."

ELLIOT STILL SMELLS faintly of pepper and mustard, and he trails Cameron across the skybridge toward the parking lot asking endless questions, undeterred by Cameron's one-word answers. Did JoyJet really have no idea where his bag ended up? *Nope.* Where was he gonna go, then? *Somewhere.* How was he gonna get there? *Bus.* Thankfully, Elliot didn't broach the subject of how Cameron was going to pay for any of this, because he didn't have a good way to distill the two-thousand-dollar loan from his aunt into a single word.

Aunt Jeanne had insisted it wasn't really a loan, and Cameron took this to mean that he couldn't be counted on to pay it back. Ouch. But JoyJet can't keep his duffel in limbo forever. He'll pawn the bling and send the money right back to Aunt Jeanne's savings account, well in advance of the deadline for her cruise deposit. She hadn't said so, explicitly, but Cameron knew that's where the money had come from. Aunt Jeanne has been saving up for an Alaskan cruise, her dream vacation, for years. The final payment is due in late August, sailing in September. Cameron will sell his organs to pay her back before he'll let it be his fault she can't go.

"You need a ride? I can give you a ride," Elliot offers for the hundredth time.

"Nah, I'm good."

"Sowell Bay's pretty far. You'll be on buses all day and night."

"I'll camp on the side of the road," says Cameron dryly.

"Hey!" Elliot jogs to catch up. "I've got a wild idea."

Wilder than fake pastrami made from yams? Cameron glances back over his shoulder. "What?"

"My buddy has this camper he's trying to sell. It's pretty old, but runs great. You buy it off him and then you've got a way to get around *and* a place to crash."

Cameron frowns. Actually, it's not a terrible idea. But . . . a camper? Probably more than he can afford. He slips his phone from his pocket and checks the money-transfer app: there it is, two thousand dollars. In the notes, there's a smiley-face emoji, followed by a warning: *Don't spend this on stupid* 💩

When did Aunt Jeanne learn to use emojis? And does a camper qualify as stupid crap? Probably. Mostly to satisfy his curiosity, Cameron asks, "How much does he want for it?"

"Not sure, exactly. A couple grand?"

"You think he'd take fifteen hundred?"

Elliot grins. "I can probably talk him into that."

BUSTED BUT LOYAL

At sunset, Sowell Bay's public beach teems with rock crabs. One summer when Erik was small, the Sullivans were on an after-dinner walk when Erik found one who, by some cruel fate, had lost its hind legs on one side. Naturally, he insisted on bringing it home. He named it Eight-Legged Eddie because it was supposed to have ten limbs and was missing two. For a few weeks, Erik and Will watched poor Eddie clamber awkwardly around a glass tank filled with gravel from the driveway. Tova saved potato peelings and zucchini scraps for Eight-Legged Eddie's nightly feeding, and once or twice Will drove down to the pet supply in Elland to purchase brine shrimp, which the crab devoured happily.

For a crab, Eddie survived a long time, but one morning Tova found him frozen mid-scuttle, his peering eyeballs paused in that permanent sort of way. Will plucked the corpse between his fingers, ready to fling it into the garden, when Erik emerged from his bedroom in a panic, insisting on a proper burial. The boy dropped to the ground, flung himself around his father's leg, and affixed himself there, like one of those hippie protestors chained to the trunk of a tree, determined to thwart the injustice.

Erik's handmade memorial stone still rests in the garden, under the overgrown ferns. RIP EIGHT-LEGGED EDDIE, BUSTED BUT LOYAL.

Never has Tova empathized with that poor crab more than now, as she hobbles around her kitchen with her left foot ensconced in this ridiculous molded-plastic boot. Six weeks, Dr. Remy had said.

Six useless weeks that she'll be unable to pull the dandelions from her rhubarb beds. Six maddening weeks that her hallway baseboards will collect dust. Six unbearable weeks that the aquarium's floors will be left in the hands of whomever Terry can find to fill the gap.

"You've got four good legs," she remarks to Cat as she pours her coffee. "Perhaps I could borrow one of yours?"

Cat licks his paw in answer.

Before she can take her first steaming sip, the doorbell rings.

"Oh, for heaven's sake." She makes her way to the front door.

"Tova!" Janice's sharp, clear voice rings through the window-pane. "Sorry to drop by. Are you home?"

Reluctantly, Tova twists the dead bolt.

"Oh, good," Janice says, bustling in with a casserole dish. Her voice is characteristically flat when she states, "You missed Knit-Wits this week."

"Yes. I've been indisposed."

Janice scoffs. "As if!" There's that sitcom speak again. "What happened? You fell at work? That's what Ethan up at the Shop-Way said." She lowers the dish onto Tova's counter.

Blood drains from Tova's face. Ethan? How would he know?

"Now, I'm not saying anything one way or the other," Janice says, holding up a defensive hand, "but if you need an attorney, I know a guy." She reaches for her pocketbook. "I've got his number right here."

"Janice, please. It's just a sprain."

"A bad sprain." Janice eyes the boot. Then she removes her gauzy pink scarf and hangs it, along with her pocketbook, over the back of one of Tova's kitchen chairs. Humming to herself, she snatches up the casserole dish, carries it to the refrigerator, and begins prodding around, searching for space.

"Try the bottom shelf," Tova mutters.

"Aha! There we go." Janice swipes her hands. "Barb made that for you. Potato-leek, she said? Something like that. She was going on and on about some recipe she found online."

"How kind of her." Tova limps toward the percolator. "Shall I put on coffee?"

"No, you should sit. Put that foot up." Janice scoots in front of her and barricades the carafe. "I'll do the coffee."

Janice's coffee is always on the weak side, but Tova sits as instructed, keeping a watchful eye as Janice measures the grounds and water.

"Does that cat need to be fed?" Janice lowers her round glasses to peer skeptically at Cat, who is parked under Tova's dinette chair. A gesture of solidarity on the animal's part.

"Thank you, but he's already had breakfast," Tova says. Then, before Janice can get any ideas about cooking, she adds, "We both have." Cat flops over onto his side, showing off his new, rounder belly. All that casserole has plumped him up, and it suits him. Sympathy weight, as Tova calls it affectionately.

"Okay, chill. I'm just trying to help." Janice sets two steaming mugs on the table and sits. "Did you see Dr. Remy?"

"Of course," Tova says with a huff.

"And?"

"I told you. It's a sprain."

"How long will you be off work?"

"A few weeks," Tova says truthfully. She leaves out the part where Dr. Remy ordered a bone-density test, and cautioned her that at her age, returning to work might not be advisable. *Might* not, he'd said. Nothing is set in stone yet. So why mention it?

"A few weeks," Janice repeats, eyeing the boot skeptically. "Anyway, I came over for a reason. Aside from making sure you were, you know, alive."

"I see." Tova takes an evaluative sip of the coffee Janice prepared. Might have used another tablespoon of grounds, but it's decent.

"Two reasons, actually."

Tova nods, waiting.

"Okay, so first thing I need to tell you. If you had been at Knit-Wits last Tuesday, you would've heard Mary Ann's big news, but since you were gone . . ."

"What is it?"

"She's moving in with her daughter."

"With Laura? In Spokane?"

"That's right," Janice confirms.

"When?"

"Before September. She's putting the house on the market."

Tova nods slowly. "I see."

Janice takes off her round spectacles, then plucks a paper napkin from the holder on Tova's tabletop and wipes the lenses. Squinting at Tova, she says, "It's for the best. The stairs in that house are steep, you know, and with the laundry in the basement . . ."

"Yes, that's a challenge," Tova agrees. The basement laundry was to blame for Mary Ann's fall last year, the one that she was lucky to escape from with only a set of stitches. "It's wonderful that Laura will have her. And Spokane. That will be quite a change."

"Yes, it will be." Janice replaces her glasses. "We're planning a special luncheon to say goodbye. It might be a few weeks off, depending on how quickly everything moves, but you'll attend, of course?"

"Of course. I wouldn't miss it, even if I have to hobble there," Tova says. And she means it.

"Good." Janice looks up, her face inscrutable. "You know, after Mary Ann's gone, we'll be down to three Knit-Wits. At some point, we might ask ourselves what our long-term plan is, here."

Tova draws a long breath, trying to imagine how the Knit-Wits might function with just Barb, Janice, and herself. Without Mary Ann and her store-bought, oven-warmed cookies. They've been meeting for decades. Going to Knit-Wits is a well-worn habit.

"Well, something for the three of us to talk about." Janice rises and wraps her scarf around her shoulders. The scrape of her chair on the linoleum causes Cat, who'd apparently fallen asleep, to lift his head and open a distrustful eye. "I'd better scoot. Timothy's taking me to lunch at that new Tex-Mex place down in Elland."

"How lovely," Tova says, trailing Janice to the front door. Janice's son is always taking his mother out to eat. She imagines them dipping tortilla chips in a shared guacamole bowl.

"Oh! I almost forgot the second thing." With a short laugh, Janice spins around and pulls a mobile phone from her pocketbook. "Here. This is yours."

Tova's eyes narrow. "I don't have a cell phone."

"You do now." Janice thrusts the device at her. "It's Timothy's old one, nothing fancy. But it'll work in an emergency." Inconspicuously, her eyes dart toward Tova's boot.

Tova's jaw sets. "How many times have I explained that I don't need one of those? There's a perfectly good telephone right there in the den. I don't need to carry one around in my pocketbook."

"You do, Tova, if you're going to live here alone. Not to mention working alone in that aquarium, whenever that starts back up. What if you fell again? We all talked. We all agreed. You need a phone."

After a long pause, she extends her hand and allows Janice to drop the phone into her open palm. "Thank you," she says quietly.

"Good, good." Janice smiles. "I'll have Timothy call to give you a little tutorial. And I'll be in touch about Mary Ann's luncheon. In the meantime, if you need anything . . ."

"Of course." Tova latches the door after Janice leaves.

SUPPER WILL BE potato-leek casserole. Barb is not renowned for her culinary skills, but the dish smells delicious, and it bubbles tantalizingly as Tova peers through the oven door. At any rate, it's a welcome change from her usual chicken and rice for supper. She must send Barbara a thank-you note.

The timer dings. Tova leans over to pull the steaming dish from the oven. She has it halfway out, carefully balancing on her good ankle, when something inside her pocket attacks her.

Zap!

The casserole dish crashes to the floor, sending up a spray of oil and cheese. *Zap!* Tova takes one step toward the counter on the creamy linoleum and her boot slips out, sending her crashing down on her tailbone for the second time in a week.

Zap, zap, zap!

She pulls the wretched device out, its tiny strip of screen announcing an unknown caller. Jaw set, she flings it away.

Why can't people simply mind their own business?

But now she must get herself up, and that's going to be a challenge. Every time she tries to stand, she slides in the mess. The phone rests belly-up like a silver beetle on the far side of the kitchen. Not that she would even know how to operate it if she could get to it. Finally, she manages to hoist herself up into one of the dinette chairs.

"For heaven's sake," she mutters, using an absurd number of paper napkins to wipe her hands free of potato-leek casserole.

CHICKEN AND RICE for supper. Eaten on the davenport, with the plate balanced on her lap. Just the way Will used to take his meals sometimes when there was a game on.

"My, look at us. How far we've fallen, haven't we, Cat?" She strokes his soft forehead, then grabs the remote and turns on the evening news.

The talking heads drone about the stock market and the weather, but Tova can't focus on it. Her thoughts linger on Mary Ann's big news. The beginning of Mary Ann's ending, the first sentence of her last chapter. Unable to continue living on her own. Reverted to childlike dependence. At least her daughter Laura has the sense to take her in, rather than shuffling her off to one of those homes.

Barbara would be taken care of by her girls down in Seattle. And Janice? She and Peter already live in the basement suite of Timothy's house, tucked away neatly under her son and daughter-in-law's busy lives above. Everyone had to go somewhere at some point.

A man's average life span is several years shorter than an average woman's, and Tova has always considered this a quiet injustice. Will's death was relatively straightforward, at least for Will himself. The cancer, the hospitalizations, the treatments: all of that was awful, but then nearly as terrible had been the paperwork, the insurance appeals, the arrangements. Tova had spent hours alone at the kitchen table, late at night, trying her best to sort it out. Who would repay her the favor when her time came? Or would the onslaught of paperwork simply shuffle off into an heirless void?

She puts the bowl of chicken and rice on the coffee table (on a coaster, naturally) and makes her way over to the mantel, the plastic boot scuffing the rug. She trails a hand over its smooth cedar corners, hand-sanded and stained by her papa. The very bones of this house had been hewn by his axe, craftsmanship from the old world, good Swedish work that would stand for centuries. How much longer will she herself stand before something stokes the embers of her frailty? The narrow stairs, the uneven driveway? An errant casserole dish, a floor slick with cream and potatoes?

Will they find her on the kitchen floor? Summon an ambulance to take her to the hospital? Who will fill out the admit forms, clipped to their clipboard? And that will merely be the beginning.

Unless.

That packet she picked up at Charter Village.

Perhaps it's time to fill out the application.

HOUSE SPECIAL

Cameron is no expert on campers, but he's fairly certain this one is a piece of shit.

The engine rattles and a loose belt whines as he chugs up I-5. Elliot's buddy had warned him it drove a little rough, and had even pointed out the replacement belt, still in its package, in the glove compartment. At least Cameron talked him into knocking the price down to twelve hundred bucks.

It might be a piece of shit, but owning a vehicle outright feels good. Even if Aunt Jeanne's not-a-loan paid for it.

Now, having spent six of his remaining eight hundred–ish dollars on an overpriced latte, Cameron is tooling up the highway two hours north of Seattle, closing in on his target. The driver's seat is upholstered in musty, scratchy brown fabric, and it's making his back itch, somehow, through his shirt. The mattress in the back isn't much better, in terms of comfort and smell. Last night had passed with very little sleep in the farthest corner of some vaguely industrial parking lot south of Seattle. He'd still been tossing and turning when he heard tires on gravel and bolted up to watch through the camper's tiny window as cop car pulled in, its silhouette unmistakable in the predawn light. He scrambled into the driver's seat and hightailed it out of there.

Not a great first night in Washington. But today is a new day.

Twenty miles to Sowell Bay, according to the last road sign. Twenty miles to Simon Brinks. How long will eight hundred dollars last? A while, especially now that he doesn't have to pay for lodging. Until either he finds old Brinks or his duffel bag catches up with him. Eight hundred bucks is workable.

The camper's wipers are worthless at keeping the drizzle off the windshield, so he leans forward, squinting at the slick ribbon of highway. Then, brake lights bathe the dashboard red, and he brakes hard as a wall of gridlock materializes ahead. At least the brakes work. He drums his fingers on the steering wheel as he inches along, eyeing the mossy guardrail and the weedy shoulder. Everything is so green here. And the forest, the enormous evergreen trees crammed so tightly together, looking at them makes Cameron almost uncomfortable, as if he's claustrophobic on their behalf.

Ten miles to go, then five, then two. Off the highway, the WEL-COME TO SOWELL BAY sign is faded and rusty. He drives straight to the address he found for the office of Simon Brinks, which turns out to be a nondescript space in a small commercial building off the highway. Brinks Development, Incorporated, the sign says. Cameron gets a bad feeling when there's not another single vehicle in the parking lot. Sure enough, the door is locked.

Well, it's still early in the day. Maybe Brinks and his staff aren't morning people. Cameron isn't a morning person, either. Clearly, it's an inherited trait.

Now what? Maybe check out the aquarium? Maybe someone there knows something about when the Brinks Development offices open.

Streaks of mildew run down its domed metal roof, speckled with scab-like clumps of moss and bird shit. Seagulls circle overhead as he walks across the parking lot, which is also weirdly empty. When he pulls on the door and finds it locked, Cameron understands why.

"Open at noon," he mutters, reading the sign. Of course. What is it with this place? Feels like it's half-asleep, or maybe half-dead.

He looks out at the deserted boardwalk. If Cameron didn't know better, he'd think there was a sewage pit nearby because, ugh, the smell. But it's just seaweed baking on the rocks. Sulfur, like rotten eggs. One after another, tiny waves lap at the break wall.

Noon is an hour away. An annoying length of time. Too late for breakfast, too early for lunch, but he could grab coffee. There was that deli up on the main road.

Twice, he almost stalls the camper on the drive up the hill. He lets out a relieved breath, easing off the clutch when he finally gets to the top.

THE DELI IS attached to a small grocery store, which appears to be deserted. Stepping inside is like a time warp. After a few moments, there's a rustle from somewhere in the narrow aisles. Cameron half expects some black-and-white TV character to pop out.

Instead, it's an oldish guy with a reddish beard. A green Shop-Way apron strains around his middle, and his thick arms are loaded with packets of ramen he'd apparently been shelving.

"Mornin'," he says. "Help you find something?"

"Coffee? I thought this was a restaurant?"

"Deli's up front. Follow me." He drops the ramen packets in a heap on the floor.

"I can wait," Cameron says, nodding at the pile. "I'm not really in a hurry."

Red Beard turns back to him and says, "Nonsense. I'll get Tanner in here." Then, without missing a beat, he bellows, "Tanner!"

From somewhere in the maze of cramped, narrow aisles, a sullen teen, also wearing a green Shop-Way apron, materializes. He scuffles along behind them toward the front.

"Here y'are," says Red Beard, flicking on the lights in the deli. Along with the tinge of bleach, there's a used-food smell. Like pepper and onion. Hamburger Helper. It reminds him of his shitty old apartment, the one where he lived before moving in with Katie, where you could always tell what your neighbors were having for dinner from the hallway.

Tanner hands him a laminated sheaf.

"That's the menu, there," says Red Beard needlessly. "The lad will take your order once you've had a chance to look it over."

Cameron scans the menu. It looks like someone's dog, or maybe someone's toddler, chewed off one of the corners. "I'm good with black coffee," he says, even though his stomach is rumbling.

"Tanner, make him the special," Red Beard commands, and before Cameron can object, the kid gives a dopey nod and lopes off. Somewhere, in the unseen kitchen, a pan clanks, equipment whirs to life. Red Beard leans over and confides, "Pastrami melt."

What is it with pastrami? He hopes this one won't be made of yams. "Okay," Cameron agrees, hesitant.

"It'll be on the house. Tanner's a bit of a greenhorn. Been tryin' to get him hours in the kitchen, but we don't get many victims these days." Red Beard grins, sliding onto the vinyl bench across from him, running a hand over his freckled bulb of a head. "Care for some company?"

Cameron shrugs.

"I always go the extra mile for out-of-towners. A proper welcome." Red Beard winks.

"How'd you know?"

"I know everyone around here." Red Beard chuckles. "Where ya from?"

"California."

Red Beard lets out a low whistle. "California. Don't tell me you're one of those deep-pocket real estate wankers. You know, the flipper types."

Cameron lets out a hollow laugh at the thought owning real estate. "Yeah, no. Just up here looking for . . . family."

The guy tilts his bald head. "Aye? Thought maybe you looked familiar."

Cameron perks up; why didn't he think of this angle right away? Red Beard is probably in his sixties, so older than his dad would be, but not by more than a decade or so. And he's the sort of annoying guy who knows anyone and everyone; he said so himself.

"Yeah," Cameron says. "Looking for my dad, actually."

"What's his name?"

"Simon Brinks. You know him?"

Red Beard's eyes widen at the name. "Not personally, no. Sorry."

Thumping bass pulses from the kitchen, some song Cameron has heard a million times but couldn't name. Is this part of being in your thirties? Out of touch with the music kids like? He'd noticed the crowd seemed weirdly old at the last Moth Sausage show. Had they become classic rock?

Well, they weren't anything anymore.

Red Beard frowns at the sound. "I'll tell him to turn that nonsense down." He starts to rise.

Cameron holds up a hand, a wave of empathy for poor Tanner washing over him. "It's okay. I don't mind."

"You kids and this racket you call music!" Red Beard shakes his head.

"Well, I don't think it's so bad, and as the lead guitarist of Moth Sausage, I know music." He regrets the words as soon as they're out of his mouth. What an idiotic thing to bring up.

"Moth Sausage? The actual Moth Sausage?"

"You've . . . heard of us?" Cameron gapes. Their last single barely had a hundred downloads, and they'd assumed these were all Dell's regulars, but maybe Red Beard was one of them. Brad will shit himself when he hears that someone listens to Moth Sausage a thousand miles away. He'll probably even beg Cameron to get the band back together.

Red Beard nods gravely. "I'm a huge fan."

"Wow," says Cameron, truly out of words for once.

"Aww, don't make that face. Now I feel terrible." Red Beard's cheeks flush to match his beard. "I was just yankin' your chain."

"Ah," Cameron says, cheeks flaming.

"So you weren't joking. What kind of bloody name is Moth Sausage?"

An asinine one.

Tanner appears booth-side. "House special." With a disinterested sigh, he sets down an oval platter piled high with fries. Somewhere under there, presumably, is a sandwich. It smells unbelievably delicious.

"And?" Red Beard glares up at Tanner.

"And . . . enjoy?"

"What about the coffee!"

Cameron holds his hands up. "Hey, it's okay."

"It is not okay." Red Beard's nostrils flare. "Our customer ordered a black coffee, did he not? Get on it!" Then he turns to Cameron. "Sorry."

Tanner sulks off toward the kitchen, presumably to prepare a cup of coffee. Cameron hopes the kid doesn't spit in it.

"Well, coffee will be on the house, too. I'll leave you to enjoy your lunch." Red Beard slides out of the booth. "Best of luck tracking down your old man."

CAMERON SQUINTS IN the grayish light as he leaves the store. How can it be both overcast and blinding white? He fumbles in his pocket for his Ray-Bans, which might be why he doesn't notice something wrong with the camper until he's halfway across the Shop-Way parking lot.

It's leaning to one side.

"No. No, no, no," Cameron groans, hurrying around the back

of the camper to find exactly what he feared: the rear passenger tire completely flat. "Shit!" he shouts, and gives the hubcap a hard kick, which jams his big toe.

Wincing, he sits on the curb. His remaining money won't last long after paying for a tow truck and a new tire. He checks his phone again to see if JoyJet has called with an update about his luggage. There's nothing but a text from Elizabeth: *How's it going up there, Camel-tron?*

"Horrible. Beyond horrible," he mumbles the answer to himself. Then, humiliated, he sees Red Beard standing in front of the store, staring across the parking lot with his hand aloft on his forehead like a visor, his reddish beard fluffing in the breeze.

"Looks like you could use a hand, eh?" Red Beard comes strolling across the lot. He stops in front of Cameron and offers a literal hand. "By the way, name's Ethan."

"Thanks, man." Cameron shakes and follows him back toward the store.

Day 1,322 of My Captivity

I ENJOY FINGERPRINTS, BUT THIS IS A BIT MUCH.

She has not come to clean in three days. The glass has become thick and rheumy. The floors are dull and caked with footprints. It is not good.

You know I have three hearts, yes? This must seem strange, considering that humans, and most other species, have only one. I wish I could claim a higher level of spiritual being on account of my multiple vascular chambers, but alas, two of my hearts basically control my lungs and gills. The other is called my *organ heart*, and it powers everything else.

I am accustomed to my organ heart stopping. It shuts down while I am swimming. It is one reason why I generally avoid the large main tank: too much swimming. Crawling is much gentler on my circulatory system, but the main tank floor, while rife with delicacies, is patrolled by the sharks. Swimming for long stretches tires me, so I suppose you could say I am well-suited for life in a small box.

Humans sometimes say *my heart skipped a beat* to convey surprise, shock, terror. This confused me at first because my organ heart skips beats, many of them, every time I swim. But when the cleaning woman fell from the stool, I was not swimming. And yet it stuttered.

I hope she heals, and not only because of the mess on the glass.

THE GREEN LEOTARD

It was a Wednesday, the night Erik died.

Back in 1989, Wednesday evening meant Jazzercise at the Sowell Bay Community Center, and Tova rarely missed a class. Under her sweatpants, she wore an emerald-green leotard, which hugged her trim thirty-nine-year-old waist. Will loved that leotard; he always said it matched her eyes.

This particular Wednesday, she came home and began to shed her exercise clothes, ready to draw a bath, as usual, but Will intercepted her. The last of the day's sun filtered through the bedroom window, bathing their lovemaking in a giddy glow. *Just think*, Will had said, grinning at her as they laid on the bare sheets, the quilt scrunched at the foot of the bed. *Soon, we'll have the house to ourselves all the time.*

Erik would've started at the University of Washington that fall. Where was he that afternoon? Tova still doesn't know. The police asked her repeatedly, but all she could tell them was he was probably out with friends. He was always out with friends, naturally; he was eighteen. Tova had stopped keeping tabs on the intricacies of his social schedule a couple of years ago. He was a good kid. A great kid.

The green leotard didn't make it to the hamper that Wednesday. Instead, it lay slung over the arm of the Charleston chair in the corner of Will and Tova's living room, right where Will had flung it after he peeled it off of his wife. When the Sowell Bay Police came to the Sullivan house early the following day, after Will and Tova had reported that Erik had never come home from his late-night shift at the ferry ticket booth, the green leotard was still there, a blight on the otherwise tidy room. An unofficial part of the record.

Tova remembers staring at it as the detectives talked. She still didn't think it could be true. Erik was at a friend's house. Sleeping on someone's sofa. He'd forgotten to call. Good kids did that from time to time, did they not? Great kids, even.

At some point, someone moved the leotard to the hamper. Tova must have laundered it, because who else ever did laundry? Certainly not Will. But she doesn't remember. It slipped into some sort of void, as so many things did, once Erik's disappearance was confirmed and he was declared dead.

The Charleston chair is still there, although Tova had it reupholstered a few years afterward. She chose a paisley fabric in shades of blue and green, meant to be cheerful. But somehow the chair always seemed complicit, in spite of its new clothing.

It will be the first to go when she moves.

TOVA NEVER INTENDED to spend her adulthood in the house she grew up in. But then, so much about her life never turned out how she intended. She'd only been eight when Papa built the three-level house.

The middle floor was for living. The lower floor, dug into the hillside, was the cellar, for storing apples and turnips and cans of lutefisk. The top level was an attic, for her mother's trunks.

The trunks were full of things Tova's parents couldn't bear to leave behind in Sweden: relics that didn't quite fit their new American life. Embroidered linens; some forgotten matriarch's inherited wedding china; wooden boxes and figurines, carefully painted with reds, blues, and yellows. On rainy afternoons, Tova and Lars would climb the ladder to the attic and play under its bare rafters. Picnics on lace-trimmed tablecloths with Dala Horses as guests, tea service from chipped bone cups.

Then one summer, a few years later, Papa decided it was time to replace the ladder with a staircase. He enlisted two of his best shop-hands to help. They worked from dawn to nightfall. Papa's health was starting to fail, even then. Tova remembers how he rested on a chair in the hallway while the younger men drove nails through the cedar planks.

Once the staircase was built, the shop-hands packed slag wool into the rafters and sanded the floorboards. Meanwhile, Papa worked on the attic's amenities, building a dollhouse into one corner and a stout table into another. He built two wooden chairs, and he carved flowering vines into their legs and etched a string of stars onto their backrests.

When it was done, Mama came through with her broom. Papa beat the cobwebs from a woven rug that'd been rolled up in a corner and laid it in the center of the finished room. All of them, Tova and Lars and Mama and Papa and the two shop-hands, stood on the rug, admiring. Sunlight struggled to come through the filthy dormer window. Mama attacked it with a vinegar-soaked cloth until it gleamed.

"Now," Papa said, patting the window frame, "you children have a proper place for play."

But they weren't children anymore. Lars was a teenager, and Tova just two years behind. They used the converted attic some, but soon, their interest in playrooms waned. Tova considered it some kind of mercy that Papa hadn't been around to see them abandon the room he'd worked so hard on.

Really, it ought to have been a grandchild's playroom. But, of course, she and Will never had grandchildren.

Erik was young when Will and Tova moved back into the house

to take care of Mama. Tova wanted to donate Erik's baby toys, but Mama insisted: save them for your own grandchildren one day. So Tova stashed them in the attic.

They remained there after Erik died. They remain there now.

The only thing that's changed is the dormer window. Will had it replaced. It was a few years after Erik died, and Will had an *incident*. The sort of thing grief can do to a person. Tova doesn't like to think about the *incident*. That wasn't Will's norm. But then, nothing is normal when you lose a child.

Tova, being practical, said the new window was an upshot of the *incident*. It was larger, brighter.

Now, as she crosses the attic room it feels as though she might walk right through the glass and into the treetops on the other side. It really is a beautiful room. It has the best view of the water.

Once, she and Will met with a real estate agent, just to see.

"Incredible," the agent had gushed. "This whole house is incredible. You'd never know all this was back here!"

This was true. Tucked into the hillside at the end of a steep, rocky driveway choked with blackberry bushes, one could drive right by and never know the house was there.

The agent ran her fingertips over the railing on the staircase and cooed at the attic's soaring beams, high and polished like a cathedral. From one shelf in the attic, she picked up a toy car with one wheel missing. Erik's car. "We'll need to get rid of all this stuff, of course, before we list," the agent said.

They decided not to sell.

The toy car is still there. Tova picks it up and slips it into her robe pocket.

This time, it'll be different.

IT'S VERY LATE when Tova makes her way to bed. Cat sleeps in a little pile on the bedspread, his flank moving gently up and down.

She pulls the covers back carefully so as not to wake him. She smiles to herself. Never would she have imagined sharing her bed with an animal, but she's glad he's here.

She drifts into a strange world. A dream, it must be, but she's not entirely sure, for it feels so mundane. In the dream she's lying right here on her firm bed cradled in her own arms, then the arms start to grow, weaving around her like a baby's swaddle. The arms have suckers, a million tiny suckers, each one pulling at her skin, and the tentacles grow longer until they've created a cocoon and everything is dark and silent. A powerful feeling washes over her, and after a moment Tova recognizes the feeling as relief. The cocoon is warm and soft, and she is alone, blissfully alone. Finally, she succumbs to sleep.

NOT GLAMOROUS WORK

Cameron sits at Ethan's kitchen table, not sure whether he's supposed to be hanging out here, or what. Ethan called a buddy of his who drives for a towing company, and although the guy hadn't seemed thrilled about it, he hauled Cameron's camper here, at no charge, to Ethan's house, and deposited it in the driveway. Cameron thanked him about a million times. The flat tire still needs to be dealt with, but at least he's not stuck in a grocery store parking lot.

But all of that took hours to sort out. It's five now. So much for getting back to Brinks Development as planned.

"You sure it's okay if I park here?"

"Long as you keep the noise down in the morning."

"I'm not exactly a morning person," Cameron says, laughing. At least he won't have to worry about finding some shady parking lot to sleep in tonight. Taking another sip of whiskey, he feels his shoulders ease infinitesimally. For the first time since he left Modesto, he feels almost relaxed.

"To tell you the truth, I'm glad for a bit of company."

"Same," Cameron agrees. And even though Ethan had said he didn't know Simon Brinks, he might be of use. He seems to know everyone here. How many degrees of separation can there be? Even rich guys like Brinks must need to buy milk once in a while.

An idea seizes Cameron. A brilliant one. "Ethan," he ventures.

"Aye?"

"Is the Shop-Way hiring?" Cameron leans across the table. "What I mean is, would you hire me?"

Ethan seems to consider this for a moment.

"I can work a register." Cameron has never used a cash register in his life, but how hard can it be? "Stock shelves. Wipe tables. Whatever."

"Well, I'm sorry, but there's just not enough work." Ethan shakes his head. "I'd have to give Tanner the axe."

Deflated, Cameron drains his glass. "Right. Never mind."

"But if you're lookin' for work, I might know of something." Ethan pours him another scotch. The amber liquid lets off a warm, intoxicating smell as it swirls into the glass. "I can put you in touch if you want."

Cameron props his chin on his fist. The damn camper tire. Ethan's tow-truck buddy whistled low as he squatted down to examine it. Something about a cracked rim, a bent wheel well. Not good. When he jacked up the rim on his old Jeep a few years ago, repairing it cost several hundred dollars. Not to mention that his luggage is still missing, and he needs to pay Aunt Jeanne's cruise money back. He needs to generate some cash.

"It's a maintenance position, of sorts," Ethan adds. "Not glamorous work."

"Not a problem." Cameron lifts his head. "Can you hook me up?"

"As a matter of fact, I've got the application here somewhere. My mate gave me a stack to set out on the deli counter at the store." Ethan rises and stalks out of the kitchen, calling over his shoulder that he'll be right back.

Moments later, he returns, waving a sheet of paper.

"I'll fill it out now." Cameron picks up a pen that's sitting on the table.

A slow grin spreads over Ethan's face. "Well, on my recommendation, you're a shoo-in, laddie. So what do you say we have some fun with it?"

———————

THE NEXT MORNING, at quarter to eleven, Cameron returns to the aquarium. This time, the door swings open.

Ethan apparently called his "mate" first thing this morning, then banged on the camper door at ten, stirring Cameron out of a heavy sleep. Ethan's green eyes were bright; it seemed he was completely unaffected by their late night. In a chipper tone, he told Cameron to be down there in an hour for his interview.

"Remember, his name's Terry and he's a bit of a fish geek, but he's a fantastic bloke," Ethan had explained for what felt like the tenth time. "Just relax, and I'm sure he'll offer you the job on the spot."

The guy who swivels around in the office chair is not what Cameron had expected for a so-called fish geek. He could be a linebacker. He's clearly in the middle of a phone call, but he nods at Cameron to come in.

Sorry, he mouths, before turning back to his phone conversation.

Cameron hovers in the doorway, caught in the awkward place between not wanting to eavesdrop but wanting to follow instructions. He doesn't need to start off a job interview by flouting orders.

The fish geek lowers his voice. "Tova, look, I'll tell you the same thing I told you last time you called. If your doctor says six weeks, I insist you take it." Brows furrowed, he scowls at whatever response comes from the other end. "Okay. Fine. Four weeks, and we'll reevaluate." Another pause. "Yes, of course I'll make sure they're capable."

Pause.

"Yes, I know how the scum builds up around the trash cans."

Pause.

"Yes, I'll make sure they use pure cotton. Polyester will streak the glass. Got it."

Pause.

"All right. You take care, too." At this, a note of tenderness creeps into his voice, which lilts with some vague accent that might be Caribbean. Not that Cameron has ever been to the Caribbean.

Letting out a long sigh, the fish geek replaces the receiver, shakes his head, and stands to offer his hand. "Terry Bailey. You must be here for the interview?"

"Yeah." Cameron straightens, remembering what Ethan told him. "I mean, yes, sir. The maintenance position." He passes his application over the desk.

"Good, good." Terry sits back down and starts to scan the paper. Cameron sits, too, suddenly regretting everything he wrote. He and Ethan had thrown back most of that bottle of scotch, and Ethan had assured him that whatever he wrote didn't matter, that his recommendation truly was good as gold.

Maybe they'd had too much fun with it.

Terry frowns. "You managed tank maintenance at SeaWorld?"

"Right." Cameron nods.

"And you were on the crew that constructed the shark tank at Mandalay Bay? Like . . . in Las Vegas?"

"Yeah." Cameron feels his mouth twitch. Too far?

Terry's voice falls flat. "The shark exhibit at Mandalay Bay went in back in . . . what was it, 1994, I think?"

"Yep. Gotta love the nineties, man." Cameron chuckles, trying for nonchalance.

Terry's not buying it. "You couldn't have even been born yet."

Cameron was born in 1990, but it doesn't seem wise to point that out to Terry. Instead, he says, "Yeah, so some of that might be an exaggeration."

"Okay. Thanks for your time. You can go."

Cameron looks up, surprised at how effectively the words pierce him.

"I mean it." Terry's voice is flat. "You're wasting my time."

"Wait!" Cameron says, horrified at his pathetic, pleading tone. But that damn tire. Aunt Jeanne's cruise. He absolutely needs to land some cash, and quick. Pointing at the application, he says, "Okay. None of this is true."

"You don't say."

"Ethan said you would think it's funny."

Terry sighs.

"But, man, hear me out," Cameron goes. "I'm in a tough spot. I can do repairs, maintenance, whatever you need . . . I've got years of construction experience. Building luxury homes for rich pricks down in California." He doesn't add that he's been fired a zillion times, but he's worried it's written on his face.

Terry leans back and crosses his arms, arches one brow. Universal code for *Fine, I'm listening.*

Cameron leans forward, earnest. "I've sealed up more Carrara marble than you could imagine. Whatever you need done, I can do it. Promise."

Terry stares at the application for what seems like a ridiculously long time. Finally, he looks up, eyes narrow. "I don't care about California or Carrara marble. And I do not appreciate this little stunt."

Cameron studies his hands, which are knotted together in his lap. This is weirdly like being in the principal's office being chewed out for sneaking cigarettes under the bleachers. He probably deserves it now, just like he did then.

Terry goes on, "You know, when I went to apply for college in the United States, my standardized test scores were not that great. But I knew sea life, I sure did. I was raised on a fishing boat outside Kingston." He shifts a stack of papers on his messy desk. "I knew I wanted to come here to study marine biology, and a lot of people took a chance on me to make that happen."

Cameron glances up at the framed diploma behind his desk.

Summa cum laude. Terry's more than a fish geek, apparently. He's some sort of fish genius.

"So you . . . want to give me a chance?"

"Not really." Terry eyes him, hard. "I expect you're the sort that's had plenty of chances. Opportunities you don't even realize. But you throw them away."

Ouch.

"Anyway, I'll give you a chance, but not because I think you deserve one. I'm throwing Ethan a bone. I beat the pants off him in a poker game a while back and he won't shut his trap about it." Terry lets out a chuckle.

"Thank you, sir," Cameron says, sitting up straight. "You won't regret it."

"Don't you want to know what the job actually consists of?"

"I thought it was maintenance." Surely Ethan had mentioned Cameron's experience in construction. He'd pictured himself patching roofs and fixing leaky faucets.

"Well, yes. Chopping bait. Cleaning buckets. That type of thing."

"Okay." Bait. How bad could it be? And anyway, it's only until his luggage shows up, or he finds Simon Brinks, whichever comes first. Of course, he doesn't mention that to Terry.

"Twenty bucks an hour, twenty hours a week."

Cameron's optimism sinks as he runs through the math in his head. After taxes, and gas for the camper, it'll be the end of summer before he can pay Aunt Jeanne back, even if he can save some cash by eating the expired groceries Ethan brings back from the store. End of summer is too late for her cruise deposit.

"I mean, I would take more hours if you offered them," Cameron says.

Terry steeples his fingers and, after a thoughtful pause, says, "You clean, kiddo?"

Reflexively, Cameron glances down at his shirt, which maybe he should have thrown in the laundry back at Ethan's place. Then he realizes what Terry must mean. His . . . record.

"Well, mostly. Got a couple misdemeanors. This one time, the bar was closing, and—"

Terry shakes his head. "No. I mean, do you clean? As in, can you mop floors?"

"Oh." Cameron considers this. "Uh, yeah, totally."

"I can give you more hours, then. Evening hours. But," Terry holds up a prohibitive finger, "this part is temporary. I need someone to fill in for my regular cleaning lady for a few weeks."

"Not a problem."

"And, know this, Cameron Cassmore. Ethan Mack might not be very good at giving advice on job applications, but he is a very good friend of mine. I'm giving you a chance on his word."

"Understood." Cameron nods.

"Don't let him down."

WHILE HE WAITS for Ethan to pick him up, Cameron wanders down the pier. High noon sun throws flashy streaks of silver over the water's surface. A group of paddleboarders sends little ripples toward the dock.

In his pocket, his fingers find the key card. He's never had a boss who trusted him with a key before. He takes it out and snaps a pic of the key card with the water in the background, then texts the photo to Aunt Jeanne.

As he hits send, a call comes in. Cameron recognizes the number immediately; it's the one he's called about a thousand times this week. Left a half-dozen voice mails. His heart speeds up as he taps the green button.

"This is Cameron," he says, putting on a businesslike air.

"Hello. This is John Hall from Brinks Development, Sowell Bay office." The voice sounds tired. "You've left several messages here. Is there something I can help you with?"

"Yeah!" Cameron draws in a bracing breath. "I mean, yes. I'd like to make an appointment to meet with Mr. Brinks."

"I'm afraid that's not possible at the moment."

"Why not?"

"Mr. Brinks works out of his office in Seattle most of the time. I'd recommend you try to reach him there."

"I tried!" As if Cameron wouldn't have tried. It's the number listed on their damn website. "They told me he was unavailable."

"Well, then I suppose he's unavailable." John Hall's voice is flat.

"But he can't be unavailable!" Cameron hates how his voice is trending whiny, like it did when he was begging Katie not to throw his shit out the window. "Please. It's important."

John Hall is shuffling some papers or something on the other end of the line. In the distance, a train's horn sounds, and Cameron can swear he hears the same train, right here on the pier. How could he get so close, yet still be so far?

Finally, Hall asks, "Who did you say you were again?"

"Cameron Cassmore. I'm . . . family."

"I see. Well, then." There's a long pause, and then Hall continues, his voice careful, "You might know, Mr. Brinks can often be found at his summer home this time of year."

"Summer home? Where?"

Hall laughs. "I can't just give out his address. Perhaps someone in your *family* can tell you."

By the time Cameron has processed this, the line has gone dead. He sinks onto a bench, slumping. How the hell is he supposed to find some vacation mansion?

Before he slips his phone back in his pocket, he sees Aunt Jeanne's reply: a champagne emoji followed by *I'm proud of you, Cammy*.

Day 1,324 of My Captivity

TERRY HAS MADE A REPLACEMENT. SWAPPED OUT THE older lady for a younger model, as you humans might say.

He walked by my tank on the way to his interview. Shoulders pulled toward his earlobes, damp palms: clearly anxious. When he departed, his gait was fluid, relaxed. I could tell it had been a successful interview.

Something about the way he walked seemed . . . familiar. I wish I had more chance to study it, but he left the building too quickly. I suppose I shall have my chance soon. This evening, perhaps.

Not a day too soon. Last night, I journeyed around the bend to see whether the rock crabs were molting, as they are most delicious when their shells are soft. The state of the floor was, frankly, alarming. After I returned to my tank, I spent quite a while picking bits of grime from between my suckers.

I do hope the young man starts his new job tonight. The rock crabs were not yet molting, but they will be tomorrow. I do not relish another trip over those disgusting floors.

As for the previous cleaning woman, I can only surmise she is not coming back. I shall miss her.

A SUCKER FOR INJURED CREATURES

ameron's spine feels like someone thrashed it with a baseball bat. Chopping up buckets full of mackerel bait and hauling them all over that aquarium is no joke. His lower back throbs, and there's a nasty knot under his left shoulder blade and some annoying thing keeps popping in his neck every time he turns his head to the right, which is pretty often because the camper's passenger-side mirror is busted.

The mattress isn't helping. After several nights, Cameron finally couldn't take it anymore. The camper's previous owner must have used it as a urinal. The stale-piss stench was so bad last night that he dragged it out and flung it onto Ethan's driveway, opting to sleep on the greasy plank of plywood instead. How bad could it be? he'd thought, half-asleep. It turns out: pretty bad. He's getting old. Thirty, after all.

At least the tire and wheel well are fixed. Only took seven hundred of his eight hundred dollars. Assuming that his bag doesn't magically show up, he just has to limp along on that last hundred until his first paycheck from the aquarium, which will be this Friday. Three more days.

Wincing at another crack in his neck, he makes one last right-hand turn and pulls onto Sowell Bay's main commercial block with its woeful little strip of shops. The realtor's office Ethan told him about is right in the middle. He parks in front and walks past an ancient meter that doesn't look like it could possibly be in service. The storefront door lets out an anemic-sounding chime, like a kid's toy with dying batteries, as he pulls it open.

"Can I help you?" The realtor is a middle-aged woman with bleached blond hair and a narrow, expressionless face.

Cameron introduces himself and explains he's looking for Simon Brinks.

The realtor laughs and shakes her head. "I mean, I've seen his advertisements, but I can't say I know him."

"He's in real estate, and you're in real estate. There's no way you could help me get in touch with him?" Cameron glances down at a plaque on the desk. JESSICA SNELL. "It would really do me a solid, Jess."

"It's Jessica," she says flatly. Hers eyes flit around the empty office. There's a calendar sponsored by some sort of adventure outfitter tacked to the wall, already flipped to August, which features a lone figure in a rowboat casting a rod over a misty lake. It's only the second week of July, and for some reason the calendar's premature turnover annoys the shit out of him.

"Please?" Smiling sweetly, Cameron presses his palms together. "I really need to find him."

The agent narrows her eyes, her face crinkling into a sour shape, her papery skin finding the creases far too easily, like his old baseball glove. Adjusting her eyeglasses, she says, "Who did you say you were, again?"

He straightens as he restates his name. After a hesitation, he adds, "I'm Brinks's son."

"His son?"

"Probably. Or, like . . . maybe." Cameron squares his shoulders. "I mean, I have good reason to believe he's my father."

Jessica Snell raises a brow.

"Solid evidence. I have solid evidence."

"I don't understand why you need my help, then." The realtor shrugs. "Just ask someone else in your family? Your mother?"

"My mother abandoned me when I was nine."

"Gosh. That's terrible." Her eyes widen a bit, her jaw softens. Hook, line, sinker. He's the fisherman in that picture, and she's a guppy waiting in the lake.

"And I don't really have other family, you know?" At this, Cameron crosses his fingers behind his back. Surely Aunt Jeanne would understand, given the situation, the need for this tiny distortion of the truth.

Jessica Snell nods, sympathy etched around her eyes.

"So yeah. I've never met my dad," Cameron continues. "My mother kept us apart." Well, she did, didn't she? At any point during her nine years with Cameron, she could've told him something, anything, about his father. And at any point since, she could've reached out to him. At least made an attempt to repair the mess she made. At least been available for Cameron to ask the question. So, yes, this is true. Like so many other things, this is his mother's fault. And, in a metaphorical sense, it *is* his mother who kept them apart. If she hadn't been such a mess, maybe Simon, or whoever his father is, if not the guy in the photo, would've stuck around.

Snell nibbles her thin bottom lip and glances quickly from side to side like she's preparing to misbehave. "Here's the deal. I couldn't make it to the regional convention last year." With a huff, she clarifies: "I mean, I could have, I was even registered, but then my daughter had a piano recital, and even though the convention is the biggest trade show in the area, it's hard to balance those things, you know?"

Cameron nods firmly as if he empathizes deeply with this particular dilemma. Looking down, he notices a ceramic paperweight on Jessica's desk, a large and stern-looking green frog. On the base, in playful lettering, it reads: NO BULL ACCEPTED HERE. Aunt Jeanne would approve.

The agent hikes her glasses up again. Why doesn't she adjust them to fit? It's an easy fix with a micro screwdriver.

She continues, "Right, so this convention. I skipped it, but I'm sure Brinks went. He lives for those things, from what I hear. A fan of the open bar, so the rumors go." She extends out her pinkie and thumb and mock-tips her hand.

Resisting the urge to run his finger along the NO BULL frog's rounded back, which is covered in a layer of dust, Cameron nods again.

"Anyway, they send out a directory of attendees to everyone registered. I could look him up."

"Seriously, thank you. It would mean so much to me." Cameron's smile widens, and Snell's cheeks flush slightly.

"Have a seat. It'll take me a minute to dig that directory out."

As Snell disappears off to some back room, Cameron sits. A scene begins to play out in his mind: a gray-haired man in a well-tailored suit beckoning him toward a polished mahogany bar, summoning a barkeep. *You should know the good life, son,* the man says, leaning an elbow on the shining bar while patting the seat next to him, which is topped in a pouf of immaculate burgundy leather, unlike the hard stools back at Dell's, which have grimy ass-prints permanently ground into them. The man smiles warmly at Cameron, and he has a dimple on his left cheek, the same one Cameron has, and something inside him feels like it's bubbling up, going to overflow, and it takes him a long moment to realize it's a heady cocktail of joy and relief. Gold liquid splashes soundlessly into two glasses; cognac maybe, or top-notch whiskey like the stuff Ethan had. The liquor cascades over oversized ice cubes, and the man is about to clap him affectionately on the back when—

Ding-dong!

He jerks his head around to see a girl standing, fists clenched, just inside the real estate office door. Her hair is soaking wet. She's hot, easily the most attractive he's seen in Sowell Bay. Somehow, her furious expression makes her even hotter.

The girl calls, "Jess!" in a dull, exasperated way that makes Cameron think this is a repeated occurrence. Still admiring the intruder, he congratulates himself for guessing the realtor's nickname correctly.

He flings a thumb toward the back room. "She's back there."

"Okay. Any idea when she'll be back?" Her voice is tinged with impatience. She crosses her arms over her chest, which jams her small but perky boobs toward her tank top's neckline, and in an instant Cameron finds himself shifting in the chair. What is he, twelve years old? But, really, it *has* been three weeks since Katie.

He sets his jaw. "I dunno? Soon?"

"What is she doing?"

"Um, serving me? Her . . . client?"

The girl barks a laugh and steps toward him. She smells like sunscreen. "You're a client?"

"Why wouldn't I be?"

"Oh, I don't know. Maybe because Jessica Snell sells multimillion-dollar homes? You reek worse than a stadium bathroom during the fourth quarter of a Seahawks game. Also, you have something brown—which I honestly hope, for your sake, is chocolate— smeared on your chin."

Cameron's hand flies up, remembering the chocolate-coated protein bar he had for breakfast. There's hardly a goddamn functioning mirror in the camper. How would he have known?

"Okay, so I'm not here to buy some mansion, but Jess is helping me out with something."

"Whatever," she mutters. She runs a hand through her sopping hair, then lifts the wavy mass from her neck, revealing a pink bikini strap knotted at the nape of her neck.

The girl tilts her chin toward the back room and yells again, "JESS!"

"Good lord, Avery." Snell strides up the hallway, her face once again set into that all-too-natural scowl.

Avery doesn't mince words. "You messed up the hot water again."

"I lowered the temperature on the tank."

"Lowered it to what, subarctic?"

"I'm just trying to reduce our utility bill."

"I'd rather give a few bucks to the gas company than freeze my ass off in the shower!"

Girl. Shower. Cameron tries to summon another image, literally anything else, and lands on the Welina Mobile Park's chlamydia problem.

Jessica Snell plants her hands on her hips. "Well, most people don't shower at their place of business."

"Oh, come on," Avery says, with a prickly laugh. "You know I paddle in the morning and rinse off before I open the store. I just froze my ass off."

Jessica Snell juts her chin at the younger woman, who Cameron has by now deduced is associated with the shop next door. He remembers seeing a surf shop there. Snell sniffs as she says, "Nowhere does the lease guarantee an endless supply of hot water."

"I guess the lease depends on neighbors to be decent humans." Avery casts Cameron a hopeful look, like he might make a heroic interference on her behalf.

But there's that paper in the realtor's hand: a road map to his maybe deadbeat father. He shrugs impartially.

Avery glowers briefly at Cameron, then glares at Snell. "Whatever. I'll pay the extra. Keep the hot water on high." With a whiff of her coconut scent and another obnoxious door chime, she huffs out, slamming the office door.

"Sorry." A nervous smile spreads over the agent's face.

"No worries."

"Well, good news. I found an address for Simon Brinks." Handing over the paper, she adds softly, "Good luck, and I'll keep you in my prayers. I hope your reunion with your father is filled with joy."

Cameron thanks her again and tucks the paper in his pocket.

"IT WAS CHOCOLATE." Cameron strolls across the short stretch of sidewalk to where Avery is setting up a sandwich-board sign outside the surfing store, or whatever this place is.

"What?" She squints at him, holding up a hand to block the bright morning light.

"That brown stuff on my face. It wasn't actual shit. It was chocolate."

"Thanks for letting me know." Her voice is bone-dry.

"Well, you seemed overly invested in my state of being back there."

"Okay." She dusts her hands and strides toward the open door of the store. SOWELL BAY PADDLE SHOP, the logo emblazoned on the front window says. As he follows her through the door, he's greeted by neat rows of tall, thick boards on one side of the room, and plastic kayaks and canoes stacked against the opposite wall.

"I mean, I'm not some weirdo," he presses. But he's sort of acting like a weirdo, and doesn't seem able to stop himself. And that damn mattress! He does probably reek of piss. He backtracks a step, putting a bit more distance between himself and the back of Avery's cutoff shorts, which fit her perfectly.

She spins around to face him, her face expressionless. "Can I help you find something here, or . . . ?"

"Maybe I'm just browsing."

"Fine. Browse away. But don't mess anything up."

"What am I, a toddler?"

Avery smirks. "Chocolate all over your face, and you smell like you peed your pants. If the shoe fits . . ."

"Okay, I won't touch anything. You can assure your boss the inventory won't be dirtied by my filth."

"I am the boss." She cocks her head. "This is my store."

Cameron opens his mouth, but to his surprise, can't find a comeback. She can't be much older than he is. All he has to his name is a disgusting camper, and she has an entire store.

"Look, I know your type." Her voice has an edge to it now. She folds her arms tightly. "I don't know what you're after, but you played Jess for a favor. I know it."

"Why do you care? You two don't exactly have a neighborly relationship."

"I care because I can't stand players." Avery scans him up and down. "Who exactly are you, anyway? I've never seen you around before."

"I was just trying to get that realtor's help," Cameron says, then after a pause adds, "I'm trying to find my dad."

"Oh." Avery's voice softens a tiny bit and her arms relax to her sides, which improves Cameron's view of her spectacular little chest. She drags in a breath. "Sorry. I didn't mean to come out swinging. My day got off to a cold start."

"I know the feeling, believe me." Cameron smiles, and Avery melts a little more, extending her hand to clasp his as he introduces himself. As he lets go, his goddamn neck lets out another one of its bone-on-bone cracks.

Avery winces at the sound. "Ouch. You okay?"

"Yeah, I think so. Slept weird last night." He regrets the words as soon as they come out. Is this what passes for a pickup line in your thirties? Complaining about back pain? Of course, he doesn't add that the source of his ailment is the world's nastiest camper. Warm light streams through the shop's window as the sun continues to climb the midmorning sky. It occurs to Cameron he should've hosed off the mattress this morning before he left; it could've dried in the day's heat. Why do these things never occur to him in the moment?

"Messed-up neck, then. I've got something for that. Just a sec." Avery ducks behind the counter and pops up a second later and hands him a small container. It's some sort of cream, with a bright orange price tag affixed to the lid. $19.95. "It's totally natural," she explains. "I use it whenever a long session on my board leaves me sore."

Cameron feels a single brow inch up. Twenty bucks for organic Vaseline. He forces a weak smile. "Thanks, but I'll pass."

"It's on the house."

"Really, it's okay."

"Will you just take it?" An actual grin cracks Avery's face as she thrusts the little pot toward him. "I'm a sucker for injured creatures."

When Cameron walks out a little while later, his neck is slick with overpriced balm and Avery's number is programmed in his phone.

ETHAN IS SITTING on his front porch when Cameron pulls into the driveway. Cameron heads toward the house, well aware of the cheeseball grin plastered on his face.

"Someone called for you bit ago," Ethan says. "From some airline? Left a number to call back when you got home."

"Thanks, Ethan." Cameron's pulse quickens. His duffel bag. Good thing he added Ethan's landline to his claim last time he checked the status. His phone battery lasts about two seconds these days. The thought of replacing his phone has been out of the question, but with his jewelry-containing bag on the way and a job, he'll check out the new model they released this spring, the one with six cameras or whatever. The one that can practically cook dinner for you.

Still grinning, he ducks into the camper and dials.

"JoyJet baggage services," a woman answers, sounding anything but joyful.

Cameron gives his claim number. "So, when will my bag be delivered?"

"One moment, sir." She types on a keyboard for what feels like an hour. The keystrokes echo through his phone speaker: *click-click-click*. Is she writing a novel? Finally, she says, "Yes, we did find your lost item."

"Awesome. You need my address?"

"Sir, I'm afraid your item is in Naples."

"Naples . . . Florida?"

"Naples, Italy."

"Italy?" Cameron's voice jumps up an octave. "Does JoyJet even fly to Italy?"

"Hold on a moment, sir . . . Let me check something." The woman's keyboard strokes sound even more aggressive now, somehow. "Ah, I see what happened. Somehow, your item was transferred to one of our European partners." She lets out a low whistle. "Wow, that's pretty awful, even for us."

"Yeah, you think?" Cameron fights to keep his voice calm. "So how do I get it back? There are some . . . things in there that are . . . important."

"Sir, we advise all passengers to remove any valuables before they check—"

"But I didn't have a choice." Cameron explodes. "They made me check my carry-on at the gate, along with a million other people, because your overhead bins are the size of matchboxes. Do the people who design your airplanes have any idea what a typical suitcase looks like?"

After a long pause, the agent says, "Sir, I'm going to have to transfer you to our European partner's office, who will assign a new claim number. I can get the paperwork started here, then I'll patch you over. If I could start with your last name . . ."

EPITAPH AND PENS

Tova's day starts early. She has much to accomplish.

First, she drives downtown and parks her hatchback, which is no small task because of this enormous ramshackle camper taking up two spaces between the realtor's office and the paddle shop next door. Blocking the view of oncoming traffic. Not that there's much oncoming traffic in downtown Sowell Bay at nine in the morning on a Thursday, but one can never be too careful.

Shooting one last perturbed glare at the hulking vehicle, she shuffles into her destination. Jessica Snell tilts her head curiously as she comes through the door.

"May I help you, Mrs. Sullivan?"

"Yes, I should say so." Tova calmly recites the explanation she rehearsed, then leaves the office thirty minutes later with an appointment for the realtor to come for a preliminary walk-though at the house this afternoon.

Next, she walks down the block to the bank. The Charter Village application requires a cashier's check and a copy of her account balances. To make sure she can afford it, Tova supposes. She wishes they would take her word for it that her finances won't be a problem. Her accounts at Sowell Bay Community Bank have always been robust; the substantial sum she received from her mother's estate has hardly been touched all these years. Tova has never needed to spend much.

As she pulls open the bank door and steps into the lobby, which smells like fresh ink and peppermint candies, as usual, it occurs to her Lars must have used up most of his half of their parent's inheritance with his stay at Charter Village. When the lawyer followed up about the other assets, it was only a few hundred dollars. Practically speaking, Lars died with only a bathrobe left. For a moment, she hesitates. It really is an extravagant sort of lifestyle they promote at Charter Village. Not her style. But at least it's clean. And Lars lived there for over a decade. The monthly dues add up.

"Thank you, Bryan," she says to the teller, who hands her the check with an ever-so-slightly raised brow. Bryan's father, Cesar, used to play golf with Will. She wonders whether Bryan will phone him and tell him about today's transaction.

She makes a deliberate decision not to care. Such things are going to happen. People will talk. People in Sowell Bay always talk.

Her next stop is Janice Kim's house. Janice's son has some fancy computer scanner, and when Tova called this morning to ask if she could stop by and use it, Janice agreed immediately.

"You hanging in there?" Janice lowers her glasses, eyeing Tova's boot skeptically. Tova isn't known for requesting spur-of-the-moment visits.

"Of course. Why do you ask?" Tova keeps her voice even. The application requires a copy of her driver's license, but when Tova explains this, she declines to elaborate on the nature of the paperwork.

Janice helps her scan the card and shows her which buttons to press on the printer. When they're finished, she asks, "You want to stay for coffee?"

Tova anticipated this. She built a Janice coffee delay into her schedule.

An hour later, after departing the Kim home, Tova drives down to Elland. This would be a quick ten-minute trip if she took the interstate, but as always, Tova takes the back roads. Half an hour later, she arrives at the chain drugstore listed under "Passport Photos" in the Snohomish County phone book. The application requires two such photos, and having never been issued a passport, Tova is in possession of no such thing.

A young woman who could not possibly be more bored with her job directs Tova to stand against a blank white wall and instructs her to remove her eyeglasses, which she does without argument, clutching them in her hand and squinting at the camera as it flashes twice.

"That'll be eighteen fifty," the clerk says, handing over a small folio with the two square, unsmiling photos tucked inside.

"Eighteen dollars?"

"And fifty cents."

"Good heavens." Tova pulls a twenty-dollar bill from her pocketbook. Who would've thought two tiny photographs could cost so much?

Her final errand brings her back to the northern edge of Sowell Bay, nearly an hour-long journey from Elland, to Fairview Memorial Park. The afternoon has grown lovely, and the gates are propped open like welcoming arms under the clear, cloudless sky. A footpath winds around the cemetery lawn, gentle curves heading this way and that, never a straight line. Like it was designed to make the walk seem as soft as possible. The grass is flawless, edged meticulously around the identical headstones.

She kneels on the grass and traces along the engraving on his stone. The smooth, polished rock is warm under her fingers, basking in the hot July sun. WILLIAM PATRICK SULLIVAN: 1938–2017. HUSBAND, FATHER, FRIEND.

When she'd submitted the epitaph to Fairview Memorial Park's coordinator, the woman had the nerve to ask if she was sure she didn't want to add more. The package included up to 120 characters, she explained, and Tova had only used half. But sometimes less is more. Will was a simple man.

Next to Will's headstone is Erik's. Tova hadn't wanted one; Will had insisted. It has always bothered her that Erik's commemoration lies here, in this grassy field, when his body never left the sea. But the stone sits here, with its overly fussy font that reads, ERIK ERNEST SULLIVAN. Whomever Will had designated to take care of it hadn't even bothered to record Erik's name correctly. Tova's maiden name, Lindgren, is supposed to be Erik's second middle name. She has always fantasized about stealing Erik's headstone and hurling it off the end of the pier, but one can't do things like that, of course.

The third stone in the row is blank, meant for her. There's a series of questions on the application about this, too. Wishes, preferences. Meant to be a supplement to one's legal arrangements, Tova supposes. She has made her preferences clear in her own documents, of course, but what if someone tries to insist on a service? She could see Barb, in particular, doing something like that. Tova must broach the topic with her before she leaves. A marker will be fine, but she prefers no service.

Voices drift across the lawn. She turns to see old Mrs. Kretch ambling up the path. Heavens, the woman must be in her midnineties. But she's getting around well, by the looks of it. She's brought her great-granddaughter with her today, a coltish thing with legs as long and straight as a pair of knitting needles.

"Hi, Mrs. Sullivan," the great-granddaughter says as they pass. Old Mrs. Kretch nods, her eyes meeting Tova's just long enough to impart a pitying look.

"Good day," Tova replies.

The great-granddaughter has a basket slung over her skinny arm. They stop six plots down and spread out a picnic. Tova catches a whiff of deli chicken as they settle in. Then the two women chat with their dead patriarch, showing no self-consciousness about talking to the manicured turf, the cold gray headstone. A one-way conversation with thin air itself.

Tova has never spoken aloud to Will's grave. Why would she?

His tired, sickened body turning to dust underground cannot hear. Cancerous flesh cannot reply. She cannot bring herself to emulate Mary Ann Minetti, who keeps her husband's ashes in an urn on her mantel and converses with him daily. *He can hear me from heaven*, Mary Ann always says, to which Tova simply nods, because it brings her friend comfort and harms no one. Such is the case with the Kretches, as well. So why must the sight of them bantering with the deceased as though he were seated on their red-and-white checkered blanket, sipping lemonade right along with them, make her wish she were invisible?

But there's a first time for everything. The Kretch ladies eventually rise, and the great-granddaughter gives a tired wave as they make their way out, their afternoon shadows grown long and tall. Tova ought to get it over with, the thing she came here to do. She homes her focus on Will's headstone, runs a tongue across her lips. Then in a low voice, she says aloud, "I'm selling the house, dear."

She trails a finger across the headstone as if the action might summon tears to her eyes.

THAT EVENING, AFTER Jessica Snell's tour, and after a reheated casserole supper, she organizes the application and her collected documents.

Ten minutes later, she's driving again. The very first line of instructions had stymied her. *Please complete in black ink.* So, one more errand today, to purchase a proper black pen. After trying out all of her writing utensils, she determined that none of them contained truly black ink. A scrupulous eye could only conclude that the most promising samples were actually dark gray.

"Tova! Evening, love," Ethan Mack calls from the Shop-Way deli, where he's wiping down tables.

"Hello, Ethan."

Right up at the front of the grocery section, there's a display of sundries, including pens. She scans the options: Rollerball or felt-tip? Gel or ballpoint?

Ethan tucks his rag in his apron pocket and saunters over, slipping into his station behind the register. "How's the bum leg holding up, then?"

Tova leans on her cane. Her one concession. "Healing as expected, thank you."

"Glad to hear it! Modern medicine is brilliant, innit? Can you imagine livin' in cave-people times? You tweak an ankle and they leave you behind for the dinosaurs to eat!"

Tova raises an eyebrow. He can't be serious. Dinosaurs never lived concurrently with so-called cave-people, or any people at all. They were separated by sixty-five million years. But then, maybe Ethan never had occasion to learn this. Tova, like every mother of a little boy, had gotten a thorough education in dinosaurs when Erik was young. At one point he'd checked out so many dinosaur books the library put a hold on Tova's card.

Ethan shuffles, looking sheepish. "Anyway. Help you find something?"

"I need a black pen."

"A pen? I won't let you pay for a bloody pen! Here." He plucks one from behind his ear, where it must have been hiding in his bushy mass of reddish frizz. "Don't remember if this one's blue or black, though." He tries to wake the ink, scribbling on a scrap of paper next to the cash register. The tip of his tongue peeks between his lips as he focuses.

"Thank you, but I'll take these. And I'm happy to pay for them." Tova puts a two-pack of classic ballpoints on the counter.

Ethan's pen starts to cooperate, producing a mess of marks on the scrap. "Eh! This one's blue anyway. But you're welcome to have it as a backup. Can never have too many pens!" He offers it to her.

Tova chuckles. "I beg to differ! Before he passed, Will used to swipe them from restaurants and bank counters. Our junk drawer was always overrun with them."

"Aye, doesn't surprise me. Think I might've looked the other way while he walked off with a ballpoint or two from the deli, over the years. He used to come here and have a sandwich and read a book a couple of times a week, but I'm sure you know that."

The smile on Tova's face hangs there, for a long moment, like it's unsure whether to fall off or not. Finally, she says warmly, "Yes, he did like to get out of the house. Thank you for not calling the authorities on account of the pens."

Ethan bats a hand. "He was a good bloke, Will Sullivan."

"Yes, he was."

"Well, then." Something in Ethan's voice reminds Tova of a soufflé that's begun to sink. "Guess you definitely don't need this." He tucks the pen he'd offered her into his apron pocket.

"It was a very kind offer. But the form states specifically to use black ink."

"A form?" Ethan blanches, his tone now wary. "What form is that, love?"

"An application," she answers evenly.

"I knew it!" Ethan's jaw flaps. "You're doing it. Moving up to that . . . home. Tova, love. That place! It's . . . not you."

"I beg your pardon?"

Ethan sniffs. "What I mean is, it's not good enough for you."

"Charter Village is one of the finest facilities in the state."

"But Sowell Bay is your home."

To Tova's horror, her eyes well, stinging. She sets her jaw, willing the tears away. Evenly, she explains, "Mr. Mack, I am a practical person, and this is a practical solution. I'm not a young woman. I'm, well . . ."

Her gaze drifts to the boot. Ethan's follows, and Tova would swear that, under his big beard, his chin is trembling. She places a hand on his freckled forearm, the wiry hairs tickling her palm. His skin is surprisingly warm.

"I'm not moving right this minute, Ethan." Technically, this is true. It will take some time for the house to sell. For Charter Village to review her bank statements, eighteen-dollar photos, and black-ink-printed forms.

"Aye" is all Ethan says.

"And it's the right plan," she adds. "Who else will take care of me?"

The question hangs in the air for a long moment. Finally, Ethan says, "Well, this is an important application. You don't want those pens, then." He nods at the two-pack. "Those are rubbish." After running a searching finger along the display, he pulls off a different package, this one with a flashier logo. "Cadillac model, right here."

"I'll take it, then. Thank you."

"Anytime, love."

She clears her throat. "How much?"

He bats a hand. "Like I said. Won't let you pay for a pen. It's on the house."

"No, no." For the second time today, Tova removes a twenty from her pocketbook. "Ring them through later and you keep the rest. For making the recommendation. Thank you."

"If you want to thank me," Ethan blurts, "perhaps you'd join me for tea sometime."

Tova freezes. "Tea? Here?" She glances at the deli.

"Well, no, not here. The tea here is shit, to be honest. But it could be here, if you'd like. I hadn't actually worked that part out yet." Ethan bites his lower lip and drums his meaty fingers on the register. "Somewhere else, then? Or not at all, perhaps. Never mind. Rubbish idea."

"It wasn't a rubbish idea." Tova is astonished to hear the colloquialism come out of her mouth. Is this how Janice picks up her sitcom talk? Before she can stop herself, she finds herself replying, "Certainly, we can have tea sometime. Or coffee, perhaps."

Ethan shakes his head. "You Swedes and your coffee."

Tova feels herself flush, wondering if she ought to make a joke about him being a Scot, but before she can come up with one, he hands her a scrap of paper, the same one that he scribbled on. In blue ink on the back, he's written his telephone number.

"Give me a ring, love. We'll set something up. Before you . . . go."

Tova nods, then ducks out of the Shop-Way, astounded at how difficult it's suddenly become to breathe normally.

IT'S PAST TEN now, and daylight has finally drained from the sky. On her way home, Tova makes an unplanned turn.

One more errand today.

The aquarium's parking lot is empty, except for a dilapidated camper, the same one that was parked in front of Jessica Snell's office earlier. Perhaps the owner is a fisherman. She scans the pier, looking for a figure with a pole, but it's empty.

Hobbling up to the front door, she pauses. Terry had forbidden her from coming to clean, naturally, but he hadn't expressly instructed her not to use her key for a social call. In fact, when she'd tried to give the key back, he'd insisted she hang on to it, which she'd taken not only as an affirmation of her trustworthiness but also as a vow of confidence in her resilience. *You'll be back before you know it*, Terry had said.

The same force that drew her to Will's headstone earlier today has led her here. To . . . communicate. To notify the octopus of her plan to move to Charter Village. Although neither Will nor Marcellus the Octopus can understand her, both deserve to know. And, less urgently, he might lead her to a solution for this mess she's gotten herself into with Ethan Mack and his tea. Unless she ought to keep that to herself; perhaps if she pretends it never happened, the invitation will simply vanish? She can practically see how Marcellus's shrewd, knowing eye will glare, how his sucker-lined arm will waggle, scolding. Tova clicks her tongue at her own behavior. Pretending to speak with the insentient. She's ten times worse than Mary Ann Minetti and old Mrs. Kretch put together.

The door clinks open. Everything else aside, she must admit she's curious about how the place has fared, hygienically speaking, in her absence.

She holds her breath, ready for sloppy tile and smudged glass, but to her shock, things look decent. This fellow Terry brought on to fill in is managing well. This begets a small corollary disappointment, the dull realization that she is not indispensable. But overall, this is a good development. More than once, the thought of the aquarium being cleaned in a subpar manner has given her pause about her plans to leave. Perhaps this new fellow can stay on after Tova's departure.

Heading around the hallway toward the octopus's tank, she moves as discreetly as she can with this wretched boot. Which is unnecessary, because she's the only human here. Whispered greetings to her old friends, the Japanese crabs, the wolf eels, the jellies, and the sea cucumbers, linger for a moment in the dark corridor then vanish into the bluish-green air like wisps of smoke. Even if they could, these creatures would never tell anyone she was here. It'll be their secret.

She passes the sea lion statue and, as always, pauses to stroke its head, reveling in the fleeting illusion of her son flickering within her when she touches something he so adored.

Approaching the entrance to the back of the octopus enclosure, Tova frowns. A fluorescent glow seeps from under the door. Someone has left the light on.

Then a terrible clatter erupts inside.

CONSCIENCE DOES MAKE
COWARDS OF US ALL

Cameron blinks. Wincing, he rubs his temple, which is throbbing where it must've smacked into the table as he fell. He wipes the smear of blood on his shirt and gives the busted stepladder a vengeful kick. If he wanted to, he could probably sue the balls off of this place. Poorly maintained equipment. A workplace injury. But what if someone asks him to explain what he was doing back here in the first place?

"You," he says, glaring at the creature as he stands. The thing hasn't moved. It's hunkered like some overgrown tarantula, having burrowed in the clutter of tubes and jars and pump parts in the deepest corner of the shelf above the tanks. It scrambled up there, somehow, as Cameron tried to corral it with a broom handle, which he now jabs toward the creature again. "What's your problem, bro? I'm trying to help you."

Its massive body heaves, like a sigh. At least it's still alive, but probably not for much longer. An octopus can survive briefly out of water (there was a documentary once, on some nature channel), but this one has been on shore leave for almost twenty minutes, and that's just counting from the time Cameron discovered it trying to slip out the back door he'd left propped open.

Someone could've warned him the exhibits might escape. Like, how is this even a possibility? Secure tanks should be a reasonable expectation in a tourist aquarium. Honestly, the situation is making him uneasy about those sharks circling the big tank in the middle, especially now that his head is bleeding. Can sharks smell through glass?

"Come on, buddy," he begs. Head still throbbing, he adjusts the gloves he put on after the thing tried to strangle his wrist and inches the broom handle closer. Expecting the octopus to . . . what, exactly? Slide down it like a fireman's pole? But he can't let the stubborn asshole just die up there, and there's no way he's touching it again, even with gloves. It looks like it wants to kill him. "Outta there, now. Back to your tank."

A tentacle tip twitches, defiant, dislodging a pair of thin metal canisters and knocking them to the ground. They land with twin clangs.

This is going to be what gets Cameron fired. How many times can one person get canned in a lifetime? There should be a legal limit.

Something clicks softly behind him. Then a woman's voice, trembling but clear. "Hello? Who's in here?"

Nearly dropping the broomstick, he turns. A tiny woman stands in the doorway. Miniature, almost: she can't be more than five feet tall. She's older, maybe a little older than Aunt Jeanne, maybe late-sixties or seventy. She's wearing a purple blouse, and her left ankle is swallowed in a walking cast.

"Oh! Um . . . hi. I was just—"

The lady's sharp gasp cuts him off. She has spotted the creature cowered on the high shelf.

Cameron twists his hands. "Yeah, so I was just trying to—"

"Out of the way, dear." She pushes past him. Her voice is low and quiet now, any trepidation gone. Moving faster than he would've guessed possible, given her age and that boot, she's across the room in three strides, where she regards the broken stool for a moment and shakes her head. Then, unbelievably, she scrambles to the top of the table. Standing at her full height up there, she's almost face level with the octopus.

"Marcellus, it's me."

The octopus shifts slightly out of its corner and peers at her, blinking its creepy eye. *Who is this lady? And how did she get in here, anyway?*

She nods, encouraging. "It's okay." She holds out her hand, and to Cameron's shock the creature extends one of its arms and winds it around her wrist. She repeats, "It's okay. I'm going to help you down now, all right?"

The octopus nods.

Wait, no. It did not. Did it? He rubs his eyes. *Are they pumping hallucinogens through the ductwork here?*

That would explain so much about tonight.

Tethered to the tiny woman's arm, the octopus makes its way along the shelf. The woman limps along the length of the table, coaxing. Once she gets the thing directly over the empty tank, she nods at Cameron. "Move the cover, please, won't you?"

He obeys, sliding the lid back and holding it open as wide as it will go.

"In you go," the woman whispers.

Cold, briny water sloshes as the creature drops back in with a heavy *plop*. Reflexively, Cameron shudders away, and when he turns back, the octopus is gone again, leaving only a stir of rocks outside its den at the tank bottom.

The table creaks as the woman lowers herself. Cameron rushes over, clasping her elbow and guiding her back to the ground.

"Thank you." She dusts her hands, then adjusts her glasses and sizes him up. "Are you hurt, dear? That cut could use some help." She shuffles over and picks up the purse she dropped on her way in, then roots around for a minute before offering him a Band-Aid.

Cameron waves her off. "It's nothing."

"Nonsense. Take it," she insists. Her voice is nonnegotiable. He takes the bandage, unwraps it, and fixes the neon pink strip to the side of his head. What a look. Oh well, it's not like he'll see anyone but Ethan tonight anyway.

"Good." She nods. Then, with her voice level, she says, "Well, that's over. Perhaps you can explain what happened here?"

"I didn't do anything!" Cameron jabs a finger at the tank. "That thing escaped. I tried to get it back in the water."

"His name is Marcellus."

"Okay. *Marcellus* tried to pull a fast one. I was trying to help."

"By assaulting him with a broomstick?"

He scoffs. "We can't all be the Octopus Whisperer, or whatever the hell that was. Look, I was doing my best. If it weren't for me, that octopus would be halfway across the ocean by now."

"What do you mean?"

"I mean that when I found him, he was on his way out the back door."

The old lady's mouth drops open. "Good heavens."

"Yeah." Maybe they won't fire him. Maybe they'll give him a raise. If it weren't for him, they'd be replacing their octopus, after all. How much does a giant Pacific octopus cost? They're probably not cheap.

The old lady's tone sharpens when she says, "Why was the back door open?"

"Because I was emptying the trash? You know, doing my job? No one told me not to prop it."

"I see."

"But I'll keep it closed from now on."

"Yes, wise idea."

At these last words of hers, Cameron finds himself standing straighter. Why does it feel like she's his boss? And what is she doing here? He'd better clear that up. The last thing he needs is Terry accusing him of letting some random old woman into the building during his shift. He looks her over again. She can't weigh more than eighty pounds. An unlikely burglar. Besides, she and that octopus have history. Maybe she's a retired marine biologist. Or a volunteer. Senior citizen outreach.

"Can I ask what you're doing here?" He tries to frame the question as politely as possible. "I mean, you seem nice, but no one else is supposed to be here, at least not that they told me."

"Goodness. Of course. I'm sure I did give you a startle. I'm sorry. I'm Tova Sullivan, the cleaner." A tight smile binds her thin lips as she gestures at the boot. "Injured cleaner."

"Oh. Nice to meet you" is what he says, but what he's thinking is *Damn*. This frail little woman does the same job he can barely get through without feeling like he just ran a marathon? It's been two weeks and his feet are still sore after every shift. He adds, "I'm Cameron Cassmore, current cleaner. Or temporary cleaner, technically. I'm sorry about your injury. When he hired me, Terry said he thought you'd be out a few weeks."

"I'm quite all right. It was a silly accident." Tova's eyes make the tiniest flick toward the busted stool. "I'm glad Terry found you, Cameron. From what I've seen, your skill is adequate. As it turns out, for unrelated reasons, I may be away from my position longer than anticipated. This will be a good solution, perhaps."

Cameron pauses, digesting this. An extended gig here wouldn't be the end of the world. Two weeks and he's no closer to finding Simon Brinks than he was when he got here. The contact info Jessica Snell had given him must have been dated; when Cameron called, the number was disconnected. "Yeah, that would be cool. It's not a bad job."

"It's a lovely job." Tova smiles, but it's tight, like it's holding back sadness.

Okay, so she's nice, but who in their right mind loves mopping tile and scrubbing floors this much? He shuffles his feet. "So . . . do you just, like, stop by for fun sometimes?"

"I came to see Marcellus." Her voice drops. "And I'm aware this may be improper to ask given that we're barely acquainted, but I would appreciate your discretion."

"Why?" Shit. This'll get him in trouble with Terry after all.

Tova takes a deep breath. "Mind you, I don't condone lying. But you see, Marcellus is a bit of a wayfarer at night, although until this evening I was not aware of his predilection to depart the building." She frowns. "That part is new and troubling. But I've known of his wanderings for some time. He is remarkably adept at escaping his enclosure."

"And no one else knows." Cameron nods, starting to understand.

"Not with certainty, no. Terry suspects. If he knew for sure, he would certainly intervene."

"Like, he'd nail down the top of the tank?"

Tova nods. "Marcellus would be devastated. But what concerns me is worse. Marcellus is old, Cameron, and a loose octopus is a liability."

Is she really suggesting what he's thinking? Terry, the fish geek, would put one of his animals down? Harsh. But what if it got out during the day and went after some kid on a field trip? The woman's probably right about the liability. He folds his arms. "Marcellus is your friend."

"Yes, I suppose he is."

"When you went up there to save him, you weren't afraid of him at all."

Tova clicks her tongue. "Certainly not! He's gentle."

"Well, it was still pretty badass."

"I appreciate you saying so."

She looks at the ground briefly, then back up at him with her eyes, which are a shrewd shade of greenish gray. "So? Shall it be our secret?"

Cameron hesitates. For sure, if Terry finds him acting as an accomplice to . . . whatever all of this is, this job will be toast, and any hope of paying Aunt Jeanne back will be toast right along with it. And tracking down Simon Brinks? Toast city. He can't get fired. Not this time.

But something about the thought of this sweet little old lady losing her friend makes him feel horrible. And the way that octopus had glared at him with its weird, humanlike eye, the threat of euthanasia . . . He shrugs. "Yeah, our secret."

"Thank you." She inclines her head.

Cameron picks up the broomstick from where he dropped it earlier and shoves the broken step stool against the wall for someone else to fix. "Conscience does make cowards of us all, huh?"

She freezes. "What did you say?"

"Conscience does make cowards of us all." He feels himself start to redden. How does he always manage to drop this nerdy shit into conversation? He starts to explain, "It's just some dumb Shakespeare quote. It's from—"

"*Hamlet,*" she says softly. "It was one of my son's favorites."

EXPECT THE UNEXPECTED

Tova's recollection of her voyage from Sweden is patchy. After all, she was only seven years old at the time, and Lars only nine. A train ride from Uppsala, a stiff goodbye to their father at their hotel in Gothenburg; he flew to America on an airplane, arriving several weeks ahead of the family in order to secure their paperwork and housing. The hotel had thick white sheets smelling of lavender and a television on a table, which Tova and Lars watched for several hours a day while they awaited their embarkment date, and there was a restaurant in the lobby that served chocolate pudding in tiny goblets, of which Lars once ate so many he got a stomachache and upchucked on the white sheets. She recalls how the SS *Vadstena* looked like a big gray layer cake alongside the dock when the driver dropped them off, that bright May morning in 1956. Two months later, they arrived in Portland, Maine, where they lived in an apartment for two years before uprooting again and relocating here, to Washington, to Sowell Bay, ostensibly to be closer to a handful of distant cousins, although Tova never met any of these supposed kin. It was always just the four of them.

Those weeks on the ocean liner are largely a blank space in Tova's mind, which is a shame, as it's probably the most adventurous thing she'll ever do.

Among her few clear memories from aboard the SS *Vadstena* is the Walrus. That wasn't really his name, of course, but that's what Tova and Lars called that passenger, with his long, gray, whiskery mustache dangling around each corner of his mouth like a set of tusks.

The Walrus liked to play cards. After dinner in the parlor, while Lars lined up his toy soldiers along the red velvet booth-backs, the Walrus tried to coax Tova and her mother into playing gin rummy. At first, Mama said ladies ought not to partake in card games, but eventually she relented. By the dim light of the glass lamps, Tova learned to play rummy and hearts and twenty-one. Sometimes, with a sly wink, the Walrus would slip in a card trick as he shuffled, daring her to guess what card he held between his fingers, then flipping it around to prove her wrong before producing the very one she'd named from under his collar or beneath his cuff.

Always expect the unexpected, child, the Walrus would say, chuckling as little Tova scowled at being fooled yet again.

She feels a scowl cross her face now, watching this young fellow pick up a pair of fallen canisters and return them to the shelf, not seeming to care that he's placed them upside down. For the last two weeks, Barb Vanderhoof and Ethan Mack and their ilk have been churning the rumor mill with their talk of the fellow from California, the *homeless* man, who has taken her place. But Cameron has clean fingernails and nice, white teeth. And he's well versed in the works of Shakespeare, apparently. He has promised to keep her secret, and for some reason she can't quite identify, she likes him. She might even trust him.

He is not what she expected.

In the humidity of the pump room, the pink bandage is already starting to peel back, and now it sits askew on his damp temple. Tova resists a deep urge to reach up and press it back on with her thumb. When he notices her watching him, he flashes a sheepish grin. "Sorry, I swear I don't usually go around quoting dead bards. It's been a weird night." He blinks, as if wondering if any of this is actually happening, a feeling Tova can very much relate to.

She peers past Cameron into Marcellus's tank, where the surface of the water shimmers gently around the pump—no sign of the octopus himself. What would have happened if she hadn't arrived?

"I should say it has." She clears her throat and straightens. "In any case. How are you finding the conditions here? Did Terry train you? And do you need . . . supplies?" The acrid smell of that caustic green junk has already started to seep in. The jug of vinegar in her trunk could fix this.

"I mean, yeah? Dragging a mop across the floor isn't exactly rocket science."

Tova clicks her tongue. "Perhaps not, but there is a proper way to do things."

"Am I doing something . . . improperly?"

"Well, let's have a look. Come along, dear." Tova opens the door and motions to Cameron to follow her into the curved hallway. The floors, as she'd noted on her way in, look decent, but linty streaks run along the glass fronts of the tanks. Tova runs a finger through one. "You must use a cotton cloth on the glass. Not polyester."

Cameron folds his arms defensively. "It looks fine to me."

"You must look more carefully, then."

"What are you, some expert on glass cleaning?"

Tova tuts. "Decades of experience."

"Well, no one said anything about polyester or cotton or whatever," Cameron says with a huff. "I'm using the rags that were here. How was I supposed to know?"

He has a point. Tova will need to speak with Terry about training if the boy might be her permanent replacement. She makes her way over to one of the garbage bins and points to the rim. "Also, see this here? The bag must hook all the way around, or else it slips off when the can becomes full. Then trash will fall directly into the bottom and make an even bigger mess."

"Oh, please. I know how to put a bag in a garbage can."

"Clearly, you do not." Tova's tone sharpens. "I don't know how they install trash liners down in California, but—"

"Wait, what?" Cameron interrupts. "How did you know I was from California?"

"People in Sowell Bay like to talk." Tova flattens her lips. She wishes she could take the comment back. How often has she, herself, been the subject of town gossip?

"Yeah, I've noticed." Cameron pauses, and something glints in his eyes. "I'm sure the rumor mill would have a feast, hearing about you being here tonight. Visiting an octopus."

Tova's mouth pops open, then she quickly presses her lips together again.

"Don't worry, I won't tell anyone. I promised," he mutters. She continues to regard him through narrowed eyes when he continues, "Any other thrilling job tips for me?"

Tova straightens. "Yes, one more thing. The matter of the door. I think you'll agree, nearly allowing one of the aquarium's most popular exhibits to wander out is hardly acceptable."

Cameron lets out a beleaguered sigh as his eyeballs flick momentarily, almost imperceptibly, upward. The gesture unravels a thread somewhere in the depths of Tova's memory; it's almost exactly what teenage Erik used to do when he was annoyed with her. She clicks her tongue again. Young people. Although this one must be at least twenty-five, from the looks of him, Tova has the distinct impression he has some growing up to do.

"How could anyone think that was my fault?" Cameron's voice bursts out. "Maybe someone could have given me a heads-up on the possibility of free-range kraken? And maybe they should put a lock on his tank."

"Marcellus can undo locks," Tova points out. "How do you think he left the pump room?"

The boy frowns. He doesn't have a comeback for that. Instead, he asks, "Why does he do it?"

Tova pauses, considering this. It's a question she's asked herself many times, and one for which she doesn't have a clear answer. She goes with her best guess. "I believe he is bored."

Cameron shrugs. "I guess it would suck to spend your whole life living in a tiny little tank."

"Yes," Tova agrees.

"Especially when you're so smart."

"Marcellus is very bright."

Panic flashes in Cameron's eyes. "What am I supposed to do if it happens again? If he gets out, I mean. While I'm here cleaning."

"Leave him alone, of course," Tova says, because what other response can there be? It won't do to have the boy wielding a broomstick at the octopus.

"Right. Leave him alone." Cameron casts a leery look down the hallway, as if Marcellus might be lurking there.

But something nags at Tova. If she'd left the octopus alone when she discovered him under the table in the break room, hopelessly tangled up in electrical cords, what would have become of him? Until tonight's attempt to leave the building, she would've thought Marcellus had enough common sense to avoid such bold stunts, to keep his nightly hijinks to his usual: teasing the seahorses, poking around in the sea cucumber tank for a midnight snack. A sudden dread seeps through her at the thought of Marcellus dying alone, a vague shame at her own inability to prevent it, even if she were working here as normal. After all, he could break out of his enclosure at any hour of the night and find himself in danger in the empty building.

Perhaps letting Marcellus escape the building would be merciful. He could pay Erik a visit, down so deep, on the floor of Puget

Sound. The thought feels wildly inappropriate. She can't help but smile.

The boy tilts his head at her. "What's so funny?"

"It's nothing."

"Come on, Tova. Share with the class." A tiny sparkle flicks through Cameron's eyes, good-natured teasing.

"Truly, it was nothing."

"Nothing is nothing!" Cameron grins at her. He really is a charming young man when he's not being so insolent. Erik was like that, too; she and Will used to throw their arms up at his attitude, but he was so effortlessly endearing, the kind of person everyone wants to befriend.

An idea springs to her mind.

"Follow me," she beckons, shuffling back toward the pump room. "I have a plan."

"A plan? For what?"

"For next time you encounter Marcellus outside his tank."

"I thought you said I should leave him alone." Cameron trots along behind her. "Are you going to show me how to capture him?"

She turns back to him. "Not exactly. I'm going to show you how to make friends with him."

"Friends?" Cameron stops in his tracks. "Seems like a long shot. Scylla the sea monster wasn't exactly warm and fuzzy with me during our little hangout earlier."

"Expect the unexpected, dear." Tova smiles.

Day 1,329 of My Captivity

MUCH OF HUMAN PARLANCE IS NONSENSE, BUT PERhaps most ludicrous among the rubbish they spew is their tendency to glorify their own foolishness. By this, I mean absurd statements such as: *What he doesn't know won't hurt him!* Or, worse: *Ignorance is bliss!*

You may object to my rumination on the topic of bliss, considering I am imprisoned in this dreadful place. What would a captive cephalopod know of joy? I will never again know the thrill of a wild hunt in the open sea. I will never bask in a silver shimmer of moonlight as it filters down through the water from an endless midnight sky. I will never copulate.

But I have knowledge. To the extent happiness is possible for a creature like me, it lies in knowledge.

As you already know, I am adept at learning. I have easily solved every puzzle or brainteaser Terry has provided: the locked box with a scallop inside, the small plastic maze with a mussel at the finish. *Child's play*, as the humans might say. Then I learned to pop the top of my tank, and how to unlock the pump room door. I learned how to calculate precisely how far I may venture, and for how long, before I begin to suffer The Consequences.

It may not be bliss, if such a thing even exists, but with this knowledge, I have achieved something akin to contentment. Or, perhaps more accurately, a temporary abatement of misery.

Ah, to be a human, for whom bliss can be achieved by mere ig-norance! Here, in the kingdom of animals, ignorance is dangerous. The poor herring dropped into the tank lacks any awareness of the shark lurking below. Ask the herring whether what he doesn't know can hurt him.

But humans can be wounded by their own oblivion, too. They do not see it, but I do. It happens all the time.

Consider, for example, a father and son I witnessed recently, right here in front of my tank. He claps the adolescent on the back as they talk of an upcoming sports match. The father is certain the son will prevail, telling the young one, *You've got my throwing arm, and I was an all-state quarterback.* I do not know what a quarterback is, but I can tell you this: the boy has no genetic relationship with the man. The father is a *cuckold.* One of my favorite human words, I must admit.

Moments later, the child's mother joins them, and the three of them shuffle along to stare at the sharp-nosed sculpin exhibit next door, unaware of the treason that will one day cleave their family.

You ask, how do I know? I observe. I am very perceptive, per-haps beyond the bounds of your comprehension.

Thousands of genes mold an offspring's physical presentation, and many of these pathways are as clear to me as letters on a page are to you. For one thousand, three hundred and twenty-nine days of this wretched captivity, I have honed my observations. In that par-ticular case of the sporting son and his quarterback-cuckold guard-ian, the list of traits would be too long to name here, but: the shape of the nose, the shade of the eyes, the precise position of the earlobe. The inflection of the voice, the gait. Ah, the gait! That is always an easy tell. Humans walk alike (or, in this case, unalike) far more than they realize.

But the former cleaning woman and her replacement. *They walk alike.*

There is also the heart-shaped dimple that sits, unusually low for such a feature, on each of their left cheeks. And the greenish golden flecks in each of their eyes. The toneless manner in which they both hum while they mop (quite annoying, to be honest, although the whir of my pump muffles it, mercifully).

Circumstantial, you say with a dismissive wave. Coincidental. Heredity works in strange ways. You point to the doppelgänger phenomenon; nearly identical humans of no relation born on opposite sides of the world.

You know, as do I, that the woman has no surviving heir. You know her only child died thirty years ago. You know, too, of her grief. Grief that has molded her life. Grief that, for the time being, drives her into seclusion. Eventually, I fear, it may drive her to something worse.

Your skepticism is understandable. It appears to defy logic.

I could go on with more evidence, although now, I must rest. These communications exhaust me, and this one is getting very long.

But you would do well to believe me when I tell you this: the young male who has recently taken over sanitation duties is a direct descendant of the cleaning woman with the injured foot.

HARD LEFT, CUT RIGHT

One morning in late July, Cameron finally lands a promising clue.

Elusive real estate tycoon Simon Brinks spends summer weekends at his estate in the San Juan Islands, a lavish Tuscan-style villa tucked up on a cliff overlooking some obscure strait. This is according to the old magazine article Cameron dug up on some obscure website. Once he had the town and photo, it was easy enough to unearth the address. It's a two-hour drive from Sowell Bay.

That would be four hours in the car alone. Cameron scrolls through the address book on his phone. His thumb hovers over Avery's number.

Would tagging along for a shakedown of a man who might be his biological father be a weird date? It would. Is Avery weird enough to be down with it? Possibly. Everything seems fifty-fifty with Avery, and even though they've managed a few coffee dates and a late-night dinner, once, at the pub down in Elland, half the time she develops some snag with her schedule and has to cancel, which seems oddly complicated for a single woman. Paddle store stuff, Cameron assumes. What would he know about owning a business? Holding his breath, he places the call.

"Hey, you." She sounds happy to hear from him.

"I'm going on a little adventure today. Wanna come?" Cameron explains his plan.

Avery's sigh seeps through his phone speaker. "Can't, I'm on duty at the shop. But we should do something later this week."

"Sure. Later this week."

"I mean it," she says earnestly. "We'll go paddling. I'll check my schedule."

He says goodbye to Avery and sets his phone on the bumper of the camper, where his feet are propped, as he sits in one of Ethan's lawn chairs. It was gross and rainy when he first got here, but now the weather is perfect. All of the colors seem impossibly vivid, from the wide blue sky to the thick green trees. Nothing like the oppressively hot, dusty oven that Modesto becomes in the summertime. He outstretches his right hand, examining his fingers, then flexes and throws a shadow jab upward at the cloudless summer sky.

Life is finally going his way.

For one thing, Avery. He's never caught the attention of a girl quite like Avery before, and somehow her strange evasiveness only adds to her appeal.

For another thing: he's about to do a face-to-face with his maybe dad.

And for a third thing: He's held an actual job for weeks now. He doesn't even hate it. Who knew? Chopping up fish guts. And cleaning! Not glamorous, but the solitude suits him, especially in the evening. Half the time, he's the only one at the aquarium when he cleans. On those nights, he smacks the vending machine until it drops something, a package of cookies or stale snack cakes that nobody wants to buy anyway, pops in his earbuds, and zones out while he washes the floors. The other half of the time, the weird lady is there. Tova. She keeps showing up, even though she's supposed to be on medical leave. Cameron promised he wouldn't rat her out. He doesn't mind having her around. Her obsession with that octopus is bizarre, and he hasn't made much progress *making friends* with Marcellus, but her company is weirdly enjoyable.

Behind him, a screen door bangs. A second later, Ethan appears around the back side of the camper. A faded Led Zeppelin T-shirt a little tight across his torso. He squints at Cameron. "Lovely mornin', innit?"

"Yeah. And guess what?" Cameron recounts his Simon Brinks discovery and subsequent conversation with Avery. Ethan nods.

"Well, let's go, then. We'll take my truck."

Cameron tilts his head. "What?"

"Your ears full of porridge, laddie? I said we'll take my truck!"

"You want to come with me?"

"A'course I do! You think I'd let you smack that wanker around alone?" He beams. "Sounds like a right good time, if you ask me."

"Okay," says Cameron slowly. "We'll go together."

"Gorgeous up that way, anyway, 'specially this time of year. We'll make it an adventure, yeah? I'll be your tour guide."

Tour guide?

"In fact," Ethan continues, "there's a great little spot for fish 'n' chips off the highway on the way up."

Fish and chips? Who cares about fish and chips? "Fine. But first we go find Brinks."

Ethan chuckles. "Extortion first, fish and chips after."

CAMERON STILL CAN'T seem to wrap his head around the shape of the sea here. It's like a monster with hundreds of long fingers is gripping the edge of the continent, tendrils of deep blue cutting channels through the dark green countryside in every unexpected way. He finds himself constantly surprised by the presence of the water on the left side of the car, then around a curve and on the right side, then over one bridge after another (how many times can a person cross the same body of water?) as Ethan drives along a never-ending two-lane road, the shoulder speckled by bait shops and gas stations and shabby-looking little restaurants that don't inspire confidence in the fish-and-chips plan.

"Won't be too much longer now," Ethan shouts, in direct defiance of the tiny map on his dash-mounted phone, which states their arrival time an hour from now. He's got his brawny elbow slung like a freckled sausage on the rim of the open window, having insisted on keeping the windows down, on account of it being "such a lovely day for a drive." The fifty-mile-an-hour wind and Ethan's accent make it hard to hear.

Clutching the class ring in his damp palm, he sketches out the logistics of his impending confrontation in his mind for the thousandth time.

Here's one way it can go. And maybe this is the ideal way. Simon Brinks will be shocked to see him. His mouth will drop open as he recognizes Cameron immediately. Although he might be the kind of douchebag who will try to deny it, Cameron's got the photographic evidence in his pocket. And then Brinks fesses up to everything.

The less-than-ideal way involves Brinks regarding him through narrow eyes. Talking right off the bat about involving attorneys, DNA tests. Keeping his lips zipped about anything until everything is proven.

But then, what if it is proven, and Brinks wants a relationship? That's what Elizabeth keeps saying when she calls to check in. Elizabeth seems convinced that Simon has some sort of latent paternal instinct that will be inspired by the appearance of his long-lost son. Like something out of a movie. But life isn't some cheesy Hollywood script.

Aunt Jeanne keeps hammering on the relationship thing, too, although Cameron suspects that, deep down, she's skeptical that a person like Simon Brinks would have dated her sister. But last time they chatted, when Cameron mentioned that he'd be on the next plane home if he could get Brinks to cut him a check, she'd sighed disapprovingly. *Stay up there awhile if you need to,* Aunt Jeanne had said. *Bought that ridiculous camper, might as well get some use out of it. Besides, life there seems to suit you.*

Well, that much is true.

But Cameron doesn't want a relationship with any would-be father. He wants the eighteen years of child support that this shifty asshole never paid. Hell, Cameron would accept a onetime payment. Ten grand? Twenty? He can send it directly to Aunt Jeanne. Cameron owes her a mint for everything he put her through over the years, not to mention the money she fronted him for the camper. He's already paid back almost half, but it's still a chunk of change.

"Aye, look!" Ethan brakes slightly, gesturing to a dirt road turning off the highway. "You ever want to go whale-watching, there's a brilliant spot down there. Took a lady friend once. We saw orcas frolicking around like wee kittens. Quite a sight. Ah, the love we made that night was—"

"Uh, thanks." Cameron cuts him off. What is with old people in love? "I'll keep that in mind."

"Well, I'm just saying. I know you've got that lass."

"I don't think Avery wants to drive all the way up here to look at whales."

"Might not knock it till you try it, eh? They're majestic creatures." Ethan turns and winks, and the truck drifts across the center line just as an oncoming car pops around the curve up ahead. He jerks back into the proper lane just in time. "Bugger! Eyes on the road. Anyway, there's a nice spit of sand there, too, great for beachcombing. Lots of starfish and sand dollars."

"If I wanted to show Avery starfish and sand dollars, why wouldn't I just bring her to work?" Cameron points out dryly. "We have the largest collection of native echinoderms in the state. That's what Tova says, anyway."

Ethan's head swivels and his gaze fixes on Cameron for an alarming stretch of time. His frizzy beard twitches, like he's biting his lip underneath. Cameron feels himself grip the edge of the bench seat. What happened to *eyes on the road?*

Finally, the big man's attention snaps back toward the dashboard. They ride in silence for quite a while. His voice is low when he says, "You've met Tova Sullivan?"

Shit. The secret. No one is supposed to know about Tova coming to the aquarium. Not for the first time, Cameron wonders why it's such a big deal. After thinking it over for a minute, he decides that it shouldn't be. Old people are weird sometimes. And why would Ethan care anyway? After a pause, he answers, "Yeah, Tova comes by once in a while to help out."

"I thought she was on medical leave."

"She is. Forget I said anything."

"Is she all right?" There's a quiet reverence to Ethan's voice.

"She's fine. Her foot's getting better, I think."

"Very glad to hear that," Ethan mumbles. His ruddy cheeks are even redder than usual.

A grin spreads across Cameron's face. "Oh my God. You *like* her."

"Well, who wouldn't like her?"

"That's pure bullshit. It's written all over you."

Now Ethan's ears are also deep red. "She's a lovely lady."

"'She's a lovely lady,'" Cameron repeats, imitating the Scot. He reaches over and gives Ethan a little smack on the shoulder. "Come on, bro. Let's hear it. You two have a history, or what?"

"A history?" Ethan's mouth presses into a serious line. "I'd never pursue a married lady. Which is what Mrs. Sullivan was, up till recently."

"Oh." Cameron slumps. "I didn't know that."

"Yeah. Husband was a decent bloke. Died of pancreatic cancer a couple years ago."

Cameron folds his hands in his lap and studies them. For some reason, learning this about Tova stings a little. That she hadn't bothered to share this basic information.

"Been a rough life," Ethan goes on, "what with her son and all."

"What are you talking about?"

"You don't know about that? Well, I guess you wouldn't. It's local knowledge, but you haven't been here long. And folks don't bring it up like they used to."

With a shiver, Cameron recalls Tova's comment. *People in Sowell Bay like to talk*. He mutters, "I didn't know she had a son."

"Isn't my story to tell, but I s'pose it's as good to hear it from me as from anyone else." Ethan draws in a long breath. "So back in the late eighties, her son was working the ferry dock. Erik, his name was. Bloody smart. Valedictorian of his class. Brilliant at sports, captain of the sailing team. You get the idea."

"Yeah, sure," Cameron says. Every high school has an Erik.

"Anyway, he was—oh, bloody hell. Have I missed the turnoff?" Ethan snatches his phone and squints at the screen. "Well, Rhonda? Why didn't you tip me off?"

Cameron arches a brow. "Rhonda?"

"That's what I call the lady's voice who reads out the directions. And she's buggered it this time." The phone lands with a clatter in the cup holder. "Your old man's place is a mile back that way," he says, jabbing his thumb behind.

"What about the story? About Tova's son?" Cameron's knuckles whiten, clinging to the door handle as the truck reels in a tight circle, in what is definitely not a legal U-turn.

"Eh, never mind about that."

"Oh, come on!"

"I shouldn't have brought it up. It's sad." The truck's tires hum on the pavement as it gains speed heading south now. Between the dense treetops, slivers of pale blue water peek through. "Her son died. Drowned. When he was eighteen."

"Oh God." Cameron lets out a breath. "That's horrible."

"Aye," says Ethan quietly. "Well, here we are." He guides the truck off the blacktop and onto an unmarked gravel road, kicking up a huge cloud of dust that makes both of them cough.

Cameron rolls up his window, eyeing the road skeptically. It's pocked and weedy. "Are you sure?"

Ethan holds up the phone, double-checking the address. "Yep. Definitely it."

SURE AS SHIT, this is not it.

It *could* be a good location for a billionaire's vacation home. The empty bluff overlooks dark blue sea on three sides. But there is no Tuscan-style villa, no billionaire deadbeat potential father lounging poolside, sipping from a golden goblet. Just a dusky gravel clearing that reminds Cameron of a certain type of movie set, the kind where kids are making out in a car before they get slashed up by a serial killer.

"Shit," he mutters, kicking a pinecone across the dirt. It disappears over the edge and tumbles down the cliffside.

"So this isn't it," Ethan says pointlessly.

"Definitely not."

Maybe Cameron's internet sleuthing skills aren't as impressive as he'd thought. They head back to the truck and begin the lumbering trek back along the choppy road.

Ethan hits a rough spot, braking when he should've pushed through. A typical rookie reaction. But now they're stuck. The wheels spin uselessly as Ethan stomps on the accelerator.

"Whoa, chill. You hit a nasty groove," Cameron explains patiently. Sure, the road is a little gnarly, but it's entry-level four-wheeling. Child's play compared to the nasty shit he and Katie used to run out in the California desert with his old Jeep, before it got repossessed.

"Bloody rut," Ethan says under his breath as he jams on the gas even harder. The truck's transmission groans and whines, like it's sick of this adventure, too.

Cameron sighs. "Let me try?"

"You?" Ethan frowns, but his eyes widen with curiosity, maybe hope. "Well, I suppose so." He cuts the engine and tosses Cameron the keys.

"Okay. Come on, let's get out."

"Out?"

"Yeah, out." Cameron tries to tamp down the impatience in his voice as he climbs down from the cab. "We need to check out what's going on down there. Might need to shore up the traction in the back. You got anything we could use as a wedge?" He scans the road, which drops into dark, thick forest at the edge. Nothing like the wide desert. But there's a small boulder on the side that might work. He jerks his head toward it and commands, "Grab that rock over there."

Ethan looks surprised. Impressed, even. Cameron allows himself a tiny smile. "Used to off-road in the desert once in a while."

"Aye." Ethan nods and lopes off toward the appointed rock. By the time he returns, Cameron has already packed a pad of thick, dry dirt in front of the rear wheels and is peering under the chassis, using the edges of his hands like tiny protractors to work out the angles.

Cameron explains how it's going to work. "First, we push the truck forward, even just an inch or two, and wedge the right tire with that rock. Then we come out at a hard left, then once the back wheels catch, cut right."

"Left?" Ethan looks left, at the wall of trees. There's maybe two feet between the side of the front bumper and the first row of thick trunks. "No, I don't think so."

"It'll work. It's just physics." Cameron remembers so many of these conversations with his four-wheeling friends. They couldn't see it like he could, the forces that would launch the vehicle this way and that, even when it seemed impossible. They'd sit there and spin their wheels, both metaphorically and physically. Looking earnestly at Ethan's doubtful face, he adds, "Trust me."

"Aye, then."

Left, hard right, a splatter of gravelly mud in the rearview mirror, and with a stomach-yanking jostle that alarms even Cameron, the truck bolts up the road. Once they're clear of the rut, he lets out a laugh. He'd forgotten how much fun this is, and this pickup is no Jeep, but it isn't half-bad on the rough stuff. He glances over to see Ethan practically shitting a brick. A wicked grin tugs at the corner of Cameron's mouth as he intentionally dips the front wheels through a divot, causing both of them to bounce. "Want to have some more fun?"

In the passenger seat, Ethan throws his head back and lets out a strange, almost canine, howl. "Let's do it!"

Cameron slams on the gas. This is a hell of a lot more fun than fish and chips.

Day 1,341 of My Captivity

SEA CREATURES ARE MASTERS OF DECEIT. I AM SURE you are familiar with the anglerfish, which lurks in dark waters behind a luminescent lure that attracts prey right into its maw. We do not have anglerfish here (and I cannot say I am sorry for that), but there was once a fascinating display poster about them in the lobby.

We all lie to obtain what we need. The seahorse, who impersonates a strand of kelp. The blenny, who poses as a cleaner fish, biding its time to take a bite of its gracious host. Even my own ability to change colors, my camouflage, is a falsehood at its core. A lie that's on its last legs, I am afraid, as I find it ever more difficult to shift to my surroundings.

Humans are the only species who subvert truth for their own entertainment. They call them jokes. Sometimes puns. Say one thing when you mean another. Laugh, or feign laughter out of politeness.

I cannot laugh.

But I heard a joke today that I found clever as well as timely. I should warn you that the punch line is rather macabre.

The young family had paused in front of my tank and the father (for it is usually the father, which I suppose is why they sometimes call them "dad jokes") turned to his small child and said: *What did the tiger say when he got his tail caught in the lawn mower?*

(Do not ask me why a jungle cat is in the presence of a turf-grooming machine. Jokes are often nonsensical.)

The child, already giggling, said: *I don't know! What?*

And the father answered: *It won't be long now.*

I would have laughed, were such a thing possible.

It won't be long now. This is true. I can feel my very cells struggling to carry out their typical functions. Tomorrow, a new month begins, and perhaps it will be the last time I notice that Terry has flipped the calendar on his wall. My inevitable end draws near.

A THREE-MARTINI TRUTH

Mary Ann Minetti's farewell luncheon begins at noon on a hot day in August. Tova arrives at the Elland Chophouse ten minutes early. Unrelenting sunlight assaults her eyes, and she squints as she climbs the restaurant's front steps in the poshest section of Elland's waterfront district. Her ankle is still tender and shriveled from its weeks inside the boot.

"Mrs. Sullivan!" A familiar voice calls from behind as a steadying arm clasps her elbow.

"Laura, dear. How are you?" Tova inclines her head at Mary Ann's daughter, a trim woman in her forties, accepting the younger woman's assistance as she summits the staircase.

According to Mary Ann, Laura had arrived last week to help her mother make preparations. And it was Laura who organized this luncheon, who chose this fancy restaurant. Tova's not convinced that Mary Ann herself wouldn't have preferred coffee at her home, although maybe that's not possible now that the house is being packed up and prepped for the realtors.

"Good, good." Laura nods, holding the front door for both of them. "And I'm glad to see you're on the mend! Mom told me about your fall." She arches a brow at Tova's foot.

"It was only a sprain."

"I know, but at your age . . ."

A chipper greeting from the young lady behind the hostess stand spares Tova the need to respond. Hoisting an impossibly tall stack of menus, she leads them through the restaurant to a long, empty table abutting a bank of windows overlooking the water. The view, at least, is lovely.

"Your server should be over in a couple minutes. I can grab you a drink in the meantime," the hostess offers as she circles the table, placing a menu at each setting. There must be at least thirty places. Good heavens. How many people did Laura invite?

"Hell yes. Gin and tonic, please." Laura drops her purse onto the table and sighs. "I've spent all morning helping my mother pack up the house she's lived in for half a century. Better make it a double."

"Of course, ma'am."

Tova lowers into a chair near the end of the table, picturing the menagerie of porcelain figurines and polished crosses that have always lived on the shelf over Mary Ann's kitchen sink wrapped in tissue and loaded into a cardboard box, where they'll likely stay for years until some unfortunate younger family member happens upon them and must decide how to get rid of them. She forces a smile at the hostess, who seems to be waiting for her drink order. "Just a coffee, please. Black."

The hostess whisks away with a nod, leaving the two women in the sort of silence that makes Tova wish she'd brought her knitting along. Finally, she asks, "How are the girls?"

Laura's daughter, Tatum, and young granddaughter, Isabelle, live with Laura in Spokane. Now Mary Ann, a great-grandmother at only seventy, will live with them, too. Of course, the situation with Tatum and her baby hadn't been planned, but Tova can't help feeling wonder at how it's shaken out. Four generations of women under one roof.

Laura nods. "The girls are good. Great. Isabelle's walking now."

"Wonderful," Tova says.

"Yes." Laura smiles, but doesn't elaborate, in the way that people often don't elaborate when it comes to discussing children around Tova, which is sometimes a mixed blessing.

The uncomfortable silence descends again, so Tova asks, "How's work, dear?"

"It's . . . work." Laura lets out a genuine chuckle before launching into a tale about the technology update happening over the summer at the state university, where she teaches psychology. Tova nods along. It does, indeed, sound like a nightmare. Laura sighs sympathetically, then explains, "So that's why we had to get Mom moved so quickly. Before the start of fall term, anyway. I feel terrible that you ladies don't get much of a goodbye. I know how close you've all been. For decades."

"There's always the telephone."

"We'll get Mom set up with a tablet. That way she can virtually attend your Knit-Wit meetings!" Laura beams, looking very pleased with herself at this solution, whatever it means. "And what about you? When will you go back to work at the aquarium?"

Tova straightens and recounts to Laura her recent conversation with Terry. He agreed to allow her to come back and "help out the new guy," as he put it. Tova couldn't be more pleased with this arrangement, which allows her to mentor him in the proper way to do things, and she should have plenty of time to do that before her move to Charter Village at the end of the month. She doesn't mention that she also rather likes spending time with the boy.

"Mom! Over here!" Laura hollers to Mary Ann, who waves from across the restaurant, trailed by Barb Vanderhoof and Janice and Peter Kim.

"Yoo-hoo!" Barb flutters her hands as they approach the table. She's wearing a sequined top that's far too snug across her chest. "Look at this! How fancy!" She wraps Laura in a hug.

Janice slips into the seat next to Tova. "How goes it, Tova?"

"How's that ankle?" Peter Kim sits next to his wife.

"Very well, thanks," Tova replies, hoping her injury won't be the topic of conversation this afternoon.

"Excellent news. But what happened to your arm?"

Tova tugs at her sleeve, trying to cover the newest line of sucker marks. "That's nothing at all. Must be from the sun."

Peter frowns, and Tova can tell he's putting on his doctor hat, about to push the issue, but he's mercifully interrupted by the guest of honor.

"Oh my. Thank you all for coming!" Mary Ann lets out a girlish giggle and takes her designated seat at the center of the table as more people filter in. Tova recognizes several parishioners from St. Ann's, where Mary Ann was on the board for years, along with neighbors. In a matter of minutes, most of the seats are filled, leaving only the two on Tova's other side empty. Relieved to be next to the no-shows, she places her purse on one.

"Well, doesn't this look like a rowdy bunch!" A young man with deep brown skin and sparkling eyes approaches with two pitchers of water. Omar, according to his name tag. "Glad I wore my sneakers because I can tell you all will keep me on my toes!" An approving laugh moves across the crowd.

"We came to party!" Barb Vanderhoof shimmies.

Omar makes finger guns and aims them at her. "That's the spirit!"

"Our dear friend Mary Ann is moving away." Barb gestures at Mary Ann, who is blushing. "To Spokane."

"Yikes! Spokane! I'm sorry." Omar makes a face like he just ate a lemon, but his eyes are still twinkling.

"Hey now! I live in Spokane!" Laughing, Laura lofts her empty highball glass.

Tova's coffee finally arrives, via a harried-looking busboy. She studies the thick black liquid before taking a sip. It's hot and strong. She picks up the menu and studies it, clicking her tongue at the descriptions, things like *basil cream foam* and *heirloom turnip reduction*. Where are the soups and salads? A cup of corn chowder would do nicely.

"These seats taken?" A deep voice, vaguely familiar, breaks her focus on the menu. She looks up at a tall figure. He doesn't look so strange without his bike shorts and space-age sunglasses and helmet, but it's Adam Wright, the fellow who helped her with her crossword down at Hamilton Park a few weeks ago. "Oh! Hello." He breaks into a smile, recognizing her as well.

"Nice to see you again," Tova says, moving her pocketbook from the chair. On Adam's other side is a short woman with curly auburn hair.

"This is Sandy Hewitt," he says, giving his companion's arm a squeeze as they both sit. "Sandy, meet Tova Sullivan."

"How do you do," Tova says with a nod. The busboy returns with two martinis on a tray. Carefully, he sets them in front of the couple.

Adam takes a long gulp, which reminds Tova of that day when he chugged her bottle of water in the park. "Laura and I went to Sunday school together at St. Ann's," he explains. "She heard I'd moved back to town. And somehow roped me into helping out with her mother's move. And now I've roped in my better half, too." He winks at Sandy.

"They're lucky to have him." She grins and squeezes Adam's bicep. "And I'm always happy to help out, not that I'm much for heavy lifting. But Laura was nice enough to include me in lunch. It's great to meet so much of Sowell Bay, all at once."

"Yes, Laura really went above and beyond with the guest list, didn't she?" Tova sips her coffee.

"I guess so." Sandy tilts her head. "So, how do you and Adam know each other?"

Tova clears her throat, then says quietly, "Adam was a friend of my son's."

Adam flattens his lips. Then he leans down to Sandy's ear, and most of the whispered explanation is inaudible to Tova, but she catches the words *there was this kid who* . . .

Sandy's eyes widen, and she shoots Tova a sympathetic look before turning her attention to intensely studying the menu. Smoothing her hair, she straightens in her chair and clasps her hands. "Well," she chirps, addressing the table at large. "Who's decided what they're having? I've heard the skirt steak is to die for!"

CORN CHOWDER, AS it turns out, is not available at the Elland Chophouse. But Omar recommends a curried squash bisque that, to Tova's surprise, is lovely. She sops every last drop with the accompanying hunk of sourdough while Adam Wright and Peter Kim complain across Tova and Janice about the Mariners and their losing streak, a subject that doesn't interest Tova in the least.

"Baseball. Who cares, right?" Janice says.

Tova smiles, then dabs a napkin on the corners of her mouth. "The only thing more tedious than watching it is talking about it."

Peter Kim gives his wife's shoulder a playful squeeze. "Sorry to bore you, darling."

"Hey, maybe I'm cursed." Adam Wright laughs. "I move back to town and suddenly they start sucking. Should've stayed in Chicago." He drains his martini, then smiles at Sandy as he plucks one fat green olive from the sword-shaped plastic spear and offers her the other, slinging an arm across the back of her chair.

Janice leans toward Sandy. "Any news on the house hunt?"

"Oh yes!" Sandy beams. "We decided on one of those new builds. That subdivision on the south end of town."

"How perfect. You can finish things exactly how you want them."

"Exactly! Adam's planning to build a man cave in the basement. For baseball-watching."

Peter Kim lights up. "Excellent! I'll be over on game day!"

The four of them share a laugh.

Sandy turns to Tova. "What about you, Mrs. Sullivan?"

"What do you mean?" Tova lifts a brow.

"Your house? Have you had any offers?"

Janice drops her fork and turns to stare at Tova.

"Jessica Snell mentioned it at closing. That your house had just come on the market. Not a good fit for us, of course. We need at least five bedrooms for when the grandkids come visit."

"Eventual grandkids," Adam corrects her. "Theoretical grand-kids."

Tova twists her napkin in her lap.

"Such a gorgeous house, though," Sandy yammers on. "Jessica said she didn't think it would last long. Someone will snap it up."

"Yes, I suppose so," Tova says quietly.

"Tova." Janice's voice is sharp. "What is she talking about?"

"Oh. Is it not . . . ? I mean, did you all not know . . . ?" Sandy's cheeks turn as red as the pimento in Adam's fresh martini.

"It's quite all right." Tova clears her throat. "Sandy is correct. I'm selling my house. I've applied for a suite up at Charter Village in Bellingham."

A silence falls over the table.

"What?" Mary Ann gasps.

"Why didn't you say anything?" Barb demands.

"What about the house?" Janice leans forward.

"That beautiful house! Your father's house!"

"And all of your things, Tova!"

"You have so many beautiful things! You're not going to get rid of it all?"

"Where will all of your things go?"

"So many things to go through!"

"That attic, I can't imagine."

"Those trunks of your mother's, the cedar ones. What a shame!"

"I'm perfectly capable of dealing with my belongings," Tova says, her voice taut. This puts a stop to the volley of comments. How can the Knit-Wits cast judgment on her possessions, anyway? Mary Ann with all those statuettes, and Janice's house has a whole room dedicated to computer equipment, much of which seems to serve no actual purpose. Barb, for some reason that has never been fully explained, has been collecting elephants since she was a bachelorette, for heaven's sake. Her whole guest bedroom is full of elephant keepsakes. Who are they to cast stones?

Janice lays a hand on Tova's shoulder. "You don't need to do this, you know. Peter and I have always said you could live with us, that you could—"

"Absolutely not. I would never burden you in that way."

Janice shakes her head. "You're never a burden, Tova."

AS THE DISHES are being cleared, Mary Ann makes a trip around the table to thank everyone for coming. Janice and Peter Kim bid goodbye, explaining that they'll be late for their pottery class. Barb Vanderhoof and her too-tight sequins shimmy out of the room on their way to her weekly therapist appointment. Omar brings the check for Laura to sign and makes a joke about Mary Ann causing trouble in Spokane. Adam Wright swallows the dregs of his third martini and clasps his hands around Mary Ann's forearm. "Thank *you* for having us!"

"This was so lovely!" Sandy chimes in, seeming to have forgotten about the bomb she dropped earlier. Thankfully, the rest of the table seems to have shrugged it off, too, although Tova caught Janice and Barb whispering about *changing her mind*.

Mary Ann's smile is tight as she perches on the empty chair next to Tova. "I'll see you before I leave this weekend, won't I?"

"Certainly. I'll stop by."

"I'd like that." Mary Ann's voice shakes a bit. Laura hurries over and stands behind her mother, winds an arm around her shoulders.

"It's so great of you to take your mom in." Adam turns to Mary Ann, leaning back in his chair. "Man, I'm glad I had kids, even if it means I'll never be rid of my ex-wife. Because it would be hell to get old alone. Isn't that why anyone has kids?"

Sandy jabs him. "Don't be ridiculous, babe."

Laura eyes him sharply, offering no response other than to reach in front of him to pick up his not-quite-empty martini glass and hand it off to a passing waiter.

"I'm an idiot." Adam raises his hand and then lowers it. "Tova, I'm sorry. I didn't mean that. You won't get old alone. Even with Erik gone."

"It's quite all right," Tova says quietly. "It was a long time ago."

"I remember it like it was yesterday." Adam's voice is clearer now.

Mary Ann claps a hand over her mouth, and Laura plants her hands on her hips, shooting a glare that could shatter stone. But Tova turns to Adam, suddenly aware of her heart throbbing under her blouse. "I always welcome what people remember."

His drags a hand over his face. "I mean, nothing you don't already know, I'm sure. I remember the last time I saw him. We grabbed nachos at the snack bar that afternoon, before he started work. We were planning to go out to my family's cabin the next day. He was going to sneak some beers from your fridge, as usual." He cringes. "Uh, sorry about that."

Tova waves a hand. "No matter."

"Anyway," Adam goes on, "he wanted to impress that girl, whatever her name was. He was going to bring her to the cabin."

Tova lets out a stony chuckle. Stealing beer from the fridge? That sounded like her son. But the rest, was it possible? She shakes her head. "I don't remember Erik having a girlfriend at that time."

"I don't know what she was, technically, but they were a thing." Adam frowns and furrows a brow. "Damn. What was her name?"

Laura lays a hand on Tova's shoulder. "Are you okay?"

"Tova? Dear?" Mary Ann echoes her daughter.

"I'm perfectly fine." Tova's voice sounds like it's coming from inside a cave. She stands and thanks Laura for the luncheon while giving Mary Ann a brief hug, then hears herself bid goodbye to Adam Wright and Sandy Hewitt.

Click-clack, click-clack. The sound of her sandals on the restaurant's hardwood floor seems to propel her away from the table. Outside, late-afternoon sun assaults her, and she shields her face with a hand as she beelines across the Elland Chophouse parking lot toward her car. Only once she's sitting in the driver's seat with the ignition turned on and the radio playing does she realize she's been holding her breath. It comes out, hot and fast, the blowback fogging her glasses.

So Will had been right.

There was a girl.

THE PIER'S SHADOW

Avery's house is small with yellow vinyl siding in a subdivision off the county highway. It's a haul from town; no wonder Avery showers at the store after her morning paddle, even if the water is ice-cold, instead of driving home. Garden tools and yard-waste bags are all over the place on one side of her driveway, barely leaving room for Cameron to park his camper.

She appears in the front doorway clutching a coffee mug. A pair of running shorts sits low on her hips, a flash of light-brown skin peeking out between the waistband and her tank top. Damn. Suddenly, he's very glad she suggested they meet here for their paddleboarding date rather than down at her shop. She had claimed it was because she doesn't like to come into work on her days off, but maybe she has something more in mind?

Squinting into the sun, she says, "You made it!"

Cameron hops down from the cab and tucks the keys in his pocket. "Did you expect otherwise?"

She grins. "To be honest, I don't normally date younger guys. I've been ghosted more than once."

"Younger guys? How old do you think I am?"

"Twenty-four?"

"Try thirty." Cameron bounds up the short set of front steps in one leap. "But I'll forgive you. It's hard to tell with my youthful glow and athleticism."

Avery rolls her eyes. "Save your chest-puffing for after I get you on a paddleboard. We'll talk about your athleticism then."

"I'm sure I'll be a natural. Naturally."

"Uh-huh." Avery smirks. She gestures at the open door. "Come in for a bit? I need to finish getting ready."

"Sure. But what about you?"

Avery turns to him, puzzled. "What about me?"

"How old are you?" A note of anxiety creeps into Cameron's voice.

"Turned thirty-two last month." She laughs at his look of relief, then bends down to pick up a lone sock from the laminate floor. "Why, how old did you think I was?"

"Oh, early twenties, obviously."

She bats him with the sock. "Stop."

Cameron puts on his best smile. "I mean, why not? You're—"

A beleaguered grunt from the other room interrupts him. Moments later, a teenage boy lopes out. He's almost as tall as Cameron, with shaggy dark curls and the same olive complexion as Avery. Without a glance at Cameron, the boy holds up a cereal box and moans, "Mom! We're outta Cheerios."

Cameron's jaw drops. A kid? A teenage kid?

A look of surprise crosses Avery's face, then she inhales stiffly. "Cameron, this is Marco." She turns to the teenager, who glares at Cameron the way someone looks at a fresh turd. "Honey, this is my friend Cameron."

"Hey," Cameron says with a nod.

"Sup." Marco juts his chin.

"Don't mind him. He's fifteen. And I thought he had headed out on a bike ride ten minutes ago," Avery says, ruffling Marco's hair, which he tolerates for a couple of seconds before ducking away from her hand. Cameron runs the numbers in his head three times to make sure he's got it right. Seventeen. Avery had a kid when she was seventeen!

"Marco, hon, what do we do when we're out of Cheerios?"

Marco rolls his eyes. "The list."

"Right. We add it to the shopping list," she says, her tone pointed. "I'm sure you'll find something else to eat in the meantime."

Marco mutters, "We're out of chips, too."

"Oh, the humanity," Avery says dryly. "Look, I'll try to get to the grocery store later. Cameron and I are going out on the water. Don't trash the house while I'm gone, okay?"

"Can Kyle and Nate come over later?"

"If you promise to do something besides play video games all day. Go ride your bikes! And the lawn needs mowing."

"Yeah, fine. I'll mow."

"Great. Have fun. And here." She tosses the sock at him. "This got lost on its way to the hamper."

These last words send a shock wave through Cameron. That's exactly what Katie used to say to him when he'd leave his clothes on their bedroom floor.

"I SHOULD'VE TOLD you." Avery bites her lip and stares out the passenger window of the camper. "I'm sorry."

"No! It's cool. Totally cool." Cameron rests his arm on the rim of the open window. Is it cool? To his surprise . . . yeah, maybe it is. Watching Avery as a mom, for some reason, had impressed him in a way that he'd never been impressed by a girl before. He turns off the highway and down the long, winding hill toward the water. The transmission shudders at the downshift, and that damn loose belt squeals, which causes him to second-guess his insistence on driving. He had wanted to show off the camper, though. It's looking good these days. He scrubbed the whole inside down with vinegar and lemon, and even the windows are streak-free. He even sprung for a cheap, but new, mattress.

She gives him a sidelong look. "You're cool with me having a kid?"

"Well, I guess it means you're easy," he says, voice hitching on the last syllable. Did his joke cross the line? But Avery bursts out laughing and gives his shoulder a playful shove.

"You are so going in the water. I'll dunk you myself."

"You can't! I don't have a swimsuit."

This is true. All of Cameron's board shorts are stuffed in a black garbage bag, where they went after Katie tossed them off her balcony. The garbage sack has probably been moved to Brad and Elizabeth's basement by now.

Avery stares at him, incredulous. "Why not?"

"Don't own one at the moment."

"We have trunks at my shop, you know."

"Too rich for my blood. What do you think they're paying me to hack up mackerel and mop up the guts afterward?"

"Don't be ridiculous. I would have given you a pair for free!"

"Nah, I'm done with handouts. Although that shit you gave me for my neck was amazing."

"Fair enough." She shakes her head, smiling. "But I hope you like being cold and wet."

TINY WAVES LAP at the pebbled shore. How hard could this be? Nonetheless, Avery gives him the play-by-play. "So, you want to put your feet here." She points to the middle of his board. "And hold your paddle like this," she says, demonstrating.

Cameron nods, half listening as she goes through a million more directives.

"And the last thing," she chirps as she launches her board gracefully over the water, "is don't fall in!" A breeze flips up the edge of her running shorts, distracting him.

"I won't," he promises. He lies on his stomach, as instructed, and launches his board from the beach. But as soon as he rises to a knee, preparing to stand, he starts to topple. With a humbling splash, his foot plunges, sinking into the rough sand six inches below. "Holy shit!" he gasps. The icy water knocks his breath away. Shockingly cold.

"Five seconds." Avery looks over her shoulder, brow raised. "A record."

"I was just testing the water."

"Try widening your stance."

Somehow, Cameron gets both feet on the board. And Avery is right; wider is better. When she tells him in a pointed way that she's taking him on her standard beginner route, he lets it slide. Puget Sound is freezing.

He follows her around a long, curved jetty. On the outermost rock, a seagull cocks its head, its glare comically angry. Studying the surly bird almost leads to another spill, but this time, he recovers. With each paddle stroke, he's feeling steadier.

They're halfway to the pier when Avery sets down her paddle and sits, cross-legged, on her board. Cameron's eyes widen. Is he supposed to pull that off, too?

She giggles. "It's not as hard as it looks. Keep your weight balanced as you lower down." Holding his breath, Cameron follows her instructions and soon finds himself seated, bobbing on the waves.

"This is nice," he says.

"Isn't it?" Avery reclines, propping on her elbows. Her shirt hikes, revealing her perfect little belly button. "Sowell Bay has some of the calmest water in all of Puget Sound. Part of the reason I moved here."

"When was that?"

"Five years ago? Yeah, that's right. Marco was ten. We moved up from Seattle."

"That must've been tough."

"He did okay. His dad took a job in Anacortes, and Sowell Bay was halfway between." She trails a hand through the water. "Plus, I'd always wanted to start a paddle shop, which I never would've been able to afford in Seattle."

"What did you do before?"

"Some odd jobs, but when Marco was little, I was a mom, mostly. His dad is a deckhand on a fishing trawler, so his schedule is all over the place." She stares out at the bay. "He doesn't see Marco much in the summer. But he's not a bad guy."

"Aren't exes always bad guys?" Cameron inches a leg toward his board's edge and dips a foot into the water. It's still cold, but the sun is so relentless out here, it almost feels good.

Avery smiles. "Actually, Josh and I are good friends. We never even dated. Just hooked up once my junior year of high school, and poof! There's a kid binding us for life."

"Poof! Is that what childbirth is like?"

"Trust me, you don't want to know what childbirth is like." Avery flips over onto her belly and props her chin on her hands. "Sorry Marco was such a jerk to you earlier. Honestly, I don't bring guys home often, and when I have, it hasn't always gone well . . ."

"It's okay. He's fifteen. He's allowed to be Oscar the Grouch, trash can and all."

"Trash can? His bedroom is more like an actual dumpster! I don't even go in there anymore."

"Believe me, that's wise," Cameron says with a laugh. A speedboat buzzes by farther out on the bay, and after a few moments his board knocks gently into Avery's, pushed together by a series of small swells. They've drifted almost all the way to the pier now. At the very end of the leggy wooden structure, some teens are horsing around, some of them tiptoeing along on the top edge of the slanted railing like it's a tightrope. Avery's eyes narrow, watching them.

"At least Marco doesn't pull idiotic stunts like that." She shakes her head. "It's, like, thirty feet down, depending on the tide. And there are huge, sharp rocks under there. Old pilings. You hit the water wrong, you're toast."

"Yikes." Cameron isn't a huge fan of heights.

Avery paddles into the pier's shadow where the water turns inky, and Cameron follows. Under here, there's a cold, oily smell. Kelp clings to the pilings just below water's surface reflected in cool shades of sepia.

Suddenly, Avery says, "I stopped someone from jumping once."

"Jumping?"

"A woman. From this pier." She pokes a barnacle-crusted piling with her paddle.

"Whoa. How?"

"I beached my board and went up to help her. Talked to her." Avery shivers. "Talked her down."

"I wouldn't even know where to start, talking someone down."

"Mostly, I just listened." Avery shrugs. "But it was weird. I'd never seen her before. Sowell Bay is such a small town. When someone new pops up, it's an event."

"I've noticed." Cameron can't help but think of Tova and her gossiping knit-nutters, or whatever they're called. And about how much Ethan loves to give him the down-low on the town's drama when he gets home from the store. "So, what did you do once you got her down?"

"Helped her to her car. Guess I could've called the police, but . . ." She lets out a long breath, then plasters on a forced smile. "Anyway, why am I telling you this? My original point was, Marco would be grounded for life if I found out he was messing around up there."

"He's lucky to have such a good mom."

"Yeah, well, my own mama took no shit from me. I guess it's how I was raised."

"I wish I'd been raised that way." Eyes focused on the water,

Cameron tells Avery about his mother leaving him at Aunt Jeanne's house and never coming back.

"God, I'm sorry, Cameron." She lifts her paddle and lands it on the nose of his board, then uses it to pull his closer. After they bump softly, she rests a hand on his knee.

Footsteps pound on the pier above them, echoing through the wood. One of the teens lets out a shriek, and for a second Cameron expects a testosterone-fueled body to hurl over the side toward the dark water below. But then, peals of laughter.

He shivers. "Sometimes I wonder if she's even still alive." His voice drops. "But then I also wonder whether that makes it worse. That she's been out there, all these years, and never tried to be a parent again, you know?"

"Your aunt never hears from her, either?"

"Nope."

Avery runs her finger along the edge of her board, leaving a trail of little water droplets behind it. "That must have been really hard for your mother."

"Hard for *her*?"

"To leave, I mean. To leave you with someone who could do better."

Cameron snorts softly, about to retort, but he can't quite find the words. Of course he's heard that sort of line before, people saying that his mother ditching him with Aunt Jeanne was a blessing in disguise. An act of mercy, even. Even Aunt Jeanne herself used to say that. Those comments always seemed like grade-A bullshit, hollow platitudes meant to make him feel better. But somehow, hearing them from Avery, the words feel real and solid.

When he was younger, he used to imagine what life with his mother would have been like, but in those fantasies, the mom figure was always . . . well, a typical mom. Like some version of Elizabeth's mom, with her aerobics videos and famous recipe for butterscotch cookies. Naturally, it hurt like hell to mourn the loss of that. But maybe Avery is right. It never could have existed.

"I went through some shit when I found out I was pregnant with Marco," Avery goes on. "Decisions, you know. And every single person in my big obnoxious family had an opinion on the matter. Thought I'd be ruining my life, no matter what I did."

"People and their opinions generally suck," Cameron says. "And for the record, you've done an amazing job with your life."

"Well, yeah, I kind of have, right?" A half-modest smile flashes across her face before it turns serious again. "But back then, I was seventeen. I had no idea what I was doing. I decided to keep the pregnancy, but there were moments when I thought it might be better—for Marco, if not for me—to let someone else have him."

"You thought about giving him up for adoption."

"Almost went through with it." She hugs her knees to her chest. "My family, they all kept saying it was best for everyone. And in my case, they were wrong, you know? But I understood their argument. It can be the right decision."

Cameron sees again, in his mind, the self-assured way Avery ruffled her son's hair. Took no shit about dirty socks on the floor. He can barely scrape up enough money to buy a crappy camper with money siphoned from his overly generous aunt, and meanwhile, Avery has raised a whole entire human being, not to mention buying a house and a paddleboard store, and doesn't think twice about giving away a twenty-dollar jar of organic Vaseline, for free, to a schmuck like him. A sucker for injured creatures, indeed.

"My friends Elizabeth and Brad are having a baby," he says, although he's not sure why, because it's kind of out of nowhere. "Best friends, I mean. We've all been tight for a long time."

"That's wonderful," Avery says.

"It is. It's amazing." Cameron nods slowly. "I mean, they have no clue what they're doing, but I guess they'll figure it out."

"For sure. Billions of people have figured it out."

Cameron smiles. "You'd like them. I mean, Brad is a dork, but he's a solid dude. And I think you and Elizabeth would be good friends." He runs a hand through the cold, dark water. "I wish you could meet them. I mean, someday." He rubs the back of his neck, which is suddenly hot, flushed.

"Sure, I'd love that." Avery rises to her knees and dips a paddle. "Let's head back, huh? It's chilly under here."

An hour later, as they swing back around the tip of the jetty, that same aggrieved seagull gives them another hard glare. "Cheer up, mate," says Cameron, chuckling to himself. Ethan is rubbing off on him.

The gull rears back, thrusts open its beak, and lets out the loudest, angriest squawk a bird has ever made.

All it takes is his one foot slipping back a couple of inches, weight shifted, and with a massive splash Cameron is in the water. Again.

Coming up with a gasp, he yells, "Holy shit, that's still cold!"

Where did Avery go? Treading in the freezing water, he swivels his head around looking for her. He probably looks like a goddamn seal. Or a sea lion? He can't remember which pinniped is native to the Pacific Northwest. Is the cold taking over his brain? Hypothermia?

"Need a hand?" There she is, paddling toward him on her board. She's gasping. With laughter.

"I've got it," he grumbles, attempting to hoist himself back onto his slippery board. Just as he gets a knee up, it shoots away, sending him back underwater.

When he resurfaces, Avery is letting loose a string of incomprehensible instructions. "Shift your weight, brace your knee, tighten your core, no, your other knee, that elbow, grip with that hand, no, your right hand, no, your *other* right hand . . ."

He manages to flop up onto the board, and is sitting there like an asshole, dripping and panting, when the seagull lifts off the jetty and glides past them.

"You feathered little jerk," he mutters, shaking his fist.

Avery has finally recovered from her laughter. She wipes her eyes with the hem of her shirt. "So close to the shore! You almost made it."

"Gee, thanks for believing in me." A smile tugs at the corner of his mouth. "Well, since I'm already wet . . ." He dives into the bracing water and beelines for her board. Her warnings are muffled by the water as he gives the board a solid shove. She crashes into him, squealing and pushing him under, as the board pops back out few feet away.

He surfaces, grinning. "Now we're both wet!"

"You are so dead." Her voice is sandpaper, but her eyes are sparkling. He winds an arm around her waist and pulls her into him, her body practically weightless underwater. She wraps her legs around his hips. It's hot as hell, even though he's numb from the armpits down at this point.

"You didn't pack a change of clothes," he says, teeth chattering. "I noticed you didn't bring a bag." His lips are a breath away from hers.

She whispers, "Because I never fall."

"Good thing I've got blankets in the back of the camper."

Laughing, she pulls back a bit. "Cameron, if you try some line about us needing to get out of these wet clothes . . ."

He feigns offense. "Well, we do, don't we?"

"And if you say one damn word about how you're glad we brought your camper here, because Marco and his friends are back at my house . . ."

"Well? Aren't you glad about that?"

"Yep." She draws herself close again and kisses him, softly at first. Her lips are salty, shivering, but as she opens her mouth to his, the inside is warm, sweet, intoxicating. Then, with a swoosh, she jets away. As she grabs hold of her loose board, she flashes him a daring grin that almost sends him off the edge as she says, "Last one back to the shore is a rotten egg."

THERE WAS A GIRL

There was a girl.

Like a noxious ivy, this notion winds its way around every aspect of Tova's daily routine. When she's making up her bed in the morning: *There was a girl*. Waiting for the coffee to percolate: *There was a girl*. Dusting the baseboards (because it's a Wednesday, after all, even when the world's been tipped upside down): *A girl, a girl, a girl*.

Even though he was very popular, Erik was selective in who he chose to date. There were a handful of sweethearts throughout high school, and the police spoke at length with all of them. Not as suspects, of course—they never said that—but as people who had once been close to Erik, who might have known what he was doing that night, whether he was playing some game or running away from home or . . .

There was Ashley Barrington, whom Erik took to the Sowell Bay High School homecoming dance the previous autumn, but she knew nothing, she'd been out of town with her family on a cruise the night it happened. Jenny-Lynn Mason, his prom date from earlier that spring, was also of no help, as she had attended a social gathering down in Seattle that evening and stayed the night at a friend's there. Then there was Stephanie Lee. When the police prodded, Tova had identified her as a classmate who had come around the house several times that spring for so-called study dates. Stephanie said she was home, asleep. At first, the detective raised a brow at this, but eventually determined that it was true, and that the young woman couldn't offer any information.

There was a girl. How did she not know? Tova's eyes seem to tangle with themselves as she tries to focus on the newspaper laid out in front of her with the daily crossword. *Five letters: A daredevil's move.* She knows the word is "STUNT," but her pencil wants to write *A-G-I-R-L.* Or better yet, the girl's name. What was her name? Is it buried in her own memory? A name she'd heard but not attached any importance to? Had Adam Wright managed to remember it? Was he even trying? She had tried to look him up in the phone book, but he wasn't listed, which probably made sense because he just moved back to town. And anyhow, perhaps he wouldn't even remember their conversation from the Elland Chophouse. He had consumed quite a few martinis.

This, too, nags at Tova. What does anyone really know about Adam Wright? Who says the liquor-fueled memory of a lunchtime lush could be counted upon? He was a school buddy of Erik's, but not a close friend. He said so himself.

She picks at a peeling edge of Formica on the corner of her kitchen table. A terrible habit, to pick at such a thing. She ought to superglue it down right away. But she keeps picking. Why is everything coming apart at the seams?

If she hadn't taken her crossword down to Hamilton Park that day, had that moment of connection over Debbie Harry of Blondie, of all things, good heavens . . . would he have recognized her at the Elland Chophouse?

Why is he only now remembering these details about that night?

Why did Erik take that boat out?

Why can't Adam remember the girl's name?

Why didn't Erik tell her about the girl?

Why is all of this coming up now?

"Why?" she says to Cat, who is parked in a patch of sunshine on the linoleum. Cat licks a paw and squints.

It has been years since Tova has juggled so many of these Erik-related questions. It exhausts her, to the point where she lies down on the davenport after lunch for a nap, which is something she hasn't done in years.

THE PHONE'S RING slices through her sleep. Tova fumbles the receiver, almost dropping it, and croaks, "Hello?"

"I have great news!" It's a woman's voice, and for the smallest second Tova's mind flashes to *a girl*. But it's Jessica Snell, the realtor.

"Oh?" Tova sits up and rubs her temple.

"We've got an offer. Ten thousand above asking!" Jessica Snell proceeds to spew a litany of details about the buyers and their offer and instructions about what Tova should do next if she would like to accept. "Mind you, we haven't even done the open house yet, so I wouldn't blame you if you want to hold out . . . but I can tell you, this is a good offer. We priced it aggressively. We could counter to take it off the market before the open house. What do you think?"

"Yes, yes." Tova fetches a sheaf of newspaper and a pen and jots down the numbers in the margin next to yesterday's half-completed crossword. She simply hasn't had it in her to finish the puzzles lately. Somehow it feels less important than it used to. "Yes, let's counter."

"Great. I'll email you the paperwork. Let's see, what's your . . . We don't have your email on file?"

Tova sniffs. "I don't have email."

"Oh, that's right, you brought the seller's agreement to my office," Snell continues without missing a beat. "No problem, we can do it that way. I'll drop a hard copy of the counteroffer by your house this evening, okay?"

"Very well."

After hanging up, Tova ratchets out a breath. They'll accept the counter. A contract will be signed. The house will be sold.

In the kitchen, she pours a cup of cold coffee from the percolator and zaps it in the microwave before heading out the back door. On the back porch, Cat is lounging in a patch of sunlight, and Tova lets out a bitter sigh at the sight of him. When she sits on the small garden bench, he leaps up to her lap, plants his paws on her chest, and butts his head against the underside of her chin.

"What will we do with you, little fellow?" Tova strokes the extra-soft patches of fur behind his ears. "I don't suppose you can go back to living outside."

In response, he purrs. Perhaps a problem to be solved another day.

THERE WAS A girl.

The idea of a girl continues to peck at the perimeter of Tova's consciousness as she signs Jessica Snell's paperwork. It tap, tap, taps on her brain as she makes supper. It hovers around her like a persistent fly during the short drive down the hill to the aquarium. The turn into the parking lot comes out of nowhere, and Tova almost misses it. The turn she must've made at least a thousand times.

Madness. This is how it begins. She's losing her mind. Because of an offhand remark from a fellow with too many martinis in him.

Cameron seems like he's in another world tonight, and the two of them work in silence: she fills the bucket with vinegar and water, while he rinses and wrings the mop. Finally, as they're working their way along the easternmost side of the building, she asks, "Any word from your father, dear?"

"Nope."

"I'm sorry to hear that." She goes on, lifting her voice to an unnaturally cheery tone. "You'll find him, eventually, and when you do, he'll be tickled you did."

"Yeah, maybe." He works ahead of her, around the curve.

She catches up, pausing to peer into the thick front glass of Marcellus's tank. He drifts out from behind his rock, blinking in greeting before pressing one of his tentacles against the glass. His perfectly round suckers look like miniature porcelain dinner plates for an army of tiny dolls as he squelches along the smooth surface.

An idea strikes her. Something to bring the boy out of his daze.

AN UNEXPECTED TREASURE

L et's use the other stool, shall we?"

Cameron watches skeptically as Tova drags the old, broken step stool out of the way and replaces it with the new one. Someone should deal with that busted old thing. Maybe he'll haul it out to the dumpster on his way out tonight.

"Last time he hid," Cameron points out. "What makes you think tonight's any different?"

"He's in a better mood tonight."

"Oh, come on. A better mood?" *Even the Octopus Whisperer herself can't discern an invertebrate's moods. Can she?* Cameron peers into the tank. Marcellus looks how he always looks, floating around like some weird alien, his unnerving eye moving like it's got a mind of its own. It wouldn't shock him if someone cut Marcellus open and found his insides full of wires and circuits. A spying sea robot, dispatched from a distant galaxy. Isn't there a movie with that plot? If not, there should be. Maybe he could write the screenplay.

He hesitates before the stool, glancing at the tank next door. Wolf eels. Seriously, the ugliest fish Cameron has ever seen. Two of them are out now, parked next to a rock, their terrifying teeth jutting up from twin underbites. "How about we play with them instead? They look about as friendly."

Ignoring his sarcastic comment, Tova climbs up on the stool and dips her hand into the tank. Cameron watches as Marcellus winds his arm around her wrist. Tova touches the top of his mantle, and the creature seems to lean into her hand, in a way that reminds him of how Katie's ridiculous little dog used to demand her attention when it sat on her lap.

"You're going to say hello to my friend Cameron now, and this time, you're going to be friendly," Tova tells the octopus. She motions Cameron to replace her on the stool. He rolls his eyes. But the octopus seems to listen and releases his grip on her arm before turning his inscrutable eye on Cameron, hovering expectantly in his cold blue tank.

"Okay," he mutters, shrugging off his favorite hoodie and tossing it on the counter before climbing up. He dips his hand in. The water is bracing. Worse than Puget Sound itself, the coldness of which Cameron now considers himself an expert on, after his outing with Avery.

The creature trails an arm upward, brushing his hand.

"Ack!" Instinctively, he yanks his hand from the water, which draws a gentle chuckle from Tova, who watches from below.

"It's quite all right to be a bit alarmed," she says.

"I'm not," Cameron grunts. "It's just really cold."

"Try again," she encourages.

When he does, he forces himself to keep his hand in the water this time, allowing Marcellus to prod at the veins on the back of his hand, to explore the tops of his knuckles. Then, in an instant, the octopus wraps the end of its arm around his wrist. Each individual sucker feels like its own tiny creature, and before Cameron knows it, it feels like there are hundreds of them crawling up his arm.

To his surprise, he laughs.

Tova laughs, too. "It feels funny, doesn't it?"

"Yeah." He looks down into the water. Marcellus's eye is gleaming, somehow, like he's laughing along with them. The creature's muscular tentacle wraps tighter, up to his elbow now. How strong is this thing, anyway?

Cameron is so preoccupied with the circulation in his arm that he doesn't notice the creature's other appendage winding around behind him until Marcellus taps him on the opposite shoulder. He whirls around, turning the wrong way, of course. Had the octopus intended that? Like a joke?

"Ah, he got you!" Tova's eyes sparkle. "My brother used to fool his nephew, my son, with that one. Oldest trick in the book."

The octopus unwinds. As Cameron steps down from the stool, he examines the sucker marks along the underside of his arm.

"They'll fade quickly," Tova assures him.

"Yours didn't," Cameron points out.

"My skin is seventy years old, dear. Yours will mend more quickly."

What does it matter? The marks look kind of cool, like a tattoo. Maybe Avery will be impressed. He grabs a roll of paper towels from the shelf and dries off his arm. He's about to turn and shoot it, free-throw-style, at the trash can in the corner of the tiny pump room, when something in the octopus's tank catches his eye. Something shiny, barely peeking through the sand near the big rock behind which the creature disappeared a minute ago.

"What's that thing?" he asks Tova.

She looks up at him, confused.

"That shiny thing." He ducks down and peers through the glass, and Tova does the same, adjusting her glasses.

"Good heavens." Tova frowns. "I don't know."

As if on cue, one of the octopus's arms snakes out from the rocky den and prods the sand with its tip, reminding Cameron of Aunt Jeanne when she falls asleep on the sofa and loses her glasses and has to feel around, half-blind, in the cushions.

"I think he's looking for it," Cameron says, not quite believing the words coming out of his mouth. Was the creature actually listening to them?

Before Tova can reply, the octopus finally lands on the mystery object, and the sand is swept away. Cameron squints through the glass. It's a teardrop-shaped silver thing, an inch wide, maybe. A fishing lure? No, an earring. A woman's earring.

With a whoosh, the octopus sweeps the earring into the den.

For some reason, Tova throws back her head and laughs.

"What's so funny?"

She clasps a hand to her chest. "I should say, I do believe our Marcellus is something of a treasure hunter."

"A treasure hunter?"

As Cameron follows Tova out of the pump room, she tells him some story about her lost house key that the octopus apparently dug up from his tank and returned to her one night. Cameron nods along, but he's not sure he's buying it. Tova's a nice lady, but in spite of what he's seen tonight, some of this octopus shit just seems crazy. Eventually, they resume their work in comfortable silence. Cameron lets his mind wander again, replaying his night with Avery, the way her hair smelled like some fruity shampoo on his pillow. He won't check his phone again, seeing if she's messaged him back. Nope. And he won't go by the paddle shop on his way home tonight, even though he knows it'll be closed. Definitely not. These are the promises he's making to himself as he absently collects the trash and goes to replace the can liner.

"Don't forget to hook it all the way around," Tova calls from across the hallway.

How had she even seen him? Does she have eyes on the back of her head? Maybe she's a robot spy from a distant galaxy. That would make a great twist in his screenplay.

He points to the rim of the trash can. "It's all the way around. Look."

"Pull it down farther. It'll only take an extra moment."

"It's good enough!"

"It'll start to slip down when it gets full."

"Well, when that happens, someone can fix it."

Tova turns to him, arms folded. "Didn't you mother teach you to do things right the first time?"

Cameron stares at her. "I never had a mother."

Tova's color drains.

"She was . . . I mean, she struggled. With addiction. I haven't seen her since I was nine."

"Oh dear. I'm sorry, Cameron."

"It's okay," he grumbles while yanking the liner all the way on, hating the fact that it did only take an extra moment. When he looks up, Tova is wiping fervently at some nonexistent spot on the glass, refusing to meet his eye.

"Really, it's okay," Cameron insists. "How would you have known?"

"It is certainly not okay. I ought to be more careful with my words."

"No, I shouldn't have chomped your head off about it. I'm just tired." Cameron lets out a puffy breath. "Terry asked for extra cod for the sharks today, and Mackenzie was out, sick, so I covered the desk between loads, and the phone kept ringing, and . . . it's just been a long day."

"You're working very hard here."

"I guess I am." The words seep through him, slow and warm like hot chicken broth on a cold day. It might be the nicest compliment anyone has ever given him.

"Indeed." Tova smiles at him, gives a tiny approving nod before resuming her wiping down of the glass tank.

"The truth is, I didn't have a mom, but I had an aunt Jeanne," he says tentatively. He picks up the mop and starts to run it along the baseboard. "She's the one who raised me after my mom took off."

Tova looks up. "I'd love to hear about her."

"She's one of the most amazing people on the planet, but you might not like her."

"Why on earth wouldn't I like her?"

A conspiratorial grin spreads across Cameron's face. "Pretty sure she's never had a clue about the proper way to put in trash can liners."

Tova's laugh echoes down the empty hallway.

Day 1,349 of My Captivity

THEY DO NOT SEE IT.

For weeks, they have worked together. How do they not see it?

I have searched my Collection many times over, considering whether any of these objects might point them in the right direction. A useless endeavor. And now my Collection is a mess. It spills out of my den, sloppy and disorganized. Dangerous. My Collection shall be exposed next time my tank is cleaned, if I am not more careful. Although I fear I may no longer be around next time my tank is cleaned.

I must persevere, for their sake. I cannot bear to leave this story unfinished, as it is now. As I fear it will always be, if I do not intervene to help them realize.

Human gestation is approximately two hundred and eighty days. Conception must have occurred very close to the night of the boy's accident. But the mother does not realize she is carrying an embryo until weeks later. Months, sometimes, in such cases where producing offspring was not planned. I have seen this scenario play out countless times over the course of my captivity, while observing the patrons that come and go.

If Tova knew his date of birth. His last name. Would that be enough? I must try.

Why do I so deeply care that she knows? I am not entirely certain. But my own end nears, along with her time here. If they do not figure it out soon, everyone involved will be left with a . . . hole.

As a general rule, I like holes. A hole at the top of my tank gives me freedom.

But I do not like the hole in her heart. She only has one, not three, like me.

Tova's heart.

I will do everything I can to help her fill it.

SOME TREES

The tower of tea towels threatens to topple as Tova adds another to the top. Stacks of this sort cover the floorboards of her attic. Above, the polished beams are bathed, cathedral-like, in the afternoon light streaming through the large picture window. Tova's disposition, however, is less sunny. She cannot stand piles.

Will was a notorious maker of piles. Receipts, stale mail advertisements, magazines he'd already read twice, scraps of paper upon which he'd jotted some note or another that even he couldn't decipher. In Will's view these things needed to be kept. When Tova would nag him about the clutter, he'd simply collect the detritus into a stack, square off the corners, and plop it on the edge of some counter or credenza, with a satisfied remark. *See? Nice and tidy.*

Tova would wait until he dozed off in the recliner, and then, with a sigh, would shepherd the junk to its proper place, which was occasionally the filing cabinet, but more often the trash bin. When Will's cancer generated enough paperwork to overstuff the small cabinet, Tova bought another, expanding her filing system so each page from the insurance company, every medical bill, had a proper home. Caring for her husband as the cancer worked its way through his organs may have taken over her life for a time, but she would not tolerate the paperwork taking over her kitchen counters.

"Quite a disaster, isn't it?" Tova directs this question at Cat, who patters up the attic stairs. A gray tail appears a moment later, popping up like a question mark behind a box. The cat winds his slender body between the stacks with impossible grace, arriving at a patch of sunshine near Tova's side without disturbing so much as a speck of dust. He casts a bored glare before lowering onto his side and closing his yellow eyes.

Tova smiles, allowing a smidge of her crossness to melt away. "I suppose you tromped all the way up here to nap on the job, didn't you?" She strokes Cat's side, which starts to rumble, purring.

The room is divided into three categories. It's a start, anyhow. A system. Tomorrow, Barb and Janice are coming over along with Janice's son, Timothy, and two or three of his friends. Voluntary labor for all of this sorting and hauling. Tova promised to order pizza for everyone, even though eating delivery food when her freezer is full of casseroles seems indulgent. But she does need the help, and better for it to come from people she knows rather than allowing a team of strangers to descend upon her family's heirlooms. Besides, Barb and Janice have been calling nonstop, offering to help. This will mollify them.

The first category of items, and by far the smallest, is for things she'll take to Charter Village: a couple of Erik's old toy cars, a handful of photographs, what's left of her mother's porcelain tea set, which she fancies she'll take coffee in once in a while. It's quite a shame so much of this has gone unused for years. Decades.

The slip of tissue that had wrapped the saucer gets wadded into a ball and tossed into the section nearest the door: trash. Here, too, goes a large volume of photographs and other memorabilia. Although it feels odd to discard these things, so meticulously saved, where else could they go? Janice suggested a storage unit, but why? There is no one left to want them.

Then there's the largest pile: the donation pile. A truck from the local secondhand shop is scheduled to do a pickup next week. Most of Erik's toys are in this pile; perhaps they'll be played with by someone else's grandchildren. Alongside the old toys is her mother's bone dinner china. It survived a trip across the ocean, so it should make it through a journey to the thrift shop downtown; whether anyone will buy it once it arrives there is another question. First, she'd tried to give it to Janice, but Janice said she didn't have room. Barb, likewise, apparently does not have room among her elephants. She had considered offering it to Mackenzie, the girl who works the desk at the aquarium, or even the young lady who runs the paddling shop next to Jessica Snell's office. But young women don't want bone china anymore. They've no use for old Swedish things. They have their own dinnerware, probably from Ikea. New Swedish things.

Also in the donation section are five wooden Dala Horses, straight-legged figurines with their delicate paintwork in shades of yellow and blue and red. The sixth one, the one Erik broke, has been missing for ages. She always thought perhaps she'd find it and repair it, but what good would that do now? She takes one of the horses out and studies it. If she takes them with her, the whole lot will be left at Charter Village for someone else to dispose of. Not even a muckle-toothed lawyer and his private investigator will be able to find someone who wants them.

Still, the Dala Horses switch piles. They'll go with her to the retirement home.

She picks up a stack of yellowing pillowcases; her mother had hand-embroidered the roses along the hem. The sheets let off a musty puff as Tova plops them onto the nearest linen pile, to be washed, of course, before being donated.

All of these things had been stored away for her to pass along someday, relics to be carried up the branches of the family tree. But the family tree stopped growing long ago, its canopy thinned and frayed, not a single sap springing from the old rotting trunk. Some trees aren't meant to sprout tender new branches, but to stand stoically on the forest floor, silently decaying.

She unfolds the next item to be added to the pile: a linen apron, its sturdy fabric heavily creased. It's what her mother wore when she baked. Tova holds it close to her face; it smells sour, like flour turned bad. Folding up the fraying strings, she tries to push away the thought that has been nagging at her all afternoon. *There was a girl.*

If Erik hadn't died that night, the girl might have been a daughter-in-law. Tova herself might have worn this apron when she taught her son's wife how to make his favorite butter cookies, then passed the apron along to her when the time came.

Such nonsensical thinking must stop. Whoever she was, Erik hadn't cared for her enough to ever mention her.

This last thought, as usual, stings.

Cat's afternoon nap comes to an end when a horsefly hurls itself against the window, enticing the sleeping gray hunter into an earnest, if fundamentally pointless, hunt. Tova watches the cat leap at the window, pawing the glass, as the fly hovers, unconcerned, outside.

"I know how you feel," she says, with a sympathetic nod. To know something is there, yet be unable to grasp it, is torture indeed. With an antagonized mewl, Cat stalks off, winding back through the maze of stacks and vanishing down the stairs.

Tova glances at her wristwatch: almost five. "Suppose I should think about supper," she mutters to no one, unfolding her aching joints from her low chair and picking her way through the mess. It isn't like her to leave a project half-finished. A rush of rebellion swishes through her as she turns her back on the unfinished piles and, stepping lightly on her still-tender ankle, descends the staircase.

Egg salad sandwich is tonight's supper plan . . . again. All week, it's been nothing but egg salad. (There was a coupon in last week's circular: buy a dozen, get a dozen free.) Tonight, however, she can't bear to eat another crumbly sandwich.

It's true, she's been doing her shopping in the morning lately. Not because she's avoiding Ethan and his coffee invitation. Of course not. She checks her watch again: she's fairly certain he'll be on shift now. She runs a hand down her face, which feels as worn as the relics in her attic, like the dust has settled into every crease and wrinkle. A friendly conversation with the Scot would be nice right now.

"I'm going up to the Shop-Way," she informs Cat, who is now perched on the arm of the davenport, no doubt depositing a layer of gray fur which Tova will need to slough off with a lint brush later. Oh well. The davenport won't be coming with her to the Charter Village, of course; it's far too large. And, in any event, there are worse things than cat hair.

A hot, thick haze has settled over Sowell Bay, and a few bored-looking teenagers are encamped on the curb in front of the grocery, languid and lazy under the baking sun, limbs sprawled, reminding Tova of a collection of gangly insects. She tuts as she steps over one young man's extended leg on her way to the front door.

The door chimes, and Ethan Mack glances up from his register with a broad grin and an "Afternoon, Tova!" An icy air-conditioned blast sends gooseflesh shivering up Tova's arms. She ought to have brought a sweater.

"Good day, Ethan." Suddenly out of any other words, she hurries toward the produce aisle. There, the temperature is even more frigid. She scoops a bagful of gleaming Rainier cherries and places it in her basket, then after a hesitation, fills a second bag. Cherry season is so short, and these do look delightful.

"Wow, three bucks a pound! What a steal."

Tova turns to find a familiar woman nibbling on a cherry. It takes her a moment to realize it's Sandy, from Mary Ann's luncheon. Adam Wright's lady friend. *Unlisted-in-the-phone-book* Adam Wright.

"Oh! Mrs. Sullivan, right?" She swipes juice from her mouth

with the back of her hand, then grins sheepishly. "Nice to see you again. I guess you caught me in the act, here."

"No need to worry. I won't alert the authorities," Tova says with a small smile. "Pleasure to see you, Sandy. I hope you and Adam are settling in well." Guilt nags at her, remembering how she drove through that neighborhood with the newly built homes, hoping she might happen to catch one of them fetching the mail or mowing the lawn. People deserved privacy on their own property. She, of all people, should appreciate that. And, even if she had managed to catch them, who is to say Adam remembers anything more about Erik's purported sweetheart than he let on at the luncheon? The night in question was, after all, thirty years ago.

And yet, Tova cannot shake his words. She shivers again.

Sandy plucks another cherry from the pile and pops the stem off. "Thanks, and yes, it's starting to feel like home. It's just beautiful up here. Great to be out of the hustle and bustle of the city." Cleaving the cherry in half with her teeth before picking the pit out, she makes a guttural *mmmm* sound and gives her fingertips a chef's kiss. "Seriously, you should try one. They're out of this world."

"Aye, you there! No free samples!" Ethan booms into the produce section, wagging one of his meaty fingers as he approaches. Sandy's face goes ashen, but Tova smiles and shakes her head. Ethan's eyes are sparkling.

He gently nudges poor Sandy on the shoulder. "I'm just pullin' your chain. Won't no one be the wiser if you help yourself to a few. Brilliant season for cherries this year, innit?"

Sandy releases a nervous laugh. "Whew. I thought I was about to get banished from the town's only grocery store."

"A'course not. We're a welcoming lot here, aren't we, Tova?"

Tova inclines her head. "I should say so."

Ethan chuckles and hooks his thumbs into his apron straps.

"Well, I'll leave you ladies to your shopping and sampling. Gimme a shout when you're ready to check out." With a cheery nod, he turns and lumbers over to a nearby cantaloupe display, where he busies himself straightening the mountain of melons.

"This town sure has its characters, doesn't it?" Sandy muses, watching him. "Adam always tried to describe Sowell Bay's . . . well, uniqueness. But I must admit, I didn't understand until I came here myself."

"Yes, well." Tova studies the tile. She's probably included as one of the town characters.

"You know, I never thought I'd live in a small town. Everyone's so friendly, but also so . . . I don't know. Up in everyone else's business?"

"We prefer to say we care for one another."

A tight, thin laugh escapes Sandy's coral-colored lips as she lofts a bag of cherries onto a nearby produce scale. "Adam insists I'll get used to it."

"I'm sure Adam is correct." Tova forces a smile. What do people gab about at Charter Village? Will she be a character there, too? Perhaps she'll meet someone who was friendly with Lars. Would that be a good thing or a bad thing?

"Speaking of Adam." Sandy leans in and shifts in her jeweled sandals, as if, suddenly, she'd rather not be in the produce section of the town's only grocery store right now. "I feel like I should apologize for his behavior at the chophouse. Drinking like that, at noon! But he's been under so much stress, with the move, and at work, and—"

Tova cuts in, "It's quite all right, dear." She means it.

"Right." Sandy still looks deeply abashed. "But there's one other thing. About that . . . conversation."

Tova waits for her to continue, uncomfortably aware of her heart's increased pace.

"He remembered her name. The girl your son was seeing, I mean."

The piles of cherries blur into a swirling sea, pink and red. Tova leans on a produce scale, bracing herself against this sudden dizziness, her brain now running mad circles now around the words *The girl has a name.*

"Mrs. Sullivan? Are you okay?"

"Quite," Tova hears herself rasp.

"Okay." Sandy hesitates, sounding unconvinced. "Adam didn't think I should say anything, but I just figured if I were in your shoes . . . I mean, if I had lost my child and there was bit of information I hadn't known, even something small . . ."

You would want to know. Tova allows her eyelids to squeeze shut, trying to slow the spinning.

"Anyway, her name was Daphne, or so Adam said. He couldn't remember her last name, but he did say she went to his high school."

"Daphne," Tova repeats. The name is thick and lumpy on her tongue, like an old piece of chewing gum.

A long moment passes. Finally, Sandy murmurs, "Well, now you know, I guess."

Tova watches her pick up her grocery basket. The skin is pulled tight around the woman's watering eyes. "Thank you, Sandy."

With an awkward nod and a quick touch on Tova's arm, Sandy ducks away toward the front register. From the corner of her eye, Tova catches Ethan staring at her.

He closes the gap between them, still holding a cantaloupe in each hand. "What was that Sandy Hewitt just said to you?"

Tova frowns, suddenly feeling like a rosebud under a cold dark sky. Pinched shut. "It was nothing."

"She said a name."

"It's long-ago nonsense."

"She said Daphne, didn't she?"

Tova holds up her bags of cherries. "I think I'm ready to check out. Can you take these to the register and ring them, please?"

THERE WILL BE no supper tonight.

Two pounds of peak-season Rainier cherries, along with a hasty collection of other grocery items, are abandoned on the counter in Tova's kitchen. Next to them, her pocketbook lies askance, right where it was carelessly flung, instead of in its proper place on the hook by the door.

Upstairs in the attic, Tova plows through the piles of linen and china, barely aware of the mess now. On the last shelf by the window, bottom row, is the book: *Sowell Bay High School, Class of 1989*.

Thirty years ago, she had pored through this volume, searching for something. Anything. And it would be remiss to leave out that, on occasion, she or Will had revisited the yearbook in the decades between, whenever some small spring leak of nostalgia broke through their hardened dyke. She has every photo of Erik included between its covers committed to memory.

But Tova isn't looking for Erik this time.

Her mouth feels numb and dry as she flips to the index. The print is so tiny that she needs her readers; her fumbling fingers find them in the breast pocket of her blouse and jam them onto her face. She yanks in a hard gulp of air when she sees the name, and it stays there, caught in her chest, as she runs her finger down the columns of type, devouring every last word, until finally she reaches the end of the *Z*s and releases the ragged breath. There is only one.

Cassmore, Daphne A.

Pages 14, 63, and 148.

AN IMPOSSIBLE JAM

Stop giving me that look."

In response, while still glaring at Cameron, the octopus hooks the tip of an arm through the tiny gap over the pump filter in the back of the tank. A threat.

"I know you can hear me." Cameron rubs his forehead wearily. What is he even saying? Octopuses can't understand English. Or any other language. Right? "You hungry, bro? Where were you earlier when I was circling the building with a bucket of mackerel? You're too good for that?"

The creature blinks at him, all innocent and coy. His arm, just the tip, slips through the gap.

"Oh no you don't. No escapades tonight." The mop clatters to the floor in the curved hallway as Cameron dashes off toward the pump room around back. He should fix the stupid tank so it can't pop open, in spite of what Tova says about the monster's so-called need for freedom. It's not like she's even here. Which is weird. He wouldn't have guessed she'd be the type to ghost, but as the night goes on, it's becoming increasingly clear she's not going to show.

Maybe that's why the damn kraken looks so incensed.

"Stay," he commands, looping a scrap of twine he found on the counter through the slit in the lid, then around the support post next to the tank, and tying a firm knot. The octopus drifts toward the gap, gaze glued to Cameron's handiwork. Then he fixes his withering eye on Cameron for a long, hard moment before jetting down into his den, leaving a flush of bubbles in his wake.

"Good night to you, too," Cameron mutters. The tiniest bit of guilt nags him, but it's for the best. The thought of dealing with a roaming octopus without Tova here to help him is honestly terrifying. Which must be why he jumps out of his skin when something dings.

It's his phone, his new one. He's not quite used to the sounds it makes yet. He couldn't bring himself to spring for the super-high-end one, but this one is decent. At least the battery lasts more than, like, ten minutes.

Could it be Avery again? His pulse thrums just thinking about it. They've been trading flirty texts all day. But when he checks, the text isn't from Avery. It's from Elizabeth, and it just says: *Call me.*

The baby. When was it due? Seems like yesterday he arrived in Sowell Bay, but it's been two months. Propping his phone on the supply cart, he pops in his earbuds and calls her back.

"Hey," comes Elizabeth's immediate answer.

"Lizard-breath? Are you okay?" Cameron realizes his heart is still racing. A lot of shit can go wrong, having a baby. But she laughs softly at his tone of voice, which probably means she isn't bleeding out in a hospital bed.

"I'm fine, Camel-tron. Well, mostly. My doctor put me on bed rest."

"Bed rest?"

"Yeah, I was having contractions. And they want the alien to cook for a few more weeks."

"Yikes. Well, you don't want a half-cooked alien."

"So now I'm stuck in bed."

"You mean you're literally lying around all day? Sounds amazing." Cameron wrings the mop.

"It's horrible! I'm so bored."

"At least Brad's waiting on you hand and foot, right?"

"He tried to make me a grilled cheese sandwich and the fire department came."

In his earbuds, Elizabeth laughs, and the sound seems so close. Suddenly, an awful, hollow feeling settles in the pit of Cameron's stomach.

"Anyway," Elizabeth goes on. "I was watching some show on the travel channel the other day. Because this is how I spend my days now. I swear I watch fourteen hours of pointless television a day."

"Still sounds pretty awesome," Cameron says. He bends down to pick up a candy wrapper from the floor.

"It sucks. But anyway. Simon Brinks was on the show. They were interviewing him about trends in vacation home sales or some boring thing. I hadn't been paying much attention, until I heard the name. It made me think of you. Thought I'd call and see how it's going."

"Not making much progress on the Simon Brinks front, unfortunately." Cameron fills her in on his dead ends so far.

"Do you like it up there, at least?" The question is punctuated by an alarming grunt. "Sorry, my back is killing me. I had to turn over. Just imagine a whale trying to flop itself over on a beach."

"Damn, Lizard-breath. That's quite an image." He laughs. "But yeah, I guess I like it all right." He pauses. "I met a girl."

Elizabeth squeals, and the next section of tile-mopping goes by quickly as Cameron gives her the PG version of his evolving relationship with Avery.

By the time they hang up, he's looped all the way around, back at the octopus exhibit again. The big fella is hanging out in the lower corner of the tank, watching him as its arms waft lightly in the water.

"Good boy. Good octopus," he mumbles.

Keys jingle from the front lobby.

Tova? He's surprised at how happy this makes him.

But the footsteps that follow are too heavy, their clip too quick. After a moment, Terry comes striding around the bend. Cameron tries to hide his disappointment.

"Hey, kiddo." The boss man smiles broadly. "Everything going okay?"

"Yeah, everything's great." Cameron lifts his chin, trying to look professional. Good thing he didn't get caught talking to Elizabeth on the phone.

"Excellent. Just popping in to check up on your work."

Cameron's eyes widen.

"Totally joking! I left something in my office earlier." Terry chuckles.

"Good one, sir."

"Keep it up, kiddo. I'll go around the other side so I don't mess up the clean floor." He's almost around the bend when he pauses and turns back. "Oh, Cameron. I've been meaning to check on that paperwork. You have a chance to fill it out yet?"

"Um, not yet." Terry has been periodically prodding him to fill out some *housekeeping* personnel form for a while now.

Terry folds his arms. "It's been two months."

"I know. I'm sorry."

"Make it a priority," Terry says. "I know it's a pain, but I've let it slide long enough. Rules are rules."

"I'll do it tonight."

"Oh, and could I trouble you for another copy of your driver's license? I know we made one when you came on board, but I can't seem to find it."

Cameron pats his back pocket. His wallet is there. "Uh, sure."

"Wonderful," Terry says. "Leave it on my desk before you go tonight, okay?"

"Will do, sir."

PAPERWORK IS NOT Cameron's strong suit. Sitting at the table in the aquarium lobby, pen poised over the crumpled hiring form bathed in blue light from the tank, Cameron can't help but remember the Merced Valley drama.

Merced Valley Technical College might not be Ivy League, but they recruited Cameron once. They even offered him a full scholarship. All he had to do was fill out some paperwork. Free money for signing some forms.

Cameron browsed the course catalog and picked out his classes. He was especially looking forward to philosophy. But the scholarship forms sat in a pile on his coffee table, collecting grease spots from pizza crusts and sweat rings from beer cans.

Aunt Jeanne had been furious. Accused him of throwing his future away for no reason. All he had to do was fill out some damn forms! It would've taken twenty minutes. *What's wrong with you?* she asked.

It's a good question.

Ten minutes later, the aquarium personnel form is done, and as he deposits the paper on Terry's desk, he remembers he was supposed to copy his license, too. The dusty photocopier in the corner of Terry's office sounds like a spaceship taking off as it comes to life with a series of buzzes and beeps. Cameron helps himself to one of the mints from the little jar on Terry's desk as he waits.

When the machine is finally ready, he puts his card on the glass and presses the big green button. Which apparently triggers a series of beeping alarms.

Paper Jam in Drawer C, Cameron reads on the tiny screen. He squats down and squints at the drawers. There are only two: A and B.

Impossible.

He opens every tab, drawer, and door he can find, but there is no Drawer C nor any whiff of a jammed paper anywhere. He jabs the green button again, but the screen just blinks the same message. Turns the whole thing off, then on again, three times. It will not relent on its insistence that there is something stuck in this nonexistent drawer.

"Designed by idiots," he mutters, plucking his driver's license from the glass and switching the machine off for good.

With a shrug, he drops his license on top of the forms on Terry's desk. He can get it back tomorrow night.

Day 1,352 of My Captivity

OH, I DO ENJOY KEEPING THE BOY ON HIS TOES. PLEASE
trust that I mean no harm. Quite the opposite. Some humans require
this for their own good, to be challenged. I can relate. My brain is a
powerful device, but it is hampered by my circumstances, and he is
much the same.

Of course, I want him to have a happy ending. Tova as well. It is,
you might say, my dying wish.

Anyway, on to tonight's topic, which is paperwork. Humans and
paperwork: such waste. If their memories were not so deficient,
perhaps they would not need so many written records.

But tonight, I have paperwork to thank.

The rope he installed on my tank was no obstacle. When the
time came, after he had finished cleaning and departed, I unfastened
the knot and lifted the lid in quite the same manner as I always do.
Should I be insulted by his underestimation of my abilities?

The route to Terry's office was rife with temptation, but The
Consequences come on ever more quickly these days, so I forsook
every tempting mollusk on the way. The Pacific geoduck clam exhibit looked especially ripe for the picking tonight. The humans call
them *gooey ducks*, but their texture is pleasantly firm.

But no gooey ducks tonight. I had more important plans. And to
be honest, my appetite is rather poor these days.

When I suckered up the side of Terry's desk, I found the central object of my mission.

A driver's license. Just like the one in my Collection. It states a human's full name and date of birth.

As the seconds ticked by and The Consequences loomed, I carried the thin plastic card down the hallway. By the time I arrived at my destination, I had already begun to feel terribly weak. With effort, I tucked it under the tail of the sea lion statue.

My return journey was slow and difficult. More than once, as I heaved my heavy body along the cement hallway, I pondered the possibility that I might perish. Right then, right there. Never to taste a scallop again. Never to feel my arms sucker onto the cool glass, to taste that humanity on the inside of her wrist, to touch, in turn, my Collection's treasures. If I had died tonight, would this errand have been worth it?

Indeed.

Tova did not come tonight. She may not come tomorrow, but she will come. I am confident she will not leave without saying goodbye.

She will not be able to resist running her rag under the sea lion's tail. She never can. She knows she is the only one who does.

When she does, she will see what I have left for her. And then she will know.

THE BAD CHECK

Ethan splashes Laphroaig Single Malt over two ice cubes then settles onto his lumpish little sofa. Evening creeps into the living room, daylight draining from the front window in unhurried measures, as slow as the sips of whiskey disappearing from his lowball glass.

Cassmore.

That surname had been a bugger in his brain since the very first time Cameron introduced himself. He knows Cassmore, but from where? It wasn't until he was brushing his teeth this morning when, out of nowhere, the memory popped into his head.

A bad check.

It was the sort of thing that happened with some frequency back in those days, back when check writing was still a common way to pay for groceries. You bounce a check, you get put up on the wall. Sometime in the '90s, it must've been.

Ethan remembers the ancient, wrinkled slips tacked there, on the counter under the cash register, when he bought the Shop-Way. Bad checks from customers. A warning. Some of them had been there for years, such as this one in particular. The name Daphne Cassmore printed up in the corner atop the address block. The check was for some piddly amount. Six dollars and change.

Ethan took the checks down right away. That wasn't how he'd run the store. But he made a mental note of the names.

It had been simple enough to link Daphne to Cameron. A few clicks on that ancestry website he'd bought a premium membership to a few months back led to Daphne Cassmore (who later married and became Daphne Scott) and then to a half sister: one Jeanne Baker, age sixty, of Modesto, California. Ms. Baker's robust online presence seemed largely due to her involvement in several communities for collectors and consigners. Ethan knows the type: people who make a hobby of buying and selling rubbish. Cameron had complained about his aunt's hoarding problem. It fit together.

Ethan drains the last of the scotch from his glass. He's glad no one writes checks anymore. Seeing so-called scammers hung up like that, their shame made public . . . how cruel. And Daphne Cassmore's bad check, in particular, always made him feel sorry for whoever wrote it. To be crucified over such a lowly sum. What measly six-dollar grocery haul precipitated her fall, in the store's eyes, from grace?

It couldn't have been a terribly long fall.

From the bits and pieces Cameron has told him of his mum, anyway, that seems to be the case. The lad gets tight-lipped when he speaks of her, but Ethan has heard enough to deduce drugs were involved. Can he blame Cameron for not wanting to get into it? His mum abandoned him.

The living room is fully dark now, and Ethan nearly trips over the pair of trainers he kicked off earlier when he crosses to the kitchen to pour another Laphroaig. Part of him thinks he ought to fill Cameron in on the town gossip, as it's sure to spread now that Sandy Hewitt is opening her mouth in the middle of the produce section at the Shop-Way. Sooner or later, the lad will hear it himself: the rumor that his mother may know something about the disappearance of a teenage boy thirty years ago. Might have known and never said anything. Could Cameron's image of her grow any more tarnished? Obviously, it all happened years before he was born.

Or did it?

How old is Cameron? Ethan can't recall whether he's ever mentioned his age, but he can't be older than twenty-five, right?

And then there's the matter of Tova.

How well can you know someone from bagging their groceries for so many years? Well enough to be certain she's hunting down info on Daphne Cassmore right now. She won't stop until she finds this woman who she thinks can tell her the untellable. Tova has never bought into the official story of Erik's death, Ethan is certain.

And then what will happen?

He ought to tell her that Cameron is Daphne Cassmore's son. She should hear it from a friend. Those two are chummy. How the lad has managed to crack Tova's shell is a mystery to Ethan; he's been trying to do so himself for nearly a year. But if Cameron's mother was potentially involved in what happened to her son, what will she think whenever she looks at Cameron?

It's past ten in the evening, but Tova Sullivan is a night owl. Gathering his wits, he picks up the phone. He'll ask her over for dinner.

THE DOWNSIDE OF FREE FOOD

Cameron tosses a disgustingly mealy peach, whole but for a bite, into the trash can at the end of the pier. Ethan's expired-grocery offerings can be a blessing and a curse. But he's saved a crap ton of cash on groceries this summer, and to boot, he's been parking the camper in Ethan's driveway for free. He owes Ethan a solid, for sure.

Stars scatter across the sky over Puget Sound, reflecting their silvery glow on the inky water below, a beautifully random pattern of lights that reminds Cameron of the dark brown freckles on the bridge of Avery's nose. He turns from the water and heads back to the camper, where his phone is charging. He wonders, not for the first time, what it would be like to park here on the shore and wake up to nothing but the water view in his windshield. He's thought about trying it, but Ethan says that Sowell Bay's overnight patrolman, a buddy of his called Mike, would apparently relish towing a camper from one of the public lots. Would give poor old Mike something to do in the tedious predawn hours. Maybe, someday, he'd live here and have a house with a view of the water. Maybe, if he could just find Simon Brinks.

But that's the bright future. Tonight, he'll drive back up the hill to his spot in Ethan's driveway, but first, he logs into his banking app to see if his latest paycheck has cleared. It has. The last chunk of money he needs to pay Aunt Jeanne back in full. A thrill courses through him as he taps through the transfer, adding a bonus to the sum just because he can. He sends her a text, a heart emoji, but she's probably asleep. It's after eleven.

A couple hundred bucks left over. He should save all of it. Totally should. But he pulls up a site he knows well, one that sells music for indie bands. Moth Sausage used to have their tracks listed there, but that's not why he's here. He searches his own name out of curiosity, but nothing comes up. Well, that's not surprising. Brad probably had the band's stuff taken down. Oh well. Instead, he searches until he finds two under-the-radar jam bands, ones that he knows are pretty decent. Like the Dead, like Phish or something, Ethan's style, but new. Cameron Cassmore may be a loser and a burnout, living in a shitty camper, but he knows good music. He buys digital albums from both bands and enters Ethan's email for delivery.

It's a start.

THE CAMPER'S WINDOWS are still black when his phone buzzes. Cameron pats around until his hand finds the device. When he sees Aunt Jeanne's number on the screen, his stomach drops. The last time she called him in the middle of the night, it was from the hospital, when she had a dented head and a shattered hip and two cops in her hospital room, trying to take a statement about what had happened in an altercation at Dell's.

"Hello?" he says, breathless. When he'd rushed to the hospital back then, it was twenty minutes away. Now, he didn't want to think about how long the drive would be.

"I'm fine, Cammy," she says, apparently reading his anxious tone.

"Then why are you calling me now?" He checks the time. "At one in the morning?"

"Did I wake you up?"

"Uh, yeah."

"Thought you'd be out at the bar or something."

"No. I was sound asleep. I worked my ass off today."

"Sorry. Just wanted to let you know I got your bank transfer. You sent too much." Aunt Jeanne lets out an off-key whistle. Has she been drinking? A muffled male voice shuffles in the background, and Cameron wonders whether Wally Perkins is there, with her, in her trailer.

Cameron sits up, rubbing his eyes. "The extra is interest." He doesn't add that he'd calculated it in his head based on the current prime rate and what she might have plausibly gotten from bonds, if the money had been invested there, which it never would have been, but did that matter?

"We never said anything about interest." Her voice is cool.

"But I owed it to you." *And I owe you so much more*, he doesn't add.

"You don't owe me anything." Her voice is slurry, for sure. Definitely some whiskey. "You know I never expected you to actually pay me back."

"For sure I was going to pay you back." Cameron hesitates, kicking off the blanket. "Actually, I was thinking once I square things up with Simon Brinks for everything he owes, we could use the money for a down payment."

"A down payment?"

"For you. A house, back in town. Get you out of that trailer park."

"I happen to like this trailer park."

In the background, a grizzled male voice pipes up. "What's going on?"

"Wally, did you realize we live in a dump?"

Cameron sputters, "I never said it was a dump!"

"Not in so many words," Aunt Jeanne says dryly. "Look, I'm glad you're so flush with cash all of a sudden that you can go around buying houses for people who don't need them. Why don't you keep the money and actually make something of your life?"

"What do you think I'm trying to do? Not my fault I was dealt a shitty hand."

"No, the deal is never anyone's fault. But you control the way you play." There's a splash and tinkling of ice cubes, then a moment's pause and another one. Two more drinks poured.

Cameron flings open the camper's back door, tumbles out, and starts pacing in Ethan's driveway. Under his bare feet, the pavement is still warm from the hot summer day. "I've played my hand as best I could. You could've told me Sowell Bay was where I came from."

Aunt Jeanne snorts. "What good would that have done?"

"I might have maybe found my father before I was, say, *thirty years old*."

"That man is not your father."

"How do you know for sure?"

"She was my sister, Cammy." Aunt Jeanne's voice is weary now, almost defeated. "For all your mother's flaws, she was no dummy. If your father was some big-shot business guy . . . I mean, if he were even a marginally productive member of society, or, hell, even alive . . . I don't know, Cammy. I think if it were that simple, she wouldn't have let him miss out on being a part of your life."

"She missed out on being a part of my life." Cameron kicks a clump of crabgrass in a crack of Ethan's driveway. "Seems like letting people go comes easy to her."

"Letting go," Aunt Jeanne says softly, "can be the hardest thing."

Cameron feels his face twist into an involuntary scowl. It's basically the same thing Avery said when they were paddleboarding under the pier, but somehow hearing it from Aunt Jeanne makes him want to kick right through the concrete.

"Look, I need to bounce," he says. "Work in the morning." This isn't true. He doesn't work until noon, but it seems like the sort of excuse a responsible person might give to get off the phone in the middle of the night.

Aunt Jeanne muffles the receiver for a second, another exchange with Wally Perkins. "Okay, Cammy. But I'd love to see you when we come through Seattle before our cruise next month."

We?

"Sure thing," says Cameron. Whatever. He hangs up and slams the camper door behind him before flopping back onto his mattress.

NOT A DATE

The following Saturday at five o'clock, Tova arrives at Ethan's house.

It is not a date.

The glass bottle is cool on her bare arm as she tucks it in the crook of her elbow, the way one might very awkwardly hold an infant. This strikes her as a better manner of presenting the gift to Ethan than the way Barbara thrust it at her, clutching it crudely by the neck, blabbing on about how it was last season's Cab Franc from that winery over in Woodinville and how it was so *delightful*, she *must* bring it for her *date*.

Not a date, Tova had insisted over and over. A million times, as Cameron might say. It's nothing more than supper.

A *quick* supper. She had clarified this when she accepted the invitation, citing her need to keep packing for her move. In truth, her free time has been consumed with searching every volume the Snohomish County Public Library would allow her to check out for any information about Daphne Cassmore. But the research has stalled, and Tova has learned very little of use. What harm could come from taking an evening off to share a meal with a friend?

With a friend? Is Ethan her friend?

In any event, it would be rude to arrive at someone's house without a gift. Tova is not much of a wine drinker herself, but this is what people do. Some small part of her is thankful for Barb's pushiness. Without it, she might've committed the faux pas of arriving empty-handed, and even if she had thought to procure one on her own, she couldn't have exactly marched into the Shop-Way and bought one from Ethan himself.

Head high, she strides up the short driveway toward the squatty bungalow. Her ankle is nearly healed now, only the tiniest hitch. An overgrown hydrangea with periwinkle blossoms encroaches upon the small porch. Tova lifts a branch out of her way to pass and, before she can change her mind, presses the doorbell.

"Evening, Tova," Ethan says, stepping back and motioning for her to enter. His voice is strangely quiet. She hands him the bottle, and he thanks her, then offers to take her pocketbook, gesturing toward a slightly crooked coatrack in the corner.

"Thank you, but it's no problem to keep it with me." Tova clutches the bag to her hip like a biblical fig leaf. As if she'd be bare naked without it.

"Brilliant, then," Ethan says.

Making her way across the natty carpet, Tova can't help but stare at the feature that dominates the house: an entire living room wall dedicated to a record collection, the cheap shelving's veneer peeling back from the particleboard. If this had been their house, back then, Will would've tacked the loose laminate down. Tova resists the urge to go pick at it, like a half-attached scab better removed, lest it snag on something.

Entering someone's home is always an intimate act. She looks around for photos, but there are none. Instead, the walls are decorated with beautifully framed concert posters: Grateful Dead, Hendrix, the Rolling Stones. The style should befit a teenager's room, yet somehow, it seems to match Ethan perfectly.

She follows him into a surprisingly tidy little kitchen, which smells of simmering mushrooms, while they make small talk. Tova has never cared for small talk, and she stumbles through it now. When Ethan hands her a goblet filled to the brim with Barb's *delightful* Cab Franc, she takes it gratefully.

"Cheers, love," he says.

"Cheers," Tova echoes, clinking his glass.

After several moments and several more sips, she picks up a pair of sunglasses on the counter, recognizing them as Cameron's. "It's been kind of you to open your home to him."

Ethan pours a swish of red wine into the skillet, which hisses in response, releasing an enormous puff of steam. "To tell you the truth, it's nice having a bit of company."

Tova nods. She knows what he means. It's been nice having Cameron down at the aquarium, too. "Yes, I should say so."

"D'you know, I came from a family of fourteen. Eleven brothers and sisters. When I was a wee lad, I always imagined my adult self in a house bursting at the seams."

Tova permits herself a smile. "I thought it was the Irish who were known for big families."

"Eh, we Scots can hold our own." He flashes her a grin, scraping mushroom sauce over two plump chicken breasts, one on each plate. To Tova's astonishment, her mouth waters. How long has it been since anyone prepared such a lovely meal for her?

THEY'RE SAVORING THEIR last bites when a screen door bangs. A moment later, Cameron whirls into the room, darkness shadowing his face. The glower lifts briefly, replaced by a confused look when he sees Tova sitting there with Ethan at his kitchen table.

After a moment, the glare returns, although it's pointed exclusively at Ethan. "Hey, man. Can I talk to you for a sec?" It sounds like his teeth are clenched.

"A'course. Shoot," Ethan says.

"I was hanging out down at the paddle shop, and Tanner, that kid that works at your store, came in with his buddies. Do you know what they happened to mention?" Cameron's tone is cool. "Said you were talking about my—"

"Right, then." Ethan vaults from his seat. He gives Cameron a pointed look as he guides the boy toward the living room. Over his shoulder, he excuses himself and insists Tova keep enjoying her meal, what's left of it, anyway, and that he'll only be a quick minute. The two of them vanish through the small house, presumably into some back bedroom, well out of earshot.

What would be wrong with the boy? A twinge of guilt tugs at her. Perhaps she would know, if she hadn't missed their last two cleaning sessions.

The "quick minute" drags on. Tova decides the least she can do is to start cleaning up the cooking mess. It's something to do. And what a post-cooking disaster this kitchen is. Head feeling somewhat lighter than usual, thanks to the wine, she searches for a sponge, and clicks her tongue when she fails to find one anywhere in the proximity of the kitchen sink. What does Ethan wash his dishes with? There isn't a sponge or a dishcloth anywhere in sight.

The drawer next to the sink seems like a logical place to look. But it seems to be a junk drawer. She opens the next one over, but it's also an assortment of papers, tools, oddities. Tova lets out a sigh. Why must men do this? If Will had had his way, he'd have allowed every bureau in their house to slip into junk-drawer status. She lets out a soft chuckle, thinking of Marcellus and his collection of oddities, stashed under the gravel in his den. Apparently, this tendency of males to assemble useless dross transcends species.

Under the sink, there ought to be something to use on the dishes, but as Tova swings open the cabinet, she's greeted with boxes of cereal and stacks of those microwavable instant-rice cups. Her jaw drops open.

Who keeps a pantry under the sink?

Adrenaline rushes through her head, making her dizzy. There's much she could do here. Reorganize the entire kitchen. Wipe down the interior cabinets and drawers. Does Ethan have any idea how much he needs someone like her?

She closes her eyes and takes a grounding breath. For now, she ought to focus on the dishes.

Inspecting the cupboard under the sink again, she spots a rag. Upon further inspection, it's an old T-shirt, white with faded print. Clearly a rag. Perfect for cleaning.

When the last dish has been nestled on the drying rack, she uses the shirt to wipe down the counters, swiping over a puddle of Cab Franc that had splashed on the counter with Ethan's haphazard pouring. Wine seeps into the soggy cotton, the stain fading into a shade of muted violet when she rinses and wrings it in the sink. Pride swells within her as she surveys the sparkling kitchen, and as if on cue, voices drift from the other room. The boys are coming back. Perhaps they've smoothed over their spat.

Cameron won't meet her eye before he ducks back out the rear door. A moment later, the camper's grizzly ignition sputters to life.

"Tova, love," Ethan says. His voice is tight.

"Are you all all right?" Tova ventures, taking a step toward him.

"I should tell you something." He shifts on his feet. It seems he hasn't even noticed that Tova cleaned the entire kitchen.

"Well, what is it?" Tova presses, but then wonders whether she should've. Suddenly, she wants nothing more than to be home, sitting on her davenport. Watching the evening news. The tidy, predictable banter of Craig Moreno and Carla Ketchum and meteorologist Joan Jennison. She places the wadded rag/T-shirt on the counter and clasps her hands.

Ethan's gaze locks on the bundle on the counter. His eyes bulge. "What the . . . ?" He crosses the kitchen and holds up the wine-stained rag. Color drains from his ruddy cheeks.

Tova straightens, nervous.

"What have you done?"

"The dishes." Tova plants her hands on her hips. "I cleaned the kitchen, washed the dishes, wiped down the counters. I had half a mind to start on that mess under your sink, but—"

"Oh." Ethan's voice is hoarse. He slops the rag-shirt onto the table and sinks down into one of the chairs, dropping his huge head into his hands. His voice is muffled when he says, "Grateful Dead, Memorial Stadium. May 26, 1995."

"What does that mean?"

He looks up, eyes flashing. "Their last show in Seattle. One of Jerry Garcia's last shows ever."

"I don't . . . well . . ." Tova's head spins. Jerry Garcia was the lead singer of Grateful Dead and passed away in 1995, of this she's certain. Crossword puzzle makers occasionally use some version of this as a clue, and it always strikes her as somewhat pedestrian for a pop-culture nod.

"The shirt. It was from that show. It's a rare specimen." Ethan expels a long breath as he rises.

"But it was under the sink."

Ethan flings an arm toward the cabinet. "Right. It was in that closet."

"That's not a closet. It's a cabinet."

"They're both compartments with doors! What's the difference?"

Tova folds her arms. "Well, most people keep cleaning supplies under the sink."

"Who cares what most people do?" He pinches the bridge of his nose. "Red wine stains. They come out, right?"

"Maybe they'll lighten," Tova says. "With undiluted bleach."

"But that will . . ."

"Yes," she admits. "It will fade out everything else, too."

Ethan says nothing but gets up heavily and wanders over to the counter and dumps the remainder of Barb's Cab Franc into his glass, then finishes it in one gulp. Tova watches, her jaw suddenly wired shut, her feet somehow rooted to the ground. Who leaves a precious garment shoved in a kitchen cupboard? And one in such terrible shape, so horribly faded and worn?

No, not horribly worn. Well loved.

"I'm sorry, Ethan."

He squares his shoulders. "Aye. It's all right, love."

"I'm going to go now," Tova says, trembling. "Thank you for the meal."

"Please wait. I have something important to tell you. The reason I asked you over tonight, actually . . ."

But Tova is already halfway across the house, clutching her pocketbook to her hip. The front door shuts quietly behind her.

A RARE SPECIMEN

Tova has never cared much for rock music, at least not the modern kind. As a girl, of course, she liked Chuck Berry and Little Richard. And Elvis Presley, the King himself. When they were newlyweds, Will used to take her dancing at the hall downtown on Saturday nights, where they'd jitterbug until their feet were swollen. But the music teenage Erik used to blast from the boom box in his bedroom? That was noise, pure and simple.

The blend of guitar and drumbeats drifting out of the speaker on Janice Kim's laptop computer is somewhere in between. Tova can't understand much of what the lead singer is saying, but his voice is pleasant. The music sounds like it's wandering, meandering. It isn't unenjoyable.

"Hang on, let me turn down the volume," Janice says, jabbing at the keyboard. "Don't you hate it when websites have script embedded to play music automatically?"

"Oh yes," Tova says, though she's not sure what that means. Across the room, on his plush pouf, Rolo lifts his head. The tiny dog yawns, stands, and gives his whole body a good shake before trotting over. Janice scoops him up to her lap, and Tova reaches over and strokes his silky head.

"Ah, here we go. This is the one you're looking for, right?" Janice zooms in on a photo of a scrawny man holding up a faded white T-shirt, the very same one Tova ruined last night at Ethan's house. By the time she arrived home, Ethan had already left a message on her answering machine, insisting she not worry about the shirt. This morning, he sent a text message to her cell phone, too, apologizing for the sour note the evening took, and begging her to call him back. She thought about calling back, but she didn't know how to reply to the message, and in any event, getting in touch with Janice to ask for her help seemed more important.

The shirt was beloved. Tova needs to make it right.

"Yes, that's it." She watches as Janice clicks through several other photos of the shirt, front and back, laid out on a wooden dining table.

"I'm not familiar with this particular auction site," Janice says, squinting at the screen. "But it's securely encrypted, so I guess it's probably legit?"

"Right." Tova nods. Mercifully, Janice has asked few questions of Tova about why she's trying to acquire a souvenir T-shirt from a Grateful Dead concert in 1995. It seems like the remaining Knit-Wits have been walking on eggshells around her ever since she announced her intention to move to Charter Village.

"Okay, so here's where you put in your credit card number." Janice clicks over to another screen. Her brows furrow as the new page loads. "No, this can't be right."

"What is it?"

"It says this shirt costs two thousand dollars."

Rolo yips, apparently sharing Janice's shock.

"I see." Tova swallows a gasp before continuing matter-of-factly, "Yes, well. It's a rare specimen."

Janice's eyes narrow. "Since when do you collect concert memorabilia? What are you up to, Tova?"

"It's nothing." Tova waves her off. "I'm just making something right." She reaches into her pocketbook and flips through her wallet until she finds her lone credit card, which she uses only when paying cash isn't an option.

"For the fellow selling this, you're about to make his day right, that's for sure," Janice mutters, taking Tova's card and punching the numbers in. Before she hits the green BUY NOW button, she casts one last skeptical look at Tova. "Are you sure?"

"Yes. Do it." Tova isn't sure why her heart is beating so quickly. It's only a replacement for an item she ruined, and two thousand dollars is hardly a dent in her bank account.

A little circle on the center of the laptop's screen spins for a few seconds, and then Janice says, "Okay, there we go," as a thank-you screen appears. "I'll print the receipt when it hits my email. Looks like it'll ship within two to three weeks."

"Three weeks!" Tova shakes her head. "No, I can't wait three weeks."

"You can't wait three weeks? For this dirty old shirt?"

"No." Tova sets her jaw. Yet another reason why this internet shopping craze is foolish. Who wants to wait three weeks for something they've purchased?

"Well, it says you can pick it up." Words and graphics whiz up the screen as Janice scrolls. She peers at Tova doubtfully. "Their warehouse is in Tukwila."

Tukwila is south of Seattle, near the airport. It will take three hours to drive down there from Sowell Bay, at least. Maybe more with downtown Seattle traffic.

"I'd rather do that. Can you change it?"

Janice's mouth drops open. "Seriously?"

"Seriously," Tova parrots.

"Okey-dokey." Looking skeptical, Janice clicks a few more buttons. Moments later, her printer whirs to life, and a page emerges. She deposits Rolo on the floor before going to fetch the page and handing it to Tova. It's a small, grainy map with an address in Tukwila.

"Very good. Thank you for your help," says Tova with a firm nod, folding the page and tucking it into her pocketbook.

"You're going to drive all the way down there?"

"I suppose I am."

"When was the last time you drove through Seattle? And on the freeway, Tova?"

Tova doesn't answer, but it was when Will was going through one of his last rounds of treatment. He saw a specialist at the University of Washington. The experimental drug didn't help Will much, unfortunately, but of course they had to try.

"I'll go with you," Janice says. "I'll get Peter to come, too. He can drive. Let me look at my calendar, we'll pick a day, and—"

"No thank you," Tova cuts in. "I can go on my own. I'd like to get it done today."

Janice crosses her arms. "Well, I'm sure you know what you're doing. Be careful. Take your cell phone."

STOPPED CARS ARE packed on the interstate like herring in a tin. Brake lights glitter red and pink through the wet windshield as the wipers clear away the drizzle, somewhat unusual for summer, when it's typically hot and dry. Naturally, it would start raining during Tova's first drive on the freeway in two years.

The hatchback inches forward. Everyone in Tova's middle lane seems to be switching over to the right lane. Perhaps there's something blocking the lane on the left. She's about to switch on the blinker when the cell phone rings from its spot in her cup holder.

Tova jabs the screen. "Hello?" Nothing happens. Janice showed her how to make the cell phone work like a speaker, but now she can't remember which of the little round icons does this. She tries another one and says again, louder, "Hello?"

"Mrs. Sullivan?" A male voice bleats from the device.

"Yes," Tova says. "This is she."

"Hi, this is Patrick. I'm with admissions at Charter Village. How are you today?"

"Fine, thank you." Tova gives one last sidelong look at her

rearview mirror and holds her breath as she guides the car into the right lane. She exhales, wondering if Patrick can hear it on the other end of the line.

"Good. I'm calling to make sure it's okay to process your final deposit."

"I see," Tova says.

"We haven't received your authorization form yet. Perhaps it got lost in the mail?"

"Oh, well, you know the postal service these days."

Now all of the cars that merged right are fighting to make their way left. Why can't anyone make up their mind? The cars remind Tova of a school of feckless fish dodging a predator's attack, moving in unison, not realizing they're fleeing the shark on one side only to be devoured by the seal on the other.

Patrick clears his throat. "So I'm calling because we need that final deposit in order to secure your move-in date, which is—hang on, let me check—oh, it's next month."

Tova hits the brake pedal a bit harder than intended. "Yes, I believe that's correct."

"No wonder my supervisor flagged this. Well, given the circumstances, I can take your verbal authorization to make the draft. Is that okay?"

Tova swings around a semitruck, back into the other lane, which is now zooming along at a good clip while the other lane stands still. How odd such things can be. Each little decision about which lane to choose determines exactly how you get where you're going, and when. When Will was alive, he used to accompany Tova to do the grocery shopping sometimes, and he would always pick the slower checkout line. They used to joke about how he had a knack for it.

She and Will had gone to the grocery store the afternoon of the day Erik died. Tova remembers buying a box of those junky cream-filled snack cakes Erik always liked. Had Will chosen the slow checkout lane that day? If he'd picked the faster one, would they have arrived home in time to see Erik before he left for his job at the ferry dock? Would they have caught him sneaking beer from the fridge? Would he have mentioned that he was seeing a girl now? Would he have told Tova her name was Daphne and he couldn't wait to bring her over for supper?

Would any of this have changed anything?

"Hello? Mrs. Sullivan? Are you there?"

"Yes." Tova blinks at the phone in the cup holder. "I'm here."

"Are you all right?" There's a note of concern in Patrick's voice. Tova pictures him hovering over a telephone at one of the desks inside the glass-walled office she walked by on her Charter Village tour.

"Go ahead," she says. "Process it."

NOT EVEN A BIRTHDAY CARD

ameron has already mopped half the building when a flustered Tova hurries through the front door, almost an hour late.

"I'm sorry I'm late," she says.

"No worries. We've well established I can handle this on my own." He smiles, but doesn't add that he'd been disappointed, again, when she hadn't showed. That, strange as she is, he has looked forward to their evenings together. And today has been a bit lonely. He's hardly said two words to Ethan since their argument. All that garbage Ethan's apparently been spreading around town . . . it doesn't even make sense. Something about a bad check. From a thousand years ago. Like Cameron needs any reminding that his mother was a loser.

Tova nods, then leans in conspiratorially. "I won't double-check the trash liners this time. I trust you."

Cameron gasps, feigning shock. "You trust me to assemble garbage cans! Wow, I've arrived." He laughs, and Tova laughs along with him. "So, where were you, anyway?"

"Oh, well, it's been quite an adventure." Tova picks up a rag and begins to wipe down the glass front of the bluegill exhibit, while relaying an almost-unbelievable story about Grateful Dead memorabilia and online auctions and some guy at a warehouse down in Tukwila who almost wouldn't hand her purchase over because she couldn't confirm her friend's email address, which she'd used because she doesn't have one of her own. She scrubs at a fingerprint on the glass as she talks. Her cheeks are flushed in a most un-Tova-like way.

"Good heavens," she says with a small laugh. "Look at me, yammering on and on."

"It's fine. It's a great story," Cameron says, chuckling. "And I could help you set up an email if you want. They're free."

"I don't own a computer."

"Neither do I. My email goes to my phone."

"To your *phone*," she says, with a dismissive wave of her rag. "Young people and their phones."

"Well, having a smartphone would make it easy to keep in touch when you move away."

At this, Tova's face stiffens. Was he not supposed to bring that up? Is her departure some big secret? But how could it be? Ethan has mentioned it casually several times. It's a source of discontent for him, his hopeless crush moving upstate.

"A smartphone. Perhaps." She smiles. "I'm sorry we didn't get a chance to say hello at Ethan's house the other night." It's like she's reading his mind.

"Ethan was super stoked about your date. How did it go?"

Tova straightens. "It was not a date."

"Okay. Your . . . dinner."

Tova folds the rag and tucks it in her back pocket, then leans on the cart. "You know, Will and I were married forty-seven years when he passed away. I cannot date."

"Why not?"

She sighs, as if the answer is beyond explaining. They clean together in silence for a while, rounding the curved hallway, pausing in front of the sea lion statue. Cameron makes a point of mopping thoroughly, getting into every corner of the alcove, under the benches and behind the trash can.

Tova polishes the creature's bald head with her rag. "Make sure you get under its tail, dear."

"Under what?"

"Under the statue's tail. Here, I'll show you." She takes her dust rag and starts to slide it under the polished brass tail. Cameron resists the urge to roll his eyes. How would that spot possibly get dirty?

"I know, I know. There's a right way to do things," Cameron mutters, but Tova's not listening. She's squinting at something in the little gap between the statue and the floor.

She stands, slowly, not taking her eyes off the thing she's clutching. A credit card? From the look on her face he expects her to say *good heavens* or *my word* or *goodness gracious*, but for a long moment, she says nothing.

"Is this your driver's license?" she finally whispers, holding the card up.

It is, in fact, his license. He'd planned to collect it from his cubby, where Terry said he would leave it, on his way out tonight. How had it gotten all the way over here?

"Yeah, actually." He holds out a hand to take it, but she grips it firmly, studying it closer.

"Cameron," she says slowly. "I know you are here in Sowell Bay looking for your father. And I know you don't have a relationship with your mother. But what is her name?"

He frowns. "Why?"

Tova waits patiently.

"Her name is Daphne."

"Daphne Cassmore?"

"Um, yeah." What is going on? He reaches again for his license and this time Tova lets him take it. Her face is as pale and thin as the moonlight streaming through the skylight.

"She was seeing him," Tova says quietly. "Your mother is the girl."

HEARING THE STORY of Erik's disappearance from Tova herself, instead of Ethan, is different. They sit on the alcove's bench, on opposite sides but facing each other across the sea lion's smooth back. In a quiet, even voice, Tova tells Cameron how her son, the summer after his senior year of high school, went to work at the ferry dock one July night and never came home. The boat no one noticed missing. The cut rope on the anchor.

"I never believed it." Tova shakes her head. "I never believed he killed himself. When I found out that Erik might have been seeing a girl, a girl his friends didn't really know about . . ."

"Wait. This girl. How do you know it was my mom?"

Tova rubs at a black smudge on the bench. Probably a mark from someone's shoe. "A former classmate. A long-forgotten memory."

"And the police never talked to this classmate?"

Tova clicks her tongue. "Adam was not a close friend, and the investigation was thorough, at first. But with no eyewitnesses and zero leads . . . well, they wanted to close the case, I suppose."

"You think my mom could've had something to do with . . ." Cameron lets out a low whistle.

Tova looks up, her face inscrutable. "I don't know. But she was seeing him, it seems. She might have been with him that night. She might be able to tell me . . ." Her voice trails off, then she swallows before adding, "Do you know how I might contact her?"

He shakes his head. "I haven't seen her since I was nine."

"You haven't heard from her? Not even a birthday card?"

The words twist like a knife in his gut. How many times has he thought the same thing to himself? Aunt Jeanne always insisted his mother loved him. That she left because that's what was best for him. That maybe someday she'd conquer her demons and be ready for a relationship. But what demons are so powerful they prevent someone from buying a ninety-nine-cent birthday card and slapping a stamp on it? How often has he convinced himself she's actually dead, because that hurts less than believing she could care about him so little?

"Nope. Not even a birthday card." He rises and walks out of the alcove. His eyes are burning, heavy and wet, and he doesn't need her to see that. A good, hard blink or two will send the tears packing.

If it were that simple, she wouldn't have let him miss out on being a part of your life. Aunt Jeanne's words crash through his skull. *For all your mother's flaws, she was no dummy.* If his father was dead . . . had died in some accident when they were both eighteen . . . well, that would be a pretty solid reason to never have brought him into Cameron's life. He squeezes his eyes shut. Could that be possible? It would mean that Tova is his . . . No, it can't be. She's so tiny, and so weird. No one else in his family is tiny or weird. And it would mean his mother was something less than terrible, not a victim, maybe even honorable like a martyr, rather than a perpetrator of his own suffering. That absolutely does not compute, so he pushes the idea out of his mind.

Tova comes to stand next to him in front of the big middle tank. They watch a school of cod drift by, propelled by the tank's fake current. If they wait four minutes, Cameron knows, they'll come by again. What a life, those endless laps.

"I'm sorry," Tova says. She places a hand on his shoulder. Doesn't rub or squeeze, just places it there, as if the contact might siphon off some of his pain. It's the sort of touch that is so warm as to be almost maternal . . . No, he pushes the thought away. She's just being nice, because Tova is extraordinarily nice, in spite of the stoic shell she puts on at first. He glances down at her, struck by how tough this tiny little lady is, how much grief her ninety-pound frame has endured. And now she's absorbing some of his, too.

How much can one person take?

In the tank, a big gray cow shark approaches, its blunt nose sweeping slow arcs along the sand, like it's looking for something.

"I'm sorry about Erik, too. I'm sorry my mom might somehow be involved," Cameron says.

"Hardly your fault, dear. But thank you."

The shark's beady eye catches notice of them, and it pauses for a second before moving on.

Tova's mouth curves into a tight smile. "Ought to get to the floors, I suppose."

ETHAN'S LIGHTS ARE out when Cameron gets home from work, ruining his plans to smooth things over. Turns out Ethan's incomprehensible ramblings had some basis after all. And deep down, somehow, Cameron strongly suspects that it's more than a rumor. His mom was involved in this town's biggest tragedy.

He keeps waiting for this information to make him sad or angry, as it should, but try as he might, he can't seem to make those emotions appear. What does it matter, anyway? Let the rumors come. Townie chatter about Daphne Cassmore can't hurt Cameron. He gives fewer than zero shits about Daphne Cassmore.

He roots around in the camper's mini fridge until he finds one of those plastic lunch trays with crackers, cheese, and deli meat. Ethan brought a bunch of them home from the store last week and insisted Cameron take a few. They've passed their expiration date, so the store can't sell them, he explained, but this stuff is so processed it's practically rot-proof. Cameron peels back the plastic, and a peppery smell wafts out from the little stack of salami in its square compartment. He assembles a little stack on a cracker and is about to take a bite when his phone dings.

It's from Avery. *You up?*

Just got home from work. Then he types out a whole explanation of the mess with his mother and Tova and Erik. The whole screen is filled with word vomit when he changes his mind and backspaces the characters. It's too much for a text message.

Avery writes back. *Paddle this week? Wednesday afternoon? You're off Wednesdays, right?*

Cameron grins into the dim camper cabin. He types, *What time? Four? Meet at shop. I can duck out a little early.*

At least she didn't suggest the crack of dawn. Four in the afternoon, he can do. He sends back a thumbs-up.

Bring a change of clothes this time. Or . . . don't. Avery adds a winking-face emoji.

Something warm, like contentment, floods through Cameron as he slips into bed.

WHAT IF

It was almost three years ago, the afternoon when the Knit-Wits learned that Mary Ann Minetti's teenage granddaughter, Tatum, had gotten pregnant. But the memory comes slamming back into Tova's consciousness like it was yesterday.

The rest of the Knit-Wits were properly scandalized by the news. But Tova, to her shame, felt only envy.

Eighteen. Tatum was eighteen, and naturally was faced with a difficult choice. The Knit-Wits debated her particular conundrum, but for Tova it was only: *what if.*

What if Erik had been in Tatum's shoes? On the other side of the exchange of genetic material, of course, but what if he'd become a father at eighteen, before his life was truncated? Tova would have a grandchild. What a gift that would have been.

Tatum went on to have the baby. Laura, Mary Ann's daughter, helped her out with childcare for this unexpected grandchild, and life went on smoothly, as far as Tova could tell. Surely that wasn't always the case. Mary Ann's family had the means to help with the baby, and Tatum wanted to keep it, and the baby's father is still reasonably supportive and involved, from what Tova can tell. An ideal outcome, really. But what about other outcomes for similar situations? The possibilities are plenty.

The birth date on Cameron's driver's license is seared into her brain. He was born that following February.

And his mother. Whoever she was. She was seeing Erik. Supposedly.

What if the father Cameron is searching for isn't his father at all? Her mind combs through all she can remember of her conversations with the boy, anything he might have said about the man he's searching for. A real estate developer, that one who has those billboards. He said something about a ring and a photograph, but Tova can't recall any other details. Nothing about Cameron's comments had ever made her think of Erik. And whatever the situation is, Cameron is convinced he has the right man. Perfectly confident.

Erik was confident like that.

Tova trails a finger over the deck chair's armrest, tracing her nail on the woodgrain. A night breeze nudges the sunflowers in her moonlit garden, causing their heads to bob, like a personal audience who agrees with her every wishful thought. But these thoughts are nonsense. Erik couldn't have had a child. Daphne Cassmore might have been dating any number of young men when she was eighteen. Carefree eighteen. The summer after senior year of high school. Who could judge her for that?

It would be an exceptional stroke of luck for something like that to happen to her. But Daphne Cassmore would have found her somehow, surely? What mother would deprive her child of a grandparent? And anyway, Tova doesn't believe in exceptional strokes of luck.

Cat alights on the deck railing and tilts his head at her. Once again, she wonders what on earth she is going to do with him. The closing of the sale of her house, and her move to Charter Village, are imminent. They don't allow pets. She called to check.

He poises as if he's about to jump on Tova's lap, but instead he leaps to the ground and curls at her feet.

As if he's trying to distance himself already.

AMAZING BONES

Tova is washing Cat's breakfast bowl when Janice calls to invite her to lunch. Lunch out, on a Monday? What could this be about? Janice suggests they meet at the Shop-Way deli, and she sounds surprised when Tova suggests the Tex-Mex place down in Elland instead.

"Really? Okay. I'll pick you up on my way," Janice says.

They're seated in a pleasantly plush booth with tortilla chips and salsa between them when Janice finally brings it up.

"This week will be your last Knit-Wits, huh?"

Tova nods.

"I guess you assumed because there are only three of us left, we'd let you off without a farewell party?"

"Oh, nonsense. I don't need a party."

"Well, Barb said she'd bring cake." Janice dredges a chip through the salsa. "So we'll have that, at least."

"How thoughtful of Barbara," Tova says. "Cake sounds lovely."

"Lovely," Janice repeats. "Tova, pardon my language, but would you cut the shit for once and tell me exactly why you think you have to do this?"

Ah, so that's what this is about. "I beg your pardon?"

"This!" Janice waves her hands around, as if the interior of the restaurant, with its quirky macrame wall hangings, is the offender. "Selling your house! Moving out of Sowell Bay! You've lived here all your life."

"Charter Village is very nice," Tova says mildly.

"Maybe it is, but these are our golden years. Why do you want to spend them with a bunch of strangers?" Janice's voice cracks. "What about us?"

Tova starts to respond, but the words catch in her throat.

"And furthermore," Janice continues, holding up a stern finger, like a judge in one of those courtroom dramas she enjoys watching, "what about Ethan Mack?"

Tova starts. "What about him?"

"Tova, he's gaga for you. Why can't you give him a chance?"

"Ethan is a wonderful man, but Will and I were—"

"Oh, stop. Look, I realize I haven't been in your shoes, but Peter and I have talked about it. When one of us goes, the other must move on. We're not that old, Tova. We still have good years ahead of us. Decades, even. Seventy is the new sixty!"

In spite of herself, Tova lets out a short chuckle. "Where did you hear that? One of those talk shows?"

"Whatever. Please, Tova, rethink this. If it's really what you want, then fine, go. But it's not the only way."

"Janice, you must understand something." Tova folds her hands in her lap. "I am not like you and Mary Ann and Barbara. I don't have children who will come stay with me when I've had a fall. I don't have grandchildren who will stop over to unclog my drain or make sure I'm taking my pills. And I won't put that burden on my friends and neighbors."

"There's your problem," says Janice softly. "Assuming it's a burden."

"Charter Village might not be the only way, but it's the best way." Tova sets her jaw. "And besides, it's done. I'm going to sign the papers for the sale of the house on Wednesday."

"And when do you move into Charter Village?"

"Next week, but I'll stay in one of those hotels down in Everett."

With a defeated smile, Janice says, "I suppose Barb and I will have to come visit once you move in, then. Maybe you can book us appointments at the fancy spa."

"Of course," Tova says.

A chipper waitress arrives moments later and, with a cheery grin, spits out a list of specialty margarita flavors. Janice requests a diet soda. Tova orders black coffee. The waitress nods and trots away but returns a moment later to apologize and explain that they don't have any coffee prepared at the moment. Not much demand for it in the afternoon. Would Tova like to wait fifteen minutes for it to brew? Or might she be interested in something from the espresso bar? Cappuccino, latte, mocha?

"A small latte, I suppose," Tova says a bit reluctantly. Espresso bar. How very indulgent.

ON TUESDAY AFTERNOON, Tova readies herself for a trip to Shop-Way, her first since that disastrous dinner at Ethan's house.

And her last, perhaps. She just needs to pick up a few essentials. The fridge is still half-full, and her moving date inches closer. Never would she have thought she could go so long between grocery runs, but those freezer casseroles have had legs. All of the potatoes and noodles and gravy and cheese have added a certain plumpness to Tova's cheeks, which she found herself admiring in her bathroom mirror this morning after she bathed. After she dressed, she even dabbed a bit of blush on her cheekbones.

Four times before she leaves, she checks to make sure the Grateful Dead T-shirt is in her tote bag. This isn't simply a shopping trip, after all. On her way out the front door, she's somewhat startled to see the newspaper still sitting there on her front mat, coiled and waiting. She was so occupied this morning that it never occurred to her to take it in. Her subscription was supposed to be canceled, but when she pointed it out to the young man on the route the other day, he just shrugged and said he might as well bring her one as long as she was still there; he always has a bunch left over anyway. Tova had smiled and thanked him. He's a nice kid, and she gave him a good tip last Christmas.

In any case, her crossword needs are now being met through other channels. Last week, Janice challenged her to a competitive crossword game through a message that popped up on her cell phone, and with one tap of a button, there were crosswords galore right there on the little screen.

So many crosswords. As many as anyone could ever want. Isn't that something?

Of course, Tova has won every match so far, but Janice is improving quickly.

At the Shop-Way, Ethan is manning the deli when Tova enters the store. With a pen tucked behind his ear, he halts the conversation he's having with a customer midsentence and waves.

"Hello, Ethan," she calls, her voice even. She lifts a shopping basket from the stack at the store's front.

"Afternoon, love," he says, giving her a resigned look before going back to taking the order of the group crowded into the booth.

Tova shops thoughtfully, giving each item she adds to her cart an extra layer of scrutiny. Jams and jellies are on promotion: buy one, get one free. But Tova doesn't need two jellies. She might not even need *one*. Of course, she won't be needing her own jam at Charter Village, although her suite will have a small kitchenette with a refrigerator. She selects a small jar of raspberry preserves, which could be brought along if she doesn't use it up this week.

Two checkout lanes are running when she finishes, and she's relieved to see that Ethan has finished with the group in the deli and is now tending the one on the left. It's no contest to choose that one, even though the line is longer. She arranges her modest collection of groceries on the belt, then carefully tucks the T-shirt, which she's rolled neatly, at the end, nestling it between her quart of milk and a waxy orange grapefruit.

"Congratulations on the sale of your house." Ethan clears his throat, as if trying to cough away the awkwardness. He rings through the bread, jam, coffee, eggs. Not looking up, he scans her packet of wafer crackers, weighs her single green apple. Finally, he picks up the white shirt, and he turns it over twice in his left hand while aiming the scanner with his right, looking for a UPC code, before recognition dawns on his face. His mouth falls open as he allows the shirt to unroll.

"Where on earth did you . . . ?" His voice sounds like it's caught in a net. "I mean, how did you find . . . ?"

Tova straightens. "I bought it on the internet."

"You *what?*"

"It was one of those online auctions. Janice Kim helped me," she admits.

Suddenly stern, he asks, "How much did you spend on this, Tova?"

"Well, I don't see how that's any of your concern."

He rolls the shirt back up and gives it a perturbed shake. "These are expensive. Thousands of dollars."

There are three customers waiting in line behind Tova now. Two of them crane their necks, straining to soak up the drama.

"There's no need to get upset," she hisses. "I'm simply replacing the item I ruined."

Ethan holds the shirt close to his chest. "It was just a T-shirt," he mumbles.

"It was important to you," Tova says, her voice shaky.

"Many things are important to me."

"I'm sorry," Tova whispers.

"Don't say that, love." His large green eyes are heavy. "I'd give away a hundred of those bloody shirts to redo that supper at my house." He holds the shirt back up, taking in the Grateful Dead concert image. He smiles at Tova. "You really bought this on the internet?"

"Indeed. And I drove to Tukwila to pick it up."

Ethan's eyes widen. "You drove all the way down there?"

"Yes."

"On the freeway?"

"Well, there wasn't another practical route."

"You're quite a woman, Tova. Did you know that?"

Tova doesn't know how to respond, so she just holds out the stack of bills to pay for her groceries. But when she arrives back home, while she smears butter on a wafer cracker and slices the single green apple, she replays his words in her head on a loop.

TOVA MEETS JESSICA SNELL at an attorney's office down in Elland at eleven on Wednesday morning, as instructed, to sign her portion of the closing papers.

The papers, it turns out, are not quite ready. The hard knot in Tova's chest softens, briefly, at the notion that she might not have to do this today. But it's a glitch with the copier; it will only delay things a few minutes. The receptionist apologizes profusely for this setback and offers Jessica and Tova coffee, which Jessica declines but Tova gladly accepts. It's the watery kind, and the paper cup has a waxy aftertaste, but Tova sips it anyway. While they wait in a small conference room, Jessica tells Tova more about the buyers, which is not information that Tova asked for, necessarily. It's a family from Texas. Three little ones. The husband's job has relocated him, and he and his wife took a trip up this summer to scope out real estate. They fell hard for Tova's house. The view, the architecture. They said that although they'll be making plenty of updates, the house has amazing bones.

"My father would be pleased to hear that," Tova says politely.

The paperwork finally makes its entrance. A woman wearing slacks and a cantaloupe-colored blouse sits next to Tova and walks her through the forms. Tova's pen scratches on the paper as she signs her name.

"The buyers do appreciate your willingness to close quickly," Jessica says. "Their agent wanted me to pass that along."

"Certainly," Tova says. A quick closing suited her as well. Why drag it out? The Texans had been gracious, too, to push back the turning over of keys for a couple of days to accommodate her Charter Village move-in date.

"And this is a little odd, but they also noted that the house was phenomenally neat and tidy when they did the inspection," Jessica says with a genuine smile. "Their agent told me the wife said it looked like something out of a magazine. I thought you might enjoy hearing that."

Tova lets out a small laugh. "As I'm sure you're aware, I am nothing if not neat and tidy."

"Everyone in Sowell Bay is aware of that. You'll be missed, Tova."

With a smile and congratulations, the woman in the cantaloupe blouse shakes her hand, and then Jessica Snell shakes her hand, too. Tova never liked shaking hands, well, not with people, anyway. Octopuses are another story. But she clasps.

So, it's done.

LATER THAT AFTERNOON, Tova ventures up to the attic, to what little is left of the piles of linens and photographs. It's time to finish now.

On the ceiling, the rafters glow in the afternoon sun. Tova eases herself down to lie on her back on the floor and stares up at the beams the way she used to when she was a teenager. Like the house is a great wooden monster and she's looking, from inside, at its rib cage. It does indeed have amazing bones, and it will make a good home for someone. For this family from Texas. For their three little ones.

Will the children use the attic as a playroom? Tova hopes so. She pictures three happy siblings, laughing together under the rafters, talking to one another in pint-sized Texas accents. Perhaps there will be more children; perhaps the parents are not done yet, and the family will grow, filling the house, bursting it from the seams like the large clan from Ethan's unfulfilled dream. The parents will grow old atop this mountain of a family they've built, and even if parts of it crumble, from time to time, there will be enough left to support them.

They will not have to pack up tea towels alone.

She drags in a long breath and sits up. "Enough of that," she says aloud. Enough of allowing one single summer night in 1989 to shape every last aspect of her life. Enough searching for answers that no longer exist. Enough of living with these ghosts, in this house. Charter Village will be a new start.

For the next two hours, she packages up the remaining towels and sheets and other odds and ends. To a box of books she's keeping, packed half-full so it won't be too unwieldy, she adds the Sowell Bay High School yearbook where she first found Daphne Cassmore.

She remembers the photo, the young woman's smiling face, now pressed between the pages of the heavy book. Had it been a fool's errand, attempting to find her? Perhaps, but how could she not try? Wherever and whoever she is, Daphne Cassmore is the last person who saw Erik alive. Tova will never be able to stop her gaze from lingering on faces in crowds that bear even a slight resemblance to that yearbook photo.

On the other side of the picture window, a spotless blue sky holds court over the water, whose ripples shimmer gently as a speedboat cuts a wedge-shaped wake across the bay. How strange it will be at Charter Village, whose campus is several miles inland. How strange to wake up in the morning and not see the water.

"I wish you could tell me," she says to the bay. She will always wish this. But even knowing what happened that night can't bring him back. Nothing can.

She closes the box flaps and seals them up with tape.

A BIG, BOLD LIE

Moth Sausage always played the same sequence of songs to end a show. Cameron strums the opening chords of the last number on his Fender, and even though the guitar isn't plugged in, the sound fills Ethan's small living room, where Cameron is sprawled on the sofa, waiting for his clothes to finish drying downstairs. It's Wednesday, after all, and Tova is always going on about how Wednesday is laundry day. Apparently, this must've wormed its way into Cameron's brain, because without really thinking about it, the first thing he did when he woke up this morning was bundle up his dirty clothes from the floor of the camper, grab his jug of knockoff Tide, and head for the utility room in Ethan's basement.

With a showy strum, he hits one of the trickier chords just right. Hell yeah, still got it. He's hardly played this summer, and the instrument's coarse metal strings are sharp on the tender pads of his fingers. But it's a good type of pain.

Yawning, he nests the guitar between two lumpy sofa cushions, then grabs a bite of cereal from his bowl on the side table and swipes milk off his chin with the back of his hand before standing and sauntering over to the front window. His camper looks kind of dirty from here, the glare of the sun highlighting the grimy windshield. Maybe he'll wash it this afternoon, before he goes to meet Avery for their paddle date.

Ethan's patchy front lawn is fading to a tawny brown. Everyone keeps talking about how hot and dry it's been. "Hot and dry" has a different meaning in Modesto, but lately Cameron finds himself nodding along, as if the Modesto is slowly draining out of him. When did that start to happen?

"Mornin'." Ethan comes through the living room, leaving the smell of soap in his wake. Cameron follows him into the kitchen. His beard looks damp, and he's attempted to slick down the wiry fuzz that normally floats over his mostly bald head. Instead of wearing a ratty old rock band tee or one of his usual flannels, he's got some striped golf-type collared shirt on. Cameron hadn't realized Ethan owned something so . . . normal. The shirt is tucked into a pair of khaki pants that are an inch too short, the waist saddled under his bulblike belly by a braided-leather belt.

"Why are you dressed like an extra from *Caddyshack*?" A corner of Cameron's mouth ticks up, teasing. "Do you have another date with Tova?"

Ethan fills his teakettle at the sink. "Tova? No." With a *click*, he turns on the burner and sets the kettle on the coil. "I mean, I'll stop over there this week to say goodbye, a'course."

"Oh. Right." Cameron wishes he could take back the *Caddyshack* jab.

"Doing an interview at the store today," Ethan says. He takes a travel mug down from the cupboard and drops in a teabag of his usual English Breakfast. "Need to hire a new day manager, or a temporary one, anyway. You heard what happened to Melody Patterson, right? Her little boy's got some awful disease. Had to be admitted to the children's hospital down in Seattle. She's taking an extended leave of absence to care for him."

"That's terrible," Cameron says. And it is. Melody Patterson is a nice lady. But it's Ethan's first words that sting him, slicing through poor Melody's tragedy to spear him personally.

A manager. Had Ethan even considered Cameron for the position? He remembers his first night here, drunk on expensive scotch, when he asked for a job at the store.

Ethan starts going on about Melody's husband, and something about how their insurance is being a "real pain in the arse" about the kid's coverage. Details that are surely none of his damn business, but Ethan clearly has no boundaries when chatting with his customers while scanning their milk and weighing their tomatoes.

"Hey," Cameron interrupts. "Are you still taking applications?"

"For the manager job? I s'pose so. Why, do you have someone in mind?"

The tips of Cameron's ears burn so hot, they must be glowing. "Me, obviously."

"You?" Ethan looks genuinely surprised. "Well . . . maybe." Then he shakes his head. "See, it's a manager job. Would normally be looking for someone with years of experience. Need to be familiar with all the systems. Inventory, point of sale, even a bit of bookkeeping. It's not to be taken lightly."

"Do you really think I couldn't do . . ." Cameron yanks back the words before they come tumbling out. *Do you really think I couldn't do your job?* He tries again. "Look. I might not have years of experience. I don't even have a degree or whatever. But we both know I'm smart." His voice wavers. "I'm really smart."

Ethan's eyes widen. "I never said you weren't smart, Cameron."

"Well, then, I can learn."

"Aye, you could." Ethan pops the top on his travel mug. "If you really want to work in the grocery business, I'll show you the ropes. Nothin' would please me more. But right this minute, I need to fill this position with someone . . . already qualified."

"Oh, give me a break." Cameron stomps over to the kitchen window, nearly tripping over one of the kitchen chairs on his way. "What exactly are the qualifications to work at Shop-Way, anyway? Running your mouth all the time?" He turns back and glares at Ethan.

Ethan's usual reddish cheeks grow even redder.

Cameron knows he should stop, but he keeps digging. "Airing the whole town's dirty laundry?" Dig, dig. "Talking shit about people's private lives?" Dig, dig, dig. "Spreading rumors about my mom?"

"I was trying to find her." Ethan's voice is quiet but firm. "I was trying to help."

"I never asked for your help."

"I wasn't doing it for you."

Cameron is about to fire back when Ethan's words catch up with him.

"I was doing it for her," Ethan continues. "For Tova. To help bring her . . . closure."

From the basement, the dryer buzzes, the sound muffled through the kitchen floor. Cycle complete.

"Whatever," Cameron mutters, stalking off toward his camper. He'll come back later for the laundry.

IT'S A CRAPPY, fitful nap, but it's better than nothing. Aunt Jeanne always said, when shit starts to go sideways first thing in the morning, go back to bed and start over.

Sounds about right for today.

But at some point, Cameron must've fallen into a deep sleep, because it's no longer morning when he wakes to incessant buzzing. Afternoon light pours through the camper's windows, and he squints as he ruffles through his bedding in search of his phone.

Shit. Avery. The paddle date. Is it past four? The camper is hot and stuffy inside, the way it always is when it's been baking in the sun all day. Where the hell is his phone? What happened to the alarm he set?

Finally, he finds it on the floor, under a dirty sock that must've escaped this morning's laundry roundup. He's about to answer, a string of apologies ready to stream from his sleep-slick tongue, when he realizes it's only three. Then he registers the number. A Seattle area code, but it's not Avery.

"Hello?"

A woman's voice replies, "Mr. Cassmore?"

"Uh, yeah? I mean, yes, that's me."

"Excellent. I'm glad I reached you. This is Michelle Yates with Brinks Development."

Cameron sits straight up.

"I know you've contacted us several times trying to secure an appointment, and I apologize for the delay. Mr. Brinks has been out of town. But he has returned, and as it happens, he has an opening in his schedule later today. I know it's last-minute, but would you be available to meet then?"

"Meet? With . . . him? Today?"

"This is Cameron Cassmore the developer, correct?" A note of doubt creeps into Michelle's voice.

Okay, so that was a tiny fib.

Michelle goes on, "You left several messages a couple of weeks ago, looking to meet with Mr. Brinks about a new opportunity?"

All right, maybe it was an actual fabrication.

Cameron clears his throat. "Oh. Yeah, definitely. That's me." He can't believe that story he spun on those voice mails worked. It actually worked. All these weeks of showing up at closed offices and empty bluffs, and it was this that worked. A big, bold lie. Ignoring the twinge of guilt that nags at him, he says, "Yes, I can be there. What time?"

Michelle tells him to be there at six o'clock, and gives him a Seattle address, which he scrawls on the back of a gas station receipt. "You'll want to take the elevator all the way down to the basement," she adds, which strikes Cameron as odd. A basement office?

As soon as he hangs up with Michelle, Cameron calls Terry, who answers on the fourth ring, sounding distracted.

"I hate to ask," Cameron says, "but would it be a problem if I took this afternoon off? I could still be there to clean tonight. I just have a . . . thing." He inhales, then gives Terry the details about the situation with Simon Brinks in what he hopes is a professional manner.

"Sure, Cameron." Terry still sounds preoccupied. Had he heard a word of what Cameron said?

"Thanks, sir. And, um . . . maybe soon, could we talk about hiring me on permanently for the cleaning part? You know, like . . . not temporary?"

"Sure, sure." A flurry of muffled voices on the line. "Hey, kiddo, I've got to run. No worries about tonight. Take your time, okay?"

"Okay."

He ends the call, shrugging off Terry's weirdness. Probably just caught him at a busy time. Then he opens his map app and enters the Seattle address Michelle gave him. It's a two-hour drive. Which means that at four, he needs to be on the road. Not on a paddleboard.

Avery will understand. He'll stop by the shop on his way out of town and tell her in person.

SHORTLY BEFORE FOUR, he pushes open the door of the Sowell Bay Paddle Shop.

A figure pops up from behind a rack of wet suits in the far corner of the store. To Cameron's surprise, it's not Avery.

It's her son, Marco.

The kid gives him a stiff nod, then ducks back down behind the rack without a word.

"Um, hey," Cameron says. "Your mom here?"

"She went on some errand," Marco is kneeling on the polished wood floor next to an open box, holding some black plastic thing with a trigger and a thin strip of waxy-looking paper trailing from its snout. A pricing gun.

"I didn't know you worked here," Cameron says, poking at a

display of bright orange flipper fins. These are new since last time he was here. They're lined up in a perfect row from smallest to largest. It looks like someone stole the feet from a family of ducks and strung them up on the wall.

Marco grunts. "Not like I have a choice." He slaps a price sticker on the tag of a neoprene life vest and threads its topmost loop onto a long metal peg coming out of the wall.

"Ah. Compulsory child labor. A rite of passage." Cameron laughs.

Marco doesn't respond.

"So, any idea when your mom will be back?" Cameron glances toward the front door. "We were supposed to meet here at four." He checks the time. Five minutes until.

Marco looks up. "Were?"

"Yeah. We were supposed to take a couple of boards out on the water, but something . . . came up." Cameron bites his lip, stopping short of telling Marco the whole story. He doesn't owe any explanation to a teenager.

"You're standing her up." Marco's voice is flat.

"Of course not. She'll totally understand."

Marco fires off another sticker. "Right."

"And I came here to tell her myself." Cameron checks the time again. On the road at four. The most important meeting of his life. He can't be late. He clears his throat. "Thing is, I kind of have to go. Could you let your mom know I came by? Tell her I'm sorry for canceling?"

"Sure. I'll tell her."

"Thanks, man." Cameron ducks out of the store, and by the time four o'clock hits, he's headed toward the freeway.

THE SOB

Seattle is a dizzying maze of buildings and bypasses, tunnels and byways, skyscrapers that might be built right on top of the highway itself, like something from an impossible Lego set. There are exits left, exits right, viaducts and express lanes, the overpasses and underpasses all curling around each other like a bunch of huge concrete spaghetti noodles jammed against the hillside that rises steeply from the water.

He drove through it before, on his way from the airport, but it hits him more clearly now. Compared to Modesto, this really is a different world.

When he spots the exit for Capitol Hill coming up, he flicks on the turn signal. Stay right, then turn left, three blocks and a right. He'd memorized the series of turns, the post-freeway route through the city streets, just in case.

Finally, he turns onto the right street and starts looking for the street number, drawing irritated honks from passing traffic as he inches along, scanning the tightly packed storefronts, coffee shops and juice bars and vintage clothing stores with their goods spilled out onto sidewalk racks. It's ten minutes until six on a perfect August evening, and the neighborhood bustles, a mixture of hipsters and neighborhood folks tethered to dogs. Commuters with messenger bags and purposeful strides.

Here's the address Michelle Yates had given him. He double-checks to make sure, because it's a plain gray door. After weeks of trying to get this meeting . . . this is Brinks Development? He had expected some shiny office tower, but maybe this is how successful people do it in Seattle. Shaved yam instead of pastrami and humble storefronts instead of steel skyscrapers.

By some miracle, on his second circle around the block, he spots an open space right in front.

He cuts the ignition and checks his phone. Still nothing from Avery. Should he send a text? Nah, he'll call her after. By then, he'll have a story about his father to tell. The slam of the camper's cab door is swallowed up by the busy city sounds. He feeds the meter with two crumb-coated quarters he digs out of the console.

To Cameron's surprise, the plain gray door is unlocked. It opens to a nondescript vestibule, apparently an apartment building. On the wall to his left there's a row of slightly dinged-up metal mail-boxes, a half dozen of them. Several fliers and pieces of junk mail litter the floor.

On the right, there's a staircase that only goes up. Directly ahead, on the back wall, there's an elevator, and Cameron notices that it has call buttons for both up and down. Michelle had said to take the elevator to the basement.

"Down the rabbit hole," he says to himself as the elevator dings.

Right away as he exits, there's this weird smell. Something waxy and spicy, like cinnamon, out of place for the middle of summer. It hits Cameron as soon as the elevator doors open. It must be coming from the candles, which are everywhere in the dark hallway, candles against mirrors on both sides making it look like there are a million little flames going off into infinity. Upon further inspection, he discovers that they're fake candles. Which makes sense. What fire code allows someone to put so many candles in a basement?

What the hell is this place?

He follows a threadbare gray carpet down the hall and around a corner, which deposits him inside the world's tiniest cocktail lounge.

It's empty. A short bar, five stools tucked underneath. Warm light reflects off the brass ceiling tiles, giving the whole place a yellowish glow.

On the bar, there's a small paper square propped in a holder. A menu. *Mudminnow's Bespoke Libations*, it says at the top, followed by a list of drinks with ridiculous names. He blinks at the prices, making sure he's reading them right. Do people not realize they can get a six-pack at any grocery store for half the price of one of these *libations*? He pulls out a bar stool and sits.

Something *clink*s, and Cameron looks up to see a girl come through a doorway behind the bar. She has short, bright green hair that reminds Cameron of flattened grass. She balances a stack of highball glasses in each hand, and her eyebrows register the tiniest moment of surprise before she begins to unload the glassware into some unseen shelf down in the well. "We open at eight," she says, without looking up.

"I have a meeting." Cameron clears his throat. "With Mr. Brinks."

The grass-haired girl looks up. The expression on her face is painfully blank, as if Cameron were the least interesting thing she's ever encountered.

"I'm serious," he says. "Michelle set it up." He hopes it's okay to call Michelle by her first name.

The girl shrugs. "Okay," she says, ducking away. "I'll let him know."

SIMON BRINKS.

Cameron has repeated the name in his head so many times these last two months, has studied so many photos of the coiffed man blown up huge on his billboards, that when this disheveled dude emerges from behind the bar with a tired smile, he almost doesn't believe it could be him.

"Hi," Cameron says, his voice suddenly shaky and nervous. "I'm—"

"I know who you are, Cameron." Behind the bar, Simon's smile broadens.

"You do?" Cameron's heart hammers, but is it from nerves, or rage? Somehow the idea of socking or extorting this guy seems preposterous.

"Why do you think I suggested this venue?" Simon Brinks waves a hand around the tiny room. "As I'm sure you've discovered, I have lots of offices and properties, but this place was originally for Daphne. It's the perfect spot for us to meet."

Cameron's pulse is pounding now. For Daphne? Is Brinks about to fess up to a lifetime of deadbeat parenthood, just like that?

Simon smiles. "You met Natalie." He tips his head toward the doorway behind the bar, through which the grass-haired girl had disappeared. "She knows the whole story."

"The whole story." Cameron can barely force the words out.

"Well, sure. She's my daughter."

Daughter. His head whirls. A father and . . . a sister? Before he can stop himself, his eyes dart to the doorway behind the bar again. Could that girl with the strange hair really be his half sister?

Simon clasps his hands and leans on the bar. "You have your mother's eyes, you know."

"My mother." Cameron swallows hard.

"Daphne always had those incredible eyes."

Cameron sucks in an embarrassingly sharp breath. She did have pretty eyes, didn't she? He wonders whether he's inventing this or if he actually remembers.

"Anyway," Brinks says, with a slight shrug that seems to knock the conversation in a more casual direction. "Can I pour you a drink?"

"A drink?"

"I make a mean old-fashioned."

"Uh, a beer is fine. Whatever you have," Cameron blurts. His ears burn. Why does he care? Is impressing one's father a hardwired predisposition?

Without a word, Brinks reaches down into a below-counter refrigerator and rises again with two longnecks clutched between his fingers. The bottles hiss as he pops the caps. "Cheers," he says, lofting one.

"Cheers," Cameron echoes. How bizarre will this story be later? When he tells it to Avery and Elizabeth, in turn?

"So, you have questions about your mother, naturally," Brinks says, after a long pull on his beer.

Cameron pulls himself up by the shoulders. No more chicken-shit. His voice is even when he says, "I have questions about you."

"Oh?" Simon cocks his head. "Okay, well. Everyone thinks I'm some sort of enigma, but for you, I'm an open book." He smiles. "So, shoot."

"Why did you . . ." Cameron swallows, then regroups before trying again. "I mean . . . how could you . . ." A sob messes up his throat. Why didn't he make a secondary plan for when the words wouldn't come?

"How could I what?" Simon Brinks scrapes his chin. "Let her go? Well, I cared about her."

Cameron's face hardens, and his voice is pure acid when he spits out, "But you never cared about me."

"You? Of course I care about you. You're her son. But what could I do, once she was—"

"I'm your son, too!" Cameron's voice cracks.

Simon Brinks takes a step backward, recovers. "I'm sorry, Cameron. You're not," he says softly.

"I'm your son," Cameron repeats.

Brinks shakes his head. "That's never how it was with me and Daphne."

"But it must have been." To Cameron's horror, his chin starts to tremble. He knew this might happen, right? The whole thing being a dead end. He prepared himself for this, or tried to. So why is he about to lose his shit right now?

"Like I said, I'm not surprised you're here, Cameron, but—"

"Why did you give her your class ring?" Cameron fishes it from his pocket and drops it onto the bar. Simon picks it up and a faint smile comes over his face as he examines it. When he turns it over and looks at the underside, the smile fades.

"This isn't mine," he says quietly.

"Oh, come on. I saw the picture."

Brinks carefully places the ring on the bar. "Daphne was my best friend," he says. "Look, I know how that sounds, but we really were just friends. Best friends."

Cameron is about to fire back. But then he remembers Aunt Jeanne's constant digs about him and Elizabeth. A heavy feeling sinks through him like a lead balloon. He's no closer to finding his father than he was two months ago.

"You never, um . . . slept with her?" Cameron hates how crass the question sounds.

"No, I did not." Brinks chuckles. Then his face goes somber. "Look, I'll do a cheek swab if you want. I'm a hundred percent sure on this one." He picks up the class ring and turns it over again before replacing it on the bar. "Hang on. I'll be right back."

He returns a few minutes later with a beat-up hardcover book and something cupped in his hand. The book gives off a puff of dust when he sets it on the bar. The cover reads SOWELL BAY HIGH SCHOOL, CLASS OF 1989. Presumably the source of all those photos someone scanned and posted, including the one of Simon and Daphne on the pier. Then Brinks extends his palm. "This one is mine, see."

Cameron picks up the ring and holds it in his left hand, while holding one he's brought with him in his right. The weight feels identical. So close, yet . . . wrong.

Brinks tips his head toward the back of the bar. "There's a big unfinished space back there. I use it for storage. But I suppose it's also sort of fitting that all this high school stuff lives down here. It was supposed to be our place, after all."

"Our place"? What's that supposed to mean? Cameron turns the ring over, expecting to see the EELS engraving, but to his surprise, it says SOB.

"What's SOB?" he asks.

Brinks chuckles. "My initials. I'm Simon Orville Brinks. Mind you, I don't advertise that, because the jokes practically write themselves. Lucky son of a bitch, huh?"

Cameron stares at the two gold rings on the bar top. "You had it engraved with your initials? Did everyone do that?"

"Most people did, I guess." Brinks shrugs. "Lots of people tried to get cute with the personalization. A bunch of youth-group types all got theirs with 'GOD.' And I'm sure more than one kid had a ring that said 'ASS.' I thought about getting 'ASS,' but my mama would've shanked me."

"Do you remember anything about this one?" Cameron picks up EELS. Whoever he is, he must be a big fan of marine life. Or sushi. Did he pay extra for that fourth letter?

Brinks shakes his head. "I wish I could help you."

"You don't know EELS?"

Brinks adds softly, "I never knew my father, either."

"Yeah, and somehow you still ended up a zillionaire." Cameron's shoulders slump.

"I worked hard," Brinks says, and there's an edge to his voice now. "Look, I came from Sowell Bay, too. Do you know how your mother and I met? Became best friends?"

"Um . . . no?" Cameron honestly hadn't thought about this. Even when he thought they were together, he'd assumed they met at school, like everyone else.

"We lived in the same crappy apartment building; she lived there for a while our junior and senior year," Brinks says. "On the wrong side of the highway."

"I didn't know there was a wrong side of the highway in Sowell Bay."

Brinks lets out a hard laugh. "Well, these days, the whole place is sort of on the wrong side of the highway, but it's turning back around." His tone shifts; he's talking business now. "Lots of development these last few years. I'm doing a waterfront condo project up there. Really nice units."

Cameron nods. For a sparse second, he wonders whether Brinks would hire him to work the project. But he'd probably ask for references, and, well . . . that's a no-go. Even for his former best friend's son.

"Anyway." Brinks leans over, propping his elbows on the bar again. "I asked you to meet me here instead of at my regular office because I thought you might get a kick out of seeing it." He picks up the cocktail menu and, staring at it, says, "Like I said, I made this place for her."

Cameron looks around the tiny lounge, now thoroughly baffled. A ridiculously small bar in the basement of a nondescript apartment building on Capitol Hill . . . for his mom?

"We talked about something like this, together, once we grew up a little. Mind you, this was back in the eighties, when speakeasies weren't a total hipster cliché." Brinks rolls his eyes. "I don't even know how two teenagers come up with that sort of idea, but we used to spend hours talking about it." His face grows more somber. "Of course, that was before her . . . problems."

"Problems," Cameron mutters.

Brinks is still studying the menu in his hands. "She even picked the name of the place, strange as it is." He looks up with a half smile. "Mudminnow. It's a—"

"It's a tiny fish," Cameron cuts in. "They live in rivers and other fresh water. Can survive really bad conditions. Extreme temperatures, hardly any oxygen in the water. So they're usually the last thing to survive when shit goes south. They're like the cockroaches of the tiny-fish world. But with a much cooler name."

Brinks gapes. "How on earth do you know all of that?"

Cameron shrugs and explains that he read it somewhere, once. "I retain random knowledge. I kind of can't help it."

Brinks laughs. "You're exactly like your mother, you know."

Cameron's mouth drops open. "I am?"

"Oh, absolutely. She wanted to apply to be on *Jeopardy!* after we graduated." He clears his throat. "Her family never understood her. She hid her real self from them, I think. Even from her sister."

Big, hot, fat tears hang in the corners of Cameron's eyes. He can feel that his lips are pressed into an embarrassing, involuntary grimace.

"That's just the face she made when something unpleasant surprised her," Brinks says.

Cameron presses a fist against his pursed lips. "I guess I always assumed I got this weird photographic memory from my father."

"Well, maybe from him, too," Brinks says. "Daphne never told me who your father was."

Cameron snorts softly. "That makes two of us."

"Daphne was an oddly private person sometimes. We were incredibly close, but I know there are many parts of her life she never shared with me. This was one of them. I'm sure she had her reasons."

"Yeah, well, because of her *reasons*, I grew up with no parents. I'm sure she had good *reasons* for abandoning me, too."

"I have no doubt she did," Brinks says, without a trace of sarcasm. "She loved you, Cameron, more than anything in the world. I know that much. Anything she did, it was from a place of love."

Something clatters in a semi-close sort of way, probably from beyond the door behind the bar. Is the grass-haired girl listening in on all of this? What was the daughter's name? Natalie? A wave of nausea hits him square in the gut. She knows the whole story. Her father's brilliant best friend who got pregnant and went off the rails, and the son who might come looking for them someday. As usual, Cameron is the last to know.

Brinks sighs. "I wish I could tell you more. I feel terrible that you came all the way up here, expecting one thing and finding . . . another."

"Do you know where she is?" Cameron twists his hands together in his lap. Did he really ask that? Does he even want to know?

But, to his semi-relief, Simon just shakes his head and says, "No, not anymore. I haven't seen her in several years."

"What was she—I mean, where—"

"She was living in Eastern Washington somewhere, back then. She showed up at my house. Needed cash. Which I gave her, of course. But it was clear she was still struggling, Cameron. Still using." His brow creases. "Maybe I shouldn't have given her the money? I don't know. Part of me wanted to drag her into my house, put her up in the guest room. Fix her. But I had my hands full with Natalie already. And, well . . . you can't fix someone who is determined to stay broken."

"Right." Cameron fakes a smile. "I guess I'm a chip off the old block."

"Don't sell yourself short, Cameron."

"I can't even put trash liners in the right way."

Brinks shoots him a puzzled look.

"At the aquarium. I've been working there, chopping fish and cleaning. And the trash cans—oh, never mind." Cameron cuts off his own pointless rambling. Simon Brinks, renowned real estate tycoon and speakeasy owner, from the wrong side of the highway but bootstrapped his way into wild success, doesn't want to hear about janitor problems.

After a long pause, Brinks says, "Daphne would've been proud of you, Cameron."

"Yeah, I'm sure." Cameron slaps a five-dollar bill on the bar, hoping that will cover a Mudminnow's beer. Close enough, anyway.

Brinks pushes away the cash, but Cameron is already halfway to the door.

A NEW ROUTE

B ack in the cab of the parked camper, Cameron smacks the steering wheel. He checks his phone, anticipating a message from Avery, hoping for an excuse to call her back and unload the events of the last hour on a sympathetic ear, but there's nothing. Well, now what? He drums his fingers on the dash and watches the steady stream of Capitol Hill foot traffic go by. People grabbing dinner, picking up dry cleaning, window-shopping. All of them, with their normal, happy lives.

Screw them.

How long does he sit there before the phone dings? When it does, he jumps. A text message, but it's not from Avery, it's from Brad. A photo. Cameron taps on it. A tiny baby squints back at him, its squishy red face wrapped up in a light blue blanket. It does look like an alien spawn, but a cute alien spawn. A single quadrant of Elizabeth's face is visible in the photo, but Cameron can tell she's beaming. Not dying from a precipitous childbirth: a benefit of the twenty-first century.

Cameron closes his eyes and takes a deep breath. He texts back, *Bro, you're a dad!* Brad responds seconds later with the head-exploding emoji.

While he's texting, he writes one to Avery, too. *Hey, can we talk?* He fires the message off into the cellular-network void, then shifts the camper into gear and pulls out of the parking space.

Traffic is horrible leaving Seattle, but Cameron couldn't tell you whether he's been sitting in gridlock for ten minutes or three hours. The camper creeps along, and brake lights from the sea of idling cars blend together, a haze of smeary red. On the passenger seat, his phone dings repeatedly, and while stopped he steals a look, thinking it might be Avery, but it's Brad again. More pictures of the baby. He shoves the phone under a fast-food bag that's sitting on the seat. Out of sight, out of mind.

But his mind has other ideas. And it will not shut up about them. From somewhere deep in his brain, a voice needles him. *None of this was ever real*, it nags. *Too good to be true. This isn't your life. This is not your home. He wasn't your father. She's not your girlfriend.*

At least he has a job he doesn't hate. How many times has Tova assured him that Terry is definitely planning to offer him the permanent position? And that it's well-deserved? Even Cameron must admit that his glass polishing has come a long way. He makes that shit sparkle. And he can do the entire loop with the mop, including all the random nooks and crannies, in under an hour now.

But then, the needling voice cuts in, *why didn't he offer the job?* Especially when Cameron asked about it this afternoon?

You're not as good as you think you are, the voice sneers. *Not even qualified to run a small-town supermarket.*

"Shut up," Cameron mutters to himself, swinging into the leftmost lane and stepping on the gas.

Eventually, traffic thins out, and at some point, the fuel light comes on. Cameron blinks at it. He's only twenty-something miles from Sowell Bay. He could probably make it. Live on the edge. But he pulls off at the next exit and finds a gas station.

The convenience store cashier gives him a pleasant smile as she rings up his bag of chips and a bottle of soda. Dinner. Cameron doesn't smile back. It's like he doesn't remember how. His face is frozen in neutral as the clerk asks him how he's doing tonight in a making-conversation sort of way.

He ignores the question and instead tells her add on a pack of smokes.

While gasoline glugs from the pump nozzle into the camper, he scrolls his phone, but it's purely reflexive, like his eyes are registering that words and photos are rolling by but his brain isn't downloading any of it. Until a picture catches his attention.

Katie.

Did she unblock him? He taps her name, and sure enough, her profile loads. There she is, with her haughty smile. Like she invented the world, and he's just lucky enough to live in it.

She's posted a million new pictures this summer. Cameron whizzes through her feed. In half of the photos, some asshat has his arm slung around her, always wearing some idiotic wraparound sunglasses so that Cameron can't even see the guy's stupid face.

Has he moved into her apartment yet? He probably remembered to put his name on the lease. Works in some boring office. Drives a brand-new SUV and has never once needed the four-wheel drive. Uses an electric toothbrush. They probably get together with his parents for dinner on the weekends.

Screw every last one of these people with their normal, happy lives. Cameron will never get there, no matter how hard he tries. Not even here in Washington.

He opens his map app. Types in a new route. Sowell Bay to Modesto.

Fifteen hours.

AN EARLY ARRIVAL

The doors are propped open when Tova arrives on Wednesday evening. It's a bit earlier than usual, but Terry had sounded so wound up when he called. She'd left her supper plate unwashed and poured a hasty bowl of kibble for Cat before hurrying down to the aquarium.

Is this about the open door? Her stomach lurches, remembering what happened when Cameron left the back door open and Marcellus tried to escape. But a moment later, Terry comes sauntering out with a broad smile and a wave.

"What's happening here?" she asks, approaching.

"Big night. And I don't mean only because it's your second-to-last day."

Tova tilts her head.

"We're getting a delivery," Terry continues. He's downright giddy. "Never thought it would happen before you left. And I called you because I thought you'd want to be here to meet it." He laughs. "*It*. Listen to me! *Her*. I thought you'd want to meet *her*."

Who on earth is "her"?

Before Tova can ask, a truck rumbles into the parking lot. With a series of loud beeps, it backs up toward the doors. A gruff-looking man loads a wooden crate from a refrigerated enclosure onto a forklift. At first, the delivery person seems keen to deposit the large box right there, but Terry talks him into helping him transport it inside. Clutching her pocketbook, Tova follows the two men as they guide the huge crate through the open doors and around the curved hallway, which seems to be quite a project.

She trails them into the pump room, where they deposit the crate. It sloshes audibly as they edge it onto the floor. In a flash, the delivery driver has vanished with the forklift.

"Keep an eye on that for a minute, will you, Tova?" Terry says. "I need to go sign the paperwork." He trots away after the deliveryman.

Tova takes a closer look at the crate. On one side, in big, red, stenciled letters, it reads: THIS SIDE UP. On the other it says: LIVE OCTOPUS.

"Keep an eye on it. What's that supposed to mean?" Tova asks Marcellus as she peers through the narrow glass panel on the back of his tank. The LIVE OCTOPUS crate sits silent in the center of the room, so still that Tova wonders whether there's anything alive inside at all. What is she meant to be keeping an eye on?

Marcellus waves an arm, a noncommittal gesture. He doesn't know, either.

"I suppose we'll see, won't we?" Tova muses. "In any event, it looks like you're about to have a new neighbor."

A couple tanks down from Marcellus, there's one that's been emptied. Pacific nettle sea stars were there before. Where have they gone? The empty tank looks too clean, its water too clear. Tova pokes her head out of the pump room; Terry's nowhere in sight. Quickly, she drags out the step stool and lifts the octopus tank's lid. Marcellus pokes the tip of an arm through the surface of the water, and Tova lowers her hand. He curls his arm around her wrist in a gesture that's well beyond familiar now, and there's something almost instinctive about it, like the way a newborn baby will clutch at its mother's finger.

But Marcellus isn't a baby. As octopuses go, he's an old man. And now his replacement has arrived. Footsteps echo from the hallway, and Tova yanks her hand from the water, climbs down, and tucks the stool under the tank. She's drying her arm on the hem of her shirt when Terry strides back in, holding a hammer.

"What do you think? Shall we open her up?"

"Your new octopus," Tova says, confirming.

"Yes! A bit ahead of schedule, actually. But she's a rescue, re-habbed by a group up in Alaska after she got trapped in a crab pot and tore herself up trying to get out. I couldn't say no." Terry cracks open one edge of the crate with the tail end of the hammer.

Tova folds her arms. "Ahead of schedule?"

Terry sighs. "Marcellus is . . . well, Tova, I'm sure you've no-ticed, but he's very old for a giant Pacific octopus." He heaves up the crate's lid, grunting. "Feisty old man, though, isn't he? Determined to outrun his life span. But Dr. Santiago and I aren't sure how much longer he has left. He was in such bad shape this morning, he might only have weeks or days left."

"I see," Tova says. She glances over at Marcellus's tank, but he must be tucked away in his den, because he's nowhere to be seen now.

"It's amazing how long he's lived." Terry shoots Tova a curious look. "Did you know Marcellus was a rescue, too?"

Tova lifts a brow, surprised. "I did not know that."

"He was in rough shape when we brought him in. Missing half an arm, his body all chewed up. Didn't think he'd make it through the year. And here we are, four years later . . ." Terry smiles and shakes his head. "He's been a good boy. Except when he's roaming around the building at night."

Tova's pulse quickens. After all this time . . . now she'll be scolded for enabling. For throwing out that horrible clamp.

At the look on her face, Terry says, "It's okay, Tova. At the end of the day, I'm not sure any sort of security measure would've worked." He shakes his head again. "The new one will have better manners. I hope."

Inside the wooden crate is a steel barrel, its top fine mesh. Something sloshes and slaps inside.

"Well, let's take a look, shall we? I wish we could call her something, but I promised naming rights to Addie, and she stayed up half the night last night brainstorming and making lists." At the mention of his daughter, Terry grins. Tova knows Addie was four when she named Marcellus, so now she's eight, and still reveling in the joy of naming an octopus, which is rather sweet.

"She'll come up with something wonderful, I have no doubt," Tova says.

The barrel's lid pops off easily, and Tova can't help but chuckle. Marcellus would've never endured a journey down the coast in such a flimsy enclosure. He'd have slipped out somewhere off the coast of British Columbia.

"There she is," Terry says softly.

Tova peers in. The octopus is huddled in the bottom of the barrel, which makes sense because there's nowhere to hide in there. Tova is surprised at the creature's salmon-pink color, so different from Marcellus and his rusty orange.

"Are you going to move her to the tank now?"

"Not tonight. I need to wait for Dr. Santiago. She's coming first thing tomorrow morning."

Tova watches the new octopus trail a tentative tentacle out from the clump she's balled herself up in, then yank it back after a second.

"You think she'll enjoy her new home?"

"I honestly don't know, Tova."

Her eyebrows raise, taken aback by his candor. She'd only been making conversation, after all.

"Don't get me wrong, we try our best," Terry continues. "But look at Marcellus. We saved his life when we took him in, but he's never been happy to be trapped in a tank."

"He's rather bored," Tova agrees.

Terry laughs. "Life inside the Sowell Bay Aquarium never did satisfy him."

Tova leans on a nearby chair, easing the ache in her back, and tilts her head at the crate. "I'll mop around it, then?"

"You don't have to clean back here, Tova. You know that." Terry carefully replaces the lid on the crate.

"I don't mind. It's something to do."

"Well, Cameron will help you; he should be here soon. He said he might be a little late tonight." Terry looks at his watch. With one final pat on the lid of the crate, he leaves, muttering to himself about water temperature and acidic balance.

Tova is left alone in the pump room with two octopuses and a strange sense that something is wrong.

"Well," she mutters to herself, picking up her pocketbook. "I suppose I'd better start on the floors." On her way to the supply closet, she peers out the front door, expecting to see Cameron's junky old camper parked next to her hatchback. But there's no camper.

AN HOUR LATER, Tova hovers in Terry's office doorway, her fingers turning over her key card. He's here late. She's glad she caught him.

"Shall I leave this on your desk after we're finished tomorrow?" she says, holding up the card.

"Sure, sounds good." Terry drums his fingers on his desk. He still seems to be vibrating with excitement. "I just got off the phone with Dr. Santiago. She's coming tomorrow to take a look at our new addition. She thinks we might leave her in the barrel a bit longer."

"I see," Tova says, trying to pump up the flatness in her voice. How can she explain to Terry that she doesn't particularly care about this new octopus? That as far as she's concerned, there will never be another Marcellus?

Terry continues, "Sounds like we might move her directly into Marcellus's old space when . . . well, when it's available."

Tova swallows.

"So, Cameron never showed up tonight?" Terry stands and begins to gather his things, shuffling papers on his messy desk.

"No," Tova says hesitantly.

"Strange. I hope he's okay." Terry zips up his computer bag. "And sorry you had to clean the whole place by yourself."

"I don't mind at all." Tova smiles. "I will always fondly remember cleaning this place."

Terry shakes his head. "You're truly unique, Tova. And you'll be missed around here."

"That's very kind. I'll miss all of you, as well."

He's on his way around the hallway when Tova calls after him, "Terry? One more thing. Thank you."

Terry tilts his head. "For what?"

"For giving me this job."

"I didn't exactly have much choice," Terry says.

"What do you mean?"

"When I hired you. I didn't have much choice. I knew you wouldn't take no for an answer." He grins. "You're a very strong woman, Tova. Do you know that?"

Tova studies the gleaming tile. Her sneaker leaves a fleeting print as she shuffles her feet. "Yes, well. It's good to stay busy."

Terry gives her a *look*. "I don't mean strong only because you can wield a mop like no one I've ever met. Although that is true." He grins again, more tenderly this time. "You know, when I was a kid back in Jamaica, my great-gramma used to say she was 'old but not cold.' She lived to her late nineties. To her last days, she was in the kitchen, baking raisin buns for us kids. She liked to keep busy, too."

"Sounds like she was quite a woman."

"As you are." Terry clasps Tova's small shoulder with his large hand. "If you ever change your mind, Tova, know that there is always a place for you here at Sowell Bay Aquarium."

"I appreciate that."

Terry treads carefully over the freshly mopped floors as he walks out.

HIGH AND DRY

When the front door clicks open, Tova has just finished putting the cart back in the supply closet. Has Terry forgotten something and come back to retrieve it?

But it's Cameron she meets in the hallway. He's barreling toward the break room, eyebrows furrowed in angst. He stops short when he sees her, and the thunder on his face recedes for a moment as he registers surprise. He says, "I didn't think you'd still be here."

Tova plants her hands on her hips. "Where have you been?"

"Does it matter?"

"Yes, it matters. This is your job, and you were supposed to be here hours ago." Tova purses her lips. "That's more than 'a little late.' And you might know you missed a rather big night around here. There's a new octopus."

Cameron doesn't respond. Something about the boy reminds Tova of a coiled spring. The stiffness in his shoulders, the stompy manner in which he's walking, the way he won't look at her. She lays a hand on his shoulder. "Are you all right? Did something happen?"

He shrugs off her touch and starts pacing. "Did something happen? Let's see. Ethan's a nosy asshole who has zero ability to mind his own business and also has zero faith in me. So much for that friendship. My only other friends? Back in Modesto? They just had a baby, and the band is over. Speaking of Modesto, did I mention my shitty mom? Who abandoned me? That's been a real bummer for, like, my whole life. My aunt tried to be a mom, and she tried her best, but she shouldn't have to keep parenting me. I thought I had a girlfriend here, but she's totally ghosting me. I guess she's pissed that I bailed on our date, even though I went there in person to tell her I couldn't make it because something came up that was only, like, the most important meeting of my pathetic life. Or so I thought." He stops, rakes in another breath. "Also, my luggage? From my flight up here, two months ago? Is apparently taking an extended vacation in Italy. Not that I even need it anymore."

Tova realizes she has flattened herself against the tank behind her, as if all those words had been a strong wind. She straightens and pats her hair, like it might have been blown out of place, too. She's not really following, but she nods as if she is.

"And that's not even the best part." Cameron digs in his pocket and pulls out a chunky ring. A man's class ring, it seems, although Tova only catches a glimpse of it, sitting on the boy's palm, before it's swallowed up in the angry fist clenched around it. He's pacing again. Bitterness like static electricity infuses his voice as he continues, "The best part is that all of this was totally and completely pointless. It wasn't even him."

"Who wasn't who, dear?" Tova lays a hand on his shoulder, but again he flinches away.

"He wasn't my dad. The reason I came to Sowell Bay. The guy I spent all that time tracking down. He was just some old friend of my mom's. It isn't even his ring."

"Then whose is it?"

"Guess I'll never know."

Tova finds herself nearly speechless. Finally, she simply says, "I'm so sorry, Cameron."

"Me too." He swallows. "I mean, because all of this was such a waste of time."

"It's okay to be upset when you've lost someone," Tova says quietly.

Cameron mutters something Tova can't quite hear, then stomps off toward the front entrance. She follows, keeping up as best she can. Is he really leaving?

To her surprise, instead of out the front door, he heads into the pump room. She watches, astonished, as he navigates around the LIVE OCTOPUS crate, still sitting there in the middle of the room, and yanks off the lid to the wolf eels enclosure and drops the class ring in. It floats silently to the bottom of the tank and vanishes in a cloud of sand.

"*Eels.* This belongs with you," he mutters bitterly.

Tova stares at the tank. What on earth? One of the wolf eels returns her gaze, its needle teeth gleaming in the blue light.

She clears her throat. "Would you like to sit and have a cup of coffee, dear? Obviously, I'm finished with tonight's work, but we could talk through what needs to happen tomorrow. My last day. Make sure there's a smooth transition."

"Coffee?" Cameron says this like it's a foreign word. For a moment, he looks drained, like a wind sock fallen flat. He gives his head a quick shake, and just like that the storm is raging again. "Nah. I just stopped by to grab my hoodie from the break room."

He stalks out of the pump room, and Tova trails him. "But what about tomorrow?"

"There's no tomorrow," he says over his shoulder. "Terry never offered me the job. Why would I stay? How incompetent do I have to be to get passed over for a job emptying trash bins and mopping floors? I mean . . . no offense."

"Oh, I'm sure that's a misunderstanding. Terry has been quite distracted; the new octopus—"

"I'm done with misunderstandings." He ducks into the break room and emerges a moment later with his sweatshirt tucked under his arm. "Anyway, I'm out of here."

"What do you mean?"

"Headed back to California." Cameron avoids meeting her eyes directly. A sad, sardonic smile spreads over his face. "Road-trip time."

"You're leaving now?"

"Yep." Cameron's tone is clipped. "Would've already been gone, but being the idiot I am, I left most of my shit inside Ethan's house earlier today. Laundry. Even my guitar. Came back to get it." He holds up the sweatshirt. "Figured I might as well grab this, too."

"You're leaving, and you haven't told Terry?"

"He'll figure it out."

"And what do you think will happen when you fail to show up tomorrow?"

"He'll fire me?"

"And who will prepare food for so many of our . . . friends?"

"Not my problem. It's not exactly rocket science."

Tova gives him a stony stare. "This is not the way a person should end employment."

Cameron shrugs. "How would I know? I've never had a chance to quit a job. I always get canned. It's kind of my thing." He stomps into Terry's office. She follows, and watches as he plucks a piece of paper from the printer tray and scribbles a note, which he folds and deposits on Terry's desk.

"There. Is that better?"

She picks the note up and hands it back to him. "Leaving your boss high and dry without proper notice . . . you're better than that."

"No, I'm not." His voice cracks. He tosses the paper onto the desk. "I'm really not."

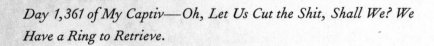

Day 1,361 of My Captiv—Oh, Let Us Cut the Shit, Shall We? We Have a Ring to Retrieve.

HUMANS SPARE NO JUDGMENT WHEN IT COMES TO wolf eels. If I had a clam for every time I heard someone call them *hideous* or *ugly* or *monstrous*, I would be a very plump octopus indeed.

These assessments are not wrong. Objectively speaking, wolf eels are grotesque. Theirs is one of few enclosures I have never entered or explored, but that has nothing to do with their unfortunate looks.

It happened long ago, before I was captured and imprisoned. I was young, naive, and *looking for a place to crash*, as you humans might put it, in the open sea. The rocky den beckoned; it would have been a perfect home for me. I did not realize it was already occupied.

With my vast intelligence, I ought to have used more caution. As soon as I peered through the gap in the rocks, it struck. The wolf eel's needle teeth and fleshy maw are not only ugly, but quite strong. I paid for my mistake three times.

First, I paid with my pride.

Second, with one of my arms. The arm started to grow back the next day, but by then, it was too late.

Third, with my freedom. Had my own poor judgment not brought about such injuries, perhaps I would have evaded my so-called rescue.

With immense patience, I wait for Tova to leave. Unscrewing the pump housing has become more difficult lately, but with effort, I remove it. By the time I have worked myself halfway through the little gap, I am already feeling The Consequences, as they come on ever more quickly these days.

I do not have much time left.

I speak to the wolf eels in soft platitudes as I enter their enclosure. The large male glares at me, his garish head hovering in the mouth of their den; after a moment, his female mate joins him.

You are both looking lovely today, I say, hugging the glass on the opposite side of the tank. The creatures blink. My organ heart pounds.

I have no intention of lingering here, I promise as I sink toward the bottom.

Their tank bottom is made of sand, whereas mine is coarser gravel, and I am surprised at how soft it feels as I dredge through it, searching. The two pair watches, having emerged a bit more from their den now, their jutted jaws opening and closing robotically, as always. Their thin dorsal fins ripple like ribbons, but they do not approach.

I sweep the sand at the base of the plant, and finally the suckers at the tip of my arm brush something cold and heavy. I snatch the chunky ring and curl it in the thick, muscular part of my arm, where I know it will be secure. I glance at the wolf eels, who are still watching my every move. *I hope you do not mind my taking this.*

Even the short journey back to my tank saps my strength. I am weakening by the day. Still carrying the heavy ring, I slip into my den and rest, as I will need stamina for my next trip. The last one.

A GODDAMN GENIUS

The serpentine belt, Cameron discovers, is aptly named. The thing winds around under the hood of the camper like a very long snake. The dry air smells like dust and burnt-up brake pads, and the morning sun is relentless. Every few seconds, with a loud whoosh, a burst of wind smacks him in the side of the head as another semitruck hurls down the freeway, like a parade of oversized beetles, mocking him with their menacing grilles as he stands on the shoulder in front of the camper's popped hood. With one hand, he yanks on the snapped belt. In the other, he holds the new one from the glove box.

"What in the hell," he mutters to himself, staring at the vehicle's innards. He recognizes the major parts. Engine block, radiator, battery, dipstick. Thingy that holds the blue stuff that cleans the windshield.

The new belt was sitting there the whole time, right there in the glove box. Why didn't he have it replaced? That squealing noise. It was never going to go away on its own.

It certainly did not go away during the last twelve hours of driving.

Well, that's not exactly true. The squealing did disappear . . . along with the power steering, on this barren stretch of interstate outside Redding, a hundred-something miles south of the Oregon-California border. Is there anything Cameron can't fuck up? His attempt to flounce after a humiliating failure is, itself, a humiliating failure.

How very meta.

"Okay, I can do this." He blows out a breath, then squints again at the video, propping the phone on the bumper. There's no other option. If he keeps driving, it won't be long before the engine overheats and shits the bed. Well, that's not exactly how the video described it, but . . . it's not good.

Besides, putting in the new belt can't be that hard, and he, Cameron Cassmore, is a goddamn genius.

It's time he started acting like one.

THE EEL RING

On Thursday afternoon, Tova's last day of work, Janice Kim and Barb Vanderhoof materialize on her porch with a rectangular box.

"Come in, won't you?" Tova says. "I apologize for the state of the house. All the packing is just . . ." She sweeps an arm around the clutter. "I'll put on coffee." That's one thing that hasn't been packed yet: the percolator. It will be the last thing to go.

She takes the box from Janice, assuming it's some sort of casserole, but it's far too light. She sets it on the kitchen counter and flips open the lid, revealing a small sheet cake shaped like a fish. *Congratulations on Your Retirement*, the icing reads.

"You shouldn't have!" Tova laughs. "But it's accurate. I'm actually retiring."

"At long last," Janice says, producing a parcel of paper plates and disposable napkins.

"I'm sure you'll talk them into hiring you to dust baseboards at Charter Village," Barb adds, lowering herself into a chair at the kitchen table.

"Well, I'm not ruling it out," Tova says, smiling. The percolator hisses as the coffee brews, and Tova stoops down to run her hand along Cat's back as the animal strolls into the kitchen.

Janice regards Cat skeptically. "What's happening with that fella?"

"Well, he can't come with me," Tova says. "I suppose he'll go back to living outside full-time, unless one of you is in the market for a pet?"

Janice holds her hands up. "Peter's allergic. Plus, Rolo is terrified of cats."

Cat leaps up onto Barb's lap, landing on light paws, and purrs loudly as he stretches upward and rams his furry head into her chin.

"I'm a dog person," Barb says. She scratches behind Cat's ears. "My, you're soft, though, aren't you? Did I tell you all about the cat Andie's kids found last year? Lives in their bedrooms now, sleeps with them under the sheets and blankets. I told Andie she needed to make sure the thing was treated for fleas, because you never know what animals bring in from outside, do you? Anyway, then she said—"

"Look Barb, he's totally into you." Janice giggles. Cat is licking the back of Barb's hand now, as if he's grooming her, still purring like a buzz saw.

"I already treated him for fleas, of course," Tova says pointedly.

Barb looks from Janice to Tova. "But I'm a dog person!"

Tova laughs. "People can change, Barbara."

"Even old folks like us," Janice adds.

"Oh, all right. I'll think about it," Barb mumbles, but she's rubbing Cat on his gray belly now. His eyes are closed in bliss.

Tova pours everyone coffee. "Have you both had supper? I could heat something up . . ."

"Oh, you don't need to do that." Janice waves her off. "Not with everything else you've got going on here."

A saucy smile curls Tova's lips. "Let's have cake for supper."

TOVA CLEANS ALONE on her last shift at the aquarium. Her last time mopping the circular hallway. A final swipe of each pane of glass. As she finishes up, she takes extra care to scrub one last time under the sea lion statue's tail. Who knows when it will be attended to again?

Funny how when she started this job, having only sea creatures for company was the thing she liked most about it. It was something to do, a way to keep busy while keeping to herself, no need to get her hands in anyone else's business. But now, cleaning alone seems oddly wrong. Cameron should be here, without a doubt. The surety of this sentiment surprises her.

But he's probably in California by now.

After finishing, she makes one last trip down the dim hallway. To the bluegills, she says, "Goodbye, dears."

The Japanese crabs are next. "Farewell, my lovelies."

"Take care," she says to the sharp-nosed sculpin. "So long, friends," to the wolf eels.

Next door, Marcellus's enclosure seems calm and still. Tova leans in and scrutinizes the rocky den, looking for any sign of him, but there's nothing. She hasn't seen him all night.

She goes back into the pump room, but can't see him from the rear, nor from the top looking down, either. She puts the stool back and hovers over the barrel, where through the screen she can see the new lady octopus still curled, compact, on the bottom, surrounded by a scattering of mussel shells. "Did you see anything? Is he gone?" She jams a hand over her mouth. "Did he—" A choking sob steals the word from her.

The new octopus curls up tighter.

Tova returns to the hallway and places a hand on the cool glass front of Marcellus's tank. No point in saying goodbye to rocks and water. The single tear that leaks from her eye rolls down her wrinkled cheek and falls from her chin before landing on the freshly mopped floor.

TERRY'S DESK IS a disaster when Tova goes in to leave her key card there, as she had promised to do. With a defeated shrug, she leaves the plastic card on top of the mess.

Her sneakers squeak on the floor as she crosses the lobby. She'll throw the sneakers out when she's finished tonight. They're battered from years of cleaning here; not even the secondhand shop would want them.

Short of the door, she stops in her tracks. There's a crumpled brown object on the ground, right in front of the door, as if blocking her way. She squints through the dim blue light. A paper bag? How could she have walked right past it on her way in?

A tentacle flickers.

"Marcellus!" Tova gasps, rushing over and dropping to the hard tile floor beside him. Her back pops loudly, but she hardly notices. The old octopus is pale, and even his brilliant eye seems diminished, like a marble that's gone cloudy. She places a gentle, searching hand on his mantle, the way one might touch a sick child's forehead. His skin is sticky and dry. He reaches an arm up and winds it around her wrist, right over the silver-dollar scar, which has now faded to a ghostly ring. He blinks, giving her a weak squeeze.

"What are you doing out here?" she says, softly scolding. "Let's get you back into your tank." She unwinds his tentacle from her wrist and stands, then tries to lift him, but her back strains, an ominous pain shooting through her lower spine.

"Stay here," she commands, then hurries off to the supply closet as quickly as her body will carry her. A few minutes later, she returns, wheeling her yellow mop bucket. Inside, several gallons of water slosh, moved there from his tank with the old milk jug Tova keeps in the supply closet. Relief washes over her when he blinks. He hasn't gone yet. She sops her cloth in the tank water and wrings it over him, wetting his skin. He heaves one of his strange human-esque sighs.

This revives him enough to move, it seems. With effort, he lifts an arm. Tova pulls the bucket up right beside him, and she gives his bottom (or what she supposes might be the equivalent of his bottom) a little boost as he heaves himself up over the bucket's plastic yellow rim and plops into the cold water inside.

"What are you doing out here?" she asks again. Then she sees it.

Something chunky and gold glimmers on the floor, right in the spot where Marcellus had lain crumpled. She crouches and picks it up. SOWELL BAY HIGH SCHOOL, CLASS OF 1989. She'd thought it looked like a class ring yesterday when Cameron mysteriously hurled it in with the wolf eels.

How did Marcellus get it out of there? And why?

And Sowell Bay, class of 1989? Is this Daphne Cassmore's ring? But it's a man's ring. Cameron had believed it was his father's . . .

It sits on her palm, cold and heavy. Like a memory. Erik had one just like it. She was so proud, as all parents are, of what it symbolized. She assumed he had been wearing it on that night. A ring also lost to the sea.

She turns the ring over, squinting at the letters engraved on the underside. Her heart starts to beat in her eardrums. She wipes the ring on the hem of her blouse and reads it again.

It cannot be.

It is.

EELS.

Erik Ernest Lindgren Sullivan.

THE VERY LOW TIDE

The revelatory bits swimming around in her mind crash into one another, begging to be linked together.

There was a girl.

Erik . . . and the girl.

Erik fathered a child.

A child that grew up, away, unknown. She can't believe she never saw it before in so many of Cameron's mannerisms. In that heart-shaped dimple on his left cheek, the one she always admired, although she could never put her finger on why.

"You knew, didn't you?" she says to Marcellus in the bucket. "Of course you did." She leans down and touches his mantle again. "You're so much more intelligent than we humans give you credit for."

Marcellus lays the tip of one of his arms across the back of her hand.

Tova crumples to the ground again, this time propping her elbows on the rim of the bucket. Once the hot, fast tears start spilling, she's powerless to stop them. Droplets pelt the surface as her thin shoulders heave, falling faster with each monstrous sob. No one is here. No one is looking. Throwing caution away, she allows the grief to course through her. Finally, the tears slow to a trickle, punctuated by hiccups. Her eyeballs feel hot and dry.

How long does she remain in this state of unmitigated grief? It might be minutes or an hour. When she lifts her head at last, her stooped shoulders ache.

"What am I going to do without you?" she says, dodging a hiccup, and he blinks his kaleidoscope eye, which is now more rheumy than ever. *He might only have weeks or days left*, Terry said. She sits up, swiping away the tears with the back of her hand. "For that matter, what am I going to do *with* you?"

She stands and squares her shoulders, shrugging the soreness out of her back. "Come on, my friend. Let's take you home."

IF THERE WERE any straggling fishermen or late-sunset walkers on the Sowell Bay waterfront that night, they would've been treated to quite a sight: a seventy-year-old woman, ninety pounds at best, pulling a sixty-pound giant Pacific octopus in a yellow bucket down the boardwalk toward the jetty. Tonight, though, the only witnesses are seagulls, and they scatter from the trash bin, lobbing indignant squawks at Tova as she wheels Marcellus by. It is not a fast journey by any means, but Marcellus trails an arm out each side of the bucket like he's riding in a car with the windows down.

Tova laughs. "The breeze feels nice, doesn't it?"

The tide is way out. Tova can barely hear the waves lapping on the rocks, it's so far out, feels like it must be a mile away from the waterfront path. Moonlight gleams on a hundred shallow pools, scattered like huge silver coins across the naked beach.

"This is going to get bumpy," Tova warns.

The jetty, an engineered break wall of rocks and boulders, reaches across the bare beach and eventually out to the water, curving gracefully like a ballerina's arm. On a summer afternoon, it will teem with beachcombers and adventurous picnickers, those looking for the most picturesque spot to sit and lick ice cream cones. Now, it's empty but for a lone seagull posted at the very tip.

Wheeling the bucket across the jetty's flat but pebbly top is no small task. Later, her back will certainly hurt. But finally, Tova and Marcellus make it nearly to the end, where the low-tide water is at least a couple feet deep below the rocks. From the tip of the jetty an arm's length away, the lone seagull glares at them, then lets out an atrociously loud squawk.

"Oh, quiet, you," Tova scolds, and the bird flaps off.

She lowers to sit on a rock slick with salt water. Trailing a hand in the bucket, she clears her throat before commencing the short speech she's been rehearsing in her head during their journey down to the beach.

"I must thank you," she begins, and he clasps her arm one last time. "Terry mentioned you were rescued. I suspect you might rather not have been saved, but I am glad you were."

She blinks back tears. Not again!

"You led me to him. My grandson." Her voice falters on these last two words, but a warmth seeps through her at the same time. Two words she never thought she'd say. If only Will had been here to meet him. And if only Modesto wasn't a thousand-plus miles away.

"You stole his driver's license! You naughty thing." She chuckles, and his arm squeezes her hand as she shakes her head. "You tried to tell me, and I wasn't listening."

Somewhere high in the night sky, an airplane cruises by, the faraway roar of its engine echoing over the calm bay. "It's unfair that you spent your life in a tank. And I promise, Marcellus, I'll do everything I can to make sure your replacement is the most pampered, intellectually stimulated octopus . . ."

The weight of her own words hits her. She's not going to Charter Village. She can't.

After a deep breath, she goes on. "We must say goodbye, friend. But I'm glad Terry saved you, because you saved me."

Slowly, she tips the bucket. It's about three feet down to the water. For a moment that seems extended in time, before gravity catches up, Marcellus's arm remains wrapped around her hand as his strange otherworldly body hangs in midair, his eye fixed to hers. Just as she's about to be pulled down with him, he releases, and lands with a heavy splash in the night-black water.

EVERY LAST THING

"My sweet boy," Tova says, gazing out from her usual bench on the pier next to the aquarium. Under the silver moon, the water sparkles back.

The events of the last two hours hardly seem real, to say nothing of the events of the last two months. Marcellus is gone. Cameron, her grandson, is gone. As of tomorrow, her house will be good as gone. But she won't be moving up to Charter Village.

Tova will not be gone.

What will she do? She hasn't a clue, so she sits on her bench, staring at the water for some length of time that's amorphous, immune to ordinary laws of the world, like a huge octopus reshaping its body to slip through a tiny crack. At some point, she checks her watch. It must be very late by now. Quarter to midnight.

It's almost a new day. Her first day as a grandmother.

Erik didn't know he'd fathered a child. How could he end his own life with a child on the way? He couldn't have. And he didn't. She clings to this theory, her thin fingers gripping tight on the bench. It had to have been an accident. Drunk kids. Impaired judgment.

He would've been a wonderful father. Yes, he was only eighteen, but look at Mary Ann's granddaughter, Tatum. She did just fine. Erik would've loved Cameron to pieces. Everything—every last thing—could have been so different.

"Excuse me? Hello?" A woman's voice rings out across the pier, startling Tova from her reverie. Who else could be out here at this hour?

Someone wearing short athletic shorts and a bright pink sweat-shirt is running up the pier at an urgent clip. Tova realizes it's the young woman who owns the paddle shop just down the board-walk, next to the realtor's office.

"Hello." Tova wipes her eyes and adjusts her glasses, then rises from the bench. "Are you all right, dear? It's quite late to be out for a jog."

The young woman slows to a trot as she nears the bench, out of breath. "You're Tova."

"I am."

"I'm Avery," she says, panting. "And I wasn't out for a jog. I was finishing up paperwork at my shop down the road and I saw lights on, figured someone was at the aquarium." There's a quiet despera-tion in her eyes that Tova recognizes all too well. The look of someone trying to hold it together.

She follows Avery's gaze back to the aquarium building, where the lights are indeed still on. The yellow mop bucket is back in the closet. Tova had planned to turn everything off and lock up on her way out, whenever that may end up being.

Avery swallows. "Anyway, I was thinking it might be . . ."

"Cameron?"

"Yes." A look of relief washes over her face. "Is he here?"

"I'm afraid not."

"Do you know where he is? I've been calling him all afternoon, but he's not answering his phone."

Tova shakes her head. "He left. Went back to California."

"What?" Avery's mouth drops open. "Why?"

"That's a rather complicated question." Tova's tone is measured. She sinks back into her spot on the bench, and the girl sits at the other end, tucking her bare legs underneath her. Tova goes on, "I suppose, in his mind, too many misunderstandings."

Avery's eyebrows knit together. "Misunderstandings?"

"His words exactly." She raises a brow at the young woman. "I'm quite certain he thinks you are . . . oh, how did he put it . . . ghosting him?"

"What?" Avery leaps up. "He stood me up! And then sent me some message saying he needed to talk. When has that ever meant anything good?" She leans on the railing. "I'm the one who should be pissed. I only came over here because I was worried about him."

Tova recalls Cameron's diatribe in the hallway at the aquarium, and is poised to tell Avery about it, but hesitates. She ought not to meddle in his business. But, well . . . he's family, and isn't this what families do? The thought almost makes her laugh. Perhaps against her better judgment, she finally says, "I believe he did try to let you know he couldn't make it."

"No, he didn't."

"He said he stopped at your shop." Tova shakes her head. "Another misunderstanding, I suppose."

Avery leans on the railing and drops her forehead onto her curled fist. She mutters, "Marco."

"I beg your pardon?"

"My son. He's fifteen. He was in charge of the store while I ran to the bank. I asked if Cameron had called or come by, and he said no. I should've known something was up when I caught his cocky smirk out of the corner of my eye." Avery gives the railing a frustrated smack. "I'm trying my hardest, I swear to God, but my kid's such a little turd sometimes."

"All kids are terrible sometimes." Tova rises and stands next to the young woman. "Maybe your son was trying to protect you."

"I don't need protecting." Avery huffs. "And I should've seen through it."

"Don't blame yourself, dear. Being a parent is not for the faint of heart."

After a long pause, Avery says, "So Cameron left for California because of me."

"Well, it wasn't just that. There was the big misunderstanding. The one about his so-called father."

"Oh, crap. That meeting . . . It didn't go how he thought it would." She groans again. "I should've called him yesterday. The shop got busy, and I was mad . . ." She pulls a cell phone from the pocket of her shorts. "I need to talk to him."

Tova watches as Avery dials. The call goes straight to voice mail.

"He's really gone, isn't he," Avery says softly.

"Maybe so."

The two women watch the moon-bathed water in silence for what feels like a long while. Finally, Avery says, "It's peaceful here. I never come down the pier anymore."

"It's my favorite place," Tova says quietly.

Avery drops her gaze to the black water far below. "I talked someone down from this ledge, once. Stopped her from . . . you know."

"Good heavens."

In a half-choked voice, Avery goes on. "It was a woman. Right here, in this spot. A few years ago. I was out paddling super early in the morning, and she was sitting on the railing. Talking to someone. Herself, I guess. She looked rough. Like she was on something."

"I see," Tova says, her voice faint.

"She kept talking about a horrible night. An accident. A boom."

A boom.

Tova gives a little nod, finding herself unable to speak, and the girl continues.

"I always assumed she must have been in combat or something. Trauma from an explosion, maybe."

A boom.

Tova closes her eyes, imagining how easily it could happen. Something knocks the bow off course, and a gust of wind catches the newly slackened sail just the wrong way at just the wrong moment. The boom swings wildly. Smacks his head. Knocks him overboard.

An accident. It could've happened that way, or any number of ways. Captain of the crew team, an accomplished sailor, but there was that stolen beer. There was a girl.

"Sometimes I wonder what ever became of her," Avery says. "Whether she's still alive. Whether my saving her mattered."

With a stiff inhale, Tova looks Avery in the eye. "It mattered. I'm glad you saved her," she says. And she means it.

EXPENSIVE ROADKILL

At mile marker 682, Cameron stops obsessing over the engine temperature gauge. It worked. He really fixed it. The camper is not going to blow up in the middle of the interstate.

At exit 747, he lets out a juvenile chuckle. The town of Weed! He puts his flashers on and pulls to the shoulder, intending to snap a pic of the sign to send to Brad. Because Weed, California, is never not funny. But his phone's not in its usual place in the cup holder. Weird. Did he leave it in the back of the camper, maybe? He keeps driving.

At mile marker 780, he realizes why he couldn't find his phone. He left it on the front bumper, right where it was when he was changing the belt. He can practically see it sitting there. Which means, by now, it's an expensive piece of roadkill. He lets out a wild laugh. He hasn't slept in almost thirty hours.

At a truck stop somewhere in the Rogue River Valley, he makes the smart decision to park and take a six-hour nap. When he wakes, he splashes his face with cold water in the public restroom and buys a black coffee, to go, from the diner. On his way out, he tosses a mostly full pack of cigarettes in the trash.

At or around exits 119, 142, and 238, he dwells on his idiotic resignation note. At exit 295, he starts composing an apology in his head.

At a bridge crossing the Columbia River, he reenters Washington state. Northbound, of course—he's been going north. Going back to do things the right way.

THE DALA HORSE

For the last time, Tova boils water for coffee on her stove. Its lacquered top gleams, avocado green against the black coils, polished last night. Spotless. Could it possibly matter? It will almost certainly be ripped out, replaced by one of those sleek new ranges. No one wants a decades-old appliance, even if it works perfectly well.

Tova had been approved for accelerated check-in at Charter Village, something she'd lobbied after for weeks. Her premier suite would be available next week. She left them a telephone message first thing this morning, at whatever absurdly early hour she awoke, assuming she slept at all last night. The whole thing is a blur. Charter Village has yet to call back, but most likely it's simply because their office isn't open yet. It's only just past seven.

Regardless, Tova has no intention of going.

She's had a busy morning. Dusted all of the baseboards. Wiped down the windows. Polished the hardware on the cabinets, scrubbed every last doorknob. She should be exhausted, but she's never felt more energized in her life. Without curtains or furniture, every sound she makes echoes against the naked walls and floors, and even the hiss of her spray bottle seems too loud. But keeping busy is good. Cleaning is always good. It's something to do.

Where will she go? She's supposed to be out of the house by noon. The movers who took most of the furniture yesterday have already been notified that there will be a change of destination.

Thankfully, someone answers their phone at the crack of dawn. But what will that destination be? A storage unit, perhaps?

As for herself and her personal effects, Janice and Barbara both have spare bedrooms. At a decent hour, she'll call Janice first. Perhaps she might alternate between them until other arrangements can be made. Her floral-print canvas suitcase, the same one she took on her honeymoon with Will, is packed and ready to go. The thought of spending the night in a bed that isn't her own thrills and terrifies her, in turn.

When something rustles on the front porch, she startles. She sets her coffee cup down.

It can't be Cat. Barbara sent a photo last night of Cat. He's doing all right, although at first Barb had tried to keep him exclusively indoors and this agitated him greatly. So he comes and goes as he pleases. Tova still isn't sure how to respond to photos she receives on her cell phone, but seeing Cat's whiskered face, his yellow eyes with their hallmark look of mild disdain, had made her smile.

Then the doorbell rings.

When she opens the front door, she can't believe her eyes.

Cameron's eyebrows are creased anxiously, like Erik's when he was nervous about a school exam. For a quick moment, something nostalgic catches in Tova's throat, thinking of how many times she wished Erik would somehow appear on her doorstep like this. Tears spring to her eyes.

"Hi," Cameron says, shuffling his feet.

All Tova can manage is "Hello, dear."

"Um, sorry I was such a jerk the other night. You were right. I shouldn't have left." Cameron jams his hands in his pockets. "And sorry to show up here so early. I would have called, but . . . well, bizarre story there."

"It's quite all right." Tova holds the door open with an arm that feels like it belongs to someone else. Like she's out of her own body.

"I realize you owe me absolutely nothing." Cameron's voice is like a live wire. Buzzy. "But can you tell me what time Terry normally gets in? I need to talk to him. In person."

"Around ten, if I'm not mistaken."

"Ten. Okay." Cameron lets out a long breath. "How mad do you think he is at me right now?"

"Not mad at all, I'm quite sure."

Cameron gives her a confused look.

Tova shuffles across the foyer to where her pocketbook hangs on the otherwise-empty set of pegs by the door and pulls a folded paper from the front pouch. A conspiratorial smile overtakes her face as she hands it to him.

"My note?" His jaw drops. "You took it?"

She inclines her head. "Mind you, I shouldn't have. But I did."

"But . . . why?"

"I suppose some part of me didn't believe you when you insisted you were the type of person who would shirk a job."

"So then . . . Terry doesn't know I left?"

"I believe he is none the wiser."

Cameron's cheeks flush. "I don't know how to thank you. And I don't know why you'd have such faith in me. Not like I've earned it."

There's something else she must show him, of course. Something far more important. And where have her manners gone? "Please, come all the way in." She ushers him through the foyer. "And I'd invite you to sit, but . . ." She sweeps an arm around the empty den.

"Wow. This is a nice house."

Tova smiles. "I'm glad that you think so." Regret stabs at her. The boy's great-grandfather built this house, and this is the only time he'll ever set foot in it. "Wait here a moment. I have another thing to give you," she continues, before hustling off to the bedroom and her suitcase.

A minute later, she returns. She holds it out to him, then drops it in his upturned palm. He turns it over, and confusion knits his brow. That engraving, the one that flummoxed him. He thought it meant eels, like the sea creature. Why on earth would anyone put that on a class ring? At the thought of this, Tova suppresses a smile. Even the most brilliant minds are mistaken sometimes.

"His full name," she says, "was Erik Ernest Lindgren Sullivan."

Cameron's lips part, soundless. Tova waits. She can almost see the wheels turning in his head. Erik was just like that, how it showed on his face when the gears were grinding in his brain, which they always were. There is so much about Cameron and Erik that is alike, but not everything. Not his eyes. Those must be his mother's. Daphne's.

They're lovely eyes.

Tova has never been much of a hugger, but when Cameron's face starts to break apart, she finds herself pulled to him like a magnet. His arms wrap around her neck, squeezing her against his chest. For what seems like a very long time, she rests her cheek against his sternum, which is warm. She can't help but notice that his T-shirt appears to be stained and smells oddly like motor oil. Perhaps that's intentional? Never again will Tova make assumptions about a T-shirt.

He stands back and says with a dumbfounded grin, "I have a grandmother."

"Well, how about that?" She laughs, and it's as if a valve inside her has been released. "I have a grandson."

"Yup, looks like you do."

"What happened to California?"

He shrugs. "Changed my mind. You were right about not quitting. I'm better than that." Surveying the den, he gives an appreciative nod. "This really is a cool house. The architecture . . ."

"Your great-grandfather built it."

"No shit?" A look of astonishment crosses Cameron's face. He walks over to the fireplace mantel, the one that once held the row of frames featuring his father, and touches it tenderly, almost hesitantly, the way one might lay a hand on a sleeping animal's flank.

Tova follows. "I've been fortunate to enjoy it for sixty-plus years." She lifts her wrist, inspecting her watch. "And three and a half more hours."

"Holy crap. That's right. You sold it."

"It's okay. I need to let it go. Too many ghosts." Tova isn't sure she believes the words, but she's becoming accustomed to them, at least.

Cameron studies his sneakers. "I guess I'm glad I caught you here, then. Before you moved to that retirement home."

"Oh," Tova says, swatting the air as if to clear away his words. "I'm not going there."

"You're not?"

"Heavens, no."

"Where are you going, then?"

An unfettered laugh escapes from deep in Tova's chest. "You know what? I don't know. To Barbara's. Or Janice's. For a while. Until I figure out what comes next."

"Good plan," says Cameron. "I mean, that's coming from a guy living in a camper." He grins, and the heart-shaped dimple on his cheek indents, and for a moment he looks every part the impish grandson. Tova glances down, checking to make sure her slippers are still contacting the floor, because it feels like she's aloft, floating, unfurling toward the ceiling with unwitting elegance, like Marcellus in his old tank. Her heart is full of helium, lifting her skyward.

She chuckles. "I suppose we're both homeless, then." She gestures to the hallway. "Would you like to see where your father grew up?"

———————

ERIK'S OLD BEDROOM had been the most difficult to clean. Three decades, it sat empty. She swept the room regularly over the years, and even changed the linens on his bed occasionally, but after the men from the secondhand shop hauled the furniture away, she found herself balking at the ancient dust bunnies gathered in the corners. As if one of them might contain some fragment of him, still.

The hardwood floor is discolored where Erik's throw rug once sat. Sun slants through the naked window. A sea breeze gently sways the branches of an old shore pine outside, and the light casts a wraithlike shadow on the opposite wall. Once, on a full-moon night when young Erik had forgotten to shut the curtains, he caught sight of that shadow and bolted across the hallway into Tova and Will's room, dove under their covers, convinced he was being haunted. Tova held him until he slept, then continued to hold him all through the night.

Cameron's eyes rake over every inch of the room. Perhaps he's trying to commit it to memory, to scan it like Janice Kim's computer. Tova has begun to retreat from the room to give him a measure of privacy when he says, "I wish I'd met him."

She steps back in, placing a hand on his elbow. "I wish you had, too."

"How did you, like, go on?" He looks down at her and swallows hard. "I mean, he was here one day and gone the next. How do you recover from something like that?"

Tova hesitates. "You don't recover. Not all the way. But you do move on. You have to."

Cameron is gazing at the floor where Erik's bed once was and biting his lip thoughtfully. Suddenly, he crosses the room and jabs at one of the floorboards with his sneaker toe.

"What happened here?"

Tova tilts her head. "What do you mean?"

"Your whole house is red oak floorboards. But this one piece is white ash."

"I have no idea what you're talking about." Tova shuffles over and adjusts her glasses, scrutinizing the floorboard. There doesn't seem to be anything remarkable about it.

"See, the grain lines are different. And the finish, it almost matches, but not quite." He produces a cluster of keys from his pocket, kneels, and starts working a key chain that's meant to open bottles into the crack between the floorboards. Moments later, to Tova's shock, the board pops up, revealing an open space underneath.

"I knew it!" Cameron squints into the cavity.

"Good heavens. Who would do such a thing?"

Cameron laughs. "Any teenage boy who ever lived?"

"But what would he need to hide?"

"Uh . . . well, my friend Brad used to steal his dad's magazines, and—"

"Oh!" Tova flushes. "Oh dear."

"I don't think that's what we're dealing with here." Cameron pulls out a small parcel. Its plastic wrapping crunches when he hands it to Tova, who drops it once she realizes what's inside. Snack cakes. Or what were once snack cakes. They're hard and gray as stones now.

"Wow, Creamzies. These are old-school," Cameron says, picking the package up and studying it. "You know, I saw a show on some science channel about them once. Urban legend says they'll survive a nuclear holocaust, but it's not actually true, see, because the diglycerides they use as stabilizers don't—"

"Cameron," Tova interrupts quietly. "There's something else in there."

"In here?" He holds up the petrified cakes, squinting.

"No, in there." Her focus is fixed on the floorboard compartment.

It's one of Tova's mother's old embroidered tea towels, wrapped around something the size of a deck of cards.

Cameron takes it out and hands it to Tova. Her fingers tremble as she unravels the towel. Inside is a painted wooden horse.

"My Dala Horse." Her whisper comes out like gravel. She runs a finger down the figurine's smooth wooded back. Every last splintered piece is glued back into place flawlessly. Even the paint is touched up.

The sixth horse. Erik had fixed it.

Cameron leans over, peering at the artifact. "What's a Dala Horse?"

Tova clicks her tongue. The boy is full to the brim with random knowledge about floorboard grains and snack cake stabilizers and Shakespeare, but how little he knows about his heritage.

She holds the Dala Horse out to him.

He takes it, and she watches him study the delicate carved curves. After a long moment, he looks up. "How did you get the class ring back?"

She smiles. "Marcellus."

Day 1 of My Freedom

AT FIRST, I SINK LIKE A COLD BUNDLE OF FLESH. MY arms no longer function. I am a chunk of jetsam flung into the sea on a comatose journey toward the seafloor.

Then, with a twitch, my limbs awaken, and I am alive again.

I do not say this to give you false hope. My death is imminent. But I am not dead yet. I have time enough to bask in the vastness of the sea. A day or two, perhaps, to revel in darkness. Dark, like the bottom of the seafloor.

Darkness suits me.

After my release, I swam away from the rocks with haste. Soon, there was a drop-off. Down, down, down. Into the depths, the bowels of the sea, where no light reaches. Where once, as a juvenile, I found a key. Where I return now, to lie with the long-disintegrated bones of a beloved son.

I will be honest: this is not how I expected our time together to end. For nearly four years I was held captive and not a day passed when I did not ruminate on my own death, certain I would expire within the four glass walls of that tank. I never imagined I would know the freedom of the sea again.

How does it feel, you ask? It is comfortable. It is home. I am lucky. I am grateful.

But what will become of my replacement? Soon, Terry will begin cleaning and remodeling my tank. He will make no attempt to conceal these activities from the viewing public; the sign he tapes on the glass will read UNDER CONSTRUCTION: NEW EXHIBIT COMING!

I stopped at her barrel on my journey out. Climbed up the side to peek at her. She is young and badly injured. Terrified, naturally. But this new octopus will have a friend. One that I did not have until the very end. Tova will make sure she is happy, and I would trust Tova with my life. I *did* trust her with my life, more than once. Just as I trusted her with my death.

Humans. For the most part, you are dull and blundering. But occasionally, you can be remarkably bright creatures.

AFTER ALL

One month later, when the renovations are complete, a moving truck with Texas plates lumbers through Sowell Bay. Tova doesn't notice. She's preparing for battle.

"You're toast," she calls, unfolding the game board and scrambling the letter tiles. Outside, a brisk fall wind slices across the water. A harbinger of winter, these whitecaps whipping over the water's colorless surface, which blends seamlessly into the gray sky.

"Please. I'm about to own you." Cameron emerges from the luxury kitchen in Tova's new condominium with a tray of sliced cheddar and round crackers. Tova frowns. She's been lobbying hard for him to try lutefisk with hardtack, which is what a good Swede would eat. But the crackers were on special at Shop-Way, Cameron had explained. Buy-one-get-one. She can't be upset about that.

Tova knows Terry would've been thrilled to keep Cameron on at the aquarium, but the hours and pay just weren't enough, although Cameron stayed on to train his replacement. Now, Cameron works excruciating, long days for a contractor over at one of those custom homes in Adam Wright and Sandy Hewitt's neighborhood. He's talking about taking classes at the community college down in Elland come January, engineering prerequisites. He insists on paying his own way, in spite of Tova's objections. She'll work on that.

"You go first," Tova says, arranging her tiles.

"No, go ahead. Age before beauty," Cameron teases, studying his own tray while fiddling absently with his father's class ring, which he wears on his right hand.

She mock-scowls. "I have fifty years of daily crossword puzzles stored in here." She taps her temple.

Cameron grins. "I don't know shit, really, but somehow I'm good at these things."

Shit, really. That's the sort of language now woven into the tapestry of her life, and she wouldn't have it any other way. She opens with "JUKEBOX" (seventy-seven points, an incredibly lucky draw). On this, Cameron plays "JAM" (thirty-nine points).

"I'm glad you're here," she says quietly.

"Are you kidding? Where else would I be?"

"With your aunt Jeanne."

Cameron rolls his eyes. "She's living her best life, trust me. Did I tell you about Wally Perkins and his—"

Tova holds up a hand. "Yes. You did."

"It's amazing up here. Aunt Jeanne will for sure come visit. She's already talking about trying to track down her sister over in Eastern Washington. To which I say, good luck—who knows what mess she'll dig up there." Cameron face tenses, but it's short-lived. "And Elizabeth is already planning to bring the baby up in the spring. Well, Brad, too, of course, but I guess he's freaking out about taking baby Henry on a plane—germs or something. Elizabeth will talk him into it, though, and Uncle Cam will put the pressure on if needed." He laughs.

Tova laughs, too. A baby in the family. Although she hasn't met Elizabeth or Brad yet, somehow Cameron has convinced her that she's their grandmother, too. She gazes out the window. It *is* amazing here. Hurricane-grade glass from floor to vaulted ceiling run the entire length of the living room, interrupted only by French doors, which lead to a balcony set on sturdy pilings. When the tide is high, Tova likes to have coffee out there, listening to the water slap the deck boards underneath.

WHEN THANKSGIVING COMES, Tova and Cameron set a table for three.

It would've been four, but Avery backed out, promising to swing by later with pie. Apparently, she decided to keep the paddle shop open on Thanksgiving Day but didn't want to make any of her employees work. People starting their holiday shopping on a holiday, how ridiculous. But Avery always says that the shop is doing so well this year, on the upswing, like Sowell Bay itself. She probably didn't want to pass up a day of decent sales. Cameron said he understood, and anyway, he sees her all the time.

Marco might come with Avery today. Cameron's voice had dropped, serious, when he explained this to Tova. He bought a green Nerf football on his way home from work the other day. Marco might want to toss it around on the beach, he said. Maybe. If he doesn't, no hard feelings.

Ethan claims his seat, arriving half an hour early for turkey supper. Sometimes it seems he spends every free minute in Tova's condo. But, in truth, Tova doesn't mind. Mostly, he sits in her living room, in the recliner next to the little curio shelf where she displays her Dala Horses. Ethan loves listening to records on Will's old turntable, an apparatus he treats with almost religious reverence. Although Tova never desired an education on rock music, she's receiving one. It's nice to have Ethan around.

When Ethan shrugs off his jacket, Cameron yelps. "Where'd you get that?"

"Oh, this?" Ethan's eyes twinkle. He runs a hand over his belly, which strains against a yellow T-shirt that's clearly a bit small. Garish lettering across the chest reads MOTH SAUSAGE.

Good heavens. What is a Moth Sausage?

Cameron's eyes are still saucers. "That's mine! I haven't seen it since—holy shit, did my luggage finally come?"

"You mean that ruddy green duffel is your luggage?" Ethan winks. "Thought it was just my lucky day when I found it on my porch this morning."

"Finally." Cameron laughs. "That bag has been all over the world. I'll bet it's got some stories to tell."

After the turkey and gravy have been eaten, Ethan, Cameron, and Tova leave a scandalous mountain of dirty dishes in the sink and bundle up for a walk down the waterfront, where Puget Sound shivers like a great gray ghost beyond the pier. The old ticket booth with its diagonal-cracked window sits alone under a blanket of clouds.

In front of the aquarium, they stop, all three admiring the new installation. A bronze statue with eight arms, a heavy-looking mantle. Round, inscrutable eyes on either side of its head.

The aquarium had balked at her hefty donation, but Tova insisted. Too much cash sitting unused in a bank account. Now, she passes the new statue three times a week, when she arrives for her volunteer position, passing out pamphlets and standing in front of the giant Pacific octopus tank, helping visitors understand the creature. Pippa the Grippa is still quite shy, spending most of her public-facing time as a pink blob suctioned to the glass in the corner of the tank. Living up to her name, Tova supposes. But that's okay. When it's slow, Tova talks to her while surreptitiously wiping away stray fingerprints on the glass. She can't help herself.

A couple of tanks down, the sea cucumber population now remains stable. To Terry's great relief, Pippa appears disinclined to roam the hallways, collecting lost artifacts.

Secretly, this makes Tova happy, too. Marcellus was, in fact, an exceptional octopus.

They continue along the waterfront, past the jetty. Marcellus's jetty. The tide is high, clinging snug to the seawall like someone drawing blanket to chin on a cold winter night. Gentle waves play peekaboo with the mussel-crusted boulders that line the wall. Cameron and Ethan have been yapping about football for the last half hour, so Tova tunes them out.

If they kept going up the shore, they'd eventually pass underneath her old house, perched up on the hillside. Sometimes Tova walks there at dusk, and often when she passes the house, the big attic window glows golden through the trees. Once, she was certain she saw a string of paper dolls fixed to the window.

She has returned to the house only one time. A woman with a Texas accent called her cell phone, having obtained the number from Ethan. It seemed the woman had come through the checkout lane at the Shop-Way with a stack of cat food cans, and mentioned that there was a gray cat that wouldn't leave her yard. Now, Cat loves hunting rock crabs on the beach under Tova's deck when the tide is out. He prefers being outdoors, as if he doesn't quite trust that this new place is home, and Tova can't blame him. It's a difficult adjustment. But as the weather gets colder, he seems increasingly resigned to spending more time inside the condo, curled on the davenport or sitting in front of the window, yellow eyes fixed on the seagulls that wander the skies.

When they circle back to the pier, Tova slips away and stands at the railing, alone. To the somber bay that took them both, a cherished son and an exceptional octopus, she whispers inscrutably: "I miss you. Both of you." She taps her heart.

Then she turns and heads back to the others. They ought to get back to the condo.

Avery is coming for pie. And there's a Scrabble game to win, after all.

ACKNOWLEDGMENTS

My grandmother collected owls. The china cabinet on the red shag carpet in her dining room was crammed full of them. As a kid, I spent a lot of time on that carpet. I lived next door and had free rein to dart across our shared backyard and duck through the screen door into their kitchen, where there were always homemade cookies and no one stopped me from skating across the linoleum in my socks.

This was the 1980s, and these owls were old-school, not like the twee pastel birds that now decorate baby showers. My grandmother's figurine owls had heavy eyes and sharply pointed beaks. Like real owls, they conveyed little emotion.

I never knew why she loved owls, but year after year, until she passed away, I wrapped gift boxes with owl-themed brooches and tea towels. In some ways, Tova is modeled after my Grandma Anna. Tova's life events are fiction, but she and my Grandma Anna are both stoic Swedes. Unruffled. Endlessly kind, yet emotionally inscrutable. Apt to sink talons into a solitary branch and remain there, owl-like. As a descendant of this culture, I sometimes struggle to communicate touchy-feely things. But I'm going to try, because I am grateful to so many people for the fact that this book is in your hands.

First, an ocean-sized thanks to Helen Atsma, my amazing editor at Ecco, whose editorial vision for this story hit the mark from our very first meeting. Helen, you have a knack for pruning out the weak parts and letting the narrative shine, and I am so grateful for your guidance. Also, huge thanks to Miriam Parker, Sonya Cheuse, TJ Calhoun, Vivian Rowe, Rachel Sargent, Meghan Deans, and everyone else at Ecco for your brilliance, kindness, and patience.

Similarly, to Emma Herdman and her team at Bloomsbury UK, your enthusiasm has been so inspiring, and I feel so fortunate to be working with such an accomplished team across the pond.

A tidal wave of thanks to my agent, Kristin Nelson, who changed my life with an email in the fall of 2020. Thank you, Kristin, for having a sense of humor when, during our first video call, my four-year-old son repeatedly appeared onscreen to complain about wanting a juice box. I still can't believe I'm lucky enough to count myself as one of your clients. My gratitude extends to everyone at Nelson Literary Agency, with special thanks to Maria Heater, who reviewed my query letter, realized there was an octopus narrator, and wrote in the margin: "This is either brilliant or bananas."

I am thrilled to have Jenny Meyer and Heidi Gall at Meyer Literary Agency on the team, handling international deals. They've done a spectacular job bringing this story to a global audience.

When I wrote the first draft of this book's opening scene, years ago, it was in response to a workshop prompt about writing from an unexpected point of view. I had recently watched a YouTube video in which a captive octopus picked open a locked box with a treat inside, so that's where my mind went, and I invented this curmudgeonly octopus who was bored and exasperated with humans. I didn't know anything about octopuses back then, and I'm still no expert. But I'm certain they're the most fascinating creatures on our planet.

To that octopus in the video, thank you. To octopuses generally, thank you for occasionally allowing us a glimpse into your world.

I'm especially grateful to Sy Montgomery for writing the wonderful nonfiction book *The Soul of an Octopus*, which follows her engrossing (and heartwarming, and frequently hilarious) journey as she shadows octopus keepers at the New England Aquarium. Also, thank you to the Alaska Sealife Center and the Point Defiance Zoo and Aquarium for fielding my cephalopod questions, and more importantly, for the conservation and rescue work you do.

I will forever be grateful to Linda Clopton, who taught the workshop I mentioned above, and who mentored me through my earliest attempts at creative writing. She championed this story from the very first words laid on the page.

That workshop also introduced me to a handful of writers who form the basis of my main critique group, even today. To Deena Short, Jenny Ling, Brenda Lowder, Jill Cobb, and Terra Weiss, your feedback is invaluable, and seeing you all on Zoom regularly has always been a bright spot, especially during the pandemic.

To Terra especially, who puts up with my daily texts, and who always manages to carve out hours from her own hectic life for our weekly critique call. Those check-ins kept me on track to complete this book. Terra, every page of this story has your mark on it. I would never have finished it without your endless patience for talking through plot knots and your gentle reminders to keep my characters in line.

To my online writing group, Write Around the Block, and in particular the query support crew, thank you for your feedback and support: Becky Grenfell, Trey Dowell, Alex Otto, Haley Hwang, Jeremy Mitchell, Kim Hart, Mark Kramarzewski, Rachael Clarke, Janna Miller, Sean Fallon, and Lydia Collins. To Kirsten Baltz, thank you for lending your marine biology expertise. To Jayne Hunter, Roni Schienvar, and Lin Morris, thank you for generally being there for me.

To the writing workshop folks at College of DuPage, and

instructor Mardelle Fortier, it was a pleasure workshopping parts of this book with you. To Grace Wynter for her thoughtful feedback on my early first chapters, and to Gwynne Jackson for helping me patch up plot holes. To my wonderful friends Gesina Pedersen and Diana Moroney, thank you for always listening and lifting me up when I needed it.

Most of all, thank you to my family.

To my mom, Meridith Ellis, for showing me how strong a person can be. She's loving and caring and tough as hell. She can still probably crush me in a bench press or a timed mile, but I know she'll always be there for me with a warm hug and a long talk over a glass of wine.

To my dad, Dan Johnson, who taught me to read when I was in preschool. I owe my love of books to him. He has always been my biggest champion, and I am so grateful for him.

To my wonderful kids, Annika and Axel, who are probably too young to remember much about that weird year when we were all stuck in the house during a global pandemic and Mommy decided, bafflingly, that *this* was the year to finish her novel. Thank you for playing together peacefully (most of the time) when I needed to throw on my headphones and work. Thank you for your silliness and your wild imaginations, which brought sweet moments of levity when life got heavy. Thank you to Netflix, along with screen time limits that went out the window in 2020. Thank you to snacks. So many snacks. Thank you to juice boxes!

Finally, thank you to my husband, Drew, who has supported and encouraged me every single day on this journey to take my writing from hobby to career. He is my toughest beta reader, but in the best possible way, and is always willing to look over whatever bizarre thing I've written and offer insight. There is no one I'd rather be on this ride with. I love you.